REPEAT AFTER ME

REPEAT AFTER ME

JESSICA WARMAN

Entangled Publishing, LLC
644 Shrewsbury Commons Ave., STE 181
Shrewsbury, PA 17361
rights@entangledpublishing.com

Entangled Teen is an imprint of Entangled Publishing, LLC.

Visit our website at www.entangledpublishing.com.

Edited by Stacy Abrams
Cover design by Elizabeth Turner Stokes
Stock art by ne2pi/Shutterstock, Sergj/Shutterstock, Svekloid/Shutterstock, mart/Shutterstock, Panimoni/Shutterstock, Sabelskaya/Shutterstock, VETOCHKA/Shutterstock
Interior design by Britt Marczak

Deluxe Edition Hardcover ISBN 978-1-64937-538-4
Standard Edition Hardcover ISBN 978-1-64937-742-5
Ebook ISBN 978-1-64937-480-6

Printed in China

First Edition September 2024

10 9 8 7 6 5 4 3 2 1

entangled teen
an imprint of Entangled Publishing LLC

ALSO BY JESSICA WARMAN

Breathless
Where the Truth Lies
Between
Beautiful Lies
The Last Good Day of the Year

For my chosen sisters: Alisa, Jen, and Idgie. I love you all.

Author's Note

Dear reader,

I'm so thrilled you have chosen to read *Repeat After Me*! In writing this book, my hope was to create characters and dialogue that felt authentic and recognizable to you, my readers. However, I also wanted to place my characters in a unique world with no consequences, like a time loop that makes every day a blank slate. Difficult life issues can be hard to discuss in our real world. But by using an extreme, satirical alternate reality with absurdist humor, I gave my characters a safe space to explore and tackle these problems. The resulting shenanigans in these pages may strike some readers as absurdly over-the-top or, perhaps, indelicate. My intention was not to minimize or make light of any serious issues or experiences, or to trivialize harsh language, but to explore what would happen in a world where nothing matters…or does *everything* matter? You be the judge.

I hope you have as much fun reading this book as I had writing it!

Best,
Jessica Warman

Repeat After Me is an upper-YA, dark humor rom-com that imagines what would happen if a group of mostly morally gray teenagers discovered their day was repeating endlessly with no repercussions or limits. However, the story contains elements that might not be suitable for all readers, including the depiction of blood, violence, death, murder, injury, choking, sexual harassment, loss of family, divorce, cheating, graphic language, drowning, drug use, alcohol use, vomiting, suicide, mistreatment of animals, disordered weight and body thoughts, bullying, and sexual activity.

But don't worry—they'll all be fine when the time loop resets...

Still, readers who may be sensitive to these elements, please take note, and take a bite of the magical ceviche...if you dare...

Prologue

My phone rang at 3:27 a.m., a full thirty-three minutes before my alarm was set to go off. I let out a tiny gasp and sat up in the dark, squinting at the cell screen. *UNKNOWN CALLER.*

Nobody calls in the middle of the night with good news.

"Hello?" My voice was faint and raspy. I couldn't force it to get any louder no matter how hard I tried; it was like trying to shout in a dream, but I knew I was awake.

There was silence, a few seconds of static. Then she spoke.

"Listen to me, Gizmo. Don't go on the trip tomorrow." I knew the voice, but I couldn't place it.

"Who is this?" My own voice was like a carbonated whisper.

"Can you hear me? It's me. Don't go, Gizmo." It was hard to make out the muffled words over the background, which was full of static. The noise faded in and out, echoing back onto itself, a dizzying kaleidoscope of sound.

"Who is Gizmo?"

"Not Gizmo. You, Emma!"

"What?" I asked. My voice grew stronger. "Who is this? What are you—"

"Ask Mom." *Click.*

I held completely still in the darkness of my bedroom. The air was saturated with a primal sense of alarm, hot and cold at the same time, a tickling deep within my reptile brain. My cat, Charles, stared at me from the foot of my bed, his eyes huge and round in the moonlight. My consciousness was gripped by vertigo, slippery and confusing, my thoughts not words but a different kind of language altogether. For an instant, I understood it. Then it was gone, a forgotten dream. As my vision adjusted to the light, I saw that everything surrounding me was perfectly normal—except that my mouth tasted like salt. I tried to shake it off. I should stop taking melatonin at night.

I was surprised to find my mom already downstairs and drinking coffee. Even with her back turned to me, I could tell she was in a bad mood. She is *not* a morning person.

Ask Mom. "Mom? Did you call my phone a few minutes ago?"

"Why would I need to call your phone?"

"I don't know. Somebody called me."

"Who was it?"

"I don't know. That's why I'm asking you."

"Jesus, Emma, it's too early for this. What did they say?" She grasped her mug with both hands and blew gently across the surface. She was still half asleep, and she couldn't have been less interested.

I hesitated. "They didn't really say much of anything."

"Well, did they leave a voicemail? If it was important, they would have left a voicemail."

"Nobody leaves voicemails anymore, Mom."

It's me. Don't go, Gizmo. The only Gizmo I'd ever heard of was the one from that old movie, *Gremlins*.

I was already packed, my suitcase waiting beside the front door. I tried to put the call out of my mind while we drove to the airport. It was still dark as Mom's Subaru sped reliably along the empty interstate, and I picked idly at my fingernails, trying to distract my racing thoughts by listening to the latest episode of my favorite true crime podcast, *It's Always the Husband*. But the call nagged at me. A small part of me hoped for a last-minute way out of the trip. Maybe we would get a flat tire and I would miss my flight. Maybe the flight would be canceled altogether.

The next thing I knew, we were standing on the curb outside and saying goodbye.

My mom didn't park the car so she could walk me inside; she pulled up to the departures area and turned on her hazard lights while I unloaded my suitcase from the trunk. She leaned against the car and yawned while she watched me.

"I guess I'll see you next week," I told her.

"Okay, kid. See you next week." After a pause, she held out her arms and pulled me into an awkward half embrace, patting me on the back like she was trying to burp a baby. My mom shows physical affection like an alien trying to mimic normal human behavior. I clung to her, which was unusual for me, but I was still so rattled from the call. Why? It was almost certainly a prank, I knew, but I couldn't figure out how or what the point might have been. Who was Gizmo? How did the caller know my name? Why now, right before this trip? It didn't make any sense. I tried to wish it away as a dream, but the evidence was right there in my call log.

"Hey," Mom said suddenly. "What's the matter? I thought you were excited for this."

"I am excited." I got the sense she was equally excited, if not more so, at the thought of her only child being halfway across the world for the next seven days. "I've never been this far away from home before. And there won't be any cell service or wifi on the island."

My mom jiggled her keys impatiently. "Don't be a baby, Emma. You'll be fine. Have fun with your friends. Get a tan. Eat some oysters. Just don't do anything stupid."

"What if—"

"*Emma.* Your grandfather survived three tours in Vietnam. Your grandmother survived being married to him after he came home. I survived both of them. You can survive for a week on the beach."

That's Mom for you. Pure tact. "I know."

"But do *not*, under any circumstances"—she pointed her finger at me—"forget to wear sunscreen on your face and neck every single day. You don't want wrinkles."

"Okay."

Ask Mom.

"Hey, Mom?" I asked as she was getting into the car. "Do you know anybody named Gizmo?"

She let out a long, exasperated sigh, like I'd asked her to recite the Gettysburg Address off the top of her head. "Gizmo? That isn't a name." She was pulling her door shut when she stopped and rolled down the window to call after me. "Emma?"

"Yeah?"

"Actually, I do remember now. Gizmo was our family code word."

As soon as she said it, I remembered, too. I felt dizzy. Family code words were a big trend on social media when I was a kid. The idea was that every family should have a secret code word to use in emergencies. Like, if a stranger approached you on the playground and said they knew your mom and she'd been in an accident and you needed to come with them right away, you could ask them your family code word to verify their story. If they didn't know the code word, you didn't go with them.

We never had a reason to use ours. We haven't talked about it in years. I hadn't even remembered it.

Until now.

Perhaps it might be said rightly that there are three times: a time present of things past; a time present of things present; and a time present of things future. For these three do coexist somehow in the soul, for otherwise I could not see them.

—*Confessions of St. Augustine*

Part 1

Emma

Monday

Auggie Marshall and I are an unlikely couple.

If someone had told me a year ago that I would spend my senior year dating him, I would have assumed they were naive or on bath salts. Someone like Auggie doesn't go out with someone like me. They go out with someone like Claire Tully, who won't even say *damn*, or Megan Shepherd, who loves Jesus and horses and Taylor Swift. People who live with parents who are still married to each other and have families that sit down to eat dinner together each night around the dining room table.

The kind of person I can never be, even if I want to. I'm not dainty and soft-spoken like Claire. I'm not talented like Megan. On paper? Sure, I'm as accomplished as the next girl: I took dance classes and piano lessons as a kid; I was a Girl Scout; I've always gotten decent enough grades, and I'm going to a good college next fall. I'm in the ski club, and I run cross country. But I'm not particularly good at any of it. I was a terrible dancer, a disaster onstage. I don't have an ear for music, which baffles me, like a foreign language I never studied. I'm the slowest runner on the cross-country team. I'm a slob. I'm weird.

I'm perfectly aware of all of this, yet I do nothing to change it. I just can't quite manage to take anything seriously enough, you know? All those years of dance and piano and theater camps and other extracurriculars are things that have happened *to* me, but I've never come close to *becoming* a dancer, or a piano player, or a runner. I'm like a knockoff of my own self.

Louis says I'm champagne and onion rings.

My mom says I'm Diet Coke, but I'll never be Coke Classic.

Mom has a whole list of commandments for girls and women. These commandments are meant to act as a guide to the shittiness of capital-r-Reality and how we women can best exploit it for our own interests. It isn't an *actual* list written on stone tablets or a legal pad, but it might as well be.

I can summarize the commandments thusly:

1) Every girl can be pretty if she puts her mind to it, but few girls are truly beautiful.

2) Being beautiful is like having a superpower because people—all people, not just straight men—are nicer to beautiful women.

3) My chestnut brown hair and light smattering of freckles on my white skin make me average at best, but never beautiful.

4) *Pretty* is temporary. *Beautiful* lasts a lifetime.

5) Because my looks have an expiration date, I need to use them to my advantage while I still can.

6) To squander my good looks would be a slap in the face to my mother, to society, and maybe even to God.

7) Yes, this is about women falling in line in a male-

dominated society, "but that's Reality, kiddo." You don't have to like it, but you ain't gonna change it.

8) There is no such thing as being too thin, unless I become thinner than her, in which case I need to put on a few pounds. (Of course, then I'm fat again, and the cycle restarts.)

9) Carbs are the devil, and they are to be avoided at all costs.

10) She's only trying to help.

I know the commandments make her seem like a one-dimensional Disney villain—like Rapunzel's mom—but there are plenty of good things about her. Besides, it's not her fault she's so insecure. When I was a kid, my dad used to joke that, when my mom turned forty, he would swap her for two twenty-year-olds. He waited until she was thirty-seven before he traded her in for a twenty-four-year-old.

Regardless of Mom's completely misguided "help," though, what Auggie and I have is somehow real. We care about each other. Maybe we even love each other. It started when we both got assigned to Max's advisory group. We didn't know each other at all—our social circles don't overlap much. But when it all began back in September, we knew it was something worth paying attention to. It got serious right away.

I still think about the first time he held my hand as we walked through the halls of our high school. It was a Monday morning. Auggie and I had gone to see a movie together the previous Friday for our first real date. He took my hand when the lights dimmed and didn't let go until the credits rolled. Then he showed up at my house on Saturday morning with flowers, and we spent the day watching Netflix and making out until our mouths went numb. It was indescribable. Electric.

But then he didn't call or text me all day Sunday, and I convinced myself I was naive for ever thinking someone as perfect as Auggie Marshall, with his halo of blond hair and angelic blue eyes, might be serious about me. I didn't sit beside him in advisory on Monday morning. I didn't even look in his direction. As we were leaving the room, he steered me around a corner and backed me gently against a row of lockers. "Why are you ignoring me? Did I do something wrong?"

"No! Look, Auggie—I didn't want you to feel awkward. It's okay."

"What's okay?"

"You know. Whatever happened this weekend—I don't want you to worry that I got the wrong idea."

"What idea is that?"

"The idea that we're boyfriend and girlfriend now just because we spent some time together. I don't want you to worry that I'm going to get obsessed with you or anything like that."

"Oh. Okay." He paused. "But what if I'm obsessed with you?"

I was melting. I was losing my goddamn mind. *I'm in* The Summer I Turned Pretty*! He's Conrad and I'm Belly and she is me and this is really happening.*

"Let me walk you to class." He took my hand. People stared. He didn't care.

That was more than eight months ago. Since then, we've spent hours in his bedroom, our lips locked together, our shirts on the floor. We've steamed up the windows of his mother's minivan plenty of times. But we've never done the full deed. We've talked about it a lot, of course. We both agree we want it to be special. It will be special.

Auggie says he loves me, and I think I love him. Is this what love feels like? In late October I typed, "What does it feel like to be in love?" into Google, and my feelings for Auggie seemed pretty close to the results.

Last weekend, after a long talk, we decided we were ready. Tonight is the night. The anticipation has been building between us all week. Auggie seems nervous, and I've found myself wondering lately if he's as sure about us as he's been telling me. I'm nervous, too, of course; I'm not exactly an expert. In fact, I have almost no idea what I'm doing. I'm a little bit terrified, if I'm being honest.

A huge part of me desperately wants to just get it over with. Virginity is such a burden.

Emma

Day 54

The weirdness of this place cannot be overstated. Everything is weird here. Louis is being weird. Auggie is being weird. Max is being weird. Things might feel more normal if we weren't so isolated—and by isolated I mean trapped. There's something terrifying about knowing we can't leave this island if we want or need to without first making arrangements for the private ferry, which I'm guessing would take a few hours or more. There is no internet and no cell service.

Before I get ahead of myself, I should explain how I got into this whole mess in the first place. Whether people believe me or not doesn't make any of this less true. I am now a living witness to the extraordinary. But how to share my story with the world? I had the idea, ages ago, to keep a diary. I imagined myself assuming my rightful place among history's most famous diarists. Virginia Woolf. Bridget Jones. Emma Davidson.

But it's hard to do that when every morning is another blank page.

It's Xavier Academy's senior class trip. Or it's one of them. Not everybody goes on the same trip. The senior class gets split up into advisory groups at the beginning of the year and competes to determine which group goes to which trip at the end of the year. All trips are not created equal, and the options change from year to year. Last year, the winners spent a week on a cruise in Central America while the losers rode donkeys at the Grand Canyon, which isn't the worst thing, but it's not a cruise. Points are calculated based on things like average GPA, number of volunteer hours completed outside school, various fundraising efforts, trivia games, and weekly intramural Frisbee tag.

It's supposed to be fun, and it is fun, but the games are also viciously competitive. Tears and occasional bloodshed are all but guaranteed. This year alone, we saw multiple bloody noses, a dislocated shoulder, and a compound shin fracture. Kids who couldn't solve a quadratic equation if their grandma's life depended on it somehow became able to craft and carry out elaborate acts of sabotage and underhandedness with the same attention to detail as a professional thief planning a bank heist.

The stakes are high enough to justify the subterfuge. While we've been at the beach all week, Ms. Miller and her team, who really shit the bed in the trivia competition and sealed their fate in last place with an embarrassing average GPA, are in the woods a thousand miles away learning how to climb mountains and go spelunking, both of which sound like punishment to me.

Our location is remote. The island is tiny and private. Gus and his daughter, Greta, are the only long-term residents. For four months out of every year, the two of them run an oyster farm on their sliver of heaven, which is barely more than a sandbar in the shape of a crescent moon in the middle of the ocean. According to Gus, before coming to the island, he taught oceanography at a university in Ireland. But there has to be more to the story.

Yes, the island is small, but it's also *his private freaking island*. He doesn't look like he can afford to supersize his meal combo, much less own his own island. I know there are plenty of millionaires (or even billionaires) out there who don't necessarily look the part within their day-to-day lives, but Gus is on a different level of decrepitude. He is a skinny old white man with a poorly trimmed white mustache that does little to hide a mouth full of mossy, overlapping teeth. His thin lips are cracked and dry, constantly dotted with white flecks of spittle. A squirrel could have suffocated in his beard, which reached almost all the way to his belly button. We've been calling him "Meth Santa" behind his back.

He is a weird guy; I got an uneasy feeling from him right away. Going to Xavier Academy all my life means I've spent a lot of time around people with money, and one thing I can tell you for sure is: the richer somebody becomes, the weirder they get. Too much money can make a person lose their humanity.

Gus and Greta live together half a mile beyond the last bungalow in a tiny yellow house attached to a large cement building the size of a middle school gymnasium. Rows and rows of tanks inside held piles of oysters, their shells green and mottled and ancient-looking, hundreds of shells in piles that were constantly being sculpted and rearranged into wavy landscapes by the currents, which were being generated by oily pumps that chuffed and were too hot to touch as they churned water to and from the sea in big, shuddering pipes.

For a few hours each afternoon, we wore heavy rubber gloves up to our elbows and packed oysters into temperature-controlled boxes to be shipped all over the world. For the first day or two, the smell was so overwhelming that a handful of us (myself included) were still gagging from inside our bungalows, half a mile downwind. By the third day, it was tolerable. Eventually we all got used to it.

Some things I have learned about oysters:

1) These bivalves provide a rich source of zinc and protein.

2) To properly shuck an oyster: First, hold the oyster flat in your palm with the hinge facing away from you. Insert

a sharp blade between the shells. Move the blade in a single, swift upward thrust to sever the connective ligament holding it shut.

3) Oysters can change genders, becoming male or female depending on environment and life cycle.

4) Cloudy fluid indicates the presence of fresh ejaculate.

5) Oysters are considered aphrodisiacs because they resemble labia folds.

6) The pearls inside oysters are created as a defense mechanism against parasites.

7) A raw, freshly shucked oyster will likely still be alive when you eat it.

8) Max's inability to "shoot" raw oysters (which is when you tilt your head back to swallow one whole) is the direct result of a traumatic event from his childhood, in which his older brother pinned him (Max) against the ground, forced his mouth open, and hocked a fully intact loogie down his throat.

9) No two oysters taste the same.

10) Oysters are gross.

Max, our advisor, is the only faculty member on the trip. A few things about him: He is a relatively young Black man who's only been teaching at our school for a couple of years, but his dad is our head of school, so it isn't like he is exactly new. He teaches senior English and intro to sociology. You know how every high school in the history of secondary education has a "cool" teacher? Max is our cool teacher, or at least he wants to be. He is one of the only faculty members who dresses casually, wearing lived-in alternative rock T-shirts and loafers without socks, and he keeps his locs in a tight bun at the back of his head. But he is also the only teacher who insists we address him by his first name, which is weird. I have enough friends.

Besides, being cool doesn't automatically make someone a good teacher. Max is kind of a lousy teacher, if I'm being honest. There are times when I get the feeling that he genuinely dislikes his job and, by extension, his students. Nobody else seems to see it; the rest of my classmates adore him. I can tell it makes them feel like real grown-ups when they call him "Max" instead of "Mr. D," as though that means anything at all. *You need to hear this amazing punk band Max turned me on to. Did you know Max volunteered for the Bernie Sanders campaign?*

It's all a bit much, don't you think? Sometimes I liked to chime in with my own "fun facts" about him: *Max still uses a hotmail email address. Max has seen Celine Dion in concert three times.* (Okay, fine—I made up the second one.)

I mean, he could have been worse. There are plenty of bad teachers at our school. For example: Before he got catfished and lost his life savings and had to retire and move back in with his kids, the head of our math department, Dr. Swisher, had never once smiled or laughed in all the years I'd known him. The assistant cheerleading coach got fired last year for sharing her Adderall prescription with some of the cheerleaders who she thought could use "extra pep." The front office secretary, Mrs. Gibson, was rumored to have a bunch of DUIs on her record.

I used to think I was being too hard on Max sometimes. Because it isn't like he's a bad guy; he is super smart, just a bad teacher, which isn't necessarily his fault. It can't be an easy job teaching high school kids at any school, but Xavier Academy is not any old school. It is an elite prep school whose alumni include senators, bestselling authors, a few professional athletes, and even a pop star. Annual tuition is as much as some colleges. The student body includes a number of brilliant, studious kids, but it's mostly made up of ordinary kids who happened to be born to wealthy parents. These parents have certain expectations for their children, and the word "ordinary" isn't part of those expectations. Which means the faculty is expected to spin straw into gold.

But I *wasn't* being too hard on him. If anything, I was being too easy on him. Sure, I used to think he was cringy, and maybe not as cool as he thought he was, but I believed he was essentially a good person. He was my teacher, so I trusted him. Maybe that was my first mistake.

Teachers are just people, you know. They lie. They let us down. But we still expect them to always do their best. A teacher keeps their students safe. Pilots don't drink on the job. Parents never hurt their children. The problem is, deep down, we know it's all bullshit. Bad teachers are everywhere; your pilot might be drunk, or depressed, or running on almost no sleep; a child's abuser is often their parent and almost always a trusted adult. So we look toward a higher authority for comfort. We tell ourselves a story where everything happens for a reason and good people always get a happy ending. We believe what we know is impossible. All of us. Even the ones who think they don't, do: everybody worships something.

Yet sometimes the impossible does happen, things that could even be called miracles: a man's cancer goes into spontaneous remission; a teenager from a tiny village in Vietnam gets knocked unconscious and wakes up speaking fluent French.

I had my own miracle once. I've never told anybody, because I know they wouldn't believe me. But it happened. A little background: I was five years old, and I was obsessed with butterflies. I had a pair of butterfly wings that I wore everywhere; I carried a net anytime I went outside in case I encountered a butterfly. My mom bought me a butterfly hatching kit. We had to send away for the cocoons, which were delivered to our doorstep after an agonizing few weeks of waiting. We set up the habitat and followed the directions carefully, but all the cocoons died, and I was devastated.

My favorite book at the time was *The Very Hungry Caterpillar* by Eric Carle. After countless hours spent poring over the book and its pictures, through a warped tangle of kid logic and complete lack of critical thinking skills, I ate several caterpillars in an attempt to poop butterflies. For a few days afterward, I peered excitedly into the toilet bowl after every number two, but it should surprise nobody to learn that no butterflies emerged fully formed from my butthole. After a week or two, I gave up hope.

And then one night all my dreams were in black and white. I dreamed I was lost in a forest. There were logs strewn all over the ground, crawling with caterpillars and butterflies. When I woke up in the morning and went to the bathroom, I looked down to see a large brown moth perched on the inner edge of the toilet bowl.

As I got older, my rational mind understood it must have been a coincidence. Of course it was a coincidence—an astronomically, incalculably unlikely coincidence.

But I'll admit, there was always a part of me that thought… *maybe*. Maybe.

Bradd

Monday

Max wants us to keep diaries all week. He said it was for extra credit, but he also said it was "nonnegotiable," which is a contradiction. In either case, I think not. Diaries are for little girls who love horsies and unmarried women with too many cats. I'm a calendar man. My father is a calendar man, and his father before him was a calendar man. If you want to know what I was doing on, say, June 10 of last year, all I have to do is refer to my notated calendar, which I keep on a shelf in my closet with all my other calendars. I've been keeping a detailed calendar since I was ten years old. Max said I wouldn't get the extra credit if I turned in a calendar. He said it had to be a diary. Oh, I'm sorry—a *journal*. So dumb. No extra credit for me, I guess. Who cares?

As the great Malvolio sang in our school's spring musical version of *Twelfth Night*: some men are born great, some men are made great, some men have greatness thrust upon them. And then there's me, with all three advantages. I'm hitting nothing but triples on my worst day.

I'm the owner of multiple patents. Twenty-three, to be exact. Soon I'll have twenty-four. Alison was actually the one who came up with a good idea today, but she said I could have it. It was an idea for a dating site where people are only allowed to list their worst qualities. Pretty great concept, right? I could patent that. You'd be surprised what a person can patent thanks to the concept of "intellectual property." As my father likes to say, "What a time to be alive."

I am crushing life. Absolutely crushing it. I am a winner. I am at the beach for a week, looking forward to graduation and college and everything else that life has in store for me. The school tried to talk up all the retreats as equally "broadening opportunities" (ha!), but they weren't fooling anybody; my group knows we won. Because of course we did: like I said, I'm a winner.

Our group—the beach group—was cautioned not to expect luxury, but I wasn't too worried; at least we were getting indoor plumbing. But we *are* kind of roughing it out here, which I can tell some people are a little disappointed by. We are on an island in the middle of nowhere. After a four-hour flight to Miami, we took a two-hour flight to someplace called Kincaid Island, which is a decommissioned military base that only gets used now for its runway and ferry services. We were in a little prop plane for that flight. Except for the pilots, we were the only ones on board. There was no flight attendant or drink service or anything like that. They didn't even close the door to the cockpit. I didn't actually think that was legal.

Because it was such a small plane, the ride was bumpy as hell, and people were starting to lose their shit left and right. Not me—I was fine. I don't get scared. But almost everyone else was terrified. It was kind of funny, if I'm being honest. I thought Auggie Marshall was going to start crying. Lucy Thomas was babbling to herself about the mechanics of flight under her breath: *It's like a boat in the sky! The plane wants to be in the air! Turbulence has never brought down a plane!* At that last one, I leaned across the aisle and said, “But don’t you think a plane crash would be turbulent?”

I thought for sure Louis Martinez was going to puke. Lily Foose *did* puke. (Why does all puke smell exactly the same?) Gianluca Spinetti, one of our exchange students—my girlfriend Alison and her friends call him the Italian Stallion—clasped his hands in prayer and repeated the rosary in frantic Italian. Besides me, Alison was the only other passenger who kept their cool, which is part of why I love her: she doesn’t get scared, either. While everybody else was freaking out, she was giggling and braiding her long blond hair into twin pigtails while we watched the *Barbie* movie on her iPad.

“Where are Barbie’s parents while all these shenanigans are going on?” I wondered out loud.

Alison thought that was the funniest thing she’d ever heard for some reason. “Barbie isn’t a teenager, babe. She’s an adult.”

“No way.”

“Yes way. Come on, Bradd,” she scoffed, “think about it. They don’t send teenagers to space.” She made a good point. Alison is clever like that.

After the second flight, we took a long ferry ride. The ferry captain had a weird accent—like, Dutch but not Dutch—and was missing his left hand. The boat was kind of small and the water was choppy as hell, and a few people *did* end up puking over the side, which was *awesome*. Puke doesn’t bother me. Body fluids in general don’t gross me out. Or bodies at all, for that matter. I would probably make an amazing doctor. Maybe a surgeon. Gynecology, even. But I’ve set my ambitions a bit higher. I’m a world-changer, my dad says.

Gus, the guy who owns the island and built everything, is supposedly some kind of billionaire science genius. But when he met us at the dock, there were visible food particles in his beard.

He smells like a hot fart and the sea. Maybe it's a weird flex? Like he has so much money that he wants everybody to know he has the freedom to give zero fucks about his surroundings or personal appearance. I kind of get it. But it's like, dude—brush your teeth and maybe run a comb through that beard? Whatever, I don't care.

But hey, I am still at the beach for a week with a bunch of my friends and my smoking-hot girlfriend. My only complaint is that I'm rooming with Auggie. The guy is like a human carbon monoxide leak. He's so boring that just seeing his face makes me want a nap. Like, I literally heard him say "fiddlesticks" once instead of "fuck." But he's also kind of a jerk, too? Like, he'll tell you to your face that he thinks you're going to Hell. First of all: not bloody likely, because I'm a great person. Second of all: aren't religious people supposed to be nice? So he's somehow both the most boring person in the world and also an asshole. A mystery wrapped in an enigma wrapped in a who-gives-a-shit. I'd off him if I could get away with it.

It's going to be a great week.

Louis

Tuesday

Because there were no curtains on our shitty windows, I was up with the sun, even though I'd barely slept the night before. I was exhausted and still feeling kind of seasick. The room felt like it was rocking back and forth as I lay in bed. My back was already killing me from being cramped into a tiny seat on the long flights, not to mention the bumpy ferry ride, and all I had for a mattress was one of those crappy slabs of foam like the ones they sell at army surplus stores, which was not a real mattress at all, if you asked me—it was a slab of fucking foam on a creaky box spring. Mine was stained with the sweat of strangers (I hoped it was sweat) and smelled like Lysol disinfectant.

Oh—and I was bunking with Connor Cackowski. I don't even know where to start with that unfortunate fact. Connor Cackowski loves two things: playing the acoustic guitar and the sound of his own voice. He's always using the word "evidently." It drives me nuts.

Evidently it's raining. Evidently I'm going to bed. He doesn't even use it correctly half the time.

The island is mostly flat and very narrow. You could walk the length in an hour and a half and go all the way across in twenty minutes on foot. There are no cars on the island; people either get around on foot or via golf cart.

Gus and his daughter, Greta, met us at the dock. Greta ran straight to Max and threw her arms around his neck. He lifted her up by the waist and spun her around, and that's when I realized the only reason we are all here in the first place is so our teacher can get laid.

Gus's intern, Steven, told us to leave our luggage right where it was and promised he'd deliver it to our bungalows while Gus and Greta gave us a tour. Everything seemed impressive at first. They led us into a big lounge area strewn with comfy sofas and a pool table. Thick, wooden beams stretched diagonally across a high, vaulted ceiling. There was a huge, double-sided stone fireplace in the middle of the room. He showed us an industrial-size kitchen that was all sleek, clean metal surfaces and carefully organized shelves.

We ate lunch in the adjacent dining hall. The food was okay. There was some fresh fruit (bananas and pineapple), but everything else was nursing-home quality and either frozen or canned, which I guess is unavoidable in a place like this. But I didn't mind because, as Gus was quick to inform us, we were promised an unlimited supply of fresh oysters at every meal.

I do love oysters.

Everything is good. Everything is fine. The isolation is a little bit eerie, if I'm being honest; there is nothing and nobody but us. We are surrounded by water as far as the eye can see in every direction. There's a helipad but no helicopter. The nearest hospital is hundreds of miles away. Our parents had to sign release forms in order for us to even get here; I'm pretty sure Max is technically my legal guardian for the week. What if somebody gets appendicitis? I guess they're shit outta luck.

Gus assured us everything would be fine, of course. "Nothing bad ever happens at the beach," he declared, which anybody who's ever seen *Jaws* knows is not true. It didn't take me long to conclude that Gus was either full of shit about everything or he was the coolest guy who'd ever lived. Within twenty-four hours of us meeting him, he told us he'd sailed around the world—alone—four times. That he'd climbed Mount Kilimanjaro and that he spoke five languages and had three PhDs. He'd been knighted by the queen. He had a photographic memory. He once saw a monk levitate.

After lunch, and after we'd all unpacked, we met in the fishery house where Gus had all his aquariums set up. We spent the afternoon listening as he and Greta told us everything there was to know about oyster farming. I'd eaten a weed gummy beforehand, so I remembered almost nothing the minute it was over.

I'm embarrassed to admit it, but I let Lily Foose give me a backrub after that. I knew it was wrong to lead her on—she's had a big crush on me for years—but my back was really sore. I've already told her I'm not interested in her romantically, and now I was opening this whole can of worms again by letting her give me a rubdown, letting her put out a sex vibe. I can't say I wasn't tempted after all that skin-to-skin contact—she had me take my shirt off and lie face down on my foam slab, and then she straddled me and slathered my back and shoulders in aloe and gave me a slow, sensual massage. If that isn't a hint, then I'm the pope.

Lily is nice and all, but she isn't my type. Still, I am only human. To prevent myself from getting aroused, I thought about the time I'd accidentally seen my abuelo's penis once, when he was in the hospital. It looked like a stuffed grape leaf. My mom saw it, too; later I overheard her telling my dad they might as well plan a trip to Australia now, because there were two things she'd never wanted to see in her life: her father's penis, and Australia. My mother is deathly afraid of kangaroos.

When Gus told us at dinner that there was going to be a meteor shower later, everybody got pretty excited. The stars here are the brightest ones I've ever seen. There's too much light pollution to see much of anything in the sky back at home. I've never seen a single shooting star, let alone a meteor shower.

Connor wasn't interested in watching the meteor shower—*evidently* he was working on a new song—so I walked to the beach alone. Somebody had brought a big blanket and spread it out on the sand. There was plenty of room for everybody.

Bradd Hazelett was there with his girlfriend, Alison Lawrence. Bradd sat with his legs spread in a *V* while Alison leaned against his chest; the two of them looked like the worst kind of Abercrombie ad: two white people who know they're hot. They were sharing a weed vape. Alison was shivering; it was chilly, and she was only wearing a flimsy pair of boxer shorts over her string bikini. She pinched the flesh around her waist. "Ugh, baby, I feel so fat."

"You aren't fat."

"Look at this." She poked at her belly button. "I look pregnant."

"You just ate dinner. It's just a food baby." Ew. These two were The Worst with capital letters. I sometimes couldn't believe they were real.

Bradd's presence alone was almost enough to make me turn around and skip the whole thing. Bradd is such a dickhead that our entire student body, including the faculty, has tacitly embraced the long-established rumor that the extra "d" in his name actually stands for "dickhead." Like, legally. I wouldn't be surprised if it ends up in the yearbook somehow. Personally, I prefer to address him with a semi-phonetic pronunciation of his name: "Brad-d." It annoys the shit out of him.

"Hey, what if I did get you pregnant? What would we name the baby?" He nuzzled his nose into her ear.

Alison didn't hesitate. "Medical Waste."

Aside from me, Bradd, and Alison, the only other people on the beach were Emma and Auggie. If you asked me to make a list of my fifty favorite people in the whole world, Emma would probably be number one. (Auggie wouldn't be on the list at all.) Emma and

I have been the closest of pals since the county-wide elementary school spelling bee in fourth grade, when the competition was down to just the two of us in the final round. I'd just misspelled "citizen," which meant that Emma only needed to spell one more word correctly in order to win, and that word was "cupboard." I remember the way she fidgeted beside me onstage in our school cafetorium as our parents watched dutifully from the audience. We'd already been neighbors for years, and she knew me well enough to know that I needed a win. Things were rough for me at home. She spelled "cupboard" as "k-u-p-p-e-r-d." The audience audibly groaned. I stared at her. She gave me the tiniest grin and a little shrug. I'll never forget it.

It was a bit awkward being the only person without a partner on the beach. But that was okay; I'd come prepared. I crept quietly behind Emma and unzipped my backpack, then I slowly removed the head and hands of what had formerly been a life-size mermaid sculpture. While nobody was paying attention—they were all staring at the sky—I placed one of the hands on Emma's shoulder. She screamed when she noticed it, an ear-splitting scream, and then she started laughing. She laughed with her whole body. It was more of a cackle, really. She's self-conscious about it, but it's adorable.

She clapped a hand to her mouth in embarrassment, trying to muffle the sound as she shook with giggles.

Beside her, Auggie gave me a dirty look. That's when Emma noticed the mermaid's head, and she completely lost it.

"You brought Maggie!" she cried. "Auggie, he brought Maggie!"

Auggie made a face like he'd just accidentally seen my abuelo's penis. "Who is Maggie?"

"Maggie the mermaid!" She couldn't stop laughing. She took one of the hands from me and used it to caress Auggie's face.

He shoved it away. "Let me guess: this is another installment in the adventures of Emma and Louis."

When my parents were trying to sell their house last year, they kind of got into it with our next-door neighbor. He was an eccentric old artist, and there was already some bad blood between him and my dad because of some lawn maintenance bullshit from years ago that involved my dad accusing the guy of being a racist and then a few of our hedges being mysteriously bulldozed down. My dad was still holding a grudge over it.

Anyway, for years this neighbor kept a mermaid, who we all knew as Maggie, displayed in his front yard. He claimed it was an art thing, but we all suspected it was more of a sex thing; he used to dress her up in elaborate costumes for every conceivable occasion and holiday. For Christmas, she was dressed as Mrs. Claus; on Easter, she was Maggie the bunny; you get the idea.

My parents happened to be trying to sell our house during Mardi Gras. Mardi Gras Maggie was topless (her nipples were huge), with bright strands of beads draped over her neck and a red Solo cup taped to her hand. My parents were convinced the house wasn't selling because nobody wants to live next door to the kind of person who puts a topless mermaid on display in his front yard, so they asked our neighbor if he would be so kind as to keep Maggie inside, just for a little while. He said no.

So late one night, Emma and I crept into the neighbor's front yard and stole her. We moved her into my parents' garage and dismembered her with a Skil saw under the cover of darkness. Nobody has ever had so much fun cutting up a body. For weeks, I kept her stashed underneath my bed in an oversize duffel bag. My neighbor nearly lost his mind; you'd have thought someone had kidnapped his only child. He was convinced my parents were responsible. Our house sold a few days later.

Six months later, Emma and I drove forty miles away and mailed Maggie's Mardi Gras beads, along with one of her fingers, to my former neighbor in an envelope with no return address.

Auggie was less than impressed by the story. "So you stole this poor man's property, and then you terrorized him, and you think that's funny."

Emma and I looked at each other. "Yes," we said in unison.

Auggie glared at me. I held out Maggie's head. "Give her a kiss, Auggie. She's lonely."

Bradd and Alison had been listening while Emma told the story. "You know what you should have done?" Bradd said, his eyes flashing in the moonlight. "You should have mailed him the nipples."

"Can I keep her head?" Emma asked. "Just for the week?"

"You should let Louis hang on to it," Auggie told her. He slung an arm around her shoulders. "So he doesn't have to be all alone." He smirked at me.

Bradd leaned over to me and stage-whispered: "You know, I could make you a nice Fleshlight from that head, dude."

Jesus Christ.

Alison

Tuesday

Mr. Crumbly, our econ professor, liked to kick off his lectures by reminding us that high school was the best time of our lives. He was overflowing with old chestnuts like *youth is wasted on the young* and *you'll only be this age once* and *enjoy it while it lasts.* I always felt sorry for him. It was like he didn't actually exist in an active sense; his whole life reeked of what he used to be, and he clung to those accolades: *I was once a star athlete. I was once a top student. I was once a handsome boy.* He'd grown up and stayed in the same town and eventually stopped growing altogether. Once he was good and fat and bald in his early forties, he left his first wife for the high school cheerleading coach. Super original.

Men are so disappointing.

By October of my senior year, I didn't recognize myself. I couldn't fathom getting through the next eight months until graduation. Most days, all I did was fantasize about getting far enough away from my past and everyone who knew me to finally see myself through my own eyes. To carve out my own identity without the weight of everyone else's expectations. I had the feeling I'd been switching out one costume for another, over and over again depending on the occasion, for my whole life.

My teachers said I was distracted. My parents assumed I was depressed and found me a good therapist. I told my therapist the truth: I was in love. But it's not what you're thinking.

I wasn't expecting it. I'd never even thought about it. But when I locked eyes with Lucy Thomas on the first day of school this year, I felt something wake up inside me—something I didn't even know about—and suddenly all I could see was her thick black hair and smooth white skin, smell her lilac perfume. I tried to push it down, to ignore it, but it was no use. I flipped. Now there are thirty-nine days until graduation. I am still in love, and I am going out of my mind. I feel like I'm trapped here; everywhere I look, I see Bradd or Lucy. I can't think straight. I need a vacation—and by "vacation," I don't mean...whatever this is.

Our parents have been duped. "Tropical getaway" my ass. There was a spider the size of a baby's fist on the ceiling in the shower with me this morning. It was literally too big to kill without having to do some major cleanup, so I tried to ignore it while I attempted to bathe. I watched from the corner of my eye as it stepped one leg at a time—quick, elegant steps with its hairy legs, legs thrumming like impatient fingers, onetwothreefourfivesixseveneight, as it crawled across the ceiling like a disembodied hand in a black glove. I hate spiders.

The island is lush and beautiful and private. The buildings are new and sturdy. Everything is high-tech and smooth and comfortable except for the bungalows, which feel like an afterthought. They are small and shitty. They have no air conditioning or hot water; our water comes from a rain barrel on the roof. There aren't any screens on the windows.

I am rooming with Emma. She isn't my first choice. She isn't my second or third choice, either—not that anybody asked. She and I used to be the best of friends when we were little girls, but that was years ago. Maybe I had something to do with the way we drifted apart. Okay, I did have something to do with it. I might be able to come up with a few things I've done over the years that weren't exactly what you'd call shining examples of friendship. I'm not perfect. I'm only a child.

In the interest of full disclosure, here is an exhaustive list of everything I have ever done that might have potentially offended Emma:

1) Elementary school. Emma wet the bed one time when she was spending the night at my house. I told some people. Kids called her "Rip Van Tinkle" for years afterward.

2) Freshman year. Emma came down with shingles. To me, this was newsworthy because my mom is a pharmaceutical rep and she told me it's super unusual for someone so young to develop shingles. It's mostly an old person's disease. I was on the staff of our school paper that year, and I'd been looking for a big scoop. My story about Emma was on the front page. Of course, I didn't use her real name. (That would have been a HIPAA violation.) The headline was: *JV Cross-Country Underdog Sidelined by Stress Shingles*. The thing is, Emma was the only JV cross-country runner absent from school that week, and she was also the slowest cross-country runner, so it didn't take a whole lot of deduction for people to correctly guess who the article was about. I'm not sure why Emma got so bent out of shape about the whole thing, but she did. She was *pissed*.

3) Junior year, three days before Homecoming. Emma had been dating this guy, Elliott Philips, for a few months. It didn't seem serious to me. Meanwhile, my friend Kelsey had spent all year nursing a huge crush on Elliott, and she was seriously depressed because nobody had asked her to

the dance. So I did what any good friend would do: I called up Elliott and laid out a hypothetical scenario in which he maybe could go to Homecoming with someone else. And okay, maybe that's what any good friend of *Kelsey's* would have done. But to be fair, I don't blame him for breaking up with Emma less than seventy-two hours before the dance so he could take Kelsey instead. I had no way of knowing Emma's dress had cost hundreds of dollars or that getting dumped at the eleventh hour for a more popular, prettier girl would absolutely devastate her. I assumed she would be able to find another date. She was not able to find another date.

4) The Incident Where I Turned Emma's Grandma into a Balloon. I'm not ready to go into detail on this one. I know I was wrong, and I've apologized more than once. Beyond that, I'm not sure what else to do. We'll leave it at that for now.

So, yeah, things between Emma and me have been strained for a long time. We've barely spoken to each other all year in homeroom. I have other friends, of course, and I have Bradd—but I've always felt bad about what happened between Emma and me.

I used to think she was going to be my Kimmie. My mom was best friends with a woman named Kimmie Carver. I called her Aunt Kimmie even though we weren't actually blood related, and she was my godmother even though my family wasn't Catholic. She and my mom liked to say they'd known each other since they were fetuses. Their mothers were good friends who'd met when they were newly pregnant.

I didn't have anyone like Kimmie in my life for a long time. I have a Bradd, but that isn't the same thing, is it? Bradd is the kind of guy who will always look great on paper. Sometimes it feels like knowing how to look good on paper is the only thing that matters in life. He is handsome and rich and charming enough that he doesn't appear immediately deranged to the casual observer. We've been dating for three years. We like each other. We trust each other. We have fun together.

But he *is* deranged, in the best possible way. For Christmas last year—get this—he gave me a Build-A-Bear that he'd hand-stuffed almost entirely with his pubes. It came with a handwritten poem—Bradd loves to write poems—that read:

When you find yourself missing your honey
If you're feeling alone and confused
Snuggle up with this bear and take comfort
His body is filled with my pubes.

Hilarious, right?

Lucy

Tuesday

I had to beg my parents to let me come on this trip, but I wasn't about to miss it. So far things are going okay. Meals are the worst, but meals are always the worst when you're the new girl who isn't allowed to wear makeup or shave her legs, so I'm used to that.

More than anything, I want high school to be over.

Alison and I had a long talk before the trip about how we're going to treat each other. She can be mean as a snake sometimes. It isn't her fault; she thinks it's how people show love. Her wires are crossed. If you pay close enough attention, you'll notice there are people like that all over the place. But even though I understand it, that doesn't make it okay. I've already explained that I expect her to be kinder. I tried to explain that kindness feels good and costs nothing. But Ali has been struggling. For months, she's been telling me she loves me and then spending the night with Bradd, only to call me crying the next morning. She keeps saying she's going to tell him, and I keep believing her. She still hasn't done it. I don't think she's ever going to do it.

I've thought about telling him myself, but it's only a thought; I would never actually go through with it. Bradd is far too intimidating. Even though I'm a gay girl, and in spite of the way he spells his name, I understand the appeal of Braddley Hazelett. He is so pretty that I can hardly look him in the eye. He is crude, and dumb, and weird; he is a jackass and a goofball; but he isn't mean. He isn't a bully.

He is also kind of the worst, but in the same way having a pet monkey would be kind of the worst. In the middle of lunch, he pulled down his pants and bent over and tucked his dick and balls between his legs to create something he called a "fruit bowl." I didn't get a good look at it because I turned my head away in time, but I wasn't born yesterday. I can imagine what might constitute a fruit bowl made of genitals. The thing that made me angry was if Bradd weren't a senator's kid, I guarantee you Max would have sent him home on the next ferry. Instead, he did nothing. If you ask me, that reinforces a dangerous double standard that has already caused far too much irreparable damage to our society. But what do I know?

It's the first time I've ever been away from home for this much time without my parents. I was never allowed to go to sleepaway camp over the summer. Not even to Girl Scout camp, which barely counts because it's like four nights maximum and the campgrounds are a twenty-minute drive from my house. I used to watch *The Parent Trap* over and over again; I dreamed of spending my summers with a hundred other girls, especially if Lindsey Lohan was one of them. I pictured us playing pranks on each other, making lifelong friendships...and yes, sometimes I fantasized about meeting my long-lost, identical twin sister. My parents told me those kinds of camps only existed in the movies. My parents were liars.

I had such high hopes for this week. I'd even thought it might be kind of cool if there were a lot of bugs, and the weather was hot and sticky, and the food was bad— I wanted it to be authentic, like a real summer camp! And there *are* a lot of bugs, and the weather *is* hot and sticky, and the food *is* terrible, but somehow it isn't as quaint and romantic as I hoped. It's mostly just unpleasant. Where's the magic?

The first problem is my roommate. Mia wasn't in my homeroom, and we didn't share any classes. She is one of two exchange students on the trip who've been with us since January. I'm sure she's a great person, smart, with a good heart and a great sense of humor, but I have no way of knowing one way or another because I've never heard her say a word. I get the impression she doesn't know much English. I've only ever seen her speak Italian to her brother, Gianluca. They're fraternal twins, both heavy smokers, both adorable and chic with the same dark brown hair and tan skin, both petite, probably because their mother had been a heavy smoker while she was pregnant. I don't even like boys, and I have a little bit of a crush on Gianluca; I think everybody has a crush on Gianluca. His name alone: Gianluca Spinetti. Come on.

Mia isn't friendly like her brother. She barely acknowledges me even though we're sharing a living space for the week. When she isn't sleeping, she spends most of her time in our room smoking cigarettes with her head stuck halfway out the window, as though the gesture does anything at all to cut back on the thick clouds of smoke that build up. She and Gianluca argue constantly. Sometimes they argue while they play chess or while they're eating, but I've never once heard them share a pleasant conversation at a normal volume. They always seem furious with each other.

I'm allergic to cigarette smoke. I tried explaining this to Mia a number of ways, but all she did was stare at me as she kept puffing away, so I finally appealed to Gianluca. He'd been wandering around the island in nothing but a linen button-down shirt, which he left open to reveal his chest, which was hairless and shiny with oil, and a pair of bikini swim trunks that left little to the imagination. He isn't what you'd call conventionally attractive—he's shorter than most guys his age, thin and wiry—imagine if Bruno Mars had been

Italian. He has a thick head of black hair, which he keeps perfectly coiffed at all times, and a ridiculous goatee. He always reeks of cologne and cigarette smoke. He is openly disdainful of Americans, shamelessly lecherous toward all women, and arrogant. Yet he is magnetic. It has to be the accent.

I explained my problem to him and asked if he could possibly convince Mia to smoke outdoors for the rest of the week. Do you know what he said to me? He said "no" with a big smile on his smug face. He was smoking as we talked. At least we were outside. He blew a series of rings in my face as he exhaled. I had a coughing fit.

"Gianluca, do you understand what I mean by an allergy?" I coughed some more.

"Yes, I understand. You have weak body. It does not like the smoke."

"Yes! So will you please, please, *please* ask Mia to smoke outside?"

"This I cannot do." He took another long drag from his cigarette.

As the child of two dentists, I couldn't help myself from asking him: "Do you realize smoking is the leading cause of death in your country? Do you have any idea how deadly it is? By the time a smoker reaches the age of seventy-five—if they even make it to that age—they have, on average, five to seven fewer teeth than average nonsmokers." (This is a true fact. I read a lot of scholarly journals. I've always preferred to read nonfiction; fiction sometimes feels like a waste of time.)

He waved dismissively. He was still smiling. His eyes were a flinty shade of blue or green, or sometimes hazel, depending on the light. He finished his cigarette, extinguishing the tip by grinding it against the bottom of his sandal before putting the butt in his shirt pocket. At least he wasn't littering.

"Lucy." He touched my cheek with a soft hand and gazed at me with pity. "You are such a gigantic, massive party pooper."

I laughed at him. "Because I like being able to breathe? Right, I'm the asshole here. All I'm asking her to do is smoke outside."

"This is why you are not cool. You are adult too soon."

"I have asthma, Gianluca!"

"What is this asthma? I don't believe. In my country, we do not have." He offered me a cigarette. "Here. You try."

"No, thank you. Those are going to kill you someday. It's a terrible way to die."

Another look of pity. "That is problem for future Gianluca. Let me tell you story: A monk is running from big tiger who chases him toward a cliff. The monk falls over cliff and finds only a small branch to hold with soft monk hands. He knows it will break soon, and he will fall and be dead. The monk looks up at tiger, who is wanting to eat him. He looks down at long drop that will make him dead. He sees big, ripe strawberry growing from branch that will soon break. Tell me, what does monk do?"

"He dies?"

He shook his head. "Think in different way. He is only dying someday, like we all do."

"I don't know. What does he do?"

"He eats strawberry." He touched my face again and tucked a strand of hair behind my ear. Ordinarily, I wouldn't have been too happy with a man putting his hands on me without my consent, but I let him slide because of his accent. "Be happy, Lucy. Eat the strawberry. Take stick from your asshole and live."

Auggie

Wednesday

It was a wild day, and now I don't feel so good. We spent part of the afternoon cleaning tanks and packing the oysters into coolers to be shipped around the world and mopping the sticky floor afterward. Gus is using us for free labor. Actually, it's worse than that—we're paying him for the privilege. But once our work was done for the day, we feasted on oysters. Gus even let us drink some white wine, which I didn't care for much.

I lost track of how many oysters I ate. It must have been at least two dozen. Eating oysters is so much more than simply *eating*. The act of shucking them, the ritual of assembly before consumption: a squeeze of lemon, a dollop of horseradish. Once I got started, I couldn't stop. People aren't kidding when they say oysters are an aphrodisiac. The sexual parallels are obvious: impaling an unassuming creature with enough force to break something open that has spent its whole life sealed shut, consuming something so fresh and delicate and sensual that it almost feels like an act of consummation. It feels like a sin to eat an oyster. Like a good sin.

I didn't expect to feel homesick, but I am. The island is so foreign and isolated; I feel unmoored. There's never a quiet moment thanks to the constant sounds of wildlife. On our first day, while we were exploring the island, we came across a deep cave eroded into a rocky cliffside. The ground inside was caked in layer upon layer of bat guano so pungent that my eyes burned. Above us were hundreds, maybe thousands, of sleeping bats. All those leathery wings and fuzzy faces and disease. Every night at dusk they awakened to fly in low circles above the trees, searching for food. One of the first things Gus told us when we arrived was that we were absolutely not to harm any living creature on the island. We were in their world, he reminded us. We were the invasive species, and we were to disturb their ecosystem as little as possible. That meant no killing spiders or squishing bugs that were as big as my palm.

The air is humid and suffocating everywhere, but it's worst in the room I'm forced to share with Bradd. He brought a bunch of different vape pens with flavors like cotton candy and butterscotch toffee and mocha mint, and he puffs on them constantly—he even slept with one clutched in his fist and took hits while he slept. He insisted he couldn't see the thick clouds in our room or smell the cloying sweetness that permeates every surface. The high humidity only makes everything smell that much worse. Bradd douses himself in DEET and cologne multiple times a day. He spends much of his time in our room fully nude, regardless of whether or not I happen to be there. He did push-ups nude. He stood with one leg on the edge of the bathroom sink and left the door open while he shaved his balls with an electric razor every. Single. Morning. He collected his loose body hair and kept it in a clear Ziploc bag.

Emma says Bradd is like if Ivanka Trump's vibrator were a person. He and I are never going to get along. There is something wrong with him. There are a *lot* of things wrong with him. In addition to the constant nudity and vaping and ball-shaving, he is absolutely obsessed with sex in general. I woke up this morning to the sound of him jacking off less than six feet away, in his little bed with the *Star Wars* sheets he'd brought from home. I pretended to be asleep. He knew I wasn't sleeping. He didn't even try to be quiet. I felt a little bit assaulted. He's extremely curious about my sexual habits. One time he asked me if I'd ever pretended to be sick so I could stay home from school all day and have "an eight-hour wankfest." He seemed shocked when I said no. "Dude, sometimes there's, like, an old season of *Adventure Time* on streaming—"

I physically recoiled. "That's a *cartoon*."

"Yeah, so? That Princess Bubblegum is *hot*, dude."

"Isn't she, like, a sentient piece of bubble gum? And I dunno, like, a teenager?"

"So what?" Bradd asked. "I'm a teenager, too."

I shouldn't have bothered engaging with him, but I was too curious not to ask. "You know about the internet, right?"

"You mean porn?" Bradd scoffed. "Don't want it, don't need it. Looking at porn is like bowling with bumpers. Too easy." He looked at me with...I want to call it a combination of admiration, disapproval, and general sleaze. "Do you look at that shit, Auggie?"

"Of course not." I said it too quickly, and he knew I was lying.

"Uh-huh. Right. That shit is dangerous, you know. It's degrading to women. And half those chicks are coerced, or trafficked, or worse." He shook his head. "I can't get off to that. Neither should you. There's no ethical way to consume pornography in the digital age unless you're involved in every aspect of production from start to finish." Bradd tapped the side of his head. "That's why God gave us an imagination. I can think of the filthiest shit I want to in my own mind, and nobody gets exploited. I could be thinking about your mom right now. I could be thinking about your *dad* right now."

My stomach was already churning from too many oysters. My skin felt clammy. All I wanted was to be left alone, but that was not in the cards. Once Bradd was gone, I stripped down to my boxer shorts, opened all the windows to let some fresh air in, and got into bed. My eyes hadn't been closed for five minutes when I heard a light tapping at my door. I tried to ignore it, hoping whoever it was would give up and go away, but the tapping grew more insistent.

"I know you're in there, Auggie." It was Shelby Tucker.

The oysters weren't the only thing making me feel sick. I had another, bigger problem.

I'm an asshole. I'm a cheater. I felt awful about it. But it happened. It was still happening.

It started innocently enough: We were selling Christmas trees last December to raise money for the Fellowship of Christian Athletes. They do it every year. It's a miserable job. Even in brutal freezing temps, you're supposed to stand around in the parking lot so you're ready to help customers when they arrive. One day it was just the two of us working the lot. The snow was coming down hard. We were closing in an hour, and we probably could have just called it a day and gone home, because who goes out in a blizzard to buy a Christmas tree? But we were both afraid of getting in trouble for leaving early.

Shelby trekked around the corner in her pink snowsuit and boots and bought us hot chocolate from a gas station to keep us from freezing. When the hot chocolate didn't work as well as we hoped, we decided to sit in my car for a few minutes with the heat blasting. The next thing I knew, her tongue was in my ear.

I tried to stop it, I swear I did, but she was so persuasive. And one thing about Shelby Tucker is that she's what my grandma would call a minx. She's one of those girls who oozes sex vibes. Everything she does, *everything*, is sexy, and she knows it.

It was just kissing. That day it was just kissing. Her hand was on my thigh. I felt like I was going to explode. I was trying to stop it, but I was too weak. She was slowly moving her hand toward my crotch when, miraculously, we were interrupted by a pair of headlights shining directly on us as a car pulled into the lot. That snapped me out of it, and I pushed her away.

That might have been the end of it. The trouble was, I'd already promised to drive her home every day, and we were going to be working shifts together at the tree lot for another three weeks. I could have asked to switch to a different shift, but that felt kind of rude. After that first day, it just sort of kept happening. Her folks were never there when I drove her home, so we got in the habit of going for a dip in their hot tub. I couldn't help it if I didn't have a swimsuit handy the first time she invited me to stay awhile.

She knew I had a girlfriend. She promised she wouldn't tell anybody about us. Obviously, this included Emma. For a while (this has been going on for months now, it has to stop), she seemed to mean it. "I'm not trying to be your girlfriend," she would reassure me. "I just want to have some fun." I lost my virginity to her on January 21. Now I don't know how to end things, and she won't leave me alone. I know I have nobody to blame but myself.

"You shouldn't be here," I told her as she pushed past me and into the room.

"I just want to talk." She made a face. "It smells like Bradd in here."

"There's nothing to talk about. I told you I can't do this anymore. It's wrong. It was a mistake."

She shook her head. "Once—maybe twice—is a mistake. This is more than that."

"Yeah, I know. This is worse."

"So that's all I am to you? A big mistake?"

"You don't need to say it like that."

"But that's the truth, isn't it?" She was flushed with anger and embarrassment. I hate confrontation. I'd do almost anything to avoid it.

"Shelby, please listen to me. I like you a lot. You're a sweet girl."

She didn't like that last part one bit. "I'm a sweet girl? Do you think I don't know what people say about me? Do you think I don't know what they call me behind my back? I know I'm Shelby 'everyone's fucked her' Tucker. Those stories aren't even true. I grew boobs before everyone else in seventh grade, and it's like everyone collectively decided I would be the class whore going forward. Nobody bothered asking me if I was interested in the role. They just decided." She stared at the floor. "I was a virgin before you."

My heart sank, and I sighed. "Shelby, you should have told me."

"Would it have made a difference?"

I didn't know how to answer the question. "Look, we can't change what happened, and I'm willing to take full responsibility. This was my fault. I should have been stronger. I know I've done a terrible thing—many terrible things—but I want to do better."

"For Emma," she said.

"Yes, for Emma."

"Because you love her."

"Yes."

"You love her so much that you've been screwing me behind her back for months. What if I decided to tell her? What do you think she would do?"

"She'd break up with me, and I would deserve it, and it would break her heart. Look, I know you hate me right now, and that's fine. You can hate me. I deserve that, too. But Emma hasn't done anything wrong, and she doesn't deserve any of this. I'm begging you, Shelby, don't hurt her just because you want to hurt me."

She laughed. "Wow. That's some argument. What a gentleman you are."

"It's the truth."

She was still staring at the floor. She wouldn't look at me. "You know, I've had a crush on you since sixth grade. I thought you really liked me."

"I do like you. But I have a girlfriend."

"What if you didn't?"

There was a long pause. "But I do."

She left without making any promises. I watched from the window as she walked away. She took about twenty paces before she ran smack dab into Bradd. I was reasonably sure she wouldn't say anything to him, and I highly doubted she would actually say something to Emma. Shelby is actually a very nice and very cool person. She doesn't deserve her reputation.

I got into bed and tried to nap. I listened to my stomach churning to digest all the oysters and wine, wondering if I should just tell Emma everything myself before she found out another way. It would have been the decent thing to do, but even as I pretended to consider it, I knew I wouldn't go through with it.

Or I could pretend the whole thing never happened. If Shelby did tell anybody, I could simply deny it. It's not like she had any proof.

I would fix this, I decided, and then I would do better. I wouldn't let it happen again. In a few weeks we'd graduate, and eventually it would all be so far in the past that my version of the truth would become real. Emma wouldn't have to find out. It would be like it never happened.

Max

Thursday

From where I'm looking at things now, which is to say near the end of my life, I have too many regrets to count. I played things too safe. I thought I had plenty of time.

I never wanted to be a teacher; I wanted to be a screenwriter. I wrote what I thought was a stellar screenplay of an original prequel to the tale of Robin Hood. More specifically the 1973 Disney *animated Robin Hood*, the best of all the Disney animated films. It didn't garner any interest. And believe me, I tried. Eventually I had to face facts: I sucked. Still, I decided to go to one last writer's conference in an attempt to keep my dream alive: Shakespeare's Women from Page to Screen. It took place over four days in Montreal. That's where I met Greta.

At the time, I was well aware—thanks to my dad, the headmaster—of how badly Xavier Academy had been hurting for funding ever since our primary donor, a man with whom you're surely familiar—

he had a popular show on a mainstream cable network—died in a way that was both undignified and hilarious. It was also disgusting. You know the famous death I'm referring to—it involved a man-size sewage pipe, a convent, and masturbation. His widow inherited everything, decided not to share another penny with our school, and became a devoted member of the aforementioned (and now very well-funded) convent.

Tale as old as time.

So there I was, pursuing a dead-end dream, wasting my degree, all the while knowing that Xavier Academy was on the verge of shutting down. My father, Xavier's first Black headmaster, was in a constant state of despair over this happening "on his watch." Not only was the school out of money, it was now inextricably associated with the aforementioned scandal. We lost a handful of faculty members and some students. Lots of Xavier Academy bumper stickers were hastily removed from Range Rovers.

Long story short: one of the conference speakers—who also taught a workshop I attended—remarked that I seemed to have a "real gift" for critiquing the work of others. It was, I'm sad to say, the only positive feedback I received all week. Thus, I started to consider returning home to teach upper-school English lit classes at Xavier Academy for pay that was next to nothing.

Greta and I shared a magical week together at the conference. She's the kind of woman people sometimes call a firecracker, which I should have realized is code for *volatile as fuck*. Would it even have mattered if I'd known? Probably not. My mom used to say I had bad taste in women. She would have been suspicious of Greta. I guess the expression is true: a mother knows.

I thought Greta and I both understood the relationship—if you could even call it that—was nothing but a fling. There was no talk of a potential future together that week. No suggestion of exchanging contact info, of trying to keep the party going. Not at first.

We mostly talked about books. Greta was like intellectual crack. She loved Kafka; I hated Kafka. She hated Proust; I loved Proust.

We argued passionately. The spark between us was electric. We even managed to flirt when we talked about my Big Moral Dilemma: Should I give up on pursuing my dreams in order to become a teacher? And at a school whose reputation was now in the toilet? Xavier Academy was a dying institution. According to my father, short of a miracle, it had another five or six years of solvency before the whole place went belly-up.

"Maybe you can be the miracle," Greta told me.

"I can't perform miracles. I can't even juggle."

"I bet those kids would love you. You're so passionate about literature. You'd be the hot young teacher. The cool teacher. All the girls would have a crush on you. Some of the boys, too. Everybody loves a hot English teacher."

"I wouldn't be comfortable with that dynamic."

"I know you wouldn't! That's what makes you so perfect for the job. You're a good guy. You're safe. And you're smart."

And even though I assumed I'd never see her again after the conference ended, I was convinced to take her advice. Not that it was difficult for her. Here's something I'm embarrassed to admit, though there's no denying it at this point: a beautiful woman can talk a person into almost anything. It's pathetic. I am pathetic. I fell hard. I played right into her hands.

Bradd

Thursday

I wanted to wait until Friday to show everyone what I've been working on all week, but I couldn't stand the excitement for another minute. I wonder if this is how a woman feels when she's getting ready to have a baby. It's basically the same thing, except my baby is not a human baby, but a groundbreaking new technology powered entirely by wind and water that will revolutionize the way couples have sex on vacation.

Once everybody was almost finished eating dinner, I stood at the head of our table and tapped my fork against the edge of my cup, trying to get everyone's attention. Nobody was interested except for Alison. I know most people don't take me seriously, and I don't mind. The greatest minds are never appreciated in their own lifetimes.

"Hey. You're being rude." Alison reached across the table to smack Lucy Thomas's book (*Slaughterhouse-Five*) from her hands, accidentally knocking over her juice in the process. "Look what you made me do, Lucy!"

Lucy glanced around the table. "I didn't make you do anything! Did you all see that?"

"Wow, Lucy. I can't believe you made Alison do that," Louis deadpanned.

"She—I—"

Auggie—above the drama, as usual—rolled his eyes but did nothing to stop everyone from piling onto Lucy. His aloofness irritates me. He thinks he's smarter, more mature than the rest of us.

Emma placed a hand on Lucy's forearm and gave her a sweet smile. "You ought to admit how selfish that was of you, Lucy. And look at the mess you've made."

Louis nodded in agreement. "This is pretty embarrassing for you."

"But—she did it! I didn't do anything!" Lucy's face was red.

"Jesus Christ, Lucy, do you hear yourself?" Louis continued. "I can't believe you're accusing Alison of spilling your drink. Alison doesn't even have *hands*."

"It's true." Alison, solemn, held up her fists. "These are made of wood."

"You know what else is made of wood? Witches. Are you a witch?" Louis asked her.

"Excuse me!" I smacked the table with an open palm. "I'm trying to share something with all of you!" I waited until they were all quiet. I reached for the Yeezy shoebox at my feet and placed it gently on the table.

"Oh! Is it a baby bunny?" Shelby Tucker asked.

It was not a baby bunny. Beaming, I slowly opened the shoebox. "Ladies and gentlemen, may I present to you my most impressive invention to date. A device so well-engineered, so brilliant, it will single-handedly revolutionize not one, not two, but *three* entire industries: sex toys, water sports, and beach travel. Now, keep in mind this is just a prototype. I have a few more tweaks to make before it's ready for mass production. But I'm close."

I held it proudly above my head, my arms extended toward them, like Rafiki holding baby Simba at the beginning of *The Lion*

King. "Friends, I give you the erotic aquatic device of the future… the *H2Blow*."

I'll admit, it isn't pretty, but that's only because my resources here are so limited. Right now it looks like an old-fashioned diver's helmet cluttered with thick, black tubing. It might appear unremarkable, but what it does is astounding.

I have invented a device that allows its wearer to give a blowjob underwater.

I gave them some backstory: I got the idea on our very first day here. Alison and I were fooling around in the lagoon, and I was thinking about how nice it would be if she went down on me. But Alison couldn't do it because she would have drowned. "As Martin Luther King, Jr. famously said, necessity is the mother of invention," I told them.

Lucy scowled at me. "*Plato* said that."

I ignored her. "So? What do you guys think?"

There was silence at first. Then Louis said, "Bradd, I think I speak for everybody here when I say…*it's about damn time*."

I felt a wave of pride. "Really?"

"Oh, yeah. Emma and I were actually talking about this very thing— Was that yesterday, Emma? I think it was yesterday. Anyway, we were both saying how it's such an obvious, widespread problem for people, it's wild nobody has considered a way to tackle it. I can't tell you how many times I've been in the ocean or in a swimming pool—or a hot tub, but that goes without saying—and I've thought, 'Man, if only someone were blowing me right now.' I mean, we can put a man on the moon, but we can't figure out a way to safely engineer an underwater blowjob? Preposterous. No—that isn't the right word. It's *shameful*, that's what it is. But today that shame becomes a thing of the past. And it's all thanks to you, my friend." Louis stood up and began to clap slowly. "Bravo," he said, solemn, pretending to fight back tears. "Bravo for the H2Blow. I just have one question."

"Shoot."

"Who is this for? Like, who do you envision as your target demographic?"

"Literally everyone on the planet."

"Oh, wow. I see." Louis paused. "Even babies?"

"Dude, don't be a sicko."

"Babies can't swim," Emma said.

"It's not for babies, Emma!"

"*Evidently*, it is, if it's for everyone," Connor Cackowski pointed out.

I knew it. They're making fun of me.

"You guys are all assholes! I've got a business plan! It doesn't involve babies! And not because they can't swim, because the whole point is that you don't need to know how to swim! Anybody can use the H2Blow!"

"Do you think maybe it's more of a niche product?" Louis continued. "It doesn't need to be for everybody. Like, it's not for people who don't like to suck dicks underwater, obviously. But that still leaves you a significant market share, because there are plenty of people who are into that."

"You know what, dude? Make fun of it all you want. I'm going to make a *fortune* with this thing. I'll laugh all the way to the bank. And once I've made my millions, I'm going to buy the most badass, luxury sailboat you've ever seen in your life, and I'm going to name it *The H2Blow*, because that's also an amazing name for a sailboat! Wind and water! And none of you assholes are going to be invited. Except you, babe," I said to Alison.

"I'm not making fun of you, Bradd. It's a brilliant product," Louis said. "You need to go on *Shark Tank*. Mark Cuban is going to lose his mind."

He *was* making fun of me, but he didn't know that I've already come up with a marketing plan involving *Shark Tank* that goes beyond the potential of the H2Blow. Suspecting the product might be considered too risqué to debut on *Shark Tank*, I came up with a concept for a spinoff called *Shark Tank After Dark*. I will go on *Shark Tank* to pitch the spinoff, and then I will pitch the H2Blow on the first episode of that spinoff. You don't have to say anything. I know it's a brilliant idea. They just sort of come to me.

Max

Thursday

A few weeks after I started teaching, the most amazing thing happened: Xavier Academy received a $22 million donation from one Sir Gus Dunnigan.

No amount of money is ever exchanged without conditions. So what are the appropriate conditions for handing over $22 million? Not handing it over to an individual, mind you, but to an institution. Gus, Greta's father, was our school's benefactor. The same Greta with whom I'd shared a magical week. One great thing about a week, in concept, is it's a finite entity. It has a beginning and an end. We had kept in touch after the conference, but I figured things would eventually peter out. We lived in two different worlds; of course it would have to end eventually, right? What I didn't know then—what I understand now—is that "beginning" and "end" are granular matters for Gus and Greta.

They didn't frame it like this at first. They claimed the money didn't come with any strings. There were *opportunities*, not *conditions*. One opportunity was presented as an invitation to bring a group of students to study at Gus's oyster farm. While the kids learned about oysters, I would be on the beach, close to Greta. What I should have known then—what I know now—is there is no known universe in which a gift of $22 million is given without *serious* strings attached. Nobody could have conceived of what existential hellscape might be attached to said strings. And even if we had sensed that something was amiss, what other options did we have? Have you turned down $22 million for anything, ever? Would you? People have done much worse for much less.

This is my problem: without consequences, there can be no stakes. The writer and theologian Saint Augustine defined time as "the tension of consciousness," which I think is pretty damn brilliant coming from a guy who was essentially a fourth-century teen blogger. This kind of thinking, I promise, doesn't lead anywhere good. Without the tension of consciousness, there can be no growth. There can still be discomfort, but it doesn't serve a purpose. How can it, when there's no point in striving for change? These kinds of questions are mindfucks indeed, mindfucks that I have lost all interest in turning over and over in my mind. I am numb to the appeal of ambition toward progress.

It started as a series of dumb accidents that I initially chalked up to general clumsiness and the diminishing eyesight that comes with approaching middle age. One too many spilled cups of coffee. Some occasional, mild trouble speaking, like my tongue no longer fit neatly inside my mouth or moved with the same precision at will. I was a healthy guy. No risk factors. My grandparents all lived into their nineties.

I found myself clinging to these truths, but they made no difference.

By the time I met Greta last year, I already knew my symptoms were caused by ALS. Remember the ice bucket challenge from social media all those years ago? That was to spread awareness about ALS. It's a heinous disease. My symptoms were still mild enough that I could hide it, but they were starting to worsen. Greta knows now, of course. So does Gus. What would be the point in lying? Greta has become my angel. I don't know if she really loves me or if she mostly pities me, and I don't care. I don't have time to sit around, trying to parse the unknowable truth of another person's heart. I don't have enough goddamn time.

I have chosen to run toward her love as long as she's willing to give it. But I am beginning to loathe her optimism. Greta still has hope. She still thinks there might be a future for us. That's why she begged me to come here. (To be clear, I did not chaperone a horde of teenagers to an isolated island because I'm passionate about shaping the minds of today's youth. As far as my obligation to these students is concerned, let me just say—and I can't stress this enough—fuck these kids.)

My father is the most brilliant person I've ever met. He's a scientist. He's doing some incredible research on longevity. Maybe he can help you.

Hope isn't always a good thing. I wish she could have accepted reality. Yet here I am.

I didn't come here expecting any miracles. I wasn't even expecting love—this thing with Greta was an explosive, unsustainable relationship, but that was okay, because I was running out of time. We spent every moment together. On Wednesday night, we ate psychedelic mushrooms and stared at the stars and laughed more than I've ever laughed, maybe in my entire life. I forgot I was dying, so for those few hours I forgot to be angry that it took the news of my impending death to make me truly live. Bittersweet, that one.

I don't remember coming in from the beach or falling asleep. I woke up the next morning alone in Greta's bed, in her room inside her father's house. I heard their voices coming from the kitchen. Lazy morning murmurings. Then she came into the room carrying a plate piled with food and a mug of coffee. She was so pretty. I couldn't stop thinking that I'll never get to see her grow old. I tried to share her optimism by thinking about it differently—*I'll never have to watch her grow old*. It didn't make me feel better.

"What do we have here?"

"Here we have some french press coffee." She handed me the mug. "It's not the bulk-order shit we serve in the mess hall—this is gourmet. And this is a seafood omelet." She made a motion like she was about to hand me the plate, but she hesitated with her arm in midair. press coffee." She handed me the mug. "It's not the bulk-order shit we serve in the mess hall—this is gourmet. And this is a seafood omelet." She made a motion like she was about to hand me the plate, but she hesitated with her arm in midair.

"What?" I said.

"There's something I want to ask you."

"Okay."

"You're going to think I'm kidding, but I'm not kidding."

"Ask me already."

She was still hesitant. "Promise you won't get mad."

"I can't promise anything."

"Max. The omelet is medicine. What I mean is there's medicine in this omelet. It wouldn't be right for me to let you eat it without telling you."

"What kind of medicine?"

She seemed to be struggling for the right thing to say. "I don't have a good answer for that. I don't know what you'd call it."

"What will it do to me?"

"Well…that's the thing. It's sort of in the pre-trial phase of development. But it can't hurt you, I promise! It can only help."

"Greta." I was impatient. (Running out of time.) "What will it do to me?"

"It will save your life."

Not the answer I was expecting. "That isn't fucking funny."

"Max, listen to me. It's real."

"There is no cure for ALS."

"This isn't a cure for ALS."

"Then what is it?"

"It's a cure for everything." She leaned in and kissed me. "It's manna from Heaven, Max. Don't you trust me?"

The question—*don't you trust me*?—bothered me. Why ask it at all? Then I thought, *Fuck it*. It's not like I had anything to lose. I could use some manna from Heaven.

Alison

Thursday

Did you know that sugar causes greater physical dependency than cocaine or heroin? It's true. I'm an addict myself. It's a crippling habit that I would love to be rid of, but I can't quit no matter how hard I try. I thought this week might be my chance to finally stop. I figured I could treat this place like my own personal rehab, since the constant temptation of all the processed, refined, high-fructose garbage modern life has to offer would be absent here. I arrived committed to completing a weeklong detox, no matter how unpleasant.

I have failed, repeatedly and without dignity. Last night I ate a tattered packet of Chick-Fil-A sweet-and-sour sauce I found at the bottom of my purse. This morning it was spoonfuls of powdered french vanilla coffee creamer.

Emma has a box of Swedish Fish hidden in her suitcase. "I could really go for something sweet," I told her, hoping she'd offer me some.

"I don't have anything," she lied.

"Is that so?"

"Yes, that is so."

"What if I told you I know you're lying?"

Emma does this thing when she's nervous or agitated, or sometimes just deep in thought, where she finds the nearest piece of fabric, the softer the better, and rubs it between the fingers on her left hand. She's done it ever since we were kids. She used to have a designated blanket with silk edging specifically for this purpose. She calls it "silking the silky." She started doing it with the edge of her T-shirt as we talked.

I don't know why seeing her do it made me so sad, but it did. It was like a wave of yearning for some long-forgotten play I'd seen years ago, so distant now that I could hardly make out the performers, while still knowing for sure Emma was among them. A play about being silly, happy kids. The sense of loss was like a tsunami that smacked and eventually receded, replaced by a growing sense of emptiness in my belly. Emma silked the silky and remained unmoved as I all but begged her to show me a little kindness.

"I know you have Swedish Fish."

"You went through my stuff?"

"I was looking for something."

"For what?"

"I don't remember. They're still there. I didn't take them."

"Listen carefully to me: I will fucking end you if you touch my Swedish Fish."

Since she wouldn't share, I talked her into coming along while I searched for a snack. The kitchen and cafeteria are attached to a lounge in a building that is kept unlocked. We walked in the dark along the uneven, pebbled path. Faint beams of moonlight filtered through the clouds and illuminated thick, gray clouds of mosquitoes gathered around our heads, only keeping a slight distance despite the DEET oozing from our pores. I could hear the waves breaking against the shore. Someone in a nearby bungalow was playing Taylor Swift's "Love Story." The moment already felt like a memory. Without thinking about it, I reached for Emma's hand to keep myself steady as we walked tentatively along the uneven path.

The lights were on in the building ahead of us. We heard muffled voices and the unmistakable, giddy laughter of drunk people coming from the lounge.

It was the adults. Gus, Greta, Max, and Steven the Intern. Steven is a graduate student, I think. He looks like a Kirkland brand Timothée Chalamet. I can't tell if he's really smart or just British. He has none of Timothée Chalamet's charm and probably none of his acting talent.

Emma and I stood close together in a darkened doorway so they couldn't see us watching them. They were playing cards. A tall bottle of liquor, nearly empty, sat in the center of the table.

The whole thing had a dreamlike quality. Part of it was the way they were gathered in the middle of the very large room, surrounded by darkness, their party lit only by a single fluorescent light glowing directly above them. It felt wrong somehow for us to watch them without their knowledge. I thought of the famous double-slit experiment, where light behaves as either a wave or a particle depending on whether or not it's being observed. I never understood how that could possibly be the case, which means I probably don't understand it at all. Does it matter if the light *knows* it's being observed? How can light know anything? It can't.

It was also strange how quiet they were being. They were laughing and talking, but their voices were low, almost hushed. Steven the Intern was seated with his back to us. His posture was stiff and tense. Greta and Max were more relaxed, even giggly. Greta was rubbing Max's leg under the table, her fingers sliding beneath the fabric of his shorts.

"I think Max and Greta are screwing," Emma whispered to me.

I held a finger to my lips. I watched Greta's hand moving like a spider on Max's leg. There was something rotten about her that I couldn't quite put my finger on.

Gus poured another round of shots while Greta reshuffled the cards and dealt everyone a new hand. The four of them clinked their glasses together. Then Gus looked up, his eyes searching the room. His gaze met mine, and he winked. It should have been playful, but honestly…it wasn't.

"Shit. Let's go," I whispered.

"What, right now?"

"Yes." I couldn't explain the feeling. Much like the light particles experiment, I knew there was something going on that I couldn't understand, and it was probably nothing good. All I wanted was to find something sweet.

We crept quietly back down the hall and into the kitchen, where we searched through the cupboards and the shelves of the walk-in freezer, but there was nothing I was excited to eat. The best thing I found was an industrial-size tub of peanut butter, which was nearly empty. I stuck my hand inside and scooped up the remnants with my fingers.

"You're like a raccoon," Emma observed.

I smirked. "Yeah, I'm adorable."

"How do you eat so much junk and stay so skinny? It's incredibly unfair."

My words were garbled by my sticky mouth. "God loves me more than he loves you."

Back at the bungalow, we both kept an eye on Emma's suitcase. Given a moment's chance, Emma knew I would steal the fish (it was amazing I hadn't done so already), and I knew she would move them to a better hiding place. "Don't you want to take a shower before bed?" I asked as she brushed her teeth with the bathroom door wide open in order to maintain her unobstructed line of sight.

She spat into the sink. "You first."

She was surprised when I agreed. "I know you're going to move them, and you should. You're right not to trust me. But I hope you'll give me another chance sometime soon."

She poked me in the sternum with the wet head of her toothbrush. "I mean it, Alison. If you touch them, I will literally mutilate you. I will pour boiling water on you in your sleep. I will seduce your dad and secretly record it and send it to your mom. I will frame your little brother for murder."

I stole them anyway. She'll get over it.

Emma

Friday

Friday morning. The bitch stole my fish.

Alison, still half asleep, clutched at her throat while she choked on a half-chewed bolus of my Swedish Fish. The sun had not yet fully risen. What sounded like some kind of big bird was making a weird, loud noise outside like *be-BLAH, be-BLAH*. Over and over again. I could only make out shadows in our room. Alison had a bad coughing fit, and then it was all over, and she was fine. She gave me a half shrug of an apology, and I knew that was all I was going to get in the way of remorse.

I hate her.

As we were getting dressed, the song "What's Up" by 4 Non Blondes started playing over her Bluetooth speaker. "Please turn this off."

"What did you say? You want me to turn it up?" She turned it up. I turned it down. She turned it up even louder. We started tussling for control of the speaker. Alison elbowed me in the chin (to be fair, it was an accident), which caused me to bite my tongue, and the speaker went flying across the room. We were both sweaty and a little bit out of breath, but Alison was smiling. She was having fun.

"You know how much I hate this song."

"I know," she agreed cheerfully. "That's why I played it."

My lord, do I hate this song. I'd rather give myself a clitoridectomy with a pair of rusty safety scissors than have to listen to it one more time. But I didn't have any rusty safety scissors on hand at the moment.

Alison played the song four times in a row as we were getting ready. She dressed herself in a red-and-white gingham crop top, cutoff jean shorts, and strappy, kitten-heeled sandals. Her hair was woven into two long braids.

"Nice outfit," I said.

"Thank you!" She beamed. "I call this look the farmer's daughter."

"You look like a prostitute at an auction for farm equipment."

She smirked. "Good. That's what I'm going for."

It started to rain while we walked to breakfast. The island was brimming with wildlife. A million creatures going about their business in the earth and trees and sky. This week I saw crabs skittering along the sand that were bigger than a grown man's outstretched palm. Gus calls them the tarantulas of the sea. I'd never thought of them that way before, and now I'll never be able to forget. I saw schools of jellyfish glugging along in the water like gobs of electric snot. Starfish in the shallow water, their bodies dense and porous as wet sponges.

The sun was bright in the sky. The rain was coming from one of the few clouds overhead, making it seem like a glitch in a simulation of the sky. We picked up our pace when the rain started coming down harder. The animals likewise scurried to safety. Dozens of little hermit crabs, their shells no bigger than blueberries, skittered in loose formation across the rocks and sand. They stopped at what seemed like random intervals, retreating into their shells before poking their heads out a moment later, their movements synchronized like they were playing a game of Red Light, Green Light.

Steven the Intern was standing in the doorway to the cafeteria. "The devil is beating his wife, ladies." He nodded at the sky.

"What the hell is he talking about? Nobody says that shit anymore." Alison turned to me, rolling her eyes.

He looked at her with bemused condescension. "Have you not heard that expression? They use it in your country's southern parts. It means that it's raining but it's sunny." He winked at her. Then he transformed his voice; instead of his British accent, he spoke with a thick country twang. "The devil's wife must like it rough." He was *vile*.

"Cool. I heard your mom likes it a little rough sometimes, too," Alison quipped. Steven's smirk vanished. He stared, gape-eyed and distracted, at her chest as we slid past him.

As I was waiting in line for breakfast, my gaze kept wandering toward Max. There was something not right about him. He was standing alone in a corner. He looked to be lost in thought, but he was scowling. His eyes were puffy and bloodshot. He was wearing the same clothes as the day before. Gus approached him and said a few words that I couldn't make out. He reached over to pat Max on the back, and Max recoiled like he was dodging an angry cobra. They exchanged a few more words. Max obviously wasn't in the mood for small talk. He had a tiny cut on his upper lip and looked like he hadn't slept.

I stepped closer in order to better eavesdrop on them. Gus, too cheerful, almost like he was enjoying Max's misery, inquired:

"How's the coffee taste this morning?"

Another pause, followed by a long sigh from Max. I tried to make it seem like I was incredibly busy putting salt on my scrambled eggs and was definitely *not* listening to them. But when I heard Max's response, which he muttered without regard for whether or not anybody might overhear him—"The coffee tastes like hot water stirred with a dead dog's dick, Gus"—my blood kind of curdled.

I didn't like that answer at all. Anybody can have a bad day—even teachers—but it's literally Max's job to be a responsible adult: to speak like a responsible adult. His title is *faculty chaperone*, for pity's sake. He shouldn't be talking about dead dog dicks.

I took a seat at the table between Louis and Auggie. My best friend, Louis, and my boyfriend, Auggie, aren't what you'd call enemies, exactly, but they also aren't friends. They manage to hide it pretty well for my sake. Okay—Auggie hides it well. Louis is not quite so magnanimous. I could actually feel his body stiffening when Auggie put his arm around my waist. He pulled me toward him and pressed my face against his chest as he kissed my forehead. "Good morning, princess."

I didn't have to look in Louis's direction to know he was rolling his eyes. That's his problem.

"Are we still on for tonight?" Auggie murmured.

Tonight. Yes. Tonight is the night. "Definitely."

"Good." Another kiss, this time on my mouth. "I can't wait."

I couldn't wait, either. Like I said, virginity is a burden. I want to get on with life.

Since it's our last day, we didn't have much of a schedule to stick to, with the exception of a plan for everyone to pile onto Gus's barely seaworthy fishing boat and go snorkeling in the nearest offshore reef after breakfast. But then Max strolled to our table. "Change of plans, kiddos. Snorkeling is canceled. You're going to pick up trash on the beach instead."

"No!" Alison howled.

Max stared at her with mild disgust, and I got the nagging sense yet again that something wasn't right with him. Max is always good for "friendly but exasperated" or *maayybe* "losing my mind but I'll manage to keep it together for these kids" on a bad day, but I've never seen him give off disgust.

Alison stared back at him. "Why are you looking at me like you just smelled a fart?"

"Because Lucy farted," Bradd said. Then he cupped a hand over his armpit and flapped his arm up and down like a bird; he made the most effortlessly robust fart noises this way, like how some people are really good at whistling by putting two fingers into their mouth.

"I didn't fart," Lucy insisted.

Max closed his eyes and held almost perfectly still, and my classmates seemed to instantly forget his presence. He stayed like that as conversations continued around him, constant and inane.

Alison nudged me. "You know who I bet had some smelly farts? Princess Diana."

"Farting is normal and healthy, and everybody does it," Lucy said quietly to herself.

"I've never told anybody this before, but I've actually never taken a shit," Louis added.

"Can we stop talking about this? People are trying to eat." That was Auggie.

"My tía couldn't go to the bathroom in public, so all her life she held it in all day every day at work and school and everywhere else, and eventually her toes fell off." Louis couldn't stop smirking. Lily Foose and I were the only ones who laughed.

Steven the Intern approached Max and tapped him on the shoulder. Max opened his eyes. For a second it almost looked like he was fighting back tears, but he quickly pulled himself together. "Do you kids understand me? Garbage pickup. It's not optional."

Alison crossed her arms. "What do you mean, *not optional*?

What's going to happen if we don't show up?"

Max sighed. "I guess nothing. But I'll be very disappointed in you."

"What happens? I'll tell you what happens." It was Steven the Intern. "I'll, uh, I'll sneak into your room in the middle of the night while you're sleeping and cut off all that pretty hair of yours."

So we hung out on the beach and picked up trash for the rest of the morning. At least, some of us did. Lily Foose shadowed Louis like it was her job. Bradd built a sandcastle. He was strolling among the garbage, looking for appropriate containers to pack full of sand, when he froze. He stared intently at the water. I followed his gaze to a small white cube that bobbed at the surface close to the shore.

Fully clothed, Bradd waded into the water until it reached past his waist to retrieve the cube. We gathered around him as he examined it. It looked like a bag of flour wrapped in clear plastic tape.

It was not a bag of flour.

Bradd held the bundle close to his chest while he told everybody a long story about the time his uncle found a brick of cocaine washed up on a beach in Miami, and "that's why he'll get arrested if he ever comes back to the United States. Not because of the manslaughter thing."

Lucy was horrified. "What are you going to do with that? Put it back! You can't keep it! You can't put that in your body!"

"Why not?" He looked around. "Let's have a party, you guys! It's our last day!"

"I would never do anything to jeopardize the structural integrity of my septum," Lucy said.

"Of course you wouldn't, Lucy. What about the rest of you? Louis? C'mon, man."

"Oh, sure—ask the Mexican guy to snort coke," Louis deadpanned. "That's rich."

We all shook our heads in silent agreement. "Bradd," Shelby Tucker said seriously, "this is a terrible idea."

"Fine"—Bradd shrugged—"more for me."

But Bradd didn't get a chance to abscond with his treasure; Steven the Intern was already jogging toward us. "You shouldn't have touched that," he said, snatching it away from Bradd. "It could be anything. It could be dangerous." He tucked it into the backpack slung over his shoulder. "Sailors call these white lobsters. Smugglers have to dump their cargo sometimes; it has to wash up somewhere. But what are they smuggling? Cocaine? Heroin? Something else? This isn't the place to take chances. It's a long journey to the nearest hospital. No, best to let me dispose of it properly."

The devil continued to "beat his wife" as the sun rose higher in the sky and the temperature climbed. We collected all the garbage littering the narrow stretch of beach. "What are we supposed to do with these?" Lucy gestured at the bags filled with trash. "They're too heavy to carry, and they'll break if we try to drag them. Should we ask Max?"

"Let's not," Louis said. "Max is the reason we had to do this in the first place."

"He's hungover," I said. "I heard him say his coffee tasted like hot water stirred with a dead dog's dick."

"That's hilarious," Louis said.

"It wasn't hilarious. It was awful. I don't want to hear my teacher say things like that."

"Why?" He looked genuinely confused. "Who cares?"

"*I* care. It feels unprofessional."

"Like walking in on Mr. Rogers while he gets a rim job from Lady Elaine."

"Wait, do you mean one of his puppets? No, not like that."

"It's exactly like that. You see, there's nothing inherently wrong with Mr. Rogers getting a rim job from Lady Elaine Fairchilde. He can be a beloved children's entertainer *and* love getting consensually rimmed by a colleague, but there's a time and a place for everything. Know what I mean?"

"You smoke too much weed, Louis."

"Yes, well, that sounds like a great idea. Why don't we do that right now?"

I shook my head. "It actually sounds like a terrible idea. Research says our brains are too underdeveloped for that shit, Louis. How'd you even get it through airport security?"

I felt unmoored by the whole exchange. (Don't think about Mr. Rogers getting a rim job from Lady Elaine. Don't think about Mr. Rogers getting a rim job from Lady Elaine.)

I couldn't stop thinking about Mr. Rogers getting a rim job from Lady Elaine. "I should check on Auggie."

Louis noted my distraction. He narrowed his eyes in subdued glee. "What's the matter, Emma?"

"Nothing."

"Are you thinking about Mr. Rogers getting—"

"No!"

"Sure you aren't." He fixed me with an expression of compassionate serenity and spoke in an even, slightly heightened pitch. "That's good, Elaine. Oh, it's a good day in the neighborhood—"

"Shut up!" I screeched, laughing. I shoved him playfully on the shoulder, which caused a shift in the energy. He looked away from me.

"I should check on Auggie," I repeated. A small part of me was aware that I didn't actually want to check on Auggie as much as I wanted to keep talking to Louis, but I tried to ignore the feeling.

"Yeah. You do that. What are you up to later?"

I paused. "Well, you know, since it's our last night and all—"

"Oh, right, sure." Suddenly he looked a little uncomfortable. "You want to be alone with Auggie."

"He's my boyfriend, Louis."

"You know he spends his summers going swimming and camping with little boys?"

"He's a camp counselor."

"I know. What kind of sicko surrounds themselves with children on purpose?"

I rolled my eyes, but I couldn't help but smile. I knew Louis didn't mind little kids; he'd loved his little brother something fierce. "Someone who's good. And kind. Did you know last summer Auggie volunteered to take on a kid with cerebral palsy? He held that kid's hand for eight straight weeks, Louis."

"Well…okay, fuck. No, I didn't know that. Now I feel bad." He paused. "Look what you did, Emma!"

"It's okay." I flicked his forehead. "Not everybody is like you, Louis, thank Christ."

He needles me like this about Auggie all the time. He always plays it off like it's only a joke, but it still bothers me. I'm happy with Auggie. Louis is supposed to be my best friend. Shouldn't he want me to be happy?

Emma

Friday

I ran into Gus while I was walking back from the beach alone. "Emily!" he greeted me. There's something about my name that confuses the hell out of old people.

"It's Emma."

"Oh, I'm sorry—so close! You must forgive me. I'm elderly, you see." I almost said something like, *Yes, I can clearly fucking see that*, but I was polite and just nodded. "Emma, I've been looking for you. Today is your lucky day. Do you have some time to spare? I have something very, very special to show you."

I looked at him warily. "Why me?"

He gave me an even smile. "Because you, my dear, look like you could use a treat!"

I watch a lot of Netflix, and I love true crime. If there's one thing I've learned, it's that you never, ever let a stranger take you to a secondary location. Gus isn't a stranger per se, but he's definitely got a significant creep factor. I told him I was busy looking for my boyfriend, but he wouldn't take no for an answer. "Auggie will find you! Please, follow me. Greta is waiting for me. She has something very special to show you. She asked for you specifically..."

Even if he was telling the truth, I still didn't want to go. Why would Greta want to see me? This is how so many girls and women get kidnapped or assaulted, or worse: we don't want to be rude, but social conditioning is hard to overcome. I followed him. It's not like I thought he was actually going to hurt me. (And he obviously didn't.) But still—what a weirdo.

The back of Gus's left hand is covered with tattoos of tentacles that wrap all the way around his fingers. Each of his three middle fingers has two tentacles, one on either side of the digit, so there are an anatomically correct eight in total. They wind like inky ribbons up the length of his arm. The rest of the tattoo is hidden by his shirt. Greta has the same tattoo on her left hand. (See what I mean? Weird.)

Spoiler alert: I'm glad I went; it was kind of the coolest weird thing I've ever seen.

I followed Gus to the big yellow building where all the aquariums are set up. There's a big red door on the far end of the room that I'd figured must lead to a closet or something. Boy, was I wrong. It leads to another huge room. Instead of rows and rows of tanks cluttered with oysters, there is one huge tank in the middle of the room. The tank itself is the size of a small room: it's at least eight feet tall and ten feet wide. It's a gigantic tank that houses a big, beautiful, terrifying, adorable octopus. Her name is Sibyl.

I've never seen an octopus up close before today. I didn't know anything about them. Unless Gus and Greta were both messing with me—which isn't out of the question—what I learned today has left me profoundly changed.

First of all, they might literally be aliens. Their DNA is so different from the DNA of every other living creature on the planet that scientists aren't sure what the hell is up. And octopuses (octopi?) are really, really, really smart.

Examples: (I watched all of this with my own eyes, or I wouldn't have believed it.)

> 1) They can change color and appearance depending on their surroundings. Gus dropped a crab into the tank for Sibyl to eat. Sibyl moved to a bottom corner of the aquarium and curled herself up beside a rock and then CAMOUFLAGED HERSELF TO LOOK LIKE THE ROCK to lure the crab into a false sense of safety. She caught and ate it right away. Poor little crab never stood a chance. I guess that's nature for ya.
>
> 2) They can solve puzzles and use tools! Greta showed me a cube that looked like one of those toys for babies where each side has a different-shaped hole—a star, a circle, etc.—and the goal is to insert the correct shape into the correct hole. Sibyl inserted each piece correctly with almost no hesitation. She is way smarter than any baby I've ever seen.
>
> 3) They have personalities! Sibyl is a fancy girl who enjoys the finer things in life. Gus put a bracelet into a mason jar, sealed the lid, and dropped it into the aquarium. Sibyl opened the jar and then PUT THE FREAKING BRACELET ON ONE OF HER TENTACLES AND HELD IT UP TO HER FACE LIKE SHE WAS ADMIRING HOW PRETTY SHE LOOKED.

Sibyl is as big as a healthy middle schooler. She has translucent red skin and bright white suction cups. There are hundreds of them in row upon row on her underside. They wiggle and contract like open, hungry mouths, seeking. She reminded me of a sentient portobello mushroom.

Gus asked me if I wanted to touch her. If I'm being honest? I sort of didn't want to. But by then I'd been hanging out for more than an hour, learning all kinds of cool octopus facts and generally having my mind blown, and I didn't want to offend Sibyl. So I climbed up the ladder beside the tank and stuck my arm in the water. Almost right away, Sibyl drifted toward me and wrapped a single tentacle around my index finger.

She did it so gently—like she could tell I was nervous. Her suction cups felt like a thousand tickly little kisses. I was so enthralled by the feeling of her touch—I know it will seem hard to believe, but I could feel it throughout my entire body. It was like there was a gentle current of electricity running through me.

I blinked slowly, and for an instant while my eyes were fully closed I thought I saw the source code of the universe blooming like fireworks in the endless space within our shared mind. I might have been a passive observer for a fraction of a second or a thousand years. There was something *maternal* about her touch. I didn't want to let go, not ever.

I stayed like that, my arm hanging over the edge of the tank while Sibyl explored my finger and hand, until my arm started to go tingly and lose feeling. Before I had a chance to ask Gus or Greta how to free myself without disturbing Sibyl, it was like she heard my thoughts somehow. She released each suction cup individually, one after the next, and each time, I felt a deliberate release, an internal sigh of yearning *(come back, Sibyl!)* combined with the bittersweet understanding that our time together couldn't last forever.

Once each suction cup was free, she gave my hand and forearm a gentle caress with the smooth edge of her tentacle and drifted away.

I was still bathing in the afterglow of the experience, barely aware of my surroundings. Then Gus climbed up the ladder, stuck his hand in the tank, and took hold of Sibyl near the top of a single tentacle, his arm gripping where it met the webbed ruching of flesh connecting her head and tentacles. She didn't try to get away from him. She floated serenely as he tugged and tightened his grip—more roughly than I would have liked—trusting him. My body was still bursting from her touch. It was like a veil had been draped over my consciousness, only to be ripped away when Gus reached into his back pocket with his free hand, pulled out a pair of gardening shears, and chopped off the better part of Sibyl's tentacle.

What had been like a beautiful dream turned into a *Black Mirror* episode in an instant. I learned that octopus blood is blue. The water bloomed an inky shade of aqua. Sibyl shrank into a corner, her body blending itself with the surrounding rocks. She seemed to disappear. In my panic, I thought I heard her screaming, but it was me.

I staggered backward and into Greta's arms. She was ready for me. She was laughing, which terrified me more than I thought was possible. Everything had been so beautiful and now it was ugly. Never go with a stranger to a second location.

In the midst of my freak-out, Gus dismounted wordlessly from the ladder and disappeared with the severed tentacle. A trail of blue blood made a staccato half-moon from the aquarium to the doorway. Greta couldn't stop giggling while she reassured me everything was okay. She was not very convincing. I was shaking and crying, and she was giggling. A little tip on crisis management that I picked up from AP Psych 101: laughing at somebody when they're crying is, generally speaking, a dick move.

"You're worried about Sibyl," Greta observed.

"He cut her arm off! Of course I'm worried!"

"Don't be. An octopus's severed limb will regenerate. Besides, Sibyl is immortal." It didn't occur to me at the moment to point out the implausibility of the latter claim. I heard "regenerate" and remembered learning about the very real ability of some animals to regrow severed limbs. For a quick minute, I felt better *(oh, Sibyl is only temporarily maimed, she'll regenerate)*. Then I felt ridiculous *(the maiming is not an exclusively cosmetic problem! She's been tortured!)*.

"But she's in pain!"

"I don't think so."

"How the hell do you know? It's not like we can ask her! And what about blood loss? What if she bleeds to death?"

"I already told you, Sibyl can't die. She's immortal," Greta repeated. She smiled a serene smile. What would have been a sweet and innocent expression five minutes earlier was suddenly unnerving.

"Um. You know that immortal means 'to live forever,' right?"

"I do."

"So what you mean is that Sibyl will live for a long time."

"No." That smile again. I started getting a reeeealll culty vibe. The father/daughter octopus tattoos were already weird; now they were downright the-power-of-Sibyl-compels-you weird. "What I mean, Emma, is that Sibyl is immortal."

So at this point I was no longer enjoying myself at all. In the span of an afternoon, I'd befriended and grown to love an octopus *(Do you want to be my mother, Sibyl? Maybe you could adopt me?)* only to watch her get maimed with zero warning. Now I was being gaslit by the maimer's daughter. Immortal my ass. Obviously, I assumed Greta was messing with me. Actually, that isn't true: I *hoped* Greta was messing with me.

There is no such thing as an immortal octopus.

And yet, as I stood there with Greta, we both turned to look into the tank. The threads of blue blood, which had been so pronounced just a moment earlier, had dissipated. The water was tinged a slight blue, but there was no obvious bleeding wound that I could see. My gaze met Sibyl's black, unblinking eyes through the thick glass and hazy water. Her eyes peered into my soul. As her tentacles rummaged through my memories, I heard her voice in my mind saying: *Remember your miracle.* And I thought of the poop moth.

My eyes were still locked with Sibyl's when Gus came prancing through the doorway. He was light on his toes, and there was a glee to his step that reminded me of Rumpelstiltskin. He held a small plastic bowl pinned between his arm and his body. "I have something very special here, Emily," he said, "something very, very special…"

"My name is Emma."

"I'm *so* sorry about that. Excuse me. Emma." But he didn't actually seem sorry at all.

Greta's hand was on my arm again. I didn't want her to touch me, but it seemed rude to push her away. I can't emphasize this enough: the whole thing was incredibly disorienting. More often than not, I was half convinced I *was* dreaming, like maybe it was one of those dreams that feels incredibly realistic.

Yeah, that's what it was. A dream. It must have been.

"Dad, let me do this," Greta said. She looked at me. She was not giggling anymore, but I could tell she wanted to. Like she was only being serious for my benefit, and this was all more or less a big game to her.

"I have a serious question to ask you, Emma. I want you to really think about it before you answer me, okay?"

Just a bad dream. But Sibyl's touch felt so *real*...and I felt so awake...

"Do you want to live forever?" Greta asked me. Just like that! Like it was a perfectly normal question!

"Sure!" I said. I didn't think it through at all. Because A, I was dreaming. And B, what are the chances of two miracles in a lifetime?

"Then you should eat this," she said. She took the bowl from Gus and handed it to me. It took a minute for me to realize that what I was seeing could even be considered food.

"What is it?"

"It's ceviche," Greta said. But it didn't look like any ceviche I'd ever had. I peered closer into the bowl. Then I gasped. You probably know where this is going, but I can assure you, I was not prepared for the reveal. It was ceviche, all right. It was *Sibyl* ceviche. Fleshy discs of pink and white looking robust and alive.

I'm dreaming, I'm dreaming, I'm dreaming. Yet I knew, deep down, it was no dream. I felt like I was in a fairy tale because this was certainly not real food; real non-fairy-tale food does not glisten, nor does it originate from an immortal octopus.

There is no such thing as an immortal octopus. I know. And yet...

"See, look at her. She's fine." Greta was pointing at Sibyl. And okay, I know this is impossible, I know nobody will believe me, but I looked and saw the octopus floating in her tank. All eight of her legs were fully intact, all grown to more or less equal lengths. I counted them three times. Then I took a bite of the ceviche. It was the most delicious thing I've ever tasted.

Emma

Friday

When the sun went down, the air grew heavy and damp, but there was no more rain. Shortly after midnight, a halo of feathered light encircled the full moon. The beach was deserted except for the crabs and bugs and other creepy-crawlies. The tide was way out. Auggie and I were alone in my bungalow. Alison was with Bradd and probably wouldn't be back for hours.

I could tell we were both nervous. We passed a thermos filled with vodka and cranberry juice back and forth between us on the bed. Auggie's sips were so small and quick that I wondered if he was actually drinking anything at all. That's something he would do—pretend to drink for my sake.

"Are you sure?" he asked suddenly.

"Of course I'm sure," I said, but when I reached for the thermos again, he pulled it back. His hands were shaking.

"Hey, maybe you've had enough."

"What do you mean? I'm fine."

"You mean you're fine for now."

"Ohhhh." My boyfriend is a kaleidoscope of virtue. He is an Eagle Scout who loves his mother. "You don't want me to be too drunk to consent."

"Well…yeah."

"Auggie." I felt warm all over, and I leaned forward until our foreheads were touching. "I'm not drunk, and I consent."

He reached past me, put the thermos on my nightstand, and turned off my light. We started kissing. Auggie used too much tongue. As usual. If I'm being honest, his kissing could use some work. He does this thing where he makes his tongue straight and hard—some might describe it as erect—and juts it in and out of my mouth in quick motions, like a lizard picking flies off a rock. I didn't want to hurt his feelings by bringing it up when we first got together. I hoped his technique would improve. It hasn't. And now it's too late to say anything.

Our mouths were sour from the cranberry juice. Before I knew it, our clothes were on the floor and our sweaty bellies were pressed together, tummies rumbling in symphony. I opened one eye to steal a peek out the window. It looked so pretty that I got distracted by the sight, sitting up on my elbows for a better look.

The halo around the moon had dissolved into a memory. A twinkling cluster of lights—a cruise ship, probably—drifted far away at sea, a million iridescent lights hovering on a fluid black ocean. I thought about all the creatures living underwater, and of Sibyl alone in her aquarium. I hadn't told Auggie about what happened; the whole matter felt a little too unconventional for him. But I'd told Louis, who was as intrigued as I'd expected. "Greta told you she could make you immortal? During some kind of ceviche orgy?"

"It wasn't an orgy."

"Let's assume it was. And you just…went along with it." He nodded. "Sure, sure, I get it. Who doesn't want to live forever?" His eyebrows rose in sudden alarm. "What if Greta is the devil? I get a witchy vibe from her, don't you? What if this is like a Monkey's Paw type of deal?"

The thought made me feel a little uneasy. "Shut up."

"Emma?" Auggie had leaned over to rummage through his pants, which were on the floor, for a condom. "Where'd you go?"

"Nowhere. I was just thinking."

He sat up. "Are you sure you're sure about this?" he repeated.

"Auggie, I'm sure. Why do you keep asking me that?" I paused. "Are *you* sure?" Was he sure?

He nodded. "I think so." He stared at the condom in his hands. He looked at me. "I really care about you, Emma. I love you. So yeah, I'm sure." His hands were still shaking as he fumbled with the wrapper.

"Let me help you," I whispered.

"It's all right, I've got it." Did he? He took a few more deep, shaky breaths as he put it on. "Okay. Are you ready?"

"I'm ready. Are you ready?"

Sex! I am about to have SEX! Sexual intercourse! Full penetration!

"Uh, just give me a minute."

I gave him a long kiss while his hands were still fumbling in his lap, in the dark. "We'll remember this night forever, Auggie."

"Uh-huh. Yup. I just need to—"

"Do you want help? I can help you."

"I don't need help! I need some better light. This thing is— Shit." Auggie stopped. He pushed himself away from my body.

"Auggie? Are you okay?" He didn't answer. It was too dark for me to make out his expression. "Did it break? What's the matter? Do you want me to turn on a light? Auggie?" A faint wheeze caught in his throat. "Auggie?"

I was about to reach for the light switch when his mouth opened wide, and I was struck by a jet of body-temperature projectile vomit. It seemed to go on forever. First I screamed, then I gagged—I cannot *stand* bodily fluids, especially vomit—then I screamed and gagged at the same time, which I had no idea was even possible before this moment.

All I could think about was making it to the bathroom. But the floor was slippery (from the vomit all over it, you see), and in my naked frenzy I slipped and fell hard on my bare ass. Auggie was still on the bed, writhing in the dark. Why didn't he *say* something? My screams turned into sobs.

I was right, all right: we'd remember this night forever.

A sliver of moonlight came shining through the open window, illuminating Auggie's face as he began to claw at his throat with his hands. Something was very wrong.

"HELP!" I screamed. Then I was scrambling to my feet again, utterly panicked, trying to find something—anything—to cover myself so I could find help. But nothing was coming easy for me. There was my panic, my fear, and—as Radiohead once said, famously—the vomit. *The vomit.*

There was a knock at the door. "Emma? I need you to put some clothes on and let me in. Auggie doesn't have a lot of time." It was Max.

I froze. In the moment, it did not occur to me to wonder how he could possibly know I was naked in there or that Auggie and I were in there together. I know that a person's first time rarely goes exactly as planned. I was prepared for any number of potential hiccups. Broken condom? There's a morning-after pill hidden in my suitcase. Premature ejaculation? Meh, there's always next time. But I don't believe *Cosmopolitan* magazine has ever covered what to do if you find yourself hosed down in your boyfriend's vomit pre-coitus, so I had to admit, I could have used some help. Also, why the hell was Auggie still not saying anything? Why hadn't he turned on the light?

Another knock. This time it was more insistent. "I need you to let me in, Emma. *Now.*"

What else could I do? I stumbled toward the bathroom, grabbed a clean towel, and wrapped it around my body. When I opened the door, Max pushed past me without saying a word and rushed toward Auggie. When he turned on the light, I let out a yowl of horror. My boyfriend was gone. In his place was a writhing, swollen mass of flesh and limbs and hair and puke. Auggie's penis was somehow both flaccid and grotesquely humongous, like a dead toad bloated with decomposition gasses. His face was swollen up so that I could barely see his eyes. He was still clawing desperately at his throat—angry red lines had risen along the length of his neck, and petechial hemorrhages (I watch a lot of *Grey's*) had turned the whites of his eyes red like a demon's—struggling to breathe. It wasn't like on TV or in the movies. There was nothing entertaining about it, and it smelled bad.

Max reached into his pocket, pulled out a syringe, and drove the needle into Auggie's upper thigh. Turning to me, he said, "He'll be okay in a few minutes."

I stared at both of them, dumbfounded. Auggie was still clawing at his throat. But I could see that he was going to be okay. I heard air whistling in his windpipe as he was finally able to pull it into his lungs again, desperate for a full breath, then another, then another. That whistling sound, I know, is going to haunt my dreams.

Max held up the now-empty syringe. "It's an EpiPen," he said. "Your loverboy here is allergic to latex."

"But how did you—"

"How did I know?" Max closed his eyes. Beside him on the bed, Auggie had caught his breath enough that he was no longer struggling to fill his lungs, although he was still…quite puffy.

"You won't believe me."

"What?" I thought of Sibyl and my miracle. It'd been a hell of a day.

"Although it's not like that matters." Now he looked me dead in the eyes. "Nothing matters, Emma. None of it."

This coffee tastes like hot water stirred with a dead dog's dick.

Auggie burst into tears. He grasped for the puke-covered blanket—oh, God, the entire *wall* behind him was splashed with vomit; there was absolutely no way I was sleeping in there until the place was decontaminated—and started to yank it upward to cover his naked body. Before that happened, he noticed his penis, which was still a blobfish, and his whole body started to heave and shudder as his tears accelerated into full-on sobs. When Max reached out and *smacked him upside the head*, I realized that, as much as I hated to admit it, our teacher was correct: whatever explanation he was about to give, I was not going to believe him.

"Quit your blubbering," he told Auggie. Then, with a terrifying grin: "Next time I'll just let you die. Would you prefer that?" He stood up and strolled to the rear door of the bungalow, which opened onto a small balcony overlooking the rocky seashore. With his back to us, he asked, "Do either of you remember when we read 'The Wasteland' in class last fall?"

I didn't remember. "Of course I remember."

"You little *liar*." He spun around to face us. His movements tonight almost seemed choreographed. "'The Wasteland' is a poem by T.S. Eliot."

"I *know* that. I just told you I remember, didn't I?"

"Right. Because you're such a studious young lady. Then of course you're familiar with Sibyl of Cumae."

I was not familiar with Sibyl of Cumae. But I was familiar with Sibyl the octopus. "I know that name. Why are you saying that name right now?"

He ignored my question. "It's okay, Emma. I know you didn't read the poem. We did discuss it in class, but if I recall correctly, you were too busy playing footsies with Stay-Puft over there to pay attention. So let me refresh your memory. According to Greek mythology, Sibyl was granted eternal life by Apollo, but she forgot to wish for eternal youth. After hundreds of years, she grew so shriveled and small that she was placed inside a jar, which was hung in the public gardens for people to gawk at. She became nothing but a freak show."

I swallowed a mouthful of bile. "I already knew that." (It may shock you to learn I did not, in fact, already know it.)

"Sure you did." Max closed his eyes. He raised his outstretched arms toward the ceiling and began to speak, but I didn't understand a word, because he was literally speaking a different language.

"Is that Spanish?" The question barely registered as a whisper.

Finally, we heard from Auggie, whose tears were beginning to slow. "I think it's German."

Max opened his eyes. Glaring at us, he said, "It's Latin and *Greek*, you absolute jackasses! We went over this for an entire week!" His voice grew louder with every word. "*For I indeed once saw with my own eyes the Sibyl at Cumae hanging in her jar*," he intoned, his speech almost trance-like, "*and when the boys asked her, 'Sibyl, what do you want?' she answered, 'I want to die.'*"

"I remember that!" Auggie almost shouted. "I remember now!"

Max ignored this. "Ask me what I want, Emma."

I shook my head *no*. Dread had pooled deep in my belly.

"Ask me what I want," he repeated, his tone more threatening now.

"Wh-What do you want?"

"What I want," he said, "is to get the fuck away from you kids." And with that, he turned again on his heel, took a running start toward the balcony, and threw himself onto the rocky shore far below.

The time present of things past is memory; the time present of things present is direct experience; the time present of things future is expectation.

—*Confessions of St. Augustine*

Part 2

Emma

Day 2

I was trapped in a nightmare.

I knew it was a nightmare, but somehow that only made it worse. The anxiety was suffocating. I needed air. I gasped as I fought my way to consciousness, fought to open eyelids that felt like lead curtains. I sat up and looked around. *I'm awake. I'm safe.* But I wasn't awake. I was trapped in a blooming tumor, each nightmare another layer of shadow.

Last night, I knew, had not been a nightmare at all. The events played out in my mind's eye once again: Auggie's swollen penis. His chin smeared with oily orange vomit. The smell. And, of course, Max's suicide. I remembered staring down at his body on the rocks, his legs folded unnaturally underneath his torso, his blank eyes wide open but unseeing. I remembered feeling something curdle inside me as Auggie—who was still nude, his palms cupped protectively around his crotch, shoulders hunched—whimpered helplessly. But after that? I couldn't remember a thing.

I finally looked at my hands. *They're real. I'm awake.* Then they began to expand like two balloons filling with water. I felt the mattress give out beneath me. I gasped as I sat up and tried to orient myself. I felt so dizzy I nearly fell out of bed. Be-*BLAH*, be-*BLAH* went a bird outside. Alison struggled and gagged and coughed a few feet away. She grasped at her throat. She spat something into her lap. She wiped away a shiny thread of saliva dangling from her chin.

Then it was all over.

Something was very wrong.

"Where did you get more of those?"

"More of what?"

"More Swedish Fish."

She coughed again. "What are you talking about? These are yours."

"What?"

"I saw you hide them under your mattress. I was spying on you while you thought I was in the shower."

"Yeah, I know." I paused. "Wait, what?"

"Are you okay, Emma?"

"Yes. I don't know." I was still too rattled from my nightmares to think straight. They felt *so* real—as real as this moment right now.

Alison's Bluetooth speaker started to play what sounded like a housecat getting eaten by a Sasquatch. I knew it all too well; it was the opening guitar riff of "What's Up," the worst song in the world. "Seriously?"

She grinned. "I love how much you hate it!" That's when I noticed her outfit: red-and-white gingham crop top, shimmery jean shorts, impractical kitten-heel sandals. Her hair fell in two braids over her shoulders. The same as yesterday.

"Why are you wearing that again?" Alison's wardrobe is meticulously curated; she would never repeat an outfit two days in a row.

She looked down at herself. "What are you talking about?"

"You wore the same outfit yesterday."

"Um, no I didn't." She pointed to an aquamarine maxi dress slung over the back of a chair. "I wore *that* yesterday."

"Don't gaslight me, Alison."

"I'm not gaslighting you, *Emma.* I packed a different look for every day this week. Yesterday's look was 'land mermaid.' Today's is 'farmer's daughter.'"

"You look like a prostitute at a state fair."

"Good. That's exactly what I'm going for."

It started to rain as we walked to breakfast. At first the droplets were fine, like mist, but it grew heavier as we turned a corner on the path, which was when I saw Steven the Intern standing ahead of us in the doorway. "The devil is beating his wife, ladies."

"That's because your mom likes it a little rough sometimes."

I froze.

"Emma, come on." Alison reached for my wrist. "You're getting soaked."

I wasn't going to panic and embarrass myself in front of everybody. But once we were inside, all I could think of was finding Greta or Gus or Max. Like Mister Rogers used to tell kids: when you're in trouble, look for the helpers. Once again, my mind's eye flashed to Max in a broken heap on the sharp rocks below my bungalow. After Auggie nearly died. After I'd tasted the ceviche of immortality. *Remember your miracle.*

I caught Lucy by the sleeve as she walked by. "Quick question: if I had a set of those day-of-the-week underwear and I always wore the correct pair on the right day, what day would it be on my underwear right now?"

She stared carefully at my face. "Are you having any numbness or tingling on your right side?"

"I'm not having a stroke."

"Are you trying to ask me what day it is?"

"Um. Sort of."

"Today is Friday."

Fuck.

I managed to hold myself together throughout the morning, for the most part. I knew it was impossible that I was still dreaming, that maybe I'd dreamed all of this, but wasn't the alternative equally impossible?

Greta and Gus never showed up for breakfast. Neither did Max. It was Steven the Intern who ordered us to the beach. He followed us all the way there and crouched behind a nearby tree, watching us intently. Throughout all of this, Auggie was cloying with his affection. It was too much.

"I think I need to lie down." I put a hand to my stomach. "I feel like I might throw up."

Auggie backed away from me. "Oh no, oh no, no, no. I can't handle body fluids." If only he knew the irony of his statement. "Go find a bathroom, Emma. Go!"

I found Max and Greta instead. They were both at Max's bungalow. At first I was relieved to see Max, very much alive, his body slouched in a chair while he smoked a cigarette. But my relief faded quickly when I locked eyes with Greta. She looked like the cat who ate the canary, barely concealing a smug grin. The tension in the air was as thick as Velveeta cheese.

"What did you do to me?" I shrieked at her. "You said I would be immortal! This isn't the same thing!"

Max stared at her in horror. "Oh, no. Tell me you didn't."

"I did. But if you'll give me a minute to explain—"

He cut her off. "You have to be fucking kidding me. She's a *child*!"

"I'm eighteen, actually."

"Fuck, Greta, you have to fix this," Max said.

She stayed calm and cool. "I've told you, we're working on it. My father needs more time—"

"I think he's had more than enough time!"

"My father needs more time," she repeated, more firmly. She looked at me. "But while you wait, you're here in paradise. You're young, Emma. You can't get sick or old. It isn't a curse; it's a gift."

I was livid. My body felt like it was on fire. "You tricked me."

"I'm sorry," she said simply. "This is bigger than you."

I looked at Max. "How could you let this happen to me? You're supposed to protect us!"

"Protect you. Right. I have some bad news about that. You see, I wake up every morning with the worst hangover of my life." He shook another cigarette from its pack and chain-smoked. "I haven't had a solid bowel movement in decades. It's diarrhea all day, every day. I have so many hemorrhoids that my asshole looks like a daisy."

"Decades?" I screeched. The word was like a gut punch. It was unfathomable to imagine I might share the same fate. I hadn't even been *alive* for multiple decades. "No. Oh, no no no no no. This can't be happening." I held my face in my hands. "You're supposed to be responsible for us. You're supposed to protect us. My mother signed a fucking waiver!"

"Look around, Emma. Does this seem like the home of someone you want looking out for you?"

To say his bungalow was a disaster would be putting it lightly. Loose papers covered in notes and sketches were arranged like a mosaic on the floor, the vision board of a madman. His nightstand was covered in pill bottles; I counted more than a dozen.

"Don't you get it? They're experimenting on us. I can't protect you. I'm as helpless as you are." He gave Greta a dirty look. "We're prisoners."

"Stop being so dramatic," Greta scoffed. "You both agreed to this." She paused. "More or less."

I could hardly stand to look in her direction. I kept my anger trained on Max. "How could you let this happen to me?"

"I didn't let it happen to you, Emma!"

"I don't believe you. You facilitated this. At best, that's serious negligence. You brought us here."

"I'm sorry. I *was* foolish. I thought I loved her." His tone was flat and hopeless.

"You thought you loved her?" I balked. "Are you fucking serious? Mr. D. *Max*." I shook my head. "This is so disappointing."

"I'm just a man."

"Yeah," I agreed, "you sure are. That's the problem."

He hung his head.

Admittedly, I should have been terrified, but I actually wasn't. None of it felt real. I wouldn't even say I was in denial, because denial implies an inability to accept reality; whatever this was, it wasn't reality to begin with. Off the top of my head, I could come up with half a dozen more plausible explanations: Maybe I'd accidentally ingested a hallucinogen. Maybe I was still dreaming. Maybe I was in a coma. Or was it possible everyone was messing with me? Could it all be an elaborate prank?

In my heart, of course I knew it wasn't a prank. Max had *died*. This was real. I pointed a finger at Greta. "I don't care how long it takes or what I have to do, but I'm going to get you. You'll pay for this."

Greta's expression settled into a serene smile. "I guess we'll see about that."

"You're a monster."

Again with the smile. So cool and calm. It chilled me to my bones. "I'm a goddess."

As if all that wasn't enough, I still had Auggie to deal with that evening. Funny how priorities can change so quickly. The desire I'd been feeling—this incredible sense of urgency to become something different, to grow into someone else—had evaporated like dew in the sun. What was once an all-consuming obsession had become a mildly annoying itch. For the first time in a very long time, sex was not my first priority; it wasn't even my second priority, or my tenth.

But Auggie didn't know that, and how could I possibly begin to explain it? The last thing I wanted was a repeat of our first try. So I avoided him; I asked Alison to tell him I had cramps and was going to skip dinner to take a nap. He showed up at my door not long afterward with some food and a handful of wilted wildflowers.

"You're sweet. Thank you." I couldn't stop picturing the way he'd looked with vomit fountaining from his swollen face. The way he'd wept over his swollen penis like a baby holding a broken crayon.

He lingered in the doorway and looked around the room warily. "Did you throw up in here?"

"Not me."

"How's your stomach?"

"They're cramps, actually. My period is early."

"Oh...*oh*. Okay. That's all right. We can wait."

"We can?"

"Of course." He unzipped his backpack and pulled out a chessboard. "Look what I found in the lounge. I was thinking I can finally teach you how to play." Auggie is extremely into chess. I've never played in my life. I'm more of a checkers girl.

"Auggie, I've had a fucked-up day. I don't know if I'm really interested in this."

"Come on," he said, "it will be fun."

It was about as fun as getting fingered by Edward Scissorhands.

Auggie is the vice president of the chess club. He takes it *very* seriously. "You can't move your rook there. You'll be in check."

"Which one is the rook?" I asked.

He sucked his teeth. "I already told you twice."

"Tell me again."

"The one you just moved."

"You mean my horsey?"

"Don't call it that. Look, Emma, I'm trying to teach you, you know, so we can play together sometimes, but you're treating it like a joke. It's annoying."

"It's annoying?" I balked. "I'm trying to remember how the pieces move. That piece"—I pointed at a knight—"looks like a horsey, so I'm calling it a horsey. So what if I call the pieces something different while I'm learning?"

"But how will you ever learn the correct names?"

"Maybe I won't."

"Then you aren't actually learning."

"Auggie, come on. This is silly."

He stared at the ceiling. "Wow," he muttered, "you really do have your period."

His words enraged me. "That's right, this is all because of my period. Oops, I've accidentally menstruated all over the chessboard. I guess that means you win." I flipped the board off the bed. The pieces scattered onto the floor.

Auggie was stunned. "What is your problem?"

"I told you, I'm having a fucked-up day."

"Okay. And how is that my fault?"

He had a point. It wasn't his fault. For a second, I thought about telling him everything that had been happening, but it would be a waste of time for plenty of reasons. "I'm sorry. I'm not myself today. Look—I think I should get some sleep. Things will be better in the morning."

It was obvious he was hurt. "So that's it? It's our last night here, and you're going to bed early?"

"Yes. But I promise, I'll explain everything tomorrow."

Once he was gone, though, the rage wasn't. I gathered up as much of Alison's stuff as I could carry in my arms: her pillow, her toothbrush, her makeup bag, her Bluetooth speaker. I walked down to the beach alone and hurled everything into the water. I got into bed and pulled the covers all the way up to my chin. I tried to fall asleep.

See you tomorrow.

Louis

Friday

This week has gone by quickly, too quickly. I don't want to go home yet. My home life isn't great right now. If I'm being honest, my home life has never been all that great.

A lot of people don't know that I used to have a little brother. He was born with severe congenital disabilities. By the time he was three years old, he'd been through something like nineteen different operations. It was never good. He never even learned to walk all that well on his own, or get to make friends, or anything like that, and then he died when he was five and I was twelve. For the last year of his life, when the end became an imminent certainty, being at home with my family made me feel like I was *almost*, but not quite, drowning. Like I was constantly using all my energy and focus to keep my face above the surface of a brackish, opaque lake.

What kind of kid loves going to school every day? Me. I was that kid. When I walked out my front door every morning, it was like my feet found the bottom of the lake. Like suddenly I was standing and the water was only up to my chin. By the time I got to school, it was more like waist-level. But even though it was such a relief to be away from my house, I didn't want to shut it out completely. I used to comb my brother's hair for him. He had thick black curls. He had a habit of twirling his fingers in his hair, which caused it to get all knotty, and I was the only one who he would let comb out his hair without screaming. It was nice. I mean, it hurt like hell—but it was comforting, too. I don't know how else to explain it. It still doesn't make sense to me.

I brought the comb to school with me every day. Sometimes I'd reach into my bookbag during class and touch his hairs that were tangled in the teeth. I just wanted to hold on to him somehow, even though I knew there was nothing I could do to stop whatever was going to happen. That was the worst feeling.

When my brother died, the feeling went away, and now it's back. When I was packing for this trip, I found the comb in my nightstand drawer and brought it with me. I don't know why. For comfort, I guess. Everything is changing; everything is ending. I'm terrified.

Emma

Day 3

I was home. I was in my own bed. I stayed there with my eyes closed, listening. Charles was hacking up a hairball in the corner of the room. My mom was walking around my bedroom, looking through my things, probably searching for a phone charger, since she's constantly losing them. She gave up after a few minutes and went into my bathroom.

Then the music started. I sat up and opened my eyes. The worst song in the world was blasting from Alison's Bluetooth speaker on the windowsill.

Alison was brushing her teeth, staring at me from the bathroom doorway.

The thought that maybe I was never going home—*never*—had been creeping at the corners of my thoughts since yesterday. I wasn't ready to contemplate the more existential implications of what was happening to me, but every familiar beat of the morning brought it closer to the forefront of my mind. It was messing with my head.

I climbed out of bed, stomped across the room, and hurled the Bluetooth speaker out the window. It broke into pieces on the rocks below. Alison's jaw dropped. Her mouth dripped with foam. "What the fuck, Emma?"

"That's for stealing my Swedish Fish."

We got dressed in silence. I stayed a few paces behind her as we walked to breakfast. She glanced over her shoulder at me a few times, as though she expected me to say something, but I didn't react.

Tiny hermit crabs crawled along in a meandering single-file beside me. Steven the Intern greeted us from the doorway. "The devil is beating his wife, ladies."

"That's because your mom likes it rough sometimes."

It was business as usual inside the dining hall. I stood away from everybody, watching as they all began their day as though anything they did mattered at all. They were all taking life so *seriously*. I thought of all the rules I'd followed so thoughtlessly over the years. All the wasted time. Now that I have all the time in the world, everything feels more urgent somehow. And then simultaneously, it all feels kind of meaningless. Maybe it can be both. All I can do is see what happens.

Our choices for breakfast were: dry cereal, scrambled eggs (they were made from dehydrated powder and tasted like paper), and, of course, oysters. None of these particularly appealed to me. I went to the kitchen and looked through the cabinets. I opened a door to what I assumed was a closet and found myself inside a sizable storage room, its walls piled to the ceiling with treasures: A gallon-size jug of marshmallow fluff! A pallet of mac and cheese! A case of champagne! A dozen jars of kalamata olives!

I took the marshmallow fluff and a bottle of champagne to my table and sat down. I used my teeth to tear the foil wrapper from the champagne cork, and then I spit it on the floor. I popped the cork and sent it flying across the room in a long arc before it landed with a *plop* in Lucy Thomas's bowl of cereal. I chugged straight from the bottle. Champagne flowed out the sides of my mouth and down my front, soaking through my shirt.

Auggie tried to take the bottle from me. "What are you doing?" he asked me through gritted teeth. "Are you out of your mind?"

I giggled. "It sure seems that way."

It had occurred to me, all of a sudden—I don't know what took so long—that I could do whatever I wanted. Nothing mattered!

But at the same time…nothing mattered.

"Emma. Look at me." He grasped my shoulders and shook me gently. "You're acting completely unlike yourself. Did you really break Alison's Bluetooth speaker?"

I let out a long belch. "Yep."

Auggie pulled me to my feet and steered me toward an empty corner. Everybody was staring at us. Max was trying to suppress a smile. Auggie gave him a helpless look of frustration; Max just shrugged.

"What in the hell… Tell me what's going on with you. Something is obviously wrong." He looked at me with concern. "Is this about tonight? Are you nervous?"

I didn't mean to do it, but his suggestion was so far from the truth that I laughed in his face.

"Thanks a lot," he said.

"I'm sorry." I took a deep breath. "Okay. I'm going to tell you why I'm acting this way."

"Please do."

"Auggie, I'm stuck in a time loop." I was still keeping a tight grip on the champagne bottle. I took another swig.

"Shut up."

"It's true. I've lived the same day three times now."

He rolled his eyes. "Fine. Don't tell me."

The champagne was starting to hit me hard on an empty stomach. I was flushed; my ears burned; I could feel my heart pounding. My thoughts raced with all the possibilities of a new reality without consequences. I wondered how many bottles of champagne I could carry to my bungalow in a single trip. I could try smoking cigarettes. I could cut off Alison's braids while she slept and leave them at Steven the Intern's doorstep. I could flirt with whoever I wanted, eat whatever I wanted, say whatever I wanted.

But what did I actually want? That was the question.

"Emma? Are you even listening to me?"

"Not really," I admitted.

"Did—did you hit your head or something? I mean it. You're starting to worry me."

"There's nothing for you to worry about. None of this matters at all. I met an immortal octopus named Sibyl. I ate a piece of her, and now I'm trapped in a time loop. This day has already happened for me, and it's going to keep happening forever."

"That's impossible."

"It sure is!" I agreed cheerfully. I took another swig of champagne. It was becoming clear that he wasn't going to match my energy.

Suddenly I had no patience for him. It was ironic how my grappling with the unfathomable concept of eternity made me want to stop wasting time.

I spotted Gianluca and Mia leaving the dining hall together, and I went running after them.

"Hey, Mia, can I have one of those?" I nodded at her cigarettes.

"Naughty girl," Gianluca said. He was such a flirt. Reluctantly, Mia shook a cigarette from her nearly empty pack and handed it to me. I wasn't a smoker; I'd never understood the appeal of cigarettes or vapes. But I figured, what the hell? I started to inhale and immediately doubled over, coughing and gagging. I caught my breath, extinguished the cigarette carefully on the pebbled path, and gave it back to Mia. It was still almost fully intact.

"You see? You are not really bad girl," Gianluca told me.

"Gianluca, you're the president of the chess club, right?" I asked him.

"I am *king* of chess club," he said proudly.

"When is your birthday?"

"I am born on seventeen of April."

"Do you have any pets?"

Mia shushed him before he could answer me. She spoke to him in rapid Italian. He shook his head and gestured wildly with his hands. They bickered back and forth. I could tell they were talking about me.

"I, uh, I will not tell you name of pets or mother's maid name or what is name of street where I grow from boy to man. You cannot know my secrets."

"Jesus Christ, Gianluca, I'm not trying to steal your identity."

He and Mia argued some more. She finally threw her hands up in exasperation and stormed away.

Gianluca shrugged. "She is grumpy grump."

"I'm not trying to trick you or anything. I just want to get to know you better. We never talk."

"We talk now. I tell you secrets."

"You don't have to tell me anything you don't want to."

"I tell you everything now. I have dog. Ask me more questions."

"Okay...what do you want to be when you grow up?"

"Money man," he said without hesitation.

"Do—do you mean like a banker?"

"Yes, banker. I will be bank. I will drive Ferrari and have beautiful wife and many children and maybe girlfriend, too."

"Really? Huh. Okay. What's your favorite food?"

"Cacio e pepe."

"What kind of movies do you like?"

"Sexy movies. I like vampires. I like American movies with shiny vampires and sexy, sexy love."

"Are—are you talking about the *Twilight* movies?"

"Yes, *Twilight*. Robert Pattinson. I am resemble him strongly, no?" He turned his head to show me his profile. "Eh? Very, very similar, yes?"

He did not look like Robert Pattinson. Like, not at all. "You could be twins."

"Yes, I know this."

"I have one more question: if you could have dinner with one person, living or dead, who would you choose?"

He didn't hesitate. "I would like to share meal with Robert Pattinson."

Naturally.

"Now I have question for you, pretty good girl. Will you make love to Gianluca?"

I was taken aback. "Oh… Oh, Gianluca, I'm sorry, but I have a boyfriend."

"Please make love to me. I yearn for you." I was pretty sure his yearning was not specific to me, but to any girl who might be willing.

"I don't think so. But that's, uh, very flattering."

He shrugged. "Is okay you reject me. I still must give it shot."

"It was nice talking to you, though."

"What can I say? I am fascinating guy."

I was officially losing it. Why not? Nothing matters! (But nothing matters.) I found a wheelbarrow perched against a shed and steered it through the double doors of the dining hall and into the kitchen, where I piled it with bottles of champagne before wheeling it down to the beach. On my way, I passed Bradd, who was by himself in the lagoon. He gazed dazedly at the calm water. The light rain pebbling its surface made a fuzzy humming sound, a din in my ears like the morning after a concert. Bradd was wearing the H2Blow in a large mesh pouch slung diagonally across his body, like a parent would wear their infant. If he noticed me, he didn't show it; he was lost in thought.

Another fifty or so paces down the beach was a sharp right curve where the tide carved a half circle into the side of a big, arched rock formation, creating a shallow cave. This was where the garbage accumulated, on what would otherwise be the loveliest spot on the entire island. Instead, it was a never-ending reminder that people are the worst. It was an absolute eyesore requiring constant maintenance or else the trash accumulated into hideous little mountains every few days.

I guided the wheelbarrow to a trash-free patch of sand close to the water, planted my butt on the damp beach, and popped another bottle of champagne. Time is a flat circle. Same as it ever was. My mom had a serious boyfriend named Curtis a few years ago who liked to say that the only thing more valuable than money is time. In hindsight, this belief probably contributed to the amphetamine habit that eventually wrecked his relationship with Mom. But he did have a point. And since I have nothing but time now, that makes me richer than Elon Musk.

Auggie was within my sights at a distance, putting more effort than necessary into the act of trash collection. It was already at least eighty degrees despite the rain. As he huffed and puffed with effort, I recalled the image of his panicky, grotesque flailing as he'd screeched, *My penis! My penis!* Vomit arching in a stream from his mouth like a garden fountain. His face all puffy, eyes swollen to slits. He'd looked like a fat, naked baby.

Louis walked toward me with a big grin on his face. "You've lost your whole damn mind." He reached for my champagne. "Share, please."

It was so easy being with him. I know people think we must be in love and we just don't realize it yet, but it isn't like that. Louis and I have known each other since nursery school. He's seen me throw up. I've seen him cry. I'm not saying I haven't thought about him in that way; *obviously* I've thought about it. But what we have is even better, because it's safe. Romance always ends with someone getting their heart broken.

"How are you getting away with all this?" he asked.

"By harnessing the forces of darkness." I waved a hand across his face. "You will remember none of this tomorrow."

Louis tilted his head back and took a few swallows of champagne.

It spilled out the corners of his mouth and onto his chin, which was rough with stubble. Sweat gathered at his hairline. He was tan, his face a little burned. He looked so…I don't know, so human. I had the urge to touch his face, his hair—longish, dark waves crowding around his ears and eyes—to hold on to him, to make sure of him. I pushed the feeling away. *Nothing matters.*

Auggie kept pausing to scowl at us from the opposite side of the beach. Louis noticed this and didn't try to hide his amusement.

"What's going on with you two? Trouble in paradise?"

"I don't know. He's getting on my nerves."

"That's a shame." Louis paused. "Hey, I need to tell you something. I've been trying to wait for a good time, but… My parents are getting divorced."

"What?" I cried. I didn't meant to react so strongly; it just happened. The news felt like a gut punch. Like my body was in free-fall. *Nothing matters, nothing matters…*

"It's true."

"But it can't be." I was already blinking back tears. I know it seems like an overreaction to the news, since they aren't my own parents. But Louis's parents made me believe in love.

It always felt like a home when I visited, and I'd been so hungry for that feeling almost my whole life. My parents divorced when I was four years old. I don't remember a whole lot from their marriage. Mostly I remember the fighting. I would put on my Dora the Explorer headphones to block out the sound and play my favorite song over and over again, for as long as it took for them to stop. (The song was "What's Up" by 4 Non Blondes. Just kidding! It was "You Don't Know You're Beautiful" by One Direction.)

They've been divorced for thirteen years now. I was young enough when it all went down that I don't have a whole lot of specific memories in the sense that I can remember the events as they happened; what I *do* remember instead is the way those things made me feel: Unsafe. Uncertain. My childhood was like trying to balance on quicksand. My dad got remarried and lives in a different state with his new family. I've never met my stepmother or step-siblings. I don't remember what my father looks like. My mom did her best, but she has her own issues. She's a story for another day.

Louis's parents seemed so different—a perfectly imperfect match made in the sacred unknown. I will admit to wishing they could be my parents, too.

I'll tell you one thing about my mom, but only one. In my AP Psych class, we read about a famous experiment called the "wire mother experiment." A guy named Harry Harlow did experiments on rhesus monkeys to learn more about the bond between mothers and their children. (Spoiler alert: You know the expression "more fun than a barrel of monkeys"? Harry Harlow's monkeys did not have much fun, nor did they have access to barrels.)

So in this particular experiment, Harry Harlow took a bunch of baby monkeys away from their real mothers and replaced them with new, inanimate "mothers." Some were made of wire and wood; others were made with wool. Each one had a face and everything. Not an actual monkey face worn like a mask; more like a doll's head mounted on a stick. You get the idea. Anyway, in the first phase of the experiment, he let each monkey choose between a wire mother—the wire was sharp!—and a wool mother who the monkeys could cuddle with. The monkeys always chose the wool mothers. Phase two was where it got interesting: when the babies were given a choice between a wire mother that had food vs. a wool mother with no food, they still chose the wool mother every time, even if it meant they starved.

My mother is a wire mother.

Louis's mother, Laura, makes me a seafood paella, which is my absolute favorite meal, every year on my birthday. She has done this since I was eight years old. She goes absolutely over-the-top apeshit with Halloween decorations every single year. Sometimes she sneaks a cigarette or two outside, when nobody else is around, and everybody pretends not to smell it on her afterward. But they don't pretend the way some families pretend not to know things by burying their heads in the sand. She knows they know, and they know *she* knows they know. They give her room to be flawed.

She seemed so happy to me. I guess not.

"It hasn't been the same since my brother died."

"So they're just giving up?"

"I don't think they're giving up, Emma. I think they tried for a long time. And if they aren't happy with each other, don't you think it will be better this way for everybody?"

"I don't understand this. Why am I more upset than you are?"

"Because you've never seen how sad they are when nobody else is around. They always tried not to show it to me, but I knew. And they deserve to be happy, don't they?"

"I guess so."

"My dad is moving out this week while I'm gone. But he's only going a few blocks away. I'll still see him every day." Louis's dad is not as vivacious or exciting as his wife, at least not outwardly. But he is kind, and he adores his wife and son. He *seemed* to adore his wife. If Laura was a little over-the-top sometimes, Mateo kept her balanced. He's vanilla ice cream; she's hot fudge. I can close my eyes and picture his face. I don't flinch at the sound of his voice. The bar is much lower for fathers, you see. All they have to do is stay.

My mom likes to remind me that all love ends in heartbreak. The deeper the love, the harder the crash. It's a cynical way to look at life. As far as I can tell from my eighteen years so far, it's also true. Think about it: Imagine you happen to stumble across your honest-to-goodness soul mate at a young age. You spend a lifetime loving each other, bearing witness to one another's journey. Best case scenario, the love endures and grows stronger over the years. Maybe it's all joy and no sorrow. Unlikely? Sure. Impossible? Probably. But pretend with me for a minute. You and your person go through life unscathed, your love guiding you like a beacon.

You grow old together. Your bodies start to fail. The world shrinks and becomes more difficult to navigate. Then one of you gets sick or injured. Your bodies become prisons. You watch each other suffer. You know how it's all going to end, you see it getting closer every day, and there's nothing you can do to stop it. Nothing. Then one of you dies, and the surviving partner is left alone with their pain. People love the expression "the only certainties in life are death and taxes." That's kind of splitting hairs, isn't it? If you zoom out on the sentiment, the message is still the same: the only certainty in life is suffering.

If somebody asks, "Is this going to hurt?" the answer is always, always yes.

Bradd

Friday

Alison was armed with every imaginable excuse to avoid beta testing the H2Blow prototype. First she said it was her fear of putting her head underwater. Then she said she didn't want to get her hair wet. She finally admitted she had some "general concerns."

"Like what kinds of concerns?"

"Structural concerns. Safety concerns."

"What's the real problem here, babe? You used to believe in me. We used to take risks together." The truth is we've been growing apart all year. I don't want to break up, but I can feel her slipping away. It hurts, man! She's my best friend. Did I actually think we were going to stay together after high school and eventually get married and have a few perfect-looking children? Who knows? Probably not, if I'm being honest. But that's the thing—it's the honesty that matters. Everything else is bullshit.

What Alison and I have is real; we accept one another; we spend time with each other because we want to. Not because our parents are friends; not because we're both exceedingly good-looking or because our families belong to the same country club or because we both look incredible in pastels. All that is just icing. Alison makes me laugh. She's a foxy little minx. She gets me. And I know she loves me—I know that for a fact. But what if she isn't *in* love with me? This is my dilemma: I'm afraid to ask her the question, because I know she'll tell me the truth.

So I tried not to think about it. I tried to focus on my work, on the H2Blow. I told myself I didn't need Alison's help anyway. I didn't need anybody's help; I have hyper-extended joints, which means I am a man of many talents. I can touch my toes; I can do a split; I can suck my own dick. I know it might seem unfair for me to be showered with so many blessings, but it's not like I asked for them. I was born this way.

I found a secluded spot in the lagoon where nobody was likely to stumble across me. I did see Emma as she was making her way to the beach. She was pushing a wheelbarrow. We didn't acknowledge each other.

So anyway, I did end up drowning. I guess I got carried away. As it turns out, Alison was correct: the H2Blow was not yet ready for retail distribution. But the goal of innovation is progress, not perfection. Look at what happened to the *Titanic*! Was it a failure just because it's sitting at the bottom of the ocean filled with second-class skeletons?

I am the James Cameron of erotic aquatic devices.

I opened my eyes. I was nestled underneath a blanket on a sofa in Gus and Greta's house. Gus was scowling down at me. Maybe he could help me fine-tune the prototype.

"The fortunate son awakens," he said.

"What happened to me? Am I dead?"

"Not anymore. You're damn lucky we found you in time, or I might be calling your parents right now with some very bad news indeed." His jaw was clenched.

"Where's Alison?"

"Alison isn't here. Son, were you paying attention to anything I just said? You drowned. You were resuscitated."

"I want Alison. Can you get her?"

"Maybe later."

"Can you get her now?"

Gus brought his hands to his face in exaggerated frustration. His fingers wriggled as he massaged his forehead. His hands were wrinkled like old leather. He wore a gold ring on his middle finger, a big, round ruby lying cushioned in the center of the thick band. The ring looked old and expensive. His shirtsleeves were rolled up, revealing the octopus tattoo that stretched from his wrist to well past his shoulder. I looked around him at the bookshelves on the wall. The books all had wordy, vaguely unsettling scientific titles like *Comprehensive Organic Transformations* and *Manipulations in Analytical Organic Chemistry* and *Deconstructing Life Through Science*.

He looked at me through his fingers. He spoke calmly, but there was a whisper of menace to his tone. "No, I will not get Alison. You and I are going to have a talk, and if you don't listen carefully, I'm going to hurt you."

His words chilled me. I tried not to let it show. "Pfffttt. You aren't going to lay a hand on me. I think my father, the *senator*, would have a problem with that."

Gus pulled his hands away from his face. His voice oozed with menace now. His eyes went flat, like a shark's. Peek-a-boo. For the first time, it dawned on me that I might be underestimating him. "You think he'd have a problem with me saving your life after you died trying to fellate yourself?"

I wanted Alison.

"I'm going to be perfectly honest with you, and you can choose to believe me now or not, but I can promise you this: you *will* believe me eventually. Maybe not immediately, because what I'm going to tell you will sound unbelievable, but I'm hoping my little preamble will convince you to give me the benefit of the doubt and accept what I'm going to tell you as the truth. Because it is the truth."

"What's a preamble?"

"You weren't breathing when we pulled you from the water. You didn't have a pulse. If you hadn't been here on this island when it happened, someone would be zipping you into a body bag right about now."

"Shut up." I remembered getting lightheaded, losing all sense of directional orientation in the water, having the sudden and in retrospect obvious realization that the H2Blow needed some kind of release valve to prevent whatever was happening. But I don't remember being scared. To be fair, it's a lot harder to be scared when you're underwater with your own dick in your mouth. There's just a lot going on.

"Don't do that, son," he said evenly. His ruby ring flashed in the light, and I reflexively flinched a little bit.

"Don't do what?"

"Don't tell me to shut up."

"Okay! I'm sorry!"

"Don't make me tell you again. What you need to do right now is pay attention and listen. You were given a highly experimental drug to save your life. I didn't want to do it, but there was no other choice. There were no other options. If we'd waited even just a few more minutes it would have been useless. You were barely dead. You were still warm. But—and this is important—make no mistake, you were not alive. No hospital on Earth could have brought you back. I injected you with a drug I've been developing here for years. I'm the only reason you're alive."

This was too much. I couldn't take him seriously. "Okay, dude. Sure." I looked around. "Where's my prototype? What did you do with it?" I tried to stand up. Gus shoved me back onto the sofa and smacked me hard across the face.

"What did I just tell you?" he yelled. "You're going to listen to me right now. As I said," he continued, "the drug is still highly experimental. Nobody outside this island even knows it exists. It isn't ready for testing on humans, not by a long shot. This isn't something that will change the face of modern medicine; it's going to change people's understanding of reality. It's going to alter the very fabric of existence." His eyes flashed with ambition.

If he was telling me the truth, I had most definitely underestimated him. The power dynamic was not in my favor, which I didn't like one bit—although I'll admit there was a small part of me that admired his entrepreneurial spirit. "Bradd, this drug is a miracle. It's the reason why you're alive right now. It's the reason you're going to stay alive. Not just for today, not just for tomorrow, because that's another thing: unfortunately, as of right now, this drug has some major, uh, limitations. It has some problems, is what I'm saying." He paused. "Complications." He held up his hands and wiggled his fingers again; this time it wasn't nearly as threatening. "Wrinkles, you might say… There are mysteries everywhere, Bradd, is what I'm saying."

I couldn't remember dying. But I couldn't remember not dying, if that makes any sense. Could he really be serious? "What the fuck did you give me? What kind of complications? What mysteries?"

He hesitated. "All the mysteries."

"So what's going to happen now? Will I be okay?" It was then I noticed Greta standing in the doorway. She had a smug look on her pretty, wild-eyed face. You know the kind of wild eyes I mean. Alison gets them, too, sometimes. I pointed at her. "You! Your dad drugged me!"

Her eyes somehow opened wider. "I know. You got yourself into some big trouble, you bad boy!"

For the first time, I was embarrassed that I'd let myself get caught up in this whole thing. But what choice did I have? I was like Benjamin Franklin, flying his kite in a thunderstorm to prove the existence of electricity.

Gus raised his voice and continued speaking over us. "The biggest issue with the drug is that it gives its recipient life, maybe even endless life, but it doesn't allow them to move forward in time. It acts as something I've been referring to as a temporal paralytic. Do you understand what that means?"

"A temporal paralytic?"

"That's right."

I looked Greta in the eye. "Is he for real?"

"He is very much for real." She said it with not a small amount of pride. She had the whitest teeth. I recognized her from somewhere, I swear to God. Maybe I'd seen her picture in a magazine somewhere, I don't know. I started to think I could feel whatever Gus had injected me with moving through my bloodstream like a burst of ants in a tunnel. Gross. What the fuck was a temporal paralytic?

"What day is today, Bradd?" Gus asked me.

"Uh…Friday."

"Correct. Ordinarily, Friday is followed by Saturday. But not for you. Not now. For you, tomorrow is going to be Friday again. And the day after that will be Friday. What I'm trying to say is get used to Friday."

Temporal paralytic. The meaning of the words clicked into place. "So what are you saying? Every day is Friday from now until forever? Am I immortal? Can I die?"

"Not forever. Nothing lasts forever," Gus said. "But yes. Forever for now."

"That's helpful," I said sarcastically.

"And no, you can't die. But in the meantime," he continued, "I wouldn't risk it."

"Pfffft. I don't think so." First of all, I still kind of didn't believe either of them. And if it *were* true, then why *shouldn't* I die? What's the harm?

"What you need to understand, Bradd, is these are uncharted waters. Nothing is certain."

It dawned on me all of a sudden that I felt absolutely fantastic. Maybe better than I'd ever felt in my whole life. I knew that I should care about whatever was happening, but I just kind of…didn't. I figured I could worry about it later. I don't know; maybe I was drunk on the nectar of discovery. I felt loopy and disoriented, but I also felt kind of like a god. I wasn't afraid of Gus or his stupid-hot daughter. "What did you do with my prototype?"

Gus's eye twitched. "Your prototype?"

"What did you do with my H2Blow? It's the erotic aquatic device that's going to revolutionize the—"

"Are you talking about the helmet you were wearing in the water?"

"Yes. It's my greatest accomplishment. It's going to revolutionize the market for erotic aquatic devices."

He actually smacked me across the face again. The nerve of this dick. Oh, I smelled a lawsuit. My father was quite litigious.

"You stole it, didn't you? You're trying to steal my prototype and pass it off as your own. You won't get away with this."

"I did not steal your prototype! It's the stupidest idea I've ever heard in my life! There is no market for erotic aquatic devices! Jesus Christ, I should have let you stay dead."

"Where. Is. My. H2. Blow?"

"Do you understand what I'm saying to you? You're in a time loop, Bradd! You're going to wake up in your room tomorrow and the H2Blow—Jesus, that's a name—will be right where you left it when you went to sleep on Thursday night. Are you hearing me?" He raised his hand, as if to hit me again.

I grabbed his wrist. "You have already hit me twice. I don't recommend doing it thrice. I come from a very well-connected and powerful family."

He stared at me. "You really don't understand who you're dealing with, do you? You need to take me seriously."

"If I tell you I understand, will you stop yelling at me? Will you stop hitting me?"

"Yes."

"Then I understand. As long as I'm under the influence of this drug, which you're telling me lasts indefinitely, you're saying I can't die. Like, even if I die, I'll just wake up again on Friday morning like nothing happened."

"That's what I'm telling you, yes."

"I believe you." I wanted to get the hell away from him. But I also wanted Alison. "Can I leave?"

"I want you to stay here for a while. You should rest. You should eat something."

"Then I want my girlfriend."

Alison

Friday

The comfort that I feel when I'm curled up in bed next to Emma: I don't have words, only feelings. It isn't anything romantic or sexual; it's just so comforting. We used to build couch forts together in her finished basement and practice french kissing on her stuffed Pikachu. We dressed up in her mom's caftans and lip synched to Miley Cyrus. Life was so much easier before boys got in the way of everything, and someday men will get in the way of everything else. It will never be the same as it used to be when we were little girls; part of growing up, as women, is being conditioned by men to see one another as rivals. What if we didn't let men have so much power? What if we simply refused to participate? It would be easy for me, but not for Emma. Some girls can't help themselves.

I started to worry when Bradd didn't show up to dinner. I love him, I do, but I won't keep looking out for him forever. I wish more people appreciated him. Even his own father doesn't understand him. Bradd is a better, kinder person than anybody gives him credit for. Bradd is harmless and straightforward: what you see is what you get.

I ran into Greta shortly after I went looking for Bradd. She told me he'd been in some kind of accident.

"Is he okay? What happened?"

She hesitated. "I'll let him explain it to you."

At Gus and Greta's house, Bradd did seem okay. But he also seemed…not okay. He was sitting up, eating a banana Popsicle, watching a DVD of the first Harry Potter movie. He looked at me, but he didn't see me. As he breathed in and out, the air he exhaled smelled like ammonia. His entire face was fixed in an expression of euphoria, mad euphoria. Something was wrong with him.

Still, I was so relieved to see him upright and breathing that I burst into tears. I rushed to his side and wrapped my arms around him. His body felt cool. The stench of ammonia was overwhelming. "What happened, baby? I was so worried about you."

He licked his Popsicle and stared at the television. "This wouldn't have happened if you had helped me with the H2Blow."

Not the goddamn H2Blow again.

"Babe, I'm sorry, but I just don't see the market potential."

Another lick. He didn't take his eyes off the screen. Harry had just boarded the train for his first trip to Hogwarts. "Choo-choo," Bradd said, motioning with his arm. "Choo-choo." He finally looked at me. "I'm going to be the H2Blow king someday, baby, and I want to make you my H2Blow queen." He bit into the Popsicle with his front teeth and immediately winced in pain. "Ohhh! Too cold!"

"Are you sure you're okay? You feel really cold, and your lips are kind of purple. Maybe I should get someone."

"No!" He grabbed my arm. "I don't need them. All I need is you. I'm okay, Al—I'm better than okay." He paused. "Can I tell you a secret?"

"Sure."

He put his lips to my ear. "I'm a god," he whispered.

"Okay." I patted him on the back. "I'm going to let you get some rest."

Greta was waiting for me outside the door. "See? He's fine."

"He doesn't seem fine. He seems concussed."

"We'll keep an eye on him. He just needs to rest. You look like you could use some rest, too."

She was right; I was exhausted.

I should have felt safe walking alone in the dark down the meandering path. There were no strangers here. There was nothing to be afraid of. There was no reason for me to hurry. Everything was fine. I kept telling myself this even as my pace quickened, even as I failed to resist the urge to lift my knees and lengthen my strides and go, fucking run, before I gave in and kicked off my sandals and took off in a hurry, arms pumping fear through my veins. I don't know why I was so scared, but I was terrified. I ran all the way back to my bungalow. The soles of my feet were raw.

Emma was asleep. I crawled into bed with her.

"Alison?" she murmured as I nestled myself behind her, taking position as the big spoon. "What time is it?"

The walls of our room were still painted with the light and shadows of sunset. The night was only beginning. "Shhh. Just sleep for now," I told her. "Let's just sleep for now."

For a little while, the two of us shared a blissful, deep sleep in each other's arms. The nap felt like being delivered to the safety of childhood again. A dreamless sleep. How could Emma not miss this as much as I did?

When I woke up, I realized I'd been unconscious for nearly an hour and a half. It was Friday evening. Emma was still fast asleep in a limp pose of half recline on her side, arms tucked against her chest like an upright bunny. Her breathing was deep and even. A dongle of drool had collected at the edge of her open mouth. She looked so peaceful.

I figured I should probably check on Bradd again. Before I left, I set the alarm on my phone for thirty minutes from now. I set it to play the song "What's Up" by 4 Non Blondes. I turned the volume all the way up and placed my phone on the pillow, beside Emma's ear. Then I kissed her on the forehead and slipped away.

Bradd

Day 2

I was up before the sun. Auggie was still fast asleep in his bed. He was resting on his side with his mouth open. For some reason, his hands were cupped protectively around his dick and balls, like he was afraid the boogeyman was going to sneak in and molest him while he slept. "I hate you," I whispered. It felt good to say it out loud, even if he couldn't hear me.

Tomorrow will be Friday. The day after that will be Friday, and the day after that. I still wasn't fully convinced yet that it was Fridays all the way down, as Gus had claimed—extraordinary claims require extraordinary evidence, as they say—but I was about to find out.

I got dressed in the dark, quickly and quietly so as not to wake Auggie, and grabbed a flashlight on my way out the door. I walked to the same beach where I'd found the white lobster, before Steven the Intern had confiscated it. There were almost two hours to go until breakfast and almost three hours until I could expect the white lobster to wash ashore—if I was truly in a time loop. But that didn't mean I had to wait around helplessly for the next three hours; the beach was buttressed by a huge coral reef maybe a hundred feet from the water's edge, which meant the white lobster was probably swirling around somewhere nearby; it was just a matter of it catching the right wave to deposit it on the beach.

I aimed the beam of my flashlight at the ocean's surface and spotted it almost immediately, a glint of shimmery white bobbing in the distance. I made my way toward it. The water never reached past my waist. I grasped it to my chest as I waded toward the shore and hurried back to my bungalow. Auggie was still sleeping, exactly as I'd left him. My hands trembled with excitement as I stashed the brick under a pile of clothes in my suitcase. It was mine now. All mine. I could hardly believe how easy it had been.

I was already aroused when I made a small tear in the plastic wrapped around the brick, deep enough for me to push a finger inside and scoop out some powder. It was damp and dense, almost like kinetic sand, and it smelled vile—like extra-pungent ammonia. The smell made my eyes water, and that was before I used my Visa card to cut it into three fat, neat lines on the surface of my dresser. I rolled up a five-dollar bill (I would have preferred to use something larger, but I only had fives and singles) and did my thing. I tilted my head back and squeezed my eyes shut, waiting.

The effect was instantaneous, yet it stretched for eons. In my mind, I saw fire and ice, bronze and steel. The rise and fall of all living creatures in the galaxy. The expansion and contraction of time; eternity and nothingness; the first gasps of consciousness colliding with inevitable decay. My dick was as hard as a lead pipe. I was dizzy; I was elated; I had never been so horny in my life. Without so much as touching myself—my hands quivered, half numb and tingling at my sides—I arched my back and braced for the imminent release.

But it never came. My body quivered at the cusp of ecstasy, riding wave upon wave of arousal but never finding relief. I was frozen. Paralyzed in an endless tunnel of death. After what felt like an eternity, I felt the heaviness returning to my physical self before I collapsed in a heap on the floor. I gasped to catch my breath. I opened my eyes.

I found myself in bed, where I'd been only moments earlier. I heard the click of our door as it closed behind Auggie. I heard his footsteps growing fainter as he walked away.

I sat up. I leaped from my bed and scrambled on all fours across the room to my suitcase. It was zipped shut again. The white lobster was inside, hidden beneath a layer of dirty clothes.

What the fuck was happening?

I didn't know. But I was going to figure it out.

Max

Day 14,987

I was jolted from a midday nap by a howl that sounded like it came from a wounded animal. It was the kind of noise you can't help but investigate right away. I followed the sound to the beach, where Alison was kneeling beside Bradd in the shallow water. Bradd was nude, facedown, his swimming trunks pulled all the way down and ballooning around his ankles. His trunks could have functioned as a makeshift life preserver, but it looked like it might be too late for that. His bare ass bobbed in the water, crack-up, his cheeks floating a few inches above the surface.

I hurried toward them and helped Alison turn him over. The H2Blow was strapped securely to Bradd's head—maybe too securely. Alison struggled to tear it away and threw it over her shoulder. Bradd's face was blue and mottled with purple. There was a mustache of foam around his nostrils. His eyes were open, but he wasn't awake.

I knelt beside him and checked for a pulse. I didn't feel anything. Alison was too hysterical to do anything but wail and cry; it was amazing there wasn't a crowd gathered around us.

"You have to calm down," I told her, which only made her more upset.

"Oh my God!" she wailed. "Baby, no!"

"Alison. Hey." I smacked her lightly across the face. She gasped and held a palm to her cheek. "You aren't helping him. I need you to get up and go find Greta." She stared at me, incomprehensive. "Alison, go find Greta. Go!"

She managed to pull herself together and took off running in search of Greta. I gave Bradd CPR. I could hear his ribs cracking beneath the thrust of the heels of my hands.

His eyes were stagnant and flat, his unseeing pupils aimed toward the sky.

CPR is physically exhausting when performed correctly. I kept going until I was out of breath and it seemed clear there was no point in continuing to try. His lights were out. He was gone.

I crumbled. I wept with rage at my own failure. I've tried to end my time here in every imaginable way, including taking matters into my own hands, to no avail. It's one thing for *me* to die here, knowing I'll wake up in the morning with the worst hangover of my life (again) yet will otherwise be fine. But these kids? Their lives aren't mine to disrupt in any version of reality. Emma was right—I'm supposed to be protecting them. The very least I can do is keep them alive. Even Bradd. He didn't deserve this. He was just a dumb, horny kid.

Bradd's eyes suddenly bulged and seemed almost to glow in his skull, and he sat up with a gasp. His whole body seized and quivered until he was a frenzied blur. I assumed he was having some kind of a seizure. Then his spine arched toward the sky, like he was being lifted into the air by an invisible hook. My ears rang. I saw a flash of light and heard a high-pitched *squawk* of terror. A large bird—a seagull—hung suspended in midair a dozen or so feet above

Bradd's naked body. The air bloomed with feathers as the bird fell, dead, into Bradd's lap. Its head rested in limp profile against his belly, a single eyeball dangling loose from its socket, held in place only by a ropy, gelatinous thread that— Oh my God. His ejaculate had struck the bird with enough force to kill it.

"Holy shit." He looked at the bird, then he looked at me. "Tell me you saw what just happened," he said, catching his breath.

"Yes, that was...quite a shot." The bird's limp body was draped across his junk like a feathered loincloth.

"I'm a god," Bradd whispered to himself. "I'm Poseidon."

"Are you okay?" All I cared about was that he was alive. Still, the lethal force of his ejaculate was...worrisome. Not to mention the fact that he was sitting up and talking at all.

"I'm more than okay." He stood, pulled up his swim trunks, and thumped his fists against his chest like King Kong. "I've never felt more alive!"

I grabbed the H2Blow. "I'm confiscating this."

"Fine with me. But I'm keeping the bird."

I've been trapped here—and by *here* I mean Friday, April 20—for decades. Time is an inscrutable kaleidoscope. I understand how it works, kind of, but if I start to think about it too hard, even after all this time, my brain starts to break. It seems clear enough to me that Gus and Greta have stumbled on sacred knowledge, something that mere humans aren't meant to mess with. Yet here we are—here *I* am—trying to make sense of the surreal, to orient myself in infinite space time. The problem is too vast and complex for me to understand; it's like trying to explain calculus to a field mouse. I still have so many questions.

For instance: While Emma and I are trapped in the same reality *now*, our realities having fused once she fed on Sibyl, what about all the Emmas who have come and gone over the decades of Fridays that passed prior to her joining me in the loop? Are we even in the same loop at all? Or is it more of a Venn diagram? Where am I in all of this? Surely there's a reality in which Emma and I went home with everybody else on Saturday, isn't there? Or maybe not. I truly don't know.

Thinking about it is enough to make anybody lose their mind. I've indulged every scenario, no matter how ridiculous. Why shouldn't I? How could anything be more ridiculous than what's already happening? I've considered that I might be in Hell or that we could all be in Hell together—maybe our plane crashed—or that I'm in a coma, and this is all a manifestation of my subconscious. One thing I'm sure of: it isn't Heaven.

Emma

Day 5

Be-BLAH, be-BLAH, went the bird outside our window as Alison choked on my Swedish Fish. Out of all the unpleasant repetition, her theft pissed me off more than anything. It was a minor offense in the overall scheme of things, I knew, but the fact she was so brazen about it filled me with rage. She knew how much I loved Swedish Fish. I love them more than I love all of my second cousins combined. Alison knew this, and it didn't make a whit of difference to her.

I glared at her. "Do you even have a soul?"

"Yes, I have a soul. Don't you remember when we both got saved?"

She was referring to the summer we went to Vacation Bible School together after third grade. We were more than best friends back then; we were practically next-door neighbors. Our little hometown is the kind where kids roam the streets with almost no adult supervision on long summer days. Very Disney Channel. My family has never been religious (my mom told me once that she briefly considered joining the Hare Krishnas back in college, but the haircut was a dealbreaker), yet somehow my mother had zero issues with her daughter accompanying all the neighborhood kids to the local Baptist church every afternoon for Vacation Bible Camp, where we were told in no uncertain terms that anyone who wasn't saved would burn in Hell.

In hindsight, my mom was never preoccupied by things like the details of exactly *how* I was spending my time outside the house, even at that young age; as long as I wasn't around, she was happy.

Bible camp could always be counted on to traumatize us kids, yet we returned year after year to make macaroni crucifix sculptures and rat on our parents for their many sins. (Janey Bennet reported to our lord and savior's proxy adults that her mom smoked funny-smelling cigarettes. Aiden Kimmel reported finding a dick pic on his dad's phone. Kids don't know when to keep their mouths shut.) I remember a lot of sobbing and snotty noses and confessing of sins and vivid, terrifying descriptions of Hell. Imagine telling a group of elementary-aged children they'll be torn limb-from-limb by a pack of rabid wolves for all eternity unless they surrender themselves to the lord.

Maybe I should have taken my commitment to our lord and savior more seriously. Maybe this is Hell. It isn't the first time I've had the thought, and it won't be the last. If someone were to ask me what kind of music they might play in Hell, I would answer instantly: "What's Up" by 4 Non Blondes, which is the song that's playing right now. I hate it so much. On occasion, hearing it actually makes me gag.

There's a very good reason for this. Something happened to me once while this song was playing. Something traumatic. I've never told anybody this story before, aside from my mom and Louis: When I was fifteen, my mom asked me if I'd like to make some extra cash by helping her friend Stephanie with some house cleaning.

Stephanie was going through a nasty breakup, and she'd let her home fall into total disarray while she was trying to pick up the pieces of her life. My mom offered my services—I actually enjoy cleaning, and I'm pretty good at it—and I foolishly jumped at the opportunity.

What my mother didn't mention was that in the wake of her breakup, Stephanie had adopted an adolescent golden retriever to keep her company. The puppy, Dixon, was already huge at two years old. From the moment I arrived, he followed me around the house as I worked. Stephanie—my mom's biggest trainwreck of a friend—offered me a Heineken Zero when I arrived because she was "out of bottled water." Then she went upstairs to "relax." She left a 4 Non Blondes album playing loudly from the surround speakers that were positioned around her living room. I didn't know how to turn it off, or even turn it down, and I wasn't about to go upstairs to ask Stephanie.

I was vacuuming the stairs when it happened. "What's Up" was blasting so loudly that I could clearly make out the tune and all the lyrics over the sound of the vacuum. I was leaning on the stairs of the first floor landing when I felt someone grasp me firmly from behind. It was Dixon.

At first I didn't realize what was happening, or why the dog wouldn't let go.

I was wearing athletic shorts; my legs were exposed all the way to my upper thigh. Dixon was humping my bare legs, and I didn't know how to make him stop.

"Help," I called weakly, frozen in horror. "Stephanie?"

It was no use. The music was too loud.

The 4 Non Blondes wailed about what might, at that moment, be going on.

I'll tell you what was fucking going on: Dixon the dog was assaulting me. He thrust his hips and pelvis against my lower half. His tail curled between my legs, waggling frenziedly, and before I knew it he'd ejaculated on my leg. I gagged and gagged and vomited

Heineken Zero onto Stephanie's carpeted stairs. I managed to get away from Dixon and ran to the first-floor bathroom, where I cleaned myself off and vomited some more. I fled Stephanie's house without saying goodbye. I went home and took a long shower, scrubbing my legs with a loofah that I then deposited directly into the garbage. It was awful.

My mother demanded to know why I'd left Stephanie's so abruptly, so I told her. She thought it was the funniest thing she'd ever heard in her life. It was not funny to me.

Hearing the song again right then kind of broke something in me. Rage bubbled in my belly. I wanted revenge.

I waited until Alison was fully dressed *(I call this look the farmer's daughter)* and she'd finished applying her makeup. I watched as she carefully parted her long hair down the middle and wove it into two braids. As we were preparing to walk out the door, I put a hand on her arm. "Wait a minute. You have a loose thread on the back of your shirt." I ducked into the bathroom and grabbed a pair of scissors from her makeup bag. "Turn around."

When her back was turned, I held both of her braids in one hand and quickly chopped them off near the base of her skull.

I clutched the braids in one fist and held her at scissor-point with my other hand. "That's what you get for stealing from me! And for that godawful song!"

She stared at the braids in disbelief. She started to cry. I strolled across the room and chucked her braids out the window. *Nothing matters.*

I was smiling as I walked to breakfast alone. I tried to brush past Steven the Intern in the doorway, but he stared me down while I approached.

"The devil is beating his wife, Steve-O."

He was stunned. "I was about to say the same thing." He paused. "Where's your friend?"

"You mean Alison? She isn't my friend. And she's still doing her hair."

I went directly to the kitchen pantry and retrieved the industrial-size jar of kalamata olives and a bottle of champagne. I carried them both to the table and sat down. Across the room, Alison wept as she spoke furiously to a bored-looking Max. She was wearing a baseball cap.

My friends stared at me. "Did you really cut all of Alison's hair?" Auggie whispered.

"Is that what she's saying?"

He nodded.

I sighed. "Of course I didn't. She did it to herself." I lowered my voice. "I'm a little worried about her. She's been acting out of character all morning."

"*Alison* has been acting out of character?" Louis was doubtful. "What's with the olives and booze?"

"They're for eating and drinking."

Auggie nudged me and nodded at the champagne. "We should save it for tonight."

"There's plenty more for tonight. Who wants mimosas?"

Tonight. I didn't want to think about tonight. I had no idea what to do. Tell him I had my period again? That hadn't worked so well last time.

Lucy Thomas gave me a disapproving look. "I don't know what you think you're doing, but Max is going to confiscate that." She meant the champagne.

"Then I guess we better hurry up and drink it."

"*Hell* yeah!" Bradd pumped his fists into the air.

Even Connor Cackowski seemed into it. "Pass it down here, Emma!"

"Ooh, evidently little Connie boy wants a drinkie," Bradd said in a mocking tone, giving Connor a hard time for no reason.

Lucy shook her head. "This isn't okay. I'm getting Max." But when she approached him—he was still talking to Alison—he waved her away. Alison glared at me. Lucy said something to Alison, and the two of them stormed off.

Max was too busy with Alison to give us any instructions on how to spend the rest of our morning. A handful of us lingered in the dining hall, drinking round after round of mimosas until we'd emptied several bottles of *delicious* champagne.

Bradd pulled his shorts down and stood at the front of the room with his junk tucked between his thighs. He kept his legs pressed together as he spread his arms like Jesus on the cross. Unlike Jesus, Bradd clutched fistfuls of oysters in both hands. "Would you shuck me?" he asked in a deep voice. "I'd shuck me."[1]

Bradd didn't seem the least bit concerned about Alison's hair or her whereabouts. He was far too amused by his own antics.

"Can I talk to you real quick, Emma?" Louis asked.

"Emma is busy right now." Even Auggie had managed to pull the stick from his ass long enough to let loose and drink some champagne. He drew me into his lap and kissed my neck.

Louis looked uncomfortable. His cheeks were flushed from the champagne. "I think Emma can answer for herself."

"Back off, dude," Auggie told him. His arms felt like tentacles constricting around my body. I felt trapped. A shudder of repulsion rippled through me as Auggie kissed my neck and shoulders. He was sloppy and sweaty and not attractive at all.

I needed air. I knew this wasn't Auggie's fault; *this* Auggie had no idea about the blobfish penis. But I was hyperventilating anyway—I excused myself and went outside. Hoping to avoid running into Alison, I cut through the vegetation instead of taking the path to my bungalow. That's how I ran into Gianluca. He was dozing in a hammock. His eyes were closed, and he snored softly. A copy of the Italian translation of *Twilight: New Moon* lay open against his chest. He didn't stir until I tapped him gently on the shoulder.

---

1 It took me a second to realize that he was doing an impersonation of Buffalo Bill from that movie *Silence of the Lambs*, where the guy dances naked in front of a camera and asks, "Would you fuck me? I'd fuck me." All I can say is, *Ew. Just ew.*

He opened his eyes and yawned. "Ciao, bella," he greeted me sleepily.

"Hi, Gianluca. I'm sorry to wake you. I hope I didn't startle you." I batted my eyelashes. I wasn't doing it for no reason; I needed to enlist Gianluca's help.

"Gianluca does not startle." He looked me up and down. "You have beautiful eyes."

"Thank you. Whatcha reading?"

"You do not recognize?" He held up the cover so I could see it better. "Is greatest love story ever told. Did you read?"

I had not read *Twilight* and had no plans to ever do so, nor had I seen any of the movies. I didn't even know the plot. "Oh, yes, I've read the whole series many times. And I've seen all the movies." I paused. "Has anyone ever told you that you look exactly like Robert Pattinson?"

Gianluca sat up slowly and stared at me with fascination. "Many people tell me. Everywhere I go, they tell me."

"The resemblance is uncanny."

He lit a cigarette. "I know this."

I stared at the sky for a minute, thinking. A light mist of rain fell around us. "This place is kind of creepy, isn't it?"

He looked around. "I am not afraid."

"But the atmosphere is creepy. And we're all alone here... It really makes me miss my dog." *Sorry, Charles. Take one for the team.*

Gianluca's expression softened. "This I understand. I, too, miss my dog."

"You know what we'd do together back home? Curl up under a blanket and watch a scary movie."

"We will watch *Twilight* movies now."

"I wish we could."

"I have every *Twilight* movie downloaded on computer. I bring with me to watch on airplane. We will watch together now and make love if you would like."

"I can't do that right now, Gianluca. I have a boyfriend." I wasn't interested in him romantically; I was interested in him strategically.

"So what? We can have secret."

"I'm not that kind of girl."

"Let Gianluca release animal inside you."

"I really don't have time right now." I paused. "I do have something to ask you, though."

"Ask me."

"Will you teach me how to play chess?"

He furrowed his brow. "And then we will make love?"

"No."

He thought about it. "I will teach you," he agreed. "I will seduce. Then we make love."

"I'm not going to sleep with you. I don't want to give you the wrong idea."

He grinned slyly. "I am full of wrong ideas."

Max

Day 14,988

It's still a mystery to me: why Emma? This is the question that drives me forward each day, convinced as I've grown that its answer holds a key that will bring me one step closer to unlocking the *why* or possibly the *how* of things. I know Emma thinks I'm holding out on her, that I know far more about what's going on than I'm willing to tell her, but she's wrong. Gus is the scientist; we're merely his lab rats.

For a long time, I had bad days and worse days. But time has healed me in ways I couldn't have anticipated. I've accepted reality, as it were. I've forgiven Greta. I've had decades to get over my initial reaction of existential agony, and I've long since stopped considering it an unforgivable betrayal. Why waste my energy holding a grudge when I can surrender to what's happening and at least get some love and companionship in the meantime? Why punish myself by turning my back on the one person on this island who (I think) truly cares about me?

Besides, nothing I can say or do will change anything. No matter how much I've begged and pouted and whined for answers, I don't get any; no matter how over-the-top my temper tantrums are, I wake up again in the same place every morning. Nothing changes. Whether I go to sleep on Friday night or throw my body off a balcony, I wake up on Friday morning again, alive. I'm still alive. And that's all that matters to Greta. Should I hold it against her that she would go to any lengths, including deceiving me, in order to keep me here with her, safe, forever? Wouldn't most of us do the same for a loved one?

Emma is new to this. She's just a kid. It would be weird if she *wasn't* freaking out. It's been entertaining to watch her blossoming understanding—I mean *really* understanding—of what it means to live a life free of consequences. This morning she cut off Alison's hair, which I'm sure was deserved. I saw little point in wasting my energy on intervening; instead, I went back to bed. I slept until the afternoon, when Emma came knocking at my door once again.

"I can't do this forever. I need answers."

I yawned. "What has it been, like, three days? You need to be patient."

"Patient for *what*?"

"You heard Greta. Gus is working on it."

"And you believe that."

It's an interesting question. "I don't have much of a choice. Neither do you."

I've accepted that I'll probably never get answers to many of my questions, but I *do* have what I'm beginning to think is a significant clue about why Greta chose Emma: before this all started, I was sorting through some school paperwork that I'd brought with me on the trip, hoping to get the bulk of my students' final grades calculated before the end of the week. That's when I came across the letters. Somebody had opened them, but it wasn't me. And one of them was missing altogether.

About the letters: I've given the same assignment to the kids in my advisory group every year that I've been a teacher: On the first day of school, I have my seniors write a letter to their future selves in which they state their goals for the year. The letter is supposed to serve as an anchor for them to keep in the back of their minds as they progress toward graduation. The idea first came to me in the middle of the night; it awakened me from a deep sleep, and I was so overcome by what an incredible opportunity for learning and reflection it could be for the kids that I couldn't risk letting the thought slip away. It was an exercise in hope and nostalgia all at once, and I was thrilled to help facilitate it for these kids, because they are the future.

I'm kidding, of course. The idea wasn't mine; it originated from the keynote speaker at an educator's conference I attended in Cleveland several years ago: "If you want to help your students grow, you need to know what motivates them. To know what motivates them requires some trickery, as they're never going to simply tell you." The whole point of the assignment is to violate their trust. I have never felt guilty for doing so, and I feel even less so now more than ever. I feel negative guilt. I wish I could travel back in time, back to the days when I respected the thoughts and feelings and privacy of these children, and punch myself in the face over and over again, and disregard the sanctity of their petty secrets, and stop myself from doing every single thing that led to me being trapped on an island with a horde of horny teenagers for all eternity.

I don't want to set a dangerous precedent for my fellow educators by giving the impression that I eventually snapped from the stressors of my circumstances, which led me to violate the trust of my students and read their private communications, thus betraying their sacred confidence in me. Until this year, I have read every letter every year, as is my right, and guess what? It has been nothing but a consistent waste of time.

Six students a year for the last decade, meaning six letters containing what should presumably be the hopes and dreams of our nation's finest youth, the outspoken prodigy of Xavier Academy, yet I struggle to recall a single poignant aspiration. Taken as a collective, the vast majority served as reassurance to me that there almost certainly is no God. A sampling of some of the goals from the letters I've collected over the years range from admirable *(Hike the Appalachian Trail)* to vapid *(Get better eyebrows by prom)* to diabolical *(Ruin Cleo Ventiglio's life[2])* to insipid *(Get revenge on Thomas F. for selling me a dab of hash that turned out to be a chicken bouillon cube/giving me herpes. Earn a GPA above 3.7 and Mr. Gillis the librarian will take me to Napa to meet his stepmom. Convince Mom and Dad to let me get a ferret. Try mint chocolate chip ice cream.)*

Because I have not had high hopes for the contents of my students' letters in many years, I was in no hurry to read this year's batch. I was surprised to realize I'd even included them with the stack of end-of-year paperwork I brought and even more surprised to find six open envelopes with only five letters among them once it finally dawned on me to do a full accounting of my belongings. Only Emma's letter was missing.

I knew it was Greta. As soon as I confronted her, she admitted it. It should go without saying the reason she took it was to keep me from knowing what it said. Control group this, scientific method that.

What could be so unique or interesting about Emma's hopes and dreams that Greta decided she ought to be part of this experiment? Hell if I know. For that matter, what's special about any of these kids? If you'd asked me the same question when I first began teaching, when I was a more optimistic man, I might have

2 This goal was so emphatically realized—you might have seen the *Dateline* special about Cleo Ventiglio—that I considered handing the letter over to the prosecution, but it turned out they already had more than enough for a conviction.

said they're all special in their own way. Even then, I would have been lying; I'm ready to admit that now, twenty-four years (plus the forty years I've been here) after the original idea, birthed by my father when he first started his role as head of school at Xavier Academy, to take the senior class on a weeklong bonding excursion before graduation.

The kids weren't all inherently special back then, and they aren't all special now. They are a malignant mass of clueless children with frenzied hormones and barely a lick of common sense among them. Bradd is destined to fail upward no matter how many times he fucks up or how badly. Alison is the brightest of all of them, but you'd never guess based on how determined she seems to squander her intellect and instead coast through life on her good looks. At some point in the last few years, she gave up on academics altogether, and now she keeps her brain on airplane mode at all times. Who knows if she's even still capable of deep thought? (I overheard Lucy telling the group she was planning to teach herself sign language over the summer after finding inspiration from a documentary about famed primatologist Jane Goodall, who taught chimpanzees to communicate via sign language. Alison's feedback: "You know, it's a shame there are so many deaf monkeys," a statement that will live rent-free in my mind for the rest of my days.)

And then there's the messy romance and psychosexual intrigue, which I know I'm not supposed to have an opinion about. I have opinions. I've spent forty years watching the same day unfold in all its potential permutations. There are some things that never change. I doubt they ever will. But I'm not about to spoil it for Emma.

I told her about my disease instead. I told her how the most precious thing in the world is time and that we're part of something so special that what Gus has discovered will potentially provide an end to aging, sickness, and even death, without any of the downsides. I believe in him; I believe him when he tells me that his discovery will change the world. But the price is so high. The cost is my whole existence. I'm alive, yes, but I am not living.

Life requires motion. It requires change. I am here, and here is all I might ever be. Day after day spent in a temporal vacuum. Some days are better than others. Some days I manage to convince myself that I've made peace with my fate. Other days, I feel nothing but helpless rage. And some days I get so frustrated that I try to end it all, knowing the attempt is hopeless. There's no escape, at least none that I've come close to finding.

"What did your letter say?" I asked.

"What letter?"

Of course she didn't even remember the assignment. I reminded her.

"You told us those letters were private!"

"They were private."

"Then how did Greta get mine?"

"She took it! It's not like you had the nuclear codes written down, Emma. But look, whatever you said in that letter, it has something to do with…something."

She had whiskers drawn on her cheeks in thick black marker. She was drunk. "That's soooo helpful. Pfft. You're kind of a loser, Max. You're kind of a jerk."

"I'm trying to help you—"

"Booooo." She picked up a full water bottle on my nightstand and turned it upside down over my bed, soaking the mattress. *"Oops."*

"Okay. You aren't allowed to drink at breakfast anymore. What did your letter say?"

She thought. "I remember. But I won't tell you."

"That's fine. Then I won't tell you anything, either."

"Like what would you tell me?"

"Nothing." I didn't tell her about Auggie and Shelby. I didn't tell her about the phone. I was in no hurry.

Alison

Friday

It took me all morning to stop crying. Bradd didn't care *at all*. He *laughed* at me when I showed him what Emma had done to my hair. Even Max didn't understand why I was so upset.

"This is assault! She assaulted me!"

Max looked hungover. His eyes were all red and puffy. "It's only hair. It will grow back," he said.

"That isn't the point!"

"Alison, I'd love to help you, but the truth is I really don't care that much."

I glared at him. "She. Assaulted. Me. You have to do something."

He sighed. "Do you have any idea why she might have done that?"

I couldn't believe him. "Are you asking me what I did to deserve this?"

"Well…I don't want to victim blame, Alison. You're clearly the victim here, in that your hair has been cut off. I'm not saying that what Emma did is okay. I'm asking you to search your heart and tell me if maybe, just maybe, you might have done *anything*—"

"I didn't do anything! Why is this so hard for you to understand? If you don't want to victim blame, then don't victim blame! I'm the *victim* here."

"So you were minding your own business, and out of nowhere Emma just—"

"Cut my hair without my consent."

Max thought about it for a minute. "Again—I'm not saying that what Emma did is okay. But I get the sense there's more to this story."

"There's nothing more to the story."

"All right, then," he said evenly, "what do you think Emma's punishment should be?"

I stared at him. "What is wrong with you?"

"Emma cut off your hair. You're upset," he said.

"Yes."

"You want retribution. Vindication. Revenge."

"I want my hair back."

"You aren't getting your hair back, Alison. I don't have that power. So tell me, what is it that you want?"

I thought about it. "I want… I want her to know that I wasn't serious. I thought we could still joke around. I guess there's a part of me that thought we were still friends."

"Does it seem like Emma wants to be your friend?"

"Not really," I admitted.

"What happened before she cut off your hair? Was there some kind of conflict?"

I remembered the song. The Swedish Fish. "She didn't have to go berserk. I would have backed off."

"You would have?" He looked at me doubtfully.

"I didn't deserve this."

"What did you deserve?" He paused. "You don't have to answer right now. Think about it and get back to me."

• • •

Lucy followed me back to my bungalow. She trimmed my ends to even them out, and the result was a shaggy bob. It didn't look half bad, if I was being honest. The issue wasn't my hair as much as it was the idea that maybe Emma really, truly doesn't like me—maybe she even hates me.

I didn't go to lunch or dinner. I didn't want to see anybody. I hid in our bungalow until Emma finally returned in the late afternoon. I was exhausted from crying.

I'm not sure what I expected from Emma. I certainly didn't expect her to be apologetic, but she was. "Everything is so fucked up right now. I feel like I'm losing my mind. And you keep stealing my Swedish Fish. I guess I just lost it."

"What do you mean, I *keep* stealing them?"

She didn't answer me. She grasped the edge of her sheet between two fingers, silking the silky.

"We used to be best friends. Don't you remember that, Emma?"

"That was years ago. Things are different now. We haven't been best friends for a long time."

I sniffled and ran my fingertips along the ends of my hair. "I guess so."

"That haircut looks good on you."

I glared at her. "I *know* it looks good on me. That isn't the point."

"I know. I'm sorry. But you stole my Swedish Fish."

"What is it with you and Swedish Fish? Jesus. I can't believe you cut my hair off over Swedish Fish."

She stared at me, and she didn't have to say anything. I already knew: this wasn't about Swedish Fish.

"So are you going to tell me what's so fucked up? Why do you feel like you're losing your mind?"

"I wouldn't know where to start."

"Is it about Auggie?" I was still playing with my new hair. I felt naked. I'd managed to recover my braids after Emma threw them out the window, before the tide had a chance to wash them away. I'd stuffed them safely inside my teddy bear along with Bradd's pubes.

"Sort of. I came here planning to lose my virginity. But it isn't going well. And now I'm not even sure I want to have sex with Auggie."

"Yeah, I don't blame you." Auggie is the definition of good on paper: Good-looking. Polite. Auggie is no match for Emma; Emma deserves someone fun, snappy, exciting. Auggie is the human equivalent of a brownie laced with ebola: he looks tasty enough, but I wouldn't want to put him inside my body.

Emma thinks she's reaching with him, but the truth is that she's settling. Auggie is ordinary. Emma is not.

"But something has to change," Emma was saying. "*I* have to change. Like a caterpillar turning into a butterfly, so I can flap my wings and fly away from here."

My gammy—that's what I used to call my grandmother—had a sister named Phyllis who was what they used to call "a real wild child." Anyway, my great-grandparents had Phyllis lobotomized. I know the practice is frowned upon now, but Bradd and I have talked a lot about how we both wish it was still an option. Imagine the peace. Maybe that's what Emma needs.

"You aren't making any sense. If you want to have sex, have sex with Auggie. He's your boyfriend. That's what he's *for*."

"I don't know." She shuddered a little bit at the thought. She was still furiously silking the silky.

"Emma, you're overthinking this. Don't you know anything about men? If you want to have sex, you can have sex. You don't need Auggie. Men are all the same; just pick one. You could have sex with Gianluca, or Louis—hell, you can have sex with Bradd if you want. He'd do it if I said it was okay. Trust me, he'll fuck anything. He fucked a conch shell the day we got here."

"I don't want to have sex with Bradd."

"That's probably for the best. He's a very selfish lover."

"I appreciate the offer, though."

"Are you sure you don't want to reconsider? He could give you the most mediocre forty-five seconds of your life."

We both laughed at this. We made brief eye contact. Emma quickly looked away.

"Can I ask you a question?" she said.

"Sure."

"What does it feel like?"

"What does what feel like? You mean sex?"

"Yes."

I thought about the question for a long time. I didn't know what kind of answer she was looking for. Because that question—*what does it feel like?*—can have all kinds of different answers, depending on how you think about it. "It feels like someone is trying to give you something and take something from you at the same time."

She sighed. "I just want to get it over with."

"So get it over with."

"I don't know if I even can. I think Auggie is allergic to latex."

"You're in luck." I rummaged through my backpack and tossed her some sheepskin condoms. "Bradd will only use sheepskin. He says he likes the hint of bestiality."

"Thanks." She seemed almost disappointed. "Aren't you on the pill?"

"Yeah. So what?"

"So why use condoms at all?"

"You're kidding me, right? Were you not listening when I said Bradd will fuck anything? If you stand in front of a mirror and say his name three times, you'll probably get chlamydia. I'm not stupid, Emma. I know what he and I have. We aren't Elizabeth Bennet and Mister Darcy."

"Doesn't that bother you?"

"Not really. There's more to life than sex. He's my best friend. We're probably better off as friends, but I don't think either of us is ready to admit it just yet. It's funny, we're like the opposite of you and Louis."

Emma stared at me. "What does that mean?"

"Come on. You know what it means."

Emma ignored the statement. She stood up. "I really am sorry about your hair," she said, "and I'm going to make it up to you." And before I knew what was happening, she got up and walked across the room to retrieve the scissors. Her hair was pulled into a low ponytail. She picked up the scissors in her right hand. With her left hand, she pulled her ponytail taut. She cut it clean through at the base of her head and tossed it into my lap.

I gazed down at it. I could feel the weight of her ponytail, the tickle of her fine, wavy hairs as they brushed my bare legs. I looked at Emma. She looked *terrible*. I shook my head—I was a little touched, if I'm being honest. "You're just full of surprises, Rip Van Tinkle, aren't you?"

"Auggggghhhhh!" Emma stomped her feet. "Don't call me Rip Van Tinkle."

"You peed the bed in your sleep." How could I *not* call her Rip Van Tinkle? It's perfect.

"Kids wet the bed sometimes! It happens!"

"I know that! So does everybody else! It's not a big deal, Emma. I'm just playing with you."

"Is it really playing if only one person is having fun?"

"Emma. Everybody loves a good nickname. You should be flattered."

She tilted her head, curious. "Tell me something. Do you think… do you actually think you're being nice? Like, do you honestly not see how mean you're being?"

"I'm being nice by being mean."

"Don't gaslight me."

"I'll gaslight whoever I want. I'll gaslight you until you beg me to gaslight you more."

"You aren't even using that word correctly, you know."

I balked. "Believe me, I know what gaslighting is. I do it all the time. It's like a magic trick."

"Oh my God. I'm leaving."

When she left, I stood up to retrieve my teddy bear again. I unzipped the back and shoved Emma's ponytail inside, next to my braids, then I pulled the zipper closed. Aside from a slightly fuller tummy, the bear didn't look noticeably different. I knew I would treasure it forever.

Some things are so special, you can't put a price on them.

Emma

Day 6

Gianluca reeked of cheap cologne and cigarettes. Somehow, it worked for him. I arrived at the common area to find him waiting, the chessboard already set up, an unlit cigarette tucked behind his ear. He wore an open chic black button-down shirt, a pair of paisley swimming trunks that left little to the imagination, and sleek leather loafers, which he wore without socks. He was the epitome of an Italian stallion.

Lucy and Alison were at the opposite end of the room, working together on a jigsaw puzzle. Alison's hair was long and lustrous again; so was mine, without the lustrous part. Alison and I looked at each other curiously. I knew we were both wondering what the other was doing—me with Gianluca, Alison with Lucy. I raised an eyebrow. She shrugged. She frowned and nodded at Gianluca. *I* shrugged.

Gianluca rested a hand lightly against my back. It might have startled me, but I'd smelled him approaching long before he'd touched me. "You learn now."

He had no way of knowing this was our third lesson together. "I understand the basics, but I have no strategy," I explained, which was true; I'd actually been picking the game up pretty quickly.

He nodded. "I am excellent teacher. You must not worry."

As we played, Gianluca kept giving me flirtatious stares. He moved his bishop; I moved my queen. His bishop captured one of my pawns; one of *my* pawns took his bishop. "Oooh-la-la, look at sexy chess moves on Emma!" He winked at me. I'd never heard anybody describe anything chess-adjacent as "sexy" until now.

"Did you let me do that on purpose?"

He gave me a wide-eyed look of innocence. "Not Gianluca!" There was something aggressively adorable about him. For a moment, I allowed myself to imagine what it might be like to have sex with him. I had the sneaking suspicion that Gianluca was either an incredible lover or a terrible one.

My best working theory for the moment was that I needed to lose my virginity in order to extract myself from the time loop I was caught up in. It wasn't a *great* theory, but it was the only one I could come up with, and it made a certain kind of sense: Max said that Greta must have chosen me because of something in my letter, so what other possibility could there be? It was already something I wanted to do, and now it seemed more urgent than ever. Sure, I was having fun living the same consequence-free day over and over again, but nothing mattered. *(Nothing mattered!)* It wasn't *real.*

But things weren't going so great between Auggie and me. I was starting to doubt we were ever going to make it across the finish line. And if not Auggie, then who? *(Don't think about Louis.)*

Gianluca may have been adorable—and he clearly would have been willing—but he wasn't my type. He was wiry and petite, whereas I was tall and sturdily built. I didn't want to lose my virginity to someone who would basically have to climb me. Also, Gianluca was maybe a little bit *too* willing for my liking.

"To play chess is like to make love," he told me, not for the first, or likely last, time.

"Oh yeah? How so?"

"Is beautiful game."

"I see." He was distracting me. I made a blunder with my horsey, and Gianluca promptly captured it.

"Remember," I told him, "you aren't going to tell Auggie about this."

"Of course, belissima. We can keep many secrets from him." He stroked my arm. He was too much.

If not Gianluca, another option *(Don't think about Louis)* was Connor Cackowski, but there was no way. I imagined it for a second: *Evidently I'm coming!* Ugh. No. No, my best option was probably still Auggie, as much as I hated to admit it. But did I really want that? I didn't care to think too hard about the answer.

Gianluca muttered to himself in Italian while we played. When we finished our game—he beat me easily, but I was definitely improving—he went outside to smoke a cigarette. I sauntered over to Alison and Lucy.

They were working on a puzzle of the Mona Lisa. They were sitting close together on the same side of the table, both of them squeezed into a single overstuffed armchair. Cozy. Also weird.

"What are you doing with Gianluca?" Alison asked without looking at me.

"He's teaching me how to play chess."

"It seems like he wants to teach you a lot more than chess."

"Well, he's only teaching me chess." This wasn't exactly true; I was also starting to pick up a little bit of Italian. It was slow, but it was happening. "Can I ask the two of you a question?" I said. They both looked at me. "If you could do anything you wanted—anything at all—what would you do?"

Alison answered without hesitation. "I'd make it illegal for girls to play the guitar."

"You *would*? Why?" Lucy asked.

"I don't know…it's just, like, come on. Do something else with your time."

Lucy gave her a serious look. "You know, I play a little guitar."

"You do?" Alison considered. "I guess that's okay."

I was lost as to what was going on between the two of them, annoyed that Alison hadn't given me a serious answer, and a little bit intrigued. "Does this rule apply to all stringed instruments or just the guitar? What about the violin?"

"The violin is fine. You use a bow to play the violin."

"What about the harp?" Lucy asked.

Alison thought about it. "No. No guitar, no harp."

"That's your answer?"

"That's my answer. What would *you* do if you could do anything?"

"I'm not sure," I said. "Maybe I would pass a law making it illegal for anybody to turn my grandma into a balloon."

Alison bristled. "You promised you would never bring that up again. I've apologized a thousand times."

"You turned her into a balloon!"

"I know! It was an accident!"

"That's enough, you two." Lucy nudged Alison. "We're still missing a corner piece. I think we're missing a few pieces, actually."

"Maybe the corner piece got misplaced. Have you checked under the seat cushion?" I asked.

"Why would it be under the seat cushion?" Alison narrowed her eyes and tilted her head. She and Lucy stood up, and Lucy lifted the edge of the cushion and peeked underneath it. She reached in and pulled out the missing corner piece.

"You're a witch," Alison whispered, stunned. "How did you know that?"

I knew because they'd found it there yesterday, and the day before that, but I wasn't going to say so. "I know things," I said smugly. "Bless you."

Lucy sneezed.

Alison looked at me, unsettled. "Witch," she whispered again. I winked at her. My work here was done for the day.

Lucy

Friday

It can be fun to have a secret. In my case, it's also necessary, so maybe it's more accurate to say that I'm trying to have fun with my secret. Results so far have been mixed. The whole mess started eighteen months ago. See, I didn't go straight to Xavier Academy from being homeschooled. That's just a lie I told people so they wouldn't ask too many questions. The truth is that I was at Saint Mary's School for Girls from preschool until midway through sophomore year. My parents were big believers in same-sex education. Fewer distractions, they said.

I was happy at Saint Mary's. I had a lot of friends. I played varsity field hockey and got straight A's. My parents were always so proud of me. I'm the only child of two overachieving parents, and that can sometimes be a lot of pressure for a kid. They put all their parenting energy and resources into me, and I don't want to disappoint them.

I guess it was inevitable I'd let them down at some point.

One of my closest friends at Saint Mary's was a girl named Charlize. Isn't that the most beautiful name? Charlize didn't come to Saint Mary's until freshman year. I fell in love with her the minute I saw her. It was the first time that I *knew*, beyond any shadow of a doubt, that I was gay.

Don't get me wrong; I always kind of suspected. But when you're raised the way I was, being straight is the default. To even *suggest* there are other, equally valid orientations simply wasn't something my family ever discussed or even acknowledged. For example: I had an uncle growing up who I realize now was definitely gay. Uncle Greg was my mom's brother. He died from brain cancer when I was twelve. I remember going to visit him and his "roommate," Howie, who also acted as a live-in nurse to my uncle in his last few months. I used to think it was so kind of Howie to put his life on hold in order to care for my ailing uncle, but it made some sense according to the kid logic of my brain at the time. They were best friends! They spent holidays together and vacationed together! They were both what my parents called "confirmed bachelors"!

I'd known Howie (I called him Uncle Howie) all my life. (That was another tell, looking back on it. Who keeps the same roommate for twelve years?) I was confused when he didn't show up for my uncle Greg's funeral. My mom told me it was because he'd moved away, but this was a lie. I spotted him at the supermarket a few months later and shouted his name in the produce section. He turned around and looked at me, then at my mother. My mom's expression was cold and unsmiling; she looked at him like he was a stranger. Uncle Howie looked like he was going to come over anyway, but at the last minute he turned and walked away. He left his cart full of vegetables sitting right there in the middle of the aisle and walked out the front door. My mom said it was probably too hard for him to see us because we reminded him of Uncle Greg. Now I know better.

I don't know how my parents figured out what was going on

between Charlize and me. All I know is that they flipped out. My dad wouldn't even look at me for weeks. My mother cried a lot. She said things like, "You were always such a girly girl!" and "How could you do this to your father and me?" as if I were deliberately making a choice to hurt them. They forbade me from ever seeing Charlize again, which went over about as well as you'd expect. So we ran away. We made it all the way to the city. My parents filed a missing person report. The police found us staying at a youth shelter in the city. That was the last time I saw Charlize. I tracked her down online shortly afterward, but she wouldn't respond to any of my messages.

I finished out the school year at home while my parents deliberated about how to best go about "fixing" me. What a relief it must have been for them when they realized the whole situation was a result of their foolish decision to send me to an all-girls school! Using that logic, they figured the solution was easy: all I needed to straighten me out (pun intended) was to spend some time around a few dicks. The only problem, as they explained it, was that I was clearly sex-crazed; what else would have driven me to get involved with another girl? Their elegant, not-at-all-cruel solution was to send me to a co-ed high school but force me to make myself as physically unappealing as possible. This meant no makeup, no shaving my legs or armpits, and no short skirts or high heels. In short, they forced me to become someone else.

Joke's on them: I'm still gay as hell. I'm just better at hiding it now. And while I had no choice but to say goodbye forever to Charlize, I've found a second chance at love with Alison.

I know what you're thinking: *that* Alison? The Alison who bullies me incessantly—that is, when she manages to come up for air in between make-out sessions with Bradd "the second 'd' stands for dickhead" Hazelett? The same Alison who doesn't even go to the beach without full makeup? I know it doesn't make sense, but that's only because nobody knows her the way I do. The truth is Alison is complex and silly and capable of incredible kindness. The truth is that nobody actually knows anybody as well as they think they do. This is our secret. It belongs to us alone. Nobody else—not Bradd, not Max, not *anybody*—has the first clue of what we're up to. Well—except for Mia. But she isn't talking. Like I said before, I'm trying to have fun with the secret. But I'll admit, it's starting to get old.

Mia was sitting by the window and smoking a cigarette when Alison and I walked into my bungalow. She looked up from her phone (I still can't figure out how she has any service here) long enough to giggle at us, then she retreated into her own little world again.

"I think she knows that you're gay for me," Alison whispered. "She knows that you're a lesbian."

Of course she knew. Alison was convinced Mia didn't know how to speak English. There's no way this was true. Mia and Gianluca have been at our school all year; they'd have to be comatose not to pick up at least a basic grasp of the language. Alison can be…Alison.

"*You* are." I kissed the tip of her nose. "The biggest lesbian."

"You're one to talk, Peppermint Patty."

"If I'm Peppermint Patty, then you're Jodie Foster."

She scoffed. "Jodie Foster isn't gay."

"Jodie Foster is definitely gay."

"Then why did she fall in love with Anthony Hopkins?"

I paused. "Are you talking about *The Silence of the Lambs*? You know that's fiction, right? And they didn't fall in love. He was a serial killer."

"And she was the FBI agent who loved him. Star-crossed lovers. Tale as old as time." She glanced suspiciously at Mia.

"Mia won't tell anybody," I reassured her.

Mia said something to us in Italian and rolled her eyes. Alison made a *V* with two of her fingers and held them up to her mouth. She stuck out her tongue and wiggled it at Mia. Mia scoffed and puffed at her cigarette and muttered to herself under her breath.

"I want to tell Bradd about us," Alison said. "I don't want to wait any longer. I want to tell *everybody*, Lucy. I'm tired of keeping us a secret. We don't have anything to be ashamed of."

I felt a twinge of anxiety. "That isn't the issue. My parents will go berserk if they catch me with another girl."

"Who cares? What's the worst they can do? You're almost an adult."

"You and Bradd have been together a long time."

"So? People break up every day."

"He doesn't strike me as the kind of guy who will be okay with his girlfriend dumping him to be with a woman. Lots of men have fragile egos. He'll take it personally."

"You only think that because you don't know him like I do." She tucked a slab of thick blond hair behind her ear. Her fingernails sparkled, pink-and-gold glitter. She was so pretty. "I thought you wanted me to tell him."

"I did. I do."

"It kind of seems like you don't."

"All I'm saying is that it's a big step. Maybe you should think about it some more before you make a decision."

"I have thought about it. I think about it all the time."

"But have you considered the possibility that—what if—what if you're just confused?" I couldn't look at her. "You know—maybe you're just experimenting. It happens a lot, especially to girls."

"Do you hear yourself? You sound like your mother."

"I know. I'm sorry." She was right; I *did* sound like my mother.

"Don't you dare tell me who I fucking am." There was a hint of anger to her tone. "I've been trying to figure that out my whole life. And now that I finally feel like I'm getting close to the truth—to understanding who I really am—you want to tell me I'm mistaken. You want to tell me I'm confused. I am not confused."

"So you're definitely a lesbian."

"Yes, I'm definitely a lesbian." She paused. "Lucy, what's the real issue here? Are you embarrassed by me or something? Even if we told some people, your parents wouldn't have to know anything about us. We don't have to keep it a secret from everybody, but we can still keep it a secret from them."

"They'll know."

"How will they know? Who's going to tell them? Bradd?" she scoffed. "Mia?" Mia extended both of her middle fingers toward Alison. "You know, I think that sneaky bitch might speak English," Alison half-whispered to me.

"Of course I can speak English!" Mia flicked her cigarette out the window and immediately lit another one. She blew the smoke in our direction. "You think I am like Americans who can speak only one language? You stupid girl with face like belly button."

Alison was agog. "My face does *not* look like a belly button."

Mia clenched her cigarette between her teeth. She stood up and lifted her shirt, shaking her midriff at us while she pointed at her belly button. "Look! Alison lives in my tummy! Belly button lesbian! Belly button lesbian!"

"Guess what I'm going to do?" Alison shouted at her, her face flushed with rage. "I'm going to wait until you get married someday, and then I'm going to fuck your husband!"

"My husband will never fuck a belly button!"

"If he's willing to marry you, he's probably willing to fuck anything with a pulse!"

"Shut up!" I screamed at them. They both froze. Mia's cigarette dangled from between her lips. Alison panted, breathless. She tried discreetly to lift her shirt and steal a quick peek at her navel. Mia quickly gathered her supplies (purse, cigarettes, lighter), slipped her feet into her sandals, and stormed out the door, slamming it hard behind her.

Like I said, secrets can be fun.

Lucy Thomas

Letter to Self

Dear Lucy,

All you have to do is make it through this year. Everything will be okay after that.

Emma

Day 7

Once again, I found myself surrounded by trash on the beach. At least there was champagne. I wasn't even sure why I was there. I asked Max why he gave us the same instructions every morning, and all he would say was, "Trust me, the beach is the safest place for you gaggle of little shits."

Auggie and Louis were both wearing gloves as they picked through separate piles of garbage a few feet apart from each other. Louis took stealthy hits from a vape pen as he half-heartedly collected the smallest pieces of debris. Auggie scowled at him. Their proximity to one another made me uncomfortable. There's always an unspoken tension when the three of us are together.

Bradd was nowhere to be found this morning. Alison and Lucy were working together, laughing and talking, which was still weird.

I made an attempt to pick up some garbage, but it felt so meaningless that I couldn't be bothered to continue; it would all be back tomorrow. I took a seat in the sand and tried to observe from a distance while I drank champagne, but it wasn't long before Auggie stepped into my sunlight.

He gazed down at me with a half grin. "Why aren't you helping us?" Auggie does this thing when he smiles that used to make me go a little berserk with lust: he lifts the corners of his mouth one at a time, left, then right. Hoo boy. It makes me feel like the first half of the grin is pure reflex, but the second half is a choice he's making just for me.

He does it right now, but this time feels different. *My penis! My penis!* Vomit arching in a stream from his mouth like a garden fountain. His face all puffy, eyes swollen to slits. He looked like a fat, naked baby.

I took a swig of champagne. "Nothing matters, Auggie. Fuck the planet."

He was shocked. "Don't say that. Just because you hate volunteering—"

"Since when do I hate volunteering?"

He cocked his head and ran his fingers through his hair and smiled wryly, playing along, still flirty. "It's okay, Emma, you can admit it. We all know that acts of service...the giving of oneself for the benefit of your fellow man...it isn't really your thing."

"That isn't true at all. Remember when I organized that huge fundraiser for adult literacy?"

"I remember when you threw a party while your mom was in Hawaii. You made everyone chip in five dollars to cover the cost of a keg. I remember how so many people showed up that you made more than enough to cover the cost, so you got the idea to donate the rest to support adult literacy in order to put it on your college applications."

"Right. That's called a fundraiser. You just literally described a fundraiser."

"Eh." He wiggles his hand in a maybe, maybe not motion. "There needs to be prior intent for it to qualify as a fundraiser."

"Agree to disagree. Sorry I'm not a Girl Scout." I nod toward Lucy Thomas. "There's one over there if that's what you'd prefer."

"What are you getting so worked up about? I'm not trying to start a fight."

"Of course you aren't. That wouldn't be very Christian of you, would it? What you *are* doing is saying the hundreds of dollars I raised for adult literacy doesn't count because I found a way to raise money where everybody had fun."

"You raised, like, a few hundred dollars for adult literacy, Emma."

"Not according to my college applications."

"So you're saying you lied on your college applications."

"I'm saying there may have been an errant zero that I failed to correct." I said I raised $8,500, when I'd only raised $850. And you know what? I don't feel any guilt. None. You can still teach, like, ten adults how to read with $850.

"Look, can we move on? I'm sorry I brought it up."

But I don't want to move on. Our tense flirtation has shifted into something less pleasant. "What are you saying? Do you think I'm a terrible person because I had the audacity to give money to charity? God, you're so right—I'm a monster."

"Why are you trying to start a fight with me?"

"I'm not trying to start a fight." Am I? I sort of am. But why? Now that I have access to Alison's sheepskin condoms, I can have sex with Auggie without endangering his life. And if what Max told me is true, and what I wrote in my letter to myself has anything to do with how I might break out of this loop, there's only one logical conclusion.

I pretended I didn't remember the assignment or what I'd written to myself, but that wasn't true. I remember, all right. My letter stating my goal for the year was short and to the point: *Emma, you need to lose your virginity*. But I wasn't about to share that with Max.

"I'm sorry," I said to Auggie. "I don't know what's wrong with me."

"You haven't been yourself all morning." He nodded at the champagne. "What's that all about?"

"Maybe I'm having an existential crisis." I sighed and stood up. "I didn't sleep well last night. I'm sorry," I repeated.

"Thank you. I appreciate that."

"Maybe I should take a nap."

"That's probably a good idea." He stepped close to me and gently wriggled the bottle of champagne from my grasp. "Maybe we should save this for later." He kissed me on the forehead, then on the lips. "Are we still on for tonight?"

It feels like someone is trying to take something from you.

Something small but loud deep inside me screamed no. I pushed the feeling aside. "Definitely."

I was halfway to my bungalow when Louis caught up with me. "Hey, where are you going?"

"To take a nap."

"No, you aren't." He held my elbow and steered me in the opposite direction. "Come with me. I want to show you something."

"What is it?"

"Just follow me. It's a surprise."

It was Louis, so I followed without further question. We talked as we walked. "What were you and Auggie fighting about?" he asked.

"We weren't fighting."

"No? You two looked pretty intense."

"It was nothing. Remember the party I had when my mom went to Hawaii for Thanksgiving with that timeshare executive?"

"The one where you raised a small fortune for adult literacy? How could I forget?"

"That's the one. Auggie said it doesn't count as legitimate philanthropy because I only donated the money as an afterthought, and I only did it to boost my college applications."

Louis nodded. "Right. So what?"

"Exactly! So what? He's always giving me these moral purity tests that are impossible to pass. Why does it matter why I donated the money?"

"Let me ask you something, Emma. Can you tell me all about everything good that Auggie does? Like, can you list his selfless deeds and squeaky-clean recreational activities?"

Not this again. "I know it seems unbelievable, Louis," I said, slowly and with exaggerated enunciation, "but there are people in this world who are just…good people—"

"No, there aren't."

"Yes, there are. They exist, and they do good things and treat other people kindly without agenda or expectation."

"Name twenty."

"Okay." I started to count on my fingers. "One: Mother Teresa."

"Wrong. Mother Teresa was one of history's greatest monsters. She believed suffering was the key to salvation. She let the people in her hospitals suffer when they didn't have to. If there's any justice in the afterlife, Mother Teresa is playing shuffleboard in Hell with Saddam Hussein right now."

I could tell from his voice that he really meant it, and in retrospect I probably should have kicked off my list with someone else—it wasn't the first time I'd heard about Mother Teresa's shortcomings. He did a whole presentation on it in our Humanities class this year, made a poster and everything. He has some strong opinions about things like suffering and end-of-life care; I know it's probably because of his brother, so I try to avoid the subject. I can see how much it hurts him. "Okay, fine." I gave it some more thought, trying to come up with someone who wouldn't indirectly remind him of the worst thing that has ever happened in his life. "Mister Rogers."

"Leave Mister Rogers out of this."

"Aha!" I punched him hard in the shoulder. "So you admit he was a good person!"

"Yes, of course I admit he was a good person. I'm not going to tell you again. Leave Fred Rogers out of this."

"I suppose he might have been a secret monster. Like another Bill Cosby. Wouldn't that be awful?"

"If that were the case—which it isn't—I wouldn't want to know."

This surprised me. Louis is usually so tickled when a beloved public figure takes a fall from grace. The further they fall, the more he enjoys it. "So, what? You're saying if anybody knows any dark, dirty secrets about Mister Rogers—"

"First of all, Mister Rogers didn't have any dirty secrets. Jesus, Emma. Secondly, if someone *did* know something bad about him... they should do the whole entire world a favor and keep it to themselves."

"So if I had evidence that, say, Mister Rogers likes to get rim jobs from Lady Elaine, I should just—"

Louis stopped in his tracks. He blinked at me. "What did you say?"

I cleared my throat and let a pause settle between us for dramatic emphasis. "I SAID," I shouted, my hands cupped around my mouth, "WHAT IF I HAD EVIDENCE THAT MISTER ROGERS LIKED TO GET RIM JOBS FROM LADY ELAINE?"

"I heard you the first time. But what made you say that?" he demanded. He was unsettled.

I shrugged. "I think about it a lot."

"You think about Mister Rogers getting rim jobs a lot," he repeated doubtfully.

"I do."

"When do you think about this?"

"I'm thinking about it right now, Louis."

We stared at each other for another long moment. Then we both burst out laughing.

"You're really something," he said, "do you know that? There's nobody else like you, Emma. You might be my favorite person in the world."

I didn't tell him—I didn't say anything, I only smiled—but inside, it thrilled me to hear him say this. His words felt like sunshine.

Even if I did have those kinds of feelings for Louis—and I'm not saying that I do—it wouldn't matter. He's made it more than clear that he has no interest in me. I wish I weren't so sure of this, but I am. There was this one night, more than two years ago, when I tried to test the waters. Just to see what would happen. We were at a party at Connor Cackowski's house. His parents were out of town for the weekend. Connor isn't exactly super popular, but he does live in an amazing house, with a swimming pool and a hot tub and a pool table. A first edition of Marilyn Monroe's *Playboy* edition was mounted in a frame behind museum glass in his father's office. The glass was made translucent that night by blooms of oily teenage boy fingerprints and the fog of their hot breath. Poor Marilyn.

There was alcohol. Connor's parents were apparently big drinkers and kept a fully stocked party house. Everybody was having a wild time. *(Evidently, someone has thrown up on my parents' Pottery Barn comforter, and someone needs to clean it up right the fuck now!)* Louis and I were hanging out in the swimming pool with a few other kids when Shelby Tucker waded over to us and began drunkenly admiring my body.

Her voice boomed. "Emma, ohmygoshhhh, your abs are cut, girl." I'd recently gotten over a bad stomach bug that had seen me lose ten pounds of water weight over three days of agony; as a result, my abs were more defined than usual. Shelby had nudged Louis. "Look at Emma! She looks so good!" She clapped her hands together. "Yay! Go, Emma!" She giggled as she sipped White Claw through a plastic straw. She waded past us toward Alison, who was bobbing in the deep end, her body draped lazily over a raft shaped like an ice cream cone.

Louis let his gaze flicker toward me for an instant. I thought I could feel something between us, but I wasn't certain. Or was I? If it wasn't certainty, it was damn close. But I was tipsy. My inhibitions were lowered, and maybe my judgment was poor. I moved closer to him until our faces were only a few inches apart. "You don't think I look good?"

I was sure what I was feeling was real. You know what I mean? You just know.

He was looking everywhere but at me. "I don't even know what you look like, Emma."

The words felt like a whip. "What does that mean?" It means no.

"It's like I know what you look like, and I could describe you to, say, a sketch artist. But you're just…just Emma. You're like an amorphous blob. I don't think about you in such, uh, superficial terms."

Nobody's love story includes prominent use of the phrase "amorphous blob." And for a moment I'd been so sure; I could have sworn there was a tangible friction between us, getting warmer. But I was wrong. *Amorphous blob.*

Never again, I swore to myself. So it was friendship. Nothing more.

Now here we were, alone together. I followed his lead amorphously and remembered that Auggie wanted me. Auggie did not think I was an amorphous blob. I recalled the feeling of his hard, pointy tongue in my mouth. In-out-in-out. It was hopelessly terrible. It would never get better. What would Louis's tongue feel like? It didn't matter. I pushed the thought away. "Where are you taking me?" We were still walking. We were almost to Gus and Greta's house when Louis turned left onto a narrow, sandy path leading into the woods.

"You'll see. We're almost there."

We reached a clearing at the end of the path. There was a small, dilapidated wooden shed with busted-out windows and no door. Looking around, I realized we were basically in Gus and Greta's backyard.

"Come on," Louis said, nodding toward the shed.

I gasped when we stepped through the doorway. Huddled in a corner on top of a small blanket, there was a mama cat surrounded by a litter of newborn kittens. I counted one-two-three-four-five-*six* small bodies, nestled side-by-side like fluffy sausages as they nursed from their sleepy mother. Her body was outstretched to accommodate their mouths as they wiggled and grasped at her nipples. They made soft mewing sounds as they drank. Their mother purred, unbothered.

"How did you find them?" I whispered, awed.

"I didn't. Greta told me about them."

I winced a little at the sound of her name. Louis didn't notice.

The kittens were so tiny, no bigger than Louis's fist. We sat on the ground and watched them silently. It was a mesmerizing sight.

Louis put his hand on my arm. "Emma, there's something I need to tell you." He had tears in his eyes.

I nodded solemnly. "Your parents," I whispered.

He looked shocked. He pulled his hand away. "How did you know about that?"

"I don't know. I—I just had a feeling."

"About my parents?"

"Yes. They're splitting up, aren't they?"

"I wanted to tell you sooner, but I didn't know how. I knew you'd be upset."

We were both crying now. One of the kittens—an orange ball of floof—wobbled unsteadily toward us. Louis picked it up and placed it in my lap. "There you go."

I rested my head on his shoulder like I've done a thousand times before. This time, he flinched a little bit. Rain fell in a fine mist outside the shack. The air inside was thick with kitten smells: fur, poop, milk. It was nice. Several empty cans of wet cat food, which had undoubtedly been supplied by Greta, were piled in another corner, licked clean.

"I had a dream about you last night," he said.

"You did?"

"Uh-huh."

"What happened?"

"Well, we were on the beach. It was low tide, and you were walking toward the ocean. The beach was littered with dozens, or maybe even hundreds, of octopuses." He paused. "Octopi? What's the plural of octopus?"

"Octopuses? Octopussies?"

"Anyway, you were on the beach with them, and you kept picking them up and throwing them into the water so they could swim away. I wasn't that far away from you, and I was scared for some reason. I don't know why, but I was afraid. I kept calling your name, but you didn't hear me. You wouldn't look back at me. I tried to shout, but it's almost impossible to shout in a dream, you know?"

What were the chances he would dream of me and an octopus? It couldn't be a coincidence. Impossible. Then again, I was starting to feel like anything was possible. Given infinite days and infinite choices, I could probably make just about anything happen if I tried hard enough.

Well—not anything.

"What happened next?" I asked.

He shrugged. "Nothing. That was the whole dream. You were walking on the beach, throwing octopuses into the sea, and I was following you."

The kittens broke away from their mother one at a time and teetered blindly toward us. They were still learning how to walk, and they weren't good at it. They fumbled and tumbled every few steps; they mewed helplessly and gazed at us with big blue eyes that were too new for them to see clearly—I remembered hearing that kittens are basically blind for the first few weeks of life. We lifted them into our laps: three in mine, three in Louis's—and they fell asleep almost instantly.

The silence was so comfortable. With the kittens asleep in our laps, we were trapped. We couldn't stand up without disturbing them, so we didn't. We sat like that for a long time. I could hear Louis's heart going *thump-thump-thump* in his chest. His sweat smelled faintly of marijuana. He shifted his weight around, forcing me to lift my head from his shoulder, and then he put his arm around me. I tucked my head against his chest. *Thump-thump-thump. Thumpthumpthump.*

Here's another truth bomb to light up your day: you don't know yourself as well as you think. Until you've been in a situation yourself, you don't know how you'll react. You might think you know—people *love* to believe that—but you don't know. Case in point: if somebody had asked me how I'd react to hearing the news (for the second time!) that my best friend's parents are divorcing, I would have said I'd be sad, of course, but devastated? Terrified? Don't be absurd. They aren't *my* parents.

Yet I felt devastated. And I was terrified. Not so much because of Louis's parents—although that was part of it—but because of everything. Something has broken that was supposed to be unbreakable. It was like trying to balance on quicksand. And what does a person instinctively do when they're trying to stay upright on unstable ground? They look for something to hold on to. In this case, Louis and I held on to each other. We held each other and cried, and suddenly the reasons why we might be crying didn't seem to matter.

My mother tells me I am an ugly crier. She has told me this many times throughout my life—probably every time I've cried in front of her. No matter how many times she repeats the observation—which I assume is made in an effort to make me stop crying—it doesn't help, it only hurts; it always hurts, each time a little worse. But I felt safe enough with Louis and the kittens to let a sliver of pain work its way outward.

At first it was the faintest sensation of a gathering dampness, a kind of emotional condensation. Slowly, then all at once: I broke.

Louis wrapped his arms around me. I felt small, so small in his arms, like he might be able to absorb me with enough pressure, absorb all the pain—because of course this wasn't only about his parents, it was about everything that was happening: this inescapable day, which I'm doomed to repeat and repeat. Is today going to hurt? You can count on it.

Emma

Day 7

I was still sobbing, my head buried in Louis's chest, when he froze. He pulled away. Just like that, the spell was broken. That's when I noticed he was looking toward the doorway. Auggie was standing outside the shack, looking in, glaring at us.

Louis practically leaped to his feet. I scrambled to gather up the kittens and place them beside their mother before I followed him outside into the clearing, where he and Auggie stared warily at each other.

"This is not what it looks like, dude," Louis said. He held up both hands in surrender.

"Yeah? Then what the fuck is it?" Auggie's whole face was red. He was sweaty. He huffed and puffed as he looked from Louis to me, then back to Louis. Glaring the whole time. Eyes smoldering with hate. There was anger, too, but the loathing was the top note, emanating from every pore.

"Listen, man. Look at Emma. She's upset, okay? She heard some bad news."

"And you happened to be right there at her side, ready to comfort her. How convenient for you. Poor Emma was all alone and sad, so Louis the hero swoops in to save her. Did you manage to cop a good feel, too?" Auggie's voice boomed above the sound of the waves beyond us as they crashed against the shore. I could feel eyes on us from somewhere behind the trees.

"Wow." Louis let his arms drop to his sides. He tilted his head like a curious dog. Was he *smiling*? "It was nothing, dude. Nothing happened."

"It's true, Auggie," I chimed in. "Louis told me something that made me really upset, and I started crying, so we—"

"*He* told you something that made you upset?" Auggie scoffed. "Again, how convenient. You knock her down so you can help her get up. Is that the plan?"

Again, the hint of a smile. "There was no plan."

"I could tell Emma something about you that would upset her, couldn't I? Should I tell her what you did?" Auggie said. I didn't have the first clue what he was referring to.

Before I had the chance to ask Auggie what he was talking about, from somewhere behind me, I heard Bradd chanting, "Fight, fight, fight!" Great. He and Alison were probably both watching, loving every minute of this.

"Look, I'm not one of those guys who thinks men and women can never be just friends. So when Emma said you were her best friend in the whole world, I thought, that's fine. I knew it going into this, and I've accepted it with a smile all year. Never said a word to either of you about it. Look at me, though, man. I mean it. Look me in the eyes. You had to know I didn't like it. Emma gets upset about something, and you're the guy she turns to every time. That's what I'm supposed to be for." Auggie looked at me, and his voice broke a little. "I love you, Emma. I want to be the one who makes you feel safe."

I nodded. "I know that."

"You think I don't know what you say about me? You think Emma doesn't tell me? I'm her boyfriend! Of course she tells me! You want her to think you don't like me because of some quality or flaw that's specific to *me*, right? That's the story you're going with. But we both know that isn't true. You'd find a problem with any guy she dated, because the only real problem you have is they aren't you." Auggie shook his head. "Just admit it. It's insulting to act like that isn't what's going on here. It's insulting to me, but it's also insulting to Emma. Do you think she's naive? Do you think everyone is naive except for you? I don't want to play this game with you anymore."

I couldn't take another minute of Auggie's ridiculous rambling. It was too humiliating. "He doesn't like me like that, Aug. He told me himself a long time ago, and I'm fine with it. It's so obvious to everyone but you that he isn't— We aren't the same. You don't need to worry about Louis and me. Ever." The three of us stared at each other. When I realized we were standing in a literal triangle formation, I took a few steps toward Auggie. I rested my forehead against his shoulder and laced our fingers together. "Let's go, okay?" I tugged at his arm. "Let's go talk alone somewhere."

If I can just make it through tonight, I can have a fresh start tomorrow morning.

We'd barely turned our backs to Louis when he said, "Wait. I need to make something clear to Auggie." Pause. "She's right. It's a friendship, that's all. I mean—think about it for a minute. I could never date Emma. It wouldn't make sense in this reality. It would redefine what is possible. And that isn't a slight against Emma in any way. Emma's a doll, obviously, we all love Emma, but that doesn't mean we all want to date her. There's nowhere for me to go with her from a relationship standpoint. There's no mystery left for me with Emma. I've known her since before she was Rip Van Tinkle." He stared at me now. "I know her better than anybody."

He was laying it on a bit thick. "Great, thanks, I think he gets the point." I led Auggie by the hand, not looking back until I was sure we'd left Louis far behind. We ducked behind an unoccupied bungalow that backed up against the forest. Auggie gave me a gentle push against the building and kissed me. When I get to feeling so good with him like this and things really start heating up, I've developed a technique in which I strategically direct his kisses onto my face, neck—anywhere but on my own mouth, to avoid the full-body desiccant effect of his firm tongue jutting in and out of my face like a meat piston.

Bad kisser or no (yes), Auggie has a gift for whispering sweet nothings. *Don't you see that Louis is lying to lull me into a false sense of security? He's crazy about you.* Auggie is wrong about Louis, but Louis is wrong about Auggie, too.

"Stop talking about Louis. I don't want to let him ruin this."

"What don't you want to let him ruin?"

"Tonight. I can't wait for tonight."

Louis

Friday

I was going to tell Emma. I wanted to tell her. But I couldn't do it. I was too scared.

Maybe some things simply aren't meant to be, and that's that.

Bradd Hazelett

September 4
Letter to self—goals for senior year

Dear Braddley, congratulations on being awesome. Your goal for the year is to invent a better mousetrap. You can do it!! #24patentsby18; #fortunateson; #senatorsson; #steakfortheson; #innovation.

Auggie

Friday

I should have punched Louis for the way his arms were wrapped around Emma, *my* girlfriend, for the way he was leaning into her, the two of them both sweaty and snotty and tearful, getting their fluids all over each other. If I hadn't interrupted them— Well, I can hardly stand to think about what might have happened. The look in Louis's eyes when I stumbled across the two of them together was the look of a man about to lose control. I should know. Would Emma have given in to him? I don't want to know the answer to that.

As much as I wanted to hit Louis, I've never been in a real fight, and I'm not excited to start now. Louis is bigger than I am—not by much, but it's enough that I'm not sure I'd be able to take him, and I wasn't about to risk it. I chose to walk away, and thank God Emma wanted to come with me. I thought it was over after that and that we could still enjoy our night together. But it wasn't over.

Emma and I were walking hand-in-hand for a romantic after-dinner stroll on the beach when we spotted them: Louis and Lily Foose. They were making out against a tree. Both of his hands were all the way under Lily's shirt, cupping her breasts.

Whore.

Emma

Day 8

Here we go again.

It was a few minutes past midnight. A halo of feathered light encircled the full moon. The beach was deserted. The tide was way out. Auggie and I were alone in my bungalow, wearing only our underwear. We passed a bottle of champagne back and forth on the bed.

I couldn't stop thinking about Louis's hands on Lily's body, whether or not he would do the same thing tomorrow, and how I might be able to stop it. All I knew for sure was that he'd never want to do it with me. As Bradd says that Armie Hammer says, the heart wants what it wants.

"Are you nervous?" Auggie asked me.

"Yes," I admitted. I was guzzling champagne like an unmarried bridesmaid at her much prettier sister's wedding reception. I belched a little in Auggie's face.

He grimaced. "C'mon, Emma, slow down a little."

I did not slow down. I took another gulp. Auggie tried to take the bottle away from me, but I held it to my chest like it was my precious infant.

"Something's wrong." Auggie hesitated. "Is this about what happened earlier with Louis?"

"Of course not. What do I care if Louis wants to hook up with Lily?"

"That isn't what I meant." He narrowed his eyes. "It's interesting how that was the first thing that popped into your head."

"It wasn't the first thing that popped into my head."

"Then why did you say it? Anyway, good for Louis, I guess. I mean, I'm not sure I've ever even heard Lily speak."

Another drink. Another belch. "What do you mean?"

"You know...she's so quiet. I guess Louis is the first one to get her to open her mouth...if you know what I mean."

"Jesus, Auggie, that's crass."

"You're one to talk."

I gave him the middle finger.

"That's nice," he said. "Very ladylike. Very mature. Anyway, when I asked if you were still thinking about what happened earlier, I meant what happened with me and Louis."

"Ohhhhh." I blew gently across the opening of the bottle to make a whistling sound. "Let's stop worrying about that." I leaned in to give him a kiss. I was drunk enough that his staccato tongue was tolerable, but my mind still wandered. I thought about his swollen penis again and couldn't suppress a laugh, which came out as a snort.

"What's so funny?" he murmured. He shifted his weight on top of me and whispered, "That's not a banana in my pocket; I'm just happy to see you."

I couldn't help it—I dissolved into giggles. Auggie sat up and gave me a disgusted look. "Seriously, what's so funny?"

I was still laughing. I couldn't stop. At the same time, the bottle of champagne we'd been drinking tilted over, spilling onto the mattress. Auggie leaped out of bed and stared down at his crotch. His boxers were soaked through.

"Well hello, there," I said to his penis, which peeked at me from the slit in his boxers like a fleshy cyclops. I gave it a *boop* with my fingertip.

"You're drunk," Auggie said flatly.

I hiccupped. "So?"

"So I don't want to do this if you're drunk."

"Auggie, come on." We were *so* close. The lambskin condoms were beside me in the nightstand. Auggie was ready, and I was ready to get this over with and get out of here. I tried to pull him back into bed, but he swatted my hand away.

"Emma, *no*." He was pulling on his pants now, getting ready to leave. "This doesn't feel right."

"Is this because of what I said earlier?" All I'd done was make the observation that Auggie is a grower, not a shower. "It's nothing to be ashamed about. It's like...like a surprise every time. You know how much I like surprises. And I read somewhere that Lin Manuel-Miranda is a grower, and he wrote *Hamilton*! He's one letter away from an EGOT!"

"It isn't about that!" Auggie snapped. He was halfway to the door when he stopped. He sighed and turned around to face me. "Emma...we should talk."

In all the history of mankind, have those three words ever preceded good news? *We need to talk; the tumor is benign. We need to talk; I'm giving you a raise and a promotion. We need to talk; I'm not attracted at all to your stepsister, and I definitely don't want to sleep with her.* See? It doesn't work that way.

"Can it wait until tomorrow?"

Alison Lawrence

Sep. 4
Letter to Self

Dear Alison,

Your goal for senior year is to figure out if the person you've become is really who you want to be. If she isn't, figure out what to do about it.

Love,

Alison

Emma

Day 9

It was a little after midnight. Outside my window, a halo of light encircled the full moon. Auggie and I were both champagne drunk. I didn't think I'd ever seen Auggie drink this much. He's not so much of a goody-goody that he eschews alcohol altogether—he's no Lucy Thomas—but he's the kind of guy who will nurse the same beer all night and exaggerate his buzz in order to fit in at parties. Tonight, though, he'd gotten a little slurry. His mood had been glum ever since his confrontation with Louis earlier today, which for some reason I'd let repeat itself. Once again, he stumbled upon the two of us in a tearful embrace and lost his shit. Once again, I smoothed things over by leaving with Auggie and turning my back on Louis. Once again, we stumbled upon Louis and Lily groping one another up against a tree in the late afternoon. I could hardly focus during my chess lesson with Gianluca.

"Hey, slow down." I tugged the bottle from Auggie's hands. "I don't want you getting too drunk to consent." I gave the bottle a gentle shake; it was almost empty. I kissed Auggie softly on the neck and tried to remember how good it used to feel to be with him.

My thoughts were racing. I couldn't close my eyes without seeing Louis's hands all over Lily. Auggie fumbled as he tried to pull his shirt over his head. *It feels like somebody is trying to give you something and take something from you at the same time. Just get it over with.*

He closed his eyes. "I don't feel so great."

"Do you want some water?"

"No. Emma, I think we should talk."

Not this again. "I thought we already talked." It was true. We'd spent most of the afternoon talking and talking and talking. It took some convincing, but Auggie seemed to calm down by the end of the day. Louis spent the afternoon avoiding us, when he wasn't busy with Lily Foose.

"I know we talked. I was there."

"Then what's the problem? There's nothing going on between Louis and me. There never has been. Never will be."

"I know." He swallowed a burp. "I know that's what you think."

"It isn't what I *think*. It's the truth."

"I can't stop going over it in my head. It wasn't right."

"But I left with you, Auggie. I chose you."

His head jerked in my direction. "Do you hear yourself? Think about what you just said to me, Emma."

"There's nothing to think about!"

"Yes, there is. You said you chose me. Maybe that's true—"

"It *is* true!"

"Let me finish." His speech was clumsy. I didn't like seeing him this way at all. *(Like Mister Rogers getting a rim job from Lady Elaine.)* His breath was damp and foul. It stunk of oysters and champagne. "I can't stop wondering what Louis was going to say before we left."

"Why does it matter what he was going to say?"

"It matters"—his tone had an edge of condescension, almost contempt, so at odds with the Auggie I thought I knew—"because saying you *chose* me implies there was a choice at all. He wasn't going to say something like, 'Emma and I have always been friends, and that's all there is to it,' because it's already been said a hundred times. So what was he all worked up about?"

"I don't know; you'd have to ask him. It was an argument. Everybody was upset. And we were already upset when you found us. He'd just told me his parents are getting a divorce. That's a big deal."

Auggie rolled his eyes. "It's a big deal if you're a kid. We're practically adults."

"How would you know how big of a deal it is? You aren't Louis."

"Yeah, well, that's another thing. You seemed a lot more upset than he did."

"Because I'd just found out! Auggie, I've known his parents most of my life. You know I don't know my dad. You know what my mom is like."

"You're missing the point, Emma. Look: the more I thought about everything, the more it didn't sit right somehow. It isn't actually about his parents. It isn't about anything you said, or even what you did, the way you were hanging on to him..." Auggie shuddered at the memory. "It's about whatever Louis didn't say."

"What do you think he was going to say?"

"I don't know," he admitted. Another burp. "I don't know what we're even doing here."

"We're having a romantic evening!" I tried to scoot closer to him, but he pushed me away.

"You didn't choose me. There was no choice for you to make." He was suddenly teary-eyed. "It isn't that you don't want Louis. It's that Louis doesn't want *you*. And if that's the case, then I'm not really your boyfriend, am I, Emma?"

"What are you talking about? Of course you're my boyfriend!"

"No. I'm your consolation prize." Auggie stood up. His legs were wobbly. His speech had the thickness of somebody who isn't used to handling their liquor. "That isn't good enough for me. If this"—he gestures between us—"if this isn't real for you the same way it's real for me, then I don't want to do it. It doesn't feel right." He paused. "You're making me feel like a piece of meat, Emma."

It feels like someone is trying to take something from you.

"I thought you wanted this."

"So did I."

We stared at each other.

"I feel like I'm going to throw up," he said.

So did I.

Emma

Day 10

Be-BLAH, be-BLAH went the bird outside our window. Alison choked and retched and made a fine recovery. She braided her hair (she really did look better with the pixie cut) while "What's Up" blasted from her Bluetooth speaker. The song barely registers with me now; I've gotten so used to hearing it every morning, at this point it's just noise. That's not to say that it's growing on me—I still hate it with the fire of a thousand suns—but I'd prefer it to a clitoridectomy.

Bradd and Auggie were not at breakfast.

"Maybe they slept in." Max yawned and sipped his coffee, unconcerned.

"How's that coffee?" I asked him.

"Same as usual." He smirked.

"Bradd never sleeps in," Alison insisted. "He has a finely tuned internal clock."

Max shrugged. "Maybe there's a carbon monoxide leak in their bungalow."

"That isn't funny."

"I thought it was funny. Fine—Louis, Emma, go check on Bradd and Auggie."

We were barely out the door when I almost ran headfirst into Auggie. He was sweaty and panting and looked like he might have a fever. His expression was wild. His breathing was shallow and quick. He rubbed his eyes with his fists and clutched at his hair and alternated between standing and kneeling with his elbows on his thighs and his face buried in his hands.

"Emma, hi… Oh, boy. Oh, God. Oh my God." He pounded the heel of his hand against his forehead. "Oh, Jesus…"

Louis looked at him with suspicion. "What's the matter with you, man? Where's Bradd?"

"Bradd…uh, Bradd is… Where's Max?"

"He's in there." Louis nodded toward the dining hall. "He's still eating breakfast. He sent us to look for you two." He took a swig from his water bottle.

"Okay, well…I need him. Now."

"Where's Bradd?" Louis asked again.

Auggie's complexion had turned a faint shade of green. "Bradd is in the bathroom."

"Is he okay?"

"Uhhh…I don't know. I don't think so. I woke up and he just— I need Max." He jogged past us toward the dining hall.

"What should we do? Should we just let him handle it?" Louis asked me.

I would have said yes, but now I was curious. "I think we should go check on Bradd."

We were almost to Auggie and Bradd's bungalow when Auggie

caught up with us. "I couldn't find Max," he said breathlessly.

"Dude, we're going inside." Louis tried to make his way to the door.

Auggie shoved past him and kept his hand on the doorknob, holding the door closed like he was afraid to show us what was inside. "I don't know how to prepare you for what you're about to see. It's so awful. Emma, I think you should let me and Louis go in by ourselves first."

"Why? Because I'm a girl?"

"Um, yeah, kind of."

Now I had to see.

Let me set the scene: The room was dark. The windows were closed, and the shades were pulled all the way down. The ceiling fan, loosely mounted on an exposed beam, went *thunk-thunk-thunk* as it spun violently on the highest setting. I smelled it before I saw it. In the same way perfume has top notes and bottom notes and other complexities, so do rooms, especially those occupied by teenagers, *especially* teenage boys. The air was heavy with the stink of dirty laundry (so, body odor) and the awful cologne Bradd applied so liberally every morning, and literal hot garbage, but among those layers I recognized the distinct smell of piss and shit, which would not be so remarkable if not for the additional sweet, acrid notes of death.

Bradd was on his back in the tub, which was filled with water. He was, unfortunately, naked. And let's just say that we bore witness to what can only be described as an impressive display of attempted contortion.

The H2Blow was strapped securely to his head, and his arms were tucked beneath his back, hands nestled under his bum. His wrists were bound for some reason. You don't question mysteries like this. It was Bradd. Of course he would become Houdini for the "sake of science."

I knew I'd recognized another smell among all the others—a bottom note, if you will, subtle but unmistakable—of fresh barf. His face was blue, and yellowish foam oozed from his nose and mouth. His glassy eyes stared at us from behind the H2Blow.

He was obviously dead.

"What the fuck?" Louis whispered, horrified.

While Auggie and Louis stared, I repositioned Bradd's body, trying not to look too closely at it, until I managed to sit him upright so I could free his wrists. His body went slack in the water. I tugged the H2Blow from his head. I was careful to breathe through my mouth the whole time.

Auggie poked Louis. "Check his pulse."

Louis had gone pale. He looked terrified and disgusted. "I don't want to touch him."

"Somebody has to check his pulse!"

"You didn't check before you went looking for help?"

"I didn't think about it! I just found him like this!"

Louis shook his head. "Get your shit together, dude. Aren't you supposed to be an Eagle Scout?"

"They don't teach you how to handle corpses in the Eagle Scouts!"

"But they teach you first aid, don't they?"

"Guys, he's dead," I told them. They either didn't hear me or didn't want to accept the truth.

Auggie clearly wasn't up for any of this. Louis was almost hyperventilating. He looked at Bradd's body with extreme reluctance. "Okay. I'm going to check his pulse." He leaned over and pressed two fingers against Bradd's neck. He waited. Then he felt Bradd's wrist. Louis looked at us, shaking his head. "Nothing. He's cold."

It was a lot to take in all at once. I didn't think about my reaction; it just happened: I started laughing. Then Louis started laughing, probably due to shock. They say laughter can be a natural response to grief and stress. But Auggie stared at us in awestruck horror.

"Someone you've known all your life is murdered, and because you don't like him, your reaction is laughter?" Auggie said, which only made Louis and me laugh harder. But Louis was visibly trembling, too. The reality (or not) of what he was seeing hadn't hit him yet.

"Oh my God, Auggie, nobody killed him," Louis said.

"What—what are you talking about? You're saying he committed suicide?"

You can't make this stuff up. "I'm saying he did it to himself. Death by misadventure."

Auggie didn't look convinced. "But if he wasn't murdered, then what about his wrists?"

"I don't know. Maybe he wanted to make it more challenging. I don't understand Bradd logic."

Once he was sufficiently convinced that Bradd's death was accidental and not murder or suicide, Auggie's entire demeanor changed. He burst into tears of relief. If it was an accident, he explained, it meant Bradd wouldn't go to Hell. "So I think we should get him cleaned up and put some pants on him before we tell Max or anybody else. We should give him back his dignity."

"That's why you want our help?" Louis asked. "To restore his dignity? He has no dignity."

"I want your help. Not hers."

One thing that really pisses me off is whenever someone refers to a person who is present as though they aren't. It's like Manners 101. Not only is it rude, it's also condescending and disrespectful and dismissive and just…ugh.

"I'm standing right here, Auggie."

He gave me a shitty look. "You shouldn't have come in here. It's indecent."

The nerve of this boy, thinking he can dictate what constitutes decency to me. "Right. Because I'm a young lady?" (I said this sarcastically because I'm not a sixty-year-old nun or a five-year-old girl.)

He scoffed. "I don't think anybody would describe you as a lady, Emma."

Louis and I glanced at each other. He cleared his throat. "Maybe you should watch your mouth, buddy."

"Since when are we buddies? You know what? It doesn't matter now. You're both here. Emma, go get a wet washcloth and clean him up. Louis and I will get him dressed."

"Oh, please. I don't think so. You can clean him up yourself." I was about to leave—not my circus, not my monkeys, as they say—but I stopped. I *should* have left, but I didn't. There was too much I wanted to say, and suddenly it felt like it couldn't wait another second. My mother tells me my need to have the last word is one of my worst qualities. (My other poor qualities are mostly physical, according to her. I do have kind of a big nose.)

I turned around to face him. "You know what, Auggie? It doesn't matter whether or not this was an accident. It definitely *was*, and I'm embarrassed for you that we had to explain it to you. But even if it hadn't been an accident, I wouldn't be worried about Bradd's soul because I don't believe in Hell. And even if I *did* believe in Hell, I don't think Bradd is in quite the same league as Hitler and Mother Teresa."

Auggie's confusion was eclipsed only by his anger. "Mother Teresa is a saint!"

I ignored him. I kept talking. "Do you know what else is embarrassing? You're a terrible kisser. *Terrible.* It feels like I'm making out with a camel."

That's when Auggie slapped me across the face. Hard.

Nobody moved. You've heard the phrase "all the air got sucked from the room"? It was like that. No sound, no motion—only the background noise of the fan's motor humming, the blades spinning—and then it was like a switch flipped, and there was nothing *but* sound and motion, but all of it was coming from Auggie: Auggie apologizing over and over again, begging me to forgive him, insisting—this is kind of funny, in a gross, sad way—that people react in unpredictable ways to enormous stress and trauma. Begging me not to tell anybody. Telling me how much he loved me.

Louis lunged at Auggie, grabbing him by the chin and backing him toward the wall. "Louis!" I shrieked.

"You. Should. Not. Have. Done. That." With each word, he slammed Auggie's shoulders against the wall.

"I'm sorry! I'm sorry!"

"Sorry isn't good enough!" Louis drew his arm back and made a fist. If Auggie had known what was good for him, he would have shut his mouth. Instead, he talked and talked and begged and rationalized his way further into trouble and out of my life.

"Look—okay, I've always wondered, but like in the way people wonder about things even though they'd never actually do them—I've wondered what it would feel like to hit a girl. And now I know I don't like it! So when you think about it, this is more like a good thing, in a way!" The more he said, the angrier Louis and I got.

Then suddenly, Auggie's eyes widened as he stared at something behind us. He raised a hand to his mouth. He was trembling.

"What is it?" Louis snapped. Auggie raised a finger and pointed behind us, where none other than Bradd was struggling to stand up, slipping on the mess of watery body fluids. He was still corpse-pale and nude. His breathing was shallow and quick. He fixed Auggie with a wild stare. "I saw what you did, motherfucker."

Auggie tried to zigzag around a distracted Louis, but he wasn't fast enough. Louis grabbed him by the shoulders and spun him around before shoving him hard. He tripped and fell backward into the shower, landing on top of Bradd. He yelped and flailed and tried to get up, but Bradd hooked an arm around Auggie's neck and pulled him close until they were cheek-to-cheek. A thick dribble of pale yellow vomit, oyster vomit, was smeared across Bradd's face.

"What kind of fucking worthless coward hits a girl?"

Auggie gagged and wriggled with his eyes wide in horror. "Help me!" he gasped, to nobody in particular.

We did not help him.

Stunned as Louis must have been, his mood remained a steady rage directed at Auggie even as he spoke to Bradd. "Are you sure you're okay?"

"I'm great, Louie. Never better. Sorry about the mess, though." He grasped a fistful of Auggie's hair.

"You were dead," Auggie managed between retches.

"Do I look dead to you, asshole?" He jerked Auggie's head back and motioned Louis closer. "You want to be a tough guy? Let's see how tough you are. Take a good shot, Louie boy."

"It was an accident, I— "

"It didn't look like an accident." Louis glanced at me. "Do you want me to kill him?"

I kind of did.

"You've made a big mistake," Bradd whispered. He drew a mustache with his bodily fluids across Auggie's upper lip before shoving his fingers into Auggie's mouth.

I had to look away. I gagged, and once I'd started gagging, I couldn't stop. Even worse—as everybody knows—gagging is contagious. I grabbed Louis's arm and pulled him outside. We stood on the front porch and caught our breath. He was bent over with his elbows on his thighs. He'd been holding on to his water bottle throughout the whole thing. He took a long drink and offered it to me.

"Are you okay?"

I nodded quickly, but my hands were shaking. It was the last thing I would have expected Auggie to do in a million years—not to mention Bradd's spontaneous resurrection. It was a lot for a Friday morning. "I thought you said he was dead."

"I thought he *was* dead!"

"You took his pulse. He wasn't breathing. You said he was cold."

"I know, Emma, but he's alive now, and that's a good thing."

"But it doesn't make sense. People don't just come back to life." Was there something more going on here? Could Bradd be involved in what was happening to Max and me? God, I hoped not. Not *Bradd*.

Louis thought about it for a minute. "It's funny," he said, "I remember being in the room when my abuelo died. He was at home. My parents and I were there visiting. We went to my grandparents' house for lunch every Sunday."

"I know. I remember."

"Every week it was the same thing: we'd eat lunch in their dining room together—it was always roast beef and mashed potatoes, every single week—and then my abuelo would fall asleep in his recliner in front of the television. On the day he died, everything happened the same as it usually did. He seemed fine. He wasn't even sick. But I remember looking over at him and knowing right away he was dead, and not because I could tell he wasn't breathing anymore. Something was just…*gone*. I don't know how else to explain it. But with Bradd, it was the exact opposite. His heart wasn't beating; he wasn't breathing; he seemed dead. But he didn't seem *gone*." He changed the subject then. "Look, I'm going to beat the living shit out of Auggie. I've gotta do it." He paused. "You're not—you won't—"

"Forgive him? Hard no. But I don't want you to beat him up."

Louis shook his head. "Somebody needs to teach him a lesson. He needs to pay."

"He'll pay. If anyone's going to hit him, though, I want it to be me."

Louis was visibly relieved. "Okay. I'm a lover, not a fighter."

"I know you are. But listen—we'll ruin his life instead." As I said it, I realized I wouldn't be able to conspire with Louis to humiliate Auggie on any long-term basis. There would be no new installment of *The Adventures of Emma and Louis*. At the end of the day, I was on my own again.

We went back inside to find Bradd and Auggie exactly as we'd left them. Auggie's eyes were squeezed shut. He was murmuring the Hail Mary prayer. Bradd flashed us a filthy grin. "I'm your God now," he told Auggie, kissing him on the cheek.

"Let him go," I said.

"Not yet. He needs to apologize first."

"I'm sorry! Emma, I'm so sorry." Auggie was pleading with me.

"I'm so sorry. I—I was in shock." He gagged again. His chin and T-shirt were smeared with puke. As soon as I noticed it, I looked away and backed out of the room.

What point was there in sticking around, anyway? "Let's get out of here," I said to Louis.

Bradd hollered at me from the bathroom. "Emma! Don't go yet! We need to talk!"

What? "Why?" I hollered back.

"It's really, really, really important!"

"Tell me."

"We need to talk privately!"

"About what?"

"It's—um— Jesus, Emma, would you just— Okay, it's about *time* that we discussed something very important. It's driving me *loopy* that we haven't talked. Do you understand me?"

I did understand him, and I wasn't happy about it. It was turning out to be a real shit morning.

Auggie staggered out of the bathroom. He'd stripped off his shirt and wiped his face, but he was still a mess. He wouldn't make eye contact as he skittered past us, crab-like, toward the door. He was suddenly more repulsive to me than ever; it was like I couldn't even remember how it had felt to be attracted to him.

"Stop," Bradd commanded. He was naked except for a towel wrapped around his waist. "Before you leave, tell Emma you're a cheating piece of shit."

Auggie froze. His body seemed to shrivel in the doorway.

"Say 'I'm a cheating piece of shit,'" Bradd repeated.

Auggie started to cry. "I'm a cheating piece of shit. I'm sorry, Emma."

"He's cheating on you with Shelby Tucker," Bradd told me.

"What?" The news felt like another slap. One look at Auggie's face told me it was true.

"She was in our bungalow a few days ago. I listened at the door. I heard everything they were saying. I could hear them perfectly because I actually have superhuman hearing. You know those hearing tests they gave us in elementary school? When I was in the first grade, I could hear the sound of a cotton ball touching a bunny's whiskers." He looked at Louis. "Louie knows the Shelby thing is true. Tell her, Louie."

I stared at Louis, my heart in my throat. My face was hot with humiliation. "You knew? And you didn't tell me?" It's a special kind of embarrassment to be the last person to know something that is nobody's business but your own.

"You know what else is true?" Auggie pointed at Louis. "Guess what he did. He did something disgusting. I saw it with my own eyes. He—"

"Oh, fuck this." Before I could blink, Louis leaped across the room and pinned Auggie to the floor. "What did I do, Auggie? Go ahead and tell her. Is it worse than beating up on your own girlfriend?"

"No," Auggie said meekly.

"That's what I thought." Louis let him go. Auggie scrambled to his feet and out the door. Louis cupped his hands to his mouth. "Keep running, you piece of shit! You can't hide from me forever! I'm coming for you!" Once Auggie was out of sight, Louis looked at Bradd. "Are you sure you're okay, man? You looked pretty dead."

"I'm great." Bradd gave him an even smile. "But if you don't mind, Emma and I have something important to discuss privately."

Louis gave us a doubtful look.

"It's true," I said.

He still wasn't sure. "Is somebody going to tell me what's going on? Because things seem pretty fucked up right now. I get the sense that I'm missing something."

"Emma will explain it all tomorrow." Bradd smirked at me. "Won't you, Emma?"

I didn't answer him. Because what else was there to say?

Emma

Day 10

I sat on Bradd's bed with my knees pulled to my chest, waiting as he took a shower. I held his *Star Wars* sheet between my fingers and silked the silky. My face still stung from Auggie's slap. I took deep breaths and tried not to cry.

Bradd emerged from the bathroom with a towel still wrapped around his bottom half. He kept the towel in place while he put on a pair of boxers in a rare display of modesty. He pulled a clean T-shirt over his head and sat down across from me on the bed.

"So…pretty bizarre morning."

I didn't say anything.

"I want to help you, Emma."

"You want to help me," I echoed.

"Yep. We're time buddies now, you and me."

Part of me felt grateful for the company, even though Bradd wouldn't have been my first choice. Or my second choice. Or my last choice. "How did you know?"

"You've been acting like someone with nothing to lose. I could tell."

"Did you meet Sibyl?"

He gave me a blank look. "Who's Sibyl?"

"Sibyl. You know—the octopus."

"You met an octopus?"

I told him everything, starting with Sibyl and our telepathic communication. I described the way her tentacle had regenerated instantly after Gus cut it off. I told him about eating the ceviche. I told him about my miracle. "So if you didn't know about Sibyl, how did this end up happening to you?"

"It all happened because of the H2Blow."

"*The H2Blow?* How? Was Alison with you?"

"Actually, I was alone. I'm quite flexible. I can—"

"Yes, I know. I saw."

"Pretty impressive, isn't it?"

"It's really something, Bradd."

"I have to bind my arms behind my back and hook my ankles around my head to stay in position. The helmet is somewhat buoyant, which wouldn't be a problem if there'd been two people involved, but I was all alone. The first time I did it, I went to the lagoon. There was a minor malfunction with the valve that snowballed into catastrophe because I couldn't get myself free so I could take the helmet off. It was scary, Emma. I knew right away that I'd fucked up, and there was nothing I could do about it."

Drowning has always seemed like an especially awful way to die. "Did it hurt?"

"If it did, I don't remember. I was scared at first, but then it was like I accepted it and all my worries disappeared and I sort of dissolved into the universe. The next thing I knew, I woke up at Gus and Greta's house. Gus was *not* cool about it." Bradd paused. "He didn't say anything about any octopus. He told me he'd injected me with a serum that causes 'temporal paralysis.'"

"And he didn't mention me at all? Or Max?"

"Nope." It was clear that Gus and Greta didn't want us exchanging notes.

"Then how did you figure out I was part of it?"

"I used my powers of deduction. It came to me a few nights ago. So every night when Auggie comes back from your room, once he thinks I'm asleep, guess what he does?" He made a jerk-off motion with his hand. "He greases the ol' tentpole. I found this strange, because I knew he was just with you, so I asked myself: why didn't Emma give Auggie a hand, so to speak? He leaves his girlfriend and ten minutes later he's burping the worm? What's that all about?"

"Did you just say 'burping the worm'?"

"Yeah. So one night I waited until he was finished practicing politics, and I pretended to wake up, and I asked him: Did something happen between you and Emma? Is she bad at sex?"

"Wait a minute. You waited until he finished?"

"That's right."

"Why not ask him before he started?"

Bradd looked at me like I was concussed. "Because it would have been rude to interrupt him, Emma. Anyway, he told me you were on your period and you didn't feel like fooling around. But the next night he told me you two got into a fight because he thinks you have a thing for Louis. Then I asked him again the *next* night, and he gave me a whole different story."

"I don't understand how that proves anything."

"I realized you were doing the same thing I've been doing: pulling on different strings to see how it changes the outcomes." He leaned forward until his face was a few inches from mine. "Emma," he whispered, "where else have you been?"

I didn't understand what he meant. "Like, on the island?"

"Yeah, but like, in history."

"What are you talking about?"

"Like, have you been to the past?"

"Bradd, no. What past? We're in a time loop. There's no past. There's no future. There's only today. That's what makes it a time loop."

"I see." He frowned. "That's interesting."

"We literally just established all this."

"Well, there's been a misunderstanding, because my experience has been a little different."

"Go on."

"First, let me ask you something else: have you died yet?"

"No."

"Oh, man… Oh, this is getting complex. Okay, remember that morning when the white lobster washed up on the beach?"

"Yes. Oh, no."

"Yes! I've been intercepting it every morning."

"Every morning?"

"Yes!"

"You fish a white brick of powder wrapped in plastic out of the ocean. You take it back to your room and put it into your body. Up your nose."

"You're goddamn right I do."

"Wow. Okay. And then what?

"Then I jerk off."

"You are… How are you a real person?"

"I would *not* recommend it, Emma. It propels me into this sexual frenzy that's like— I don't think we have the right words to describe it in English. Maybe Gianluca could describe it better. It feels like… like all the joy and pleasure that has ever existed throughout all of time is shooting from the tip of my penis. Then I pass out."

"That…sounds kind of amazing, actually."

"It is, but we're getting sidetracked. See, every time it happened, the first thirty or forty times, I'd wake up and I'd still be here on the island, in the same spot, but I'd be in a whole different point in time."

"Excuse me?" I paused. "Wait—did you just say the *first thirty or forty times*?"

"Yes, Emma. Try to keep up, okay? Infinite orgasms, more powerful than anything I've ever felt before. It was like getting a blowjob from God while I was tripping on ecstasy. The propulsion of my semen killed a bird once! But I kept running into the same problem—I was coming and coming and coming, and it was making me come unstuck in time.

"One time I woke up and there was another guy in the shower with me. Big, scary guy with a bunch of military tattoos and a cock like a baby's arm. He didn't react well to my, uh, sudden appearance. I got my ass kicked that day. I started switching up my location after that. There was a long stretch of time where, as long as I stayed in the lagoon—which I can do now, because I've worked out all the problems with the H2Blow, patent pending—I'd just wake up surrounded by turtles, which wasn't so bad, although they do bite. But that didn't last." He shuddered.

"What happened?"

"Let's just say that, sometime in the future, Gus is going to sell the island to Disney, and it's going to become a family-friendly cruise destination."

"You went to the future?"

"I went to the future and inadvertently crashed breakfast with Mickey and Minnie. And, you know, a bunch of families. Kids, parents, grandparents, all trying to enjoy their vacations. It wasn't good. An old lady threw up on me. I've never seen a bunch of little girls scream like that. I got my ass kicked that day again, this time by a bunch of very angry fathers. Even the old lady got in a few kicks. I felt like a sex offender."

"And then what? How did you get back to this day?"

He shrugged. "Eventually I'd get away from whoever was chasing me long enough to hide somewhere and fall asleep. In the morning, I'd wake up back here in bed. Finally there was one time when I came unstuck and went into the past and got chased down the beach, buck-ass naked, by a tribe of warriors who shot a bunch of arrows into my back. I died, and when I woke up, I was back here again, but it wasn't the morning. It was like no time had passed at all."

"Okay, I'm really confused."

"It was because I died," he explained. "It reset me in time somehow. So now, as long as my orgasms end in death, I stay right here in time instead of bouncing around all over the place." He beamed. "That's where my wrists come into play. Once I'm in position, I'm locked into place, like a snake eating its own tail. There's no getting out of it. I orgasm over and over again, and then I lose consciousness. Then I die. It's not as bad as you'd think; the orgasms help. And as long as I die, I don't come unstuck. If I come unstuck, I have to die to get back. It has something to do with the cocaine, I think. It…jostles things somehow."

I was intrigued, but I realized his premise had a single, glaring issue. "Bradd, I really think you're jumping to conclusions about whatever it is you're snorting."

He shook his head. "It's cocaine. My uncle told me cocaine makes you feel like God. I feel like God when I do it. Therefore, it's gotta be cocaine."

His logic seemed a tad flawed to me. "Why would cocaine jostle you around in time?"

"I don't know. I haven't figured that out yet."

"Have you told Gus?"

He snorted. "Hell no. I'm not going to be his lab rat."

"Aren't you curious? Aren't you worried there are long-term effects you aren't aware of?" As much as I didn't want to trust Gus or Greta—and I really didn't want to—surely this was relevant in a potentially enormous way.

"No way. Gus will take it from me. I'm not willing to risk it. Maybe someday, but not yet." He paused. "Probably never."

"And it only happens when you snort it?"

He nodded. The whole thing was such an unnerving new wrinkle. As if it hadn't already been enough of an impossible mystery, now we were bringing narcotics into it.

"Well gee, Bradd, have you considered just, I don't know, not doing lines of mystery powder before you masturbate? Or even—and I know this is going to sound insane—not masturbating at all?"

He snorted. "Hard pass. Besides, I'm hooked now. I couldn't stop even if I wanted to."

"You need to wean yourself off somehow. Quit screwing around with time. What if you come unstuck and you can never get back?"

"That sounds like a problem for Future Bradd."

"Bradd, you have to help me get out of here." I wanted to leave, now, more than anything in the world. I needed to go home.

He was incredulous. "You want to *leave*?"

"Of course I want to leave! Don't you?"

"Not really."

"Why not?"

"Are you kidding me right now? Emma, *we can't die*. Do you understand what that means? We can do whatever we want." Pause. "For example, maybe you could volunteer to become a pioneer of history as the first woman to successfully give an underwater blowjob."

"Oh, sure, that sounds great."

"Really?"

"No, fuckstick, it doesn't sound great. It sounds hellish. It sounds like something the devil would invent to torture women in Hell. It's never going to happen. Nobody is ever going to buy something called the H2Blow. Nobody is going to *sell* something called the H2Blow."

"People bought pet rocks."

"Pet rocks were a better idea."

He frowned. "The H2Blow is a good idea."

"Can we move on? Please?"

"Okay. You really hurt my feelings, though."

"I'm sorry about that." I actually was kind of sorry. He was just so excited about the stupid thing.

"What should we do now? Let's do something outrageous together." He ticked ideas off on his fingers. "We could build a bomb… We could—ooh, I could get really drunk and you could try taking my appendix out… We could tie up Auggie and— Emma, we could waterboard him! Come on, let's do it!"

"I don't want to waterboard Auggie." I kind of did, but I wanted to avoid having to look at him more.

"How on Earth could that not appeal to you? Are you okay, Emma?"

"I think so. I don't know."

"Hey, everything will be all right. We can look out for each other now. We're time buddies," he repeated. "You and me. What a pair!" He held up his hand for a high five.

I was not okay.

Auggie Marshall

Dear Auggie,

It's your senior year, so your goal should be an ambitious one. By the time you graduate, I hope you discover God's purpose for your life.

Fondly,
Yourself

Max

Day 15,000

Once again, there were a few missing faces at breakfast. Once again, I didn't feel like dealing with it because of the whole trapped-in-the-same-hellish-day-for-eternity situation. This time, though, my conscience got the better of me (how, I'm not sure) and I felt compelled to investigate.

I was already on alert because of Bradd's brief stint as Poseidon a few days earlier. In my heart, I already suspected the terrible truth—that Braddley Hazelett was now my permanent companion in arrested time—but I couldn't bring myself to accept it. Being with these kids at all is bad enough. I have three other adults in my world, and I don't trust any of them. As long as the kids' actions stayed predictable, though, they existed for years mostly as background noise. Then Emma got involved, which complicated things, but I could deal with it. But now Bradd, too? I couldn't bear the thought. Anyone else but Bradd. Even Connor Cackowski would have been, evidently, more tolerable.

I ran into Auggie on my way to his bungalow. "Hey!" I stood in his way. "Stop." He did. "What's going on?"

Auggie wasn't looking so hot. He wouldn't meet my eye. "Something really bad happened in my bungalow. I need to go lay down."

"I think you need to go take a shower." I could already see there were bodily fluids involved with whatever had happened inside the bungalow, which didn't surprise me one bit. Because, well, Bradd. "Tell me everyone is alive in there, Auggie."

He gagged at the word "alive" but nodded. He was starting to cry. "Can I please take a shower now?"

"Go ahead."

I found Louis waiting around outside the bungalow, also looking shaken. But when I entered, only Bradd and Emma were there. Emma was sitting cross-legged on the bed with her head against the wall and her eyes closed. Bradd was standing in the center of the room, wearing only a T-shirt and underwear. The bathroom door was wide open behind him. There was steam from a recent shower. There was an odd smell.

"What the fuck is going on?" I asked. "Emma?" She didn't respond.

Bradd grinned at me. "Emma is pissed because I'm experimenting with time travel. Don't be mad, Emma! I'm a pioneer!"

Keeping her eyes closed, Emma held up both middle fingers.

"So it's you, too," I said to Bradd.

"It's me, too," he agreed cheerfully. He held up a palm for a high five. "Time buddies!"

I could have cried.

"He creates death traps, and he handcuffs himself so he can't escape them,"" Emma muttered. "He keeps coming unstuck in time. He's addicted to cocaine."

"There's cocaine here?" This was news to me. "Where is it?"

"You can't have any," Bradd said. "You're our teacher!"

I rolled my eyes. "I'm not asking to *try some.*"

"Did you hear me?" Emma looked at me now. "He keeps coming unstuck in time when he…uh…"

"I've been calling it 'Getting a Walk-on Role in *Euphoria*,' Bradd supplied for her. "The whole multi-orgasmic-death-plus-drugs thing."

"Wait a minute. Both of you, shut up." I closed my eyes and held a finger in the air. Bradd was right—I was their teacher. I needed to take control. "Back up. Bradd, tell me everything. Start from the beginning."

Max

Day 15,001

"I have fucking had it with the two of you, do you understand? I can't believe we're having this conversation *again*." I pressed my fingertips to my temples. "For almost literally the millionth time: we have one rule here, kids! One rule!" I looked at Emma and Bradd with fury. "Do either of you want to tell me what it is?"

They stared at the ground and didn't answer me.

"Do I need to ask again?"

"No killing or dying," Bradd muttered.

"What was that?" I cupped a hand to my ear. "Emma, can you say it again for the people in the back?"

"No killing or dying," Emma echoed in a small voice.

"Yes! No killing or dying!"

"Why are you yelling at me?" Emma demanded, angry. "I haven't killed anybody!"

"Not yet. Not that I know of."

"But—but why not?" Bradd whined.

"Because you aren't God, that's why."

His expression was sly. "I'm not so sure about that, Max! I think I might be God!"

I snorted. "If you're God, then I'm AOC. Just—just listen to me, Bradd. Stop. Masturbating. To. Death."

He shook his head. "No way. My body, my choice."

Max

Day 15,002

Fuck—and I cannot possibly stress this enough—these fucking kids.

Emma

Day 30

After a lot of discussion, we decided to see if the cocaine—or whatever it was—might be the key to our escape. Bradd, Max, and I were gathered in Max's bungalow. Bradd had used a seashell to scoop a healthy portion of cocaine—we kept calling it cocaine, just for simplicity's sake—onto Max's desktop. I thought of what Lucy had said about not jeopardizing the structural integrity of her septum. I thought about Demi Lovato. I didn't want to put anything up my nose.

But what if this was the way out, or at least a clue that would help us find the way?

It made no sense. Nothing made sense. I was a virgin stuck in purgatory with a guy named Bradd and my least favorite teacher, and we were all about to ingest something together in an attempt to...understand? Escape? I was genuinely terrified. I knew I'd be fine—*nothing matters!*—but still. My hands were shaking.

I would take whatever clarity I could get, though. Of course, if it worked—which I didn't have high hopes for—that meant I was still going home a virgin. That I would still have to break up with Auggie for what he'd done to me. In other words, my problems weren't going anywhere, regardless of where I might hop around in time.

"Don't look at me," I told Bradd and Max, leaning over the desk. It felt gross doing this in front of my teacher. They both looked away. I took a tiny bit of powder on my pinkie and touched it to my tongue.

My eyes burned. I heard ringing in my ears. I felt dizzy and cold. I heard a noise. I flinched and jerked and opened my eyes to a bright light—it was Alison, pulling back the flimsy linen curtain on our window facing the ocean to let the sun shine on my face. She beamed down at me. "Good morning, Rip Van Tinkle." She was wearing a threadbare green skirt and a sheer, off-the-shoulder crop top over her bikini. Green jellies on her feet. Aquamarine earrings winking in the sun. I recognized the look immediately: land mermaid.

It was before. It was Thursday.

I couldn't get dressed quickly enough. "Why are you in such a hurry?" Alison asked, frowning at me. "Your outfit is yuck."

"What day is it?" I asked.

"It's Thursday. Why?"

I didn't answer her. I slipped on a pair of flip-flops and rushed out the door to look for Bradd or Max.

They were both in the dining hall. Bradd was chugging orange juice, preparing to burp the alphabet. Max was across the room with Greta and Gus. Greta and Max looked cozy together. Max looked happy. He didn't so much as glance in my direction.

I grabbed Bradd's arm and pulled him from his chair. "Come with me."

He tried to shake me away. "What the fuck, Emma?"

"Come with me now," I snapped, dragging him toward the door. Once we were outside, I stood facing him and looked into his eyes. "Bradd, how did you get here?"

He gave me a blank look. "On a plane, like everybody else. You were there, too." He squinted at me, a faint grin on his face. "You okay, Emma? You seem high, or manic, or…"

"You don't remember?" I wailed.

"Don't remember what?"

If he wasn't here—if this wasn't the same Bradd I'd been with moments ago in Max's room—then where did he go? My mind felt like it was melting. "You don't remember Friday, do you? Oh my God, this is a nightmare." But then it occurred to me: if this was Thursday, that meant I hadn't eaten the ceviche yet. Which meant that all I had to do was stay here and not eat the ceviche, and everything would be okay. Could it really be that simple?

"Emma, you look upset. What's wrong?" It was Greta. She smiled warmly. She didn't fool me for a second. "You're pale. Why don't you come with me, sweetie?" she asked, putting a hand on my arm.

I tried to pull away from her, but she kept her grip tight. "I'm not going anywhere with you."

Her fingernails dug into my skin. A less-than-friendly spark flickered in her eyes. "You don't have a choice."

"Will somebody tell me what's going on here?" It was Bradd.

"Emma isn't feeling well," Greta said.

"I feel fine."

"We need to check you out. Come on." She guided me toward the path that led to her house. "It's okay, Emma. I'm not going to hurt you."

"Bradd!" I shouted as she all but dragged me away.

"See ya, Emma! Hope you're feeling better soon!" He had no idea what I was talking about. Neither did Max, probably. Wherever they'd ended up, it wasn't here.

• • •

Greta brought me to her house and gave me a glass of water. I looked at it with suspicion.

"It's just water, I promise," she said.

I took a tentative sip.

"You seem lost, Emma."

I was doing my best not to let on what was happening. And how would Greta even know? Which version of Greta was I dealing with? "I'm not lost at all."

She tilted her head. "Are you sure about that?"

"I'm sure."

"Don't lie to me, Emma."

I took another sip of water. As long as I didn't consume any ceviche (or cocaine?), I figured I should be okay.

"I should never have brought you into this," Greta mused next to me.

"I don't know what you're talking about."

She looked at me doubtfully, with a hint of impatience. "I don't want to have to hurt you, Emma."

"Then don't hurt me."

"Things are getting complicated. But it will all be okay eventually—you'll see. You just have to trust me." She paused. "How did you get here?"

I still wasn't willing to admit anything. "On a plane. Then we took a ferry." I paused. I shouldn't have said what I said next—it was too much of a giveaway—but I couldn't stop myself. "I'm getting pretty homesick. I'm ready to leave."

"But you aren't feeling well," Greta said.

"I feel fine." I took another sip. It was time for me to go. I needed to get the hell away from her and stay safe for the rest of the day.

"Are you sure? You look like you might be dizzy. You're sweating. Is your heart beating fast?"

She was right. My heart went *thumpthumpthump*, pounding rapidly and erratically in my chest. A chill of pure terror washed over me. "What did you do, Greta?" I tried to stand up, but my legs were too unsteady. My teeth were starting to chatter. I felt terrible.

"I'm making a minor correction."

"What did you give me?" I looked at the water glass, gasped, and dropped it like it was hot. It shattered on the floor. I tried to stagger past Greta, but she gave me the gentlest of shoves, and I fell back onto the couch. I could feel myself fading, then everything went dark. My body felt like it was falling backward through space. I realized I was dying. Greta was sending me back.

Then there was nothing.

Bradd

Day 29

Every endless day begins the same way for me: at the beach. I've made it my business to know where to find the so-called white lobster before anybody else has a chance to notice it each morning. As I made my way to the shore, I sang a little song. The words were set to the music from my favorite song from *Beauty and the Beast*:

Little land, it's a quiet island
Every day like the one before
Little place, full of innovation
Teenage girls who say
No more!
No more, I won't use the H2Blow
No more, I come and get the blow
No more, now I don't need a woman, 'cause I've got my mouth and flex-i-bil-i-ty

Just me!
There goes my girlfriend she's so sweet and pretty
But also kind of a buzzkill
Every morning just the same
As the morning when I came
When I drowned and here's the co-caine, oh hello!

"Bonjour!" I said to the package bobbing in the water. The first time I found it, I was shaking as I snuck it back to my bungalow. I was alone that day, but I couldn't wait to show Alison the following morning. But Alison wasn't interested. Now, for about the twenty-fifth time, I tried to convince her.

"You don't know what that is. It could be cyanide," she said.

"It isn't cyanide. Come on, let's try it. I want to snort a line off your tits."

"No way. I don't even want to touch it."

"What is the deal with you lately? You used to be wild and fearless and exciting. You've changed. You won't try the H2Blow. A brick of uncut blow washes up on the beach and you want nothing to do with it. Why are you always hanging out with Lucy Thomas all of a sudden? And what's with all the jigsaw puzzles? Puzzles are for, like, Mormons and senior citizens. I thought I knew you!"

"You're right," she admitted, "I have changed."

"Well, I don't like it! I hardly recognize you."

"I don't want you to feel that way. I want you to know me. I care about you."

My stomach dropped. I knew I had to ask it. "Are—are you still in love with me?"

"I'll always love you, Bradd."

This was no good at all. "But you aren't in love with me, are you?"

"I… It isn't about you."

"Then who is it about?"

"Lucy."

It took a minute for me to piece it together. "You like girls?" I have never understood the appeal of same-sex relationships. Why bring sand to the beach?

"I don't want to hurt you. You're still my best friend. And you were right when you said you felt like you didn't know me. How could you know me when I didn't even know myself? But now I do know myself. And that means you can know the real me, too. I know it might not feel like it, but now you know me better than ever."

I was heartbroken. I did the only thing I could think of to soothe myself: I went on a drug and masturbation binge.

After so many mornings without incident, the process of retrieval has become seamless and routine: I fish the bundle from the shallow water—when I arrive at the beach at precisely 6:18 a.m., it is always near the big coral reef separating the deep sea from the calm water lapping at the shore—and hurry back to my bungalow for a little bit of what I've come to call "C&C" (use your imagination). Sometimes I black out or die—whatever that means in this fucked-up reality—but I always wake up moments later, feeling amazing. Rinse and repeat. I could do this forever.

And I'm not sharing with Emma and Max today. No way, not after yesterday's flop. It didn't even do anything to Max or me, which confirms my suspicion that whatever is happening with the cocaine, it's not the key to escaping a time loop. It's just the key to a good time.

But on this particular morning, Steven the Intern was waiting for me at the beach. The brick—my precious!—was in his arms. He gave me a big smile, showing me his crooked British teeth. "Looking for something?"

I looked around. "Me?"

"Yes, you. Maybe you're looking for this?"

I had to admit, his accent was so charming. A person can say anything with a British accent and make it sound cool and distinguished.

"You know, Steven, nobody owns the ocean. The sea belongs to all of us."

"What's your point?"

"The sea and...you know...its many treasures."

"Gus owns this island. Whatever washes up on these shores belongs to him."

"Yeah, I don't know about that. I believe maritime law adheres to the 'finders keepers' rule." I took a few steps toward him. "Why don't you go ahead and let me have that?"

"Sorry, mate. Can't do it."

"But I have a routine!"

Steven scratched his chin. "You have a routine," he echoed.

"Yes, I have a routine."

"Braddley— "

"Call me Bradd."

"What do you think this is?" He nodded at his arms.

"It's a white lobster. You know what it is."

"You think this is cocaine, do ya?"

"I know it's cocaine." Actually, that was becoming less and less true. I had assumed it was cocaine initially, sure. But I should probably mention that, until this week, I had never actually tried cocaine, so I wasn't sure what to expect. But now I've done a lot of it. I might be getting addicted. I'm not even sure I could climax without it; I certainly couldn't ejaculate with enough force to kill a seagull, and that's really where the fun is.

Who knows—maybe I'll end up in rehab someday? That's fine with me. Passages Malibu, baby. I can get sober with the stars. "Just hand it over. Please."

"Not bloody likely, mate." Not bloody likely. I love it.

"I'm an addict, man. I need my drugs."

"You don't need any more of this. You've had plenty. Bet a

bunch of funny things are happening to you, eh? Bet you feel pretty powerful after you hoover some of this up the ol' nasal passages."

"As a matter of fact, I do."

"You ever wonder why that might be?"

"Because cocaine is a powerful stimulant?"

"Yes, but I'm afraid we've got a case of mistaken identity here. This is not cocaine; this is a force, and you shouldn't be playing with it."

"What do you mean, it's a force?"

He gave me a smug look. "I'm afraid that information is classified. You wouldn't believe me, anyway."

"I don't know about that, man. There's a lot of freaky shit going on right now. I'd believe just about anything."

"Okay, then. This here? This is time. And you're coming with me."

Steven took me to Gus. He was in his lab, peering into a microscope. He scowled when he looked up and saw the two of us. Then he noticed the brick in Steven's arms.

"Got another one for you." Steven handed it to him.

"From where?"

"West side of the beach. Washed up this morning."

"Was there only one?"

"Yes, I believe so."

Gus looked forlorn. His shoulders slumped. "It isn't enough. We need more. And what is he doing here? He shouldn't be in here." He meant me.

"Our boy Braddley has been going on a little fishing expedition every morning, keeping it. Kid's got himself all twisted around. He thought it was cocaine."

Gus massaged his temples. "You absolute fucking nitwit. Do you have any idea what you've done?"

"I guess I don't! Why don't you tell me?"

Gus didn't respond.

"Are you just going to stare at me? What is this stuff if it's not cocaine?"

"It's an accelerant."

"What the hell does that mean?"

"Don't tell him anything else," Steven interrupted.

Gus glared at him. "I'm not giving anything away. And even if I do, it doesn't matter now; he's cut off." Gus looked at me. "You hear me? This isn't for you to go meddling with. It's bad enough I had to involve you at all." He paused. "Here's what's going to happen now, Bradd. You're going to tell me everything. I'll run some tests—bloodwork, imaging, DNA—and you aren't going to breathe a word of this to anybody. Understand?"

I almost told him I knew about Emma and Max and that they were onto the whole "this cocaine is perhaps not cocaine but something far more volatile and interesting" idea, but something told me to keep my mouth shut. And I was still very unhappy about the idea of losing my supply. "I can't just quit cold turkey now. I'm hooked."

"Tough shit. You've gotten yourself into quite a mess, and now you're going to help me undo it before it's too late."

I gazed longingly at the brick. "How can that be time? Time isn't, like... It's not a physical thing."

Gus glowered at Steven. "You told him this was time?" He looked at me. "Steven doesn't know what he's talking about. I told you, it's just an accelerant."

"Where did it come from?"

He shrugged. "It washes up now and then. That's all I know."

"How did you figure out that it's a—what did you call it?"

"An accelerant."

"Yeah, an accelerant. How did you figure that out?"

Steven guffawed. "How do you think, mate?"

Of course. Coke party.

It was all very interesting, but I didn't trust Gus as far as I could throw him. And I certainly didn't want him experimenting on me. "Look, I don't want you doing any bloodwork on me. I don't like needles."

"Like I already said, tough shit."

"Nuh-huh." I shook my head. "I have leverage now. You don't get to push me around like this. There's nothing in it for me."

Gus's face reddened, but he stayed calm. "Then let me compensate you for your troubles. I can pay you."

"In cocaine?"

"In dollars."

"I don't need your money."

"Everybody can use more money. Name your price."

I thought about it. The idea struck me like a bolt of lightning. "Okay, I'll do it if you invest in my company. For a million dollars, you can have a ten percent stake. But you have to publicly endorse the product. You have to take an active role in streamlining the process for mass production. You have to be my biggest champion."

"What company? You're a kid."

I raised an eyebrow. "I think you know."

"You can't possibly mean— Are you talking about the water blowjob thing? That death trap?"

"It's called the H2Blow, and it's the erotic aquatic device of the future."

"Absolutely not."

I crossed my arms. "Then I guess we don't have a deal."

Gus was silent for a long time. I was a little worried he would hit me again, or worse. "You know," he said to Steven, "I used to have the highest ethical standards. I had dignity. I was knighted by the queen, for Christsakes. And look at me now; I'm about to make a deal with the devil."

Emma

Day 31

Be-BLAH. Be-BLAH.

I woke up crying, but I wasn't sure if it was from relief (I was alive!) or sheer terror (Greta *killed* me!). For once, the routine of the day was a comfort. Swedish Fish: check. Devil beating his wife: check. Garbage on the beach: check.

And then, because nothing *truly* mattered, I allowed the rest of the day to happen exactly as it had yesterday. Dead Brad: check. Auggie slapping me: check. Louis admitting he knew about the cheating: check.

I managed to avoid almost everybody for most of the afternoon. When Louis finally found me and confronted me, I was playing with the kittens. His tall frame took up almost the entire doorway to the shed, blocking the daylight, which was starting to fade. "There you are. I've been looking for you everywhere."

I ignored him.

"Can I come in? I'm coming in."

I didn't respond. Four of the six kittens were curled up in my lap; the other two were nursing from their tired, skinny mother.

Louis sat down beside me. "You should name them." He meant the kittens.

"I already have."

"Tell me their names."

There were six kittens. Two of them were orange, one was a calico, two were tuxedo patterned, and the runt was all white except for a narrow black mustache. I pointed at it. "Well, that one is obviously Hitler."

"Poor kitty." Louis paused. "Her name really should be Kitler."

I couldn't believe I hadn't thought of it myself. "Oh, obviously. The orange ones are Frick and Frack."

"Which one is Frick and which one is Frack?"

"Nobody knows."

"I see."

"The calico is a girl. Her name is Diana."

"After Princess Diana?"

I nodded. "The people's kitty."

"You're so weird. What about the others?"

"The ones in tuxedos are both named Friday."

"Both?"

"Both."

"How will you tell them apart?"

"I'll know."

"But how?"

"I just will."

A lizard crept into the doorway as the kittens were nursing. I thought their mother was asleep. Her eyes were closed. As the lizard inched closer to her babies, the mama cat raised her head and yowled and hissed and swiped at the lizard with her claws out. The kittens wobbled and tumbled on their weak little legs. The lizard ran away, but not until after the mama had clawed deep scratches across its neck.

"You have some dirt on your forehead," Louis said. He wiped it away with his thumb.

We sat in silence for a few minutes and watched the kittens, who were nestled back into place. Finally, Louis spoke up. "Are you okay?"

For some reason, the question made me angry. "No, Louis, I'm not okay."

"I'm sorry I didn't tell you about Shelby. I should have done it right away."

"How long have you known?"

"I had my suspicions for a long time." The words—*a long time*—were like a knitting needle to my guts all over again. How long had Auggie been cheating on me? Weeks? Months?

"You should have told me."

"You would have been mad at me. You *are* mad at me. And like I said, at first I didn't know for sure. I didn't want to put myself in the middle of things if I wasn't sure."

"You should have told me as soon as you even suspected." I was so embarrassed.

"Would you have listened to me? You thought he was such a saint."

"I… You're right, I did. You tried to tell me. I should have believed you."

"I have always been an excellent judge of character. Anyway, now we can ruin his life together."

"I've wasted so much time."

"Emma, it's not like you married the guy." He fidgeted with his hands. "Did you sleep with him?"

"You know I didn't. I would have told you."

"You would have?" He was sitting so close to me that our shoulders were touching. I could smell him; he smelled like salt and sweat and shampoo. And DEET. Lots of DEET.

"Of course. I tell you everything." As I said that, I got pissed off at him all over again for keeping the secret.

"Do we have to keep talking about this? I told you, it wasn't my relationship. I didn't want to interfere."

I could tell he wasn't giving me the whole truth. "What aren't you telling me?"

He fidgeted some more. He stared at his toes. "Okay. I confronted Shelby a few months ago. We've always gotten along okay, so I figured she was more likely to admit it to me than Auggie, but she denied everything. And like I told you, I didn't have any hard proof. I used to see them flirting with each other in the back of our psych class—passing notes and shit. They weren't even supposed to be sitting together! There was a definite vibe. Some things you can just feel, you know?"

I shrugged but didn't say anything.

"I didn't believe Shelby," he continued, "so then I asked Auggie. He denied it, too, but I could tell he was lying because of how defensive he got right away. I finally convinced him to discuss it in purely hypothetical terms. He told me that if something like that had ever happened—which it hadn't—it would have been a one-time mistake that he wasn't about to make again. Hypothetically. They stopped sitting together in psych class after that, so I let it go. I made a mistake. I'm sorry."

"Nope. There's more."

"Emma, can we please let it go?"

"I thought we could tell each other anything."

"Just because we can doesn't mean we should. Look—Auggie has some dirt on me," he admitted, "and it's bad. I swore him to secrecy, and so far he's kept his promise, and I'd like to keep it that way if it's all the same to you."

"Tell me."

"It's not something I'm comfortable sharing, Emma."

"Louis."

"No. It isn't the kind of thing you can un-learn about a person."

"You're supposed to be my best friend!"

He flinched. "I am your best friend."

"If that were true…"

"It is true."

"It doesn't feel that way right now. Right now I feel humiliated, and lied to, but more than anything I feel alone."

"You aren't alone. I'm right here." And he took my hand. He seemed to do it without thinking, and as soon as our fingers made contact—he was clammy, palm damp, fingers jittery—he pulled his hand away like he'd touched something hot. "I'm sorry."

"It's okay," I said quickly. But I pulled away, too.

"I had a dream about you last night," he said. And he told me all about it again.

"What do you think it means?" I asked.

"I don't know."

"Why did you hold my hand?"

"I don't know. I just did it."

"But I'm an amorphous flesh blob."

"Excuse me?"

"You said it yourself."

"I *what*? When did I say that?"

"At Connor Cackowski's party. We were in the pool."

He was stunned. "I don't remember saying that. But I'm sure I meant it as a compliment."

"Amorphous flesh blob?" I repeated.

"Because I don't just see your face or your body, Emma. Don't you get it? I meant that you always look the same to me, because you always look beautiful."

This stopped me. He had never called me beautiful before.

"You're tall. You have long legs and a long neck. You're built like a ballerina, but you're clumsy. You aren't comfortable dancing because you feel like you take up too much space, but you're wrong.

"Sometimes your eyes are blue, and sometimes they're green. I like that you never get your nails done because you think it's a waste of time. You look sexy as hell in a turtleneck. You have the tiniest wrists I've ever seen. You don't like your nose, but it's perfect for your face. *I* like your nose."

I was barely breathing. I didn't want to move a muscle. I wanted to sit with his words forever.

For the first time, I was experiencing something I wouldn't mind experiencing again. And again.

"I look for reasons to touch you. I wanted—I want to be with you all the time. I want to have adventures with you." He took my hand again. He was still sweaty and shaky, but this time he didn't pull away, and neither did I. I was hyperaware of the way our shoulders and upper arms and thighs were touching. The air between us was electric. A fine mist of rain, barely more than a heavy dew, blurred the landscape as it fell outside the shack. It looked like a dream. It was a vibe.

"Emma? Will you look at me?" He touched my chin and gently turned my head until our faces were a few inches apart.

"You have an eyelash," he said, brushing his fingertip across my cheek. He held it to my lips. "Make a wish." I looked down. There was no eyelash.

"I don't see anything."

"You don't? I guess I just wanted to touch you."

Then I kissed him, and the world fell away.

His hands were in my hair, on my face, our mouths wet and warm and hungry to taste each other. Hands everywhere, frantic, seeking. I leaned into him with the full weight of my upper body, being careful not to crush the kittens in my lap. Louis tasted like mint and smelled faintly of deodorant and sweat, but not in a bad way. He smelled like himself. It was so familiar and comforting, aliens could have landed in the clearing and I wouldn't have noticed.

I slid my hands up the back of his shirt, underneath the damp fabric. My palms were pressed flat against the small of his back, holding on to as much of him as I could, when he abruptly pulled away. "Emma, wait."

"What's wrong?"

"Nothing. This is just happening so fast. Maybe we should take a minute."

I didn't want to take a minute. "Don't do that," I told him. "That isn't fair."

"I just need to think."

"Okay. Let's go somewhere. We could go back to my room."

He didn't say anything while he caught his breath. He stood up and looked down at me. "My parents are getting divorced. I've been meaning to tell you all week."

"I'm sorry."

"Everything is falling apart. I can't lose you, too."

"You won't lose me! Louis, I'm here right now. Please don't go. If you do, I might never get you back."

"What if we break this? It's already so close to perfect. Maybe we should leave things alone."

I could barely speak around the lump in my throat. "Y-You don't really want that."

"I don't want my heart to break. And if we do this, it will break. Maybe not right away, but someday."

"I promise I won't break your heart."

He lingered in the doorway. "I need some time to think."

I was desperate for him to stay. "But we don't have time!"

He gave me a funny look. "Of course we do. We have the rest of our lives."

As I watched him walk away, I opened my mouth to call out his name, but I couldn't make a sound. His pace grew hurried as he moved down the path and around the corner, like he'd been holding himself back from breaking into a sprint for as long as he could stand. Then he was gone. The spell was broken.

Louis

Friday

Way back at the beginning of the school year, Max had us write a letter to ourselves in which we each laid out our private goal for the year. My letter said something like: *Dear Louis, do something that scares you for once.* I still haven't done it.

What then is time? If no one asks me, I know what it is. If I wish to explain it to him who asks, I do not know.

—*Confessions of St. Augustine*

Part 3

Alison

Friday

Emma was deeply asleep. It took a minute for the tapping to register against her forehead and wake her up. *Tap tap tap tap tap.* Emma's eyeballs fluttered underneath their lids. Didn't fluttering mean a person was dreaming? Maybe the tapping felt like a raindrop, or maybe it manifested as a different kind of interruption in her dream space: a ringing phone, the need to pee, a thunderstorm, the silhouette of a burglar in the doorway.

Tap tap tap went my fingernail against her forehead. I shook Swedish Fish into my palm and emptied them into my mouth. I felt kind of bad eating them, if I'm being honest. Ordinarily, I wouldn't have thought twice about it, but I knew they were Emma's favorite. The trouble is I love them, too. I decided I'd buy her more when we got back to the United States. I'd do it as soon as we got through customs at the airport. Maybe I shouldn't have taken them in the first place. But what's done is done.

"Stop it," Emma whispered without opening her eyes. Her voice was raspy and flat.

I didn't stop. I tapped more aggressively. Emma looked at me. "What day is it?"

"It's Friday, sweetheart."

She closed her eyes, clearly not pleased by my answer for reasons I didn't understand. For a minute, I thought she was going to start crying. "I hope you choke on those," she whispered.

I threw my head back and laughed and shook another handful of fish into my mouth. Abruptly, she sat up and shoved me hard in the center of my chest. I gave an involuntary gasp of surprise, and a dense ball of gelatin lodged itself firmly in my throat. I tried to cough. It was stuck. I tried again. I felt panic creeping in.

She stared at me with pure loathing. "You think this is funny, bitch? You can't go around stealing other people's things! Ha-ha-ha-ha!" She picked up the box and shook it over my head. Swedish Fish pelted my face. "There you go! All yours now! All yours!"

Emma was officially losing her mind. She was angrier than I'd ever seen her. I grasped my neck with both hands in the universal symbol for choking, but Emma just howled with rage and lunged at me. I was too frightened and stunned to get out of the way. We both rolled to the floor. I landed with a hard *thunk* on my back. The obstruction in my windpipe stayed firmly in place.

I tried to scramble away from her without success. She caught me by the leg and elbowed her way on top of me until she was straddling me. I made the choking sign again as my eyesight blurred with tears. My only goal was air.

Emma didn't help me. She screamed in my face while I clawed at the floor and tried desperately to writhe away. "You think this is all a joke, everything, and you get away with it, and I'm tired of it! You were my best friend in the whole world and you ruined it—for what? Because you came up with a funny pun about me pissing the bed? Telling everyone to call me Rip Van Tinkle was such a clever idea that it was worth destroying our whole friendship? I loved you! And now I hate you! I don't think you even understand that sometimes! Like you think it's still all a big funny joke that I should have gotten over a long time ago. Why can't you understand that I. Do. Not. Like. You? I brought those fish for myself and you know it. That's why I hid them! But you couldn't just let me enjoy them. You couldn't just ask politely if you could have a few. I would have said no, but you could have at least asked."

Black stars burst into my field of vision. I cried without making a sound and felt true, pure terror for maybe the first time in my life.

"What's the matter, Alison?" Emma asked breathlessly. "You're never this quiet. Is this what it takes for you to finally shut the fuck up?"

I could feel myself starting to fade. What a humiliating way to die.

"What do you want me to do?" Emma asked. "Do you want me to save you?"

I nodded furiously. I pled with my eyes as tears spilled down my cheeks.

"Well, guess what? I'm not going to do it." She climbed off me, catching her breath as I sat up and tried to stand on my wobbly legs and back a safe distance away from her. At the same time, I reached out for her help. I couldn't stop myself; my will to stay alive overrode my fear.

"Aren't you a registered lifeguard?" she asked, not waiting for an answer that I was unable to give. "That means you're certified in first aid, doesn't it? Then you can save yourself for all I care." She stomped her feet and screamed like a furious child. She paced the room. She didn't help me.

How long does it take a person to choke to death? Two minutes? Five minutes? All I knew was that I didn't have much time. I could feel my heart slowing in my chest. As I stumbled around the room in a panic, I caught a glimpse of a face in the mirror, barely recognizing it as my own. My vision was too faded and blurry to make out anything but my broadest features, which were horrific enough. My throat was clawed bloody. My skin was blue. The whites of my eyes were all red. It was a bad way to go.

But hey—at least my death wouldn't involve the H2Blow.

Emma left me alone to flail. She went into the bathroom and closed the door. I staggered across the room toward the dresser and thrust my abdomen hard against the closest edge again and again, trying to give myself the Heimlich.

Finally, I succeeded. There was an audible *pop*. The blockage flew across the room and stuck to the wall. I fell into a heap on the floor and gulped air and sobbed into my hands.

Emma was running the water in the bathroom and must not have been able to hear me, but I could hear her. "She'll be okay tomorrow," she said to herself. "We'll both wake up in the morning and everything will be just like it was today. She won't remember any of this. If I had to die, at least she should, too. Who's Rip Van Tinkle now, bitch?"

I ran out the door in my bare feet and pajamas. I stumbled going down our wooden steps and barely paused. I was fueled by pure terror and adrenaline. I didn't stop until I was banging on Lucy's door with both fists.

"Emma tried to kill me," I blurted, shoving my way past her and into the room.

"Oh my God! What happened to your face?"

"Didn't you hear what I said? She tried to kill me!" I ran to the bathroom so I could get a good look at myself in the mirror. The skin around my eyes was mottled with small red dots that spread down my face along my hairline and onto my neck. Petechial hemorrhaging. It's a classic sign of strangulation, my mom tells me. She should know; she works in the medical field.

Several of my fingernails had broken off. The whites of my eyes were a startling blend of red and purple. I spat blood into the sink; I must have bitten my tongue when I was choking. I was still wearing my silk pajamas, but they were soaked in sweat. My top was halfway unbuttoned.

Mia was already gone. Lucy locked the door and got me a glass of water. Once I had calmed down somewhat, she left me alone to shower while she went to find Max. She was gone for a long time. I finished showering and changed into some of Lucy's clothes. I checked and rechecked the door, making sure it was locked. I peered out the windows. There was no sign of Emma or anybody else; they were all still at breakfast, blissfully unaware there was a killer in our midst.

Lucy returned eventually with Max. "Look at her! Look what Emma did to her!"

"Tell me exactly what happened," he said.

"Well, I was eating Emma's Swedish Fish when I started choking."

"Uh-huh, and did Emma give you permission to eat her Swedish Fish?"

"No, but I don't see how that—"

"So you stole them. Go on."

"Anyway, I started choking, and she wouldn't help me. She explicitly told me she was going to let me die."

Max seemed…annoyed? Bored? Whatever he was feeling, it wasn't the reaction I'd anticipated. "That damn kid…I can't believe her. She knows better," he muttered, more to himself than to me.

"She *knows* better?" Lucy was almost spitting with rage. "This was a crime! We need the police!"

"Do we, though?" Max was drinking coffee from a Garfield mug and nibbling on a croissant. "You look okay to me now, Alison."

"I'm not okay. I'm going to need therapy, Max."

He rolled his eyes. "You seem perfectly fine."

"Do I?" I gestured at my face and neck.

"I'm not at liberty to comment on your appearance, actually. It would be inappropriate." He took another bite of his croissant. "Okay. Here's what I'm going to do: after lunch today, we'll make Emma sit in a chair at the front of the room, and I'll let you shave her head while everyone watches."

"What is the matter with you?" Lucy asked him.

"What? No good?"

"Max. No."

He shrugged and took another bite of his croissant. He chewed with his mouth open while he talked. "Look, I'm sorry, but I don't care about any of this, like, at *all*. But I'm willing to talk to Emma to make sure this doesn't happen again. Does that sound okay?" All of a sudden, he seemed to notice that Lucy and I were sitting close together and holding hands. "Oooh, this is new. Does Bradd know? You know, Alison, you're a really smart kid. Don't waste your life trying to become one of the Real Housewives. You can do a lot better than Bradd."

Lucy seethed. "I don't know what your problem is, but you're supposed to be in charge of us. You're the adult here. Alison told you Emma tried to kill her, and it's your responsibility to do something about it, but you're treating it like a joke."

Max quietly considered her words. "Okay," he finally said, "here's what I'm willing to do. Alison, I'm going to say the first line from one of the books you were assigned to read last semester. If you can tell me the name of the book, I'll have Gus call the coast guard right now."

"What?" Lucy spat.

"I said Alison, not you." He pointed at Lucy. "You wait outside. You're too well-read."

Then it was just the two of us. "Last night I dreamt I went to Manderley again," Max said.

"Cool. I don't care."

"Not *me*. It's the first line of a book."

I didn't recognize it.

"Do you need more time to think about it?"

"I don't know the answer."

"Because you didn't do the reading assignment," he said bitterly. "Have a seat, Alison."

Max sat on the edge of the desk and lit a cigarette. "Last night I dreamt I went to Manderley again," he repeated.

"I already told you, I don't know where it's from."

"That's okay. But I want you to say it anyway."

"You want me to say the line?"

"Yes."

"Last night I dreamt I went to Manderley again."

"Say it again."

"Last night I dreamt I went to Manderley again."

"Isn't that beautiful?"

I wasn't in the mood. "I guess so."

"It's the first line of *Rebecca.* It's a book by Daphne Du Maurier. I think you would have enjoyed it."

"I don't have time to read."

He gave me a bemused look. "What about *The Great Gatsby*? Did you read that?"

"Yes." I was lying; I'd only seen the movie version, the one with Leonardo DiCaprio.

"Tell me the truth."

"Fine, I didn't read it."

"There's a part where Daisy is talking to Nick about her daughter. She tells him she hopes her daughter grows up to be beautiful and stupid, so her life will always be easy."

"So?"

"You aren't stupid, Alison. You have a good brain. Stop wasting it."

"Are you going to punish Emma?"

He gave me a nonanswer. "Why don't you do this: Take the rest of the day to relax and calm down. Stay away from Emma. Get a good night's sleep tonight, and we'll discuss this again tomorrow morning."

Emma

Day 32

I was alone in my bungalow, crying with helpless frustration, when Max knocked at the door. "Where did you go the other day?" I blurted. "What happened to you? Where's Bradd?"

"Nothing happened to me. It was like a blip." He paused. "Nothing happened to Bradd, either. I can't explain it."

"It worked for me! I went back in time! I went back to Thursday; I thought I was saved. I thought I could just not eat the ceviche and everything would be okay."

"But you're here now. So what happened?"

"Greta happened. She poisoned me. Everything went black and I passed out. I felt like I was falling through space for a long time. Then I woke up back in my room, and I tried reliving the day again, but everything went sideways with Louis and so today, I just...I don't know, I just lost it. Max, where's Bradd? Where's the cocaine? We have to try again."

Max held up a hand. "Let me stop you right there. I'm not here about that. I'm here about Alison. You almost killed her."

"But she's alive. She'll be fine."

"What's our rule, Emma? We have one rule here."

"I know the rule."

"I want to hear you say it."

I rolled my eyes. "No dying, no killing. I'm sorry. I was so angry when I woke up. Now, where's Bradd? We have to hurry!"

"Yeah, about that." He paused. "I have some bad news."

Emma

Day 33

I had my tonsils removed when I was eleven years old. It's the only time I've been put under general anesthesia. There's something magical about the process. One minute you're counting backward from ten, and the next minute you're opening your eyes, disoriented as a newborn, wondering when the procedure is going to get started.

You ask a nurse. "Honey, it already happened," she says. All that time, gone in a blink. The thing about general anesthesia is that nobody—not even anesthesiologists—fully understands how it works. To do so would require an understanding of how consciousness works. A big mystery, that one. You might even say it's *the* big mystery.

What science *does* know for sure about anesthesia is that it does two things: One, it renders the patient immobile, basically paralyzed. Two, it prevents the brain from forming new memories.

There's a terrifying, rare thing that can happen called anesthesia awareness, which is when a person is immobile but can still feel everything being done to their body. There was a *Dateline* special about this very thing a few years ago. Among the subjects they interviewed was a woman who recalled every moment of her appendectomy. Even years later, you could tell she was still carrying the trauma. You could see it on her face. I imagine it must feel like that famous short story by Harlan Ellison, "I Have No Mouth and I Must Scream."

All of this prompts the obvious question: What if we *all* feel everything happening to our bodies when we're put under? What if the only difference between me and that woman—between everyone who's ever been put under and that woman—is that we don't remember? If our body feels something, but our mind does not retain the memory, what happens to all the pain? What about all the hormones and adrenaline we produce under extreme stress? If the mind is offline, unable to process it, does it somehow still dissipate? Or does it stay with us, locked away in our subconscious as we go about life, unaware of the trauma we're lugging around?

Be-BLAH, be-BLAH, went the bird outside our window. "Hey!" went the 4 Non Blondes. Alison tapped on my forehead with her fingernail. I opened my eyes. She gazed at me with a gummy red smile. I raised my arm and, in a swift backhanded motion, smacked her so hard that her mouthful of half-chewed fish flew from her mouth and landed with a wet *plop* sound on the floor. Her eyes widened as her brain registered the smack, her face cycling rapidly through expressions: first shock, then the briefest hint of anger, then amusement. She opened her jaw wide and tilted her head back, shaking the remaining fish into her mouth, cackling like a witch while she chewed.

I sat up and shoved her. She fell off the bed and landed hard on the floor, but her smile remained. She was still holding the box of fish.

"You think this is funny, bitch? You can't go around stealing other people's things!"

"Ha-ha-ha-ha-ha!" She turned the empty box upside down and gave it a shake. "They're all mine now! All mine!"

She wasn't getting away from me again; not today. Fuck Max's rules.

I scrambled out of bed and lunged at her, catching her by surprise. I straddled her and pinned her to the floor. She was choking again. Her eyes were wide with panic as her hands moved to her throat. No matter how hard she tried, she couldn't shout or laugh or speak. She mouthed *I'm sorry, I'm sorry* with tears in her eyes. She struggled against me and tried to bring her hands to her throat in the universal "I'm choking" sign, but I held her arms against the floor.

Her lips were turning blue. "What's the matter, Alison?" I asked again. "You're never this quiet. Is this what it takes for you to finally shut the fuck up?" I released her arms from the floor; she clawed at her throat so frantically that she broke a nail, lodging a half-moon of glittery pink fingernail into the flesh of her neck. Her whole face was turning blue now.

"What do you want me to do? You want me to save you?"

She nodded. Tears were running down her face. God*damn it*. Even when she was dying, Alison looked so pretty. I felt something warm and looked down to see a wet spot spreading across her thighs as her bladder released. "Who's Rip Van Tinkle now, bitch?"

I really enjoyed saying that.

I left her alone on the floor again while I went into the bathroom, probably because there was a large part of me that couldn't bring myself to go through with murder. On the one hand, in spite of Max's "no dying, no killing" rule, it didn't seem like death was very consequential in this universe, so what was the real harm? On the other hand, if I was going to kill somebody, why not Auggie? Alison had the misfortune of being in the wrong place at the wrong time, giving me easier access to the means and opportunity, I guess.

I thought about Louis's description of his abuelo's body compared to Bradd's. Maybe I'd kill Alison and whatever intangible essence she possessed would be contained, and she'd remain whole, herself. But what if she didn't? And what if the day she died, once her essence flaked away into eternity, it became part of a new, alternate universe where Alison's parents had to mourn the death of their kid? All because she was being a bitchy teenager.

I couldn't go through with it. I guess I'm not a killer.

I didn't see her at first when I came out of the bathroom. Our front door was wide open. There was a big, ugly frog in the middle of the threshold.

"Be-BLAH, be-BLAH, be-BLAH," it croaked at me.

"You aren't a bird, you're a *frog*?" I said out loud.

"His name is Carl." Max's voice startled me. I screamed and looked around the room, but I didn't see him or Alison until he raised his head to look at me. "Close the door, will you?" He was crouched over her body in the narrow space between her bed and the wall. She was flat on her back. Completely still. Her eyes were open, flat and unseeing. She looked pretty dead to me.

"What the fuck happened? Did you do this to her?" he asked.

"Why are you even here?"

"I'm not completely incompetent, you know. I keep tabs on things. I do my best to keep the chaos to a minimum so you jackasses don't completely destroy the space-time continuum somehow. I just didn't get here in time to save her."

"I was coming out right now to help. I'll admit, I was going to kill her, but I decided not to go through with it. I didn't want it on my conscience."

"Yet I'm standing over her corpse."

"You didn't rush in to save her, either."

"I have a really bad hangover, Emma. Cut me a break."

We both stared down at Alison. "But she'll be okay tomorrow, right?" I asked. "She isn't, like, dead-dead."

"So only a little bit dead."

"Yeah."

As I looked at her, I tried to determine if her inner light—her essence, or soul, or whatever you want to call it—had gone out, but I couldn't be sure one way or another. Maybe she didn't have one. Maybe she had one, but it was dim.

"I don't want to go to Hell," I told him. I didn't even believe in Hell, but I was still afraid of it.

"I wouldn't worry about that."

"You wouldn't?" I felt tremendous relief. "Good. That makes me feel better."

"Oh, I wasn't saying that because I know there's no reason to worry; I was saying it because what's done is done." He stood up and started walking toward the door.

"Where are you going?"

He looked around. "Me? I'm leaving."

"Aren't you going to help me?"

"Help you? How am I supposed to do that?"

"I mean help me move the body."

He laughed, a full-body laugh, and shook his head. "Most definitely not. Under no circumstances will I, a Black man, take part in the disposal of a dead white teenage girl. Not happening."

"Thanks a whole lot. You're a terrible chaperone. You're a shitty English teacher, too."

"Says the girl who murdered her roommate."

"It was an accident."

"Sure it was. Hey, I'm not a shitty English teacher."

"Yes, you are."

"It isn't my fault you didn't do any of the reading."

"Maybe you should have picked better books. And it wasn't just the reading; it was everything. Fifty new vocab words every week. All the fucking sentence diagramming. Way too much Shakespeare."

"I was doing my job! You kids don't make it easy!" He closed his eyes and massaged his temples. "What am I doing here? This conversation is pointless."

"Please help me hide Alison's body."

"I can't do it, Emma. I already told you: I do not dispose of dead white girls. I've spent forty years avoiding the scenario altogether." He glanced briefly at Alison and winced.

"But it's just for today. Just this one time."

"I won't do it."

"I'm sorry I said you were a shitty English teacher."

"You were a terrible student. Your opinion means very little to me."

"I wasn't a terrible student. I got A's and B's in your class."

"Yet you somehow managed to learn nothing. Can we stop talking about this now?" His stomach rumbled loudly, and he winced in pain. "It's time for me to go vote Trump into the White House."

I stared at him. "What?"

"It's my euphemism for taking a shit. Can I use your bathroom?"

"Ew. No."

"Then I need to leave right now."

"Will you at least promise me you won't tell anybody about this?"

"Of course I won't tell anybody."

"But people are going to ask about her. We should say she has a stomach bug."

"Whatever you want, Emma." He winced again. "I have to go. The situation is becoming urgent."

"I hope you shit your pants."

It's harder than you might think to move a dead body. I couldn't leave her out in the open, where anybody would see her from the doorway the minute they turned their head. She wouldn't fit all the way under the bed. I tried to drag her into the bathroom, but I could only budge her a few inches at a time, and with tremendous effort. I also didn't enjoy having to touch her or look at her. She wasn't so pretty anymore.

I found Bradd and brought him back to the bungalow. "Don't be mad," I said before I opened the door.

He gasped when he saw her. "Aw, no!" He made blinders with his hands and looked away. "What the fuck, Emma?"

"Look, I'm sorry. Everybody dies. You do it all the time!"

"But I'm special."

"Alison is special, too, in her own way."

"Not the way she needs to be!" Was he crying? He wasn't crying. "I'm really mad at you, Emma."

"I'm sorry."

"Aw, shit. Poor Alison." He snuck a quick glance at her and grimaced. "Wow, she looks *ugly*."

"She's dead, jackass. Can you help me hide her somewhere? Maybe in the shower?"

He shook his head. "Bad idea. She's going to start smelling real gross as soon as it warms up outside. Then the flies will show up, and they'll bring their friends. They'll eat her starting with the softest tissue." He gave me a somber look. "Her eyes."

"All that will happen in a single day?"

He nodded, slowly and decisively. "Indeed it will."

"How do you know?"

"Because I've killed a bunch of people here, Emma."

Of course he had. "Like who?"

"Well, I killed your boyfriend—excuse me, your ex-boyfriend—last night."

I was oddly touched. "You did? For me?"

"I sure did. I waited until he was fast asleep, and then I crept over to him and shouted, 'Boo!' and when he opened his eyes, I stabbed him in the ear with a screwdriver."

"Jesus Christ, Bradd. Flathead or Phillips head?"

"Phillips head."

I shuddered. "That seems extreme."

"It *was* extreme," he admitted. "I didn't enjoy it. He put up quite a struggle. It was a fucking mess. And then I had to fall asleep next to the body. So I guess now I know not to do that again." He paused. "I mean I won't use a screwdriver again. Maybe next time I'll use a garrote."

"I'm not sure you ought to be killing anybody except yourself." I paused. "You probably shouldn't be killing yourself, either."

He rolled his eyes. "Okay, Mom."

"I'm serious! Don't you remember what Max said? There's only one rule: no dying, no killing."

"That sounds more like two rules to me."

"But it seems like a reasonable guideline to follow, doesn't it?" The fact was, regardless of the consequences, I didn't like having anybody's death on my conscience. Not even Alison's. Not even if it was only temporary.

Bradd scoffed. "Oh, please. Time is a flat circle. There are no rules. Now, are we moving this body together or not?"

Bradd was efficient and businesslike as we worked. He made an excellent helper, actually. We moved Alison's bed to make some room and spread her pink comforter out on the floor, and then we dragged her body to the middle of the blanket and used it to drag her across the floor instead of having to carry the dead weight. "This is how the Egyptians built the pyramids," he told me. We rolled her body up inside the blanket and secured it with a few of her own belts. We waited until the coast was clear and carried her into the woods. Bradd said a quick prayer over her body.

"I'm really sorry," I told him again.

"I know you are."

"Bradd, I need to get out of here. I want to go home. I think we can figure it out if we work together. Don't you want to go home?"

"Now that Max is trying to take all the fun out of things, I'm starting to consider it." He paused. "I do really miss my dog."

"Then help me. You're an inventor. Think creatively."

"Emma, we aren't going to figure it out. If it was the cocaine, we don't have access anymore." He paused. "It doesn't make sense that it would be the cocaine, does it? I think we might be getting jerked around."

"Of course we're getting jerked around. You think Gus or Greta is going to tell us the truth? We can't trust anything they say. But, Bradd, we still need to try to find a way out. I know you can help me. Please?"

"You literally just murdered my girlfriend." He brightened. "Hey! We're murder buddies *and* time buddies now!"

"It was manslaughter at worst, and I've told you how sorry I am three times now. At least I didn't use a screwdriver."

"That's fair. But look, I don't want you doing it again. Kill Auggie, or Lucy, or *please* kill Connor Cackowski, but Alison is off-limits. Agreed?"

"If I promise not to kill Alison again, will you promise not to kill Auggie again?"

"Come on!" He stomped his foot. "Auggie deserved it!"

"Nobody deserves that. I think we should listen to Max. We should both stop killing people. Even Auggie."

"Don't tell me how to live my life."

"Will you at least try to help me find a way out of here?"

"I mean, I'm willing to try, but I think you should keep your expectations low. I'm not a time wizard. I've never told anybody this before, not even Alison, but I can't even read a watch."

I didn't dwell on the last part. "Thank you. Can we start now?" My mind was racing as a thought hit me. "I have an idea."

"What is it?"

"I think you should meet the octopus."

I got more and more excited the closer we got to Sibyl. This felt right; this had to be it. By the time we were outside her door, I had almost completely forgotten about Alison. "I can't believe you haven't met her yet! I'm so jealous you're meeting her for the very first time! She's so pretty! She's telepathic!"

"I guess we'll see," he said, doubtful. The door to the structure containing her aquarium was deadbolted shut. It was easy enough for him to break the lock with a hammer, but it made a ton of noise.

I looked around for anybody who might have heard all the ruckus. "We're going to get caught now."

But somehow, we didn't get caught.

Sibyl's body was curled up in a corner of her tank, her tentacles piled into bumpy ropes of mottled red flesh. Each tentacle's underside was lined with rows of pulsing suction cups. Her translucent head (Greta says it's called a "mantle") was reminiscent of a bust of Nefertiti. Her eyes widened with curiosity and her gaze followed us as we approached her tank. Her tentacles unfurled, ribbonlike, and she crept toward us.

I pressed my palms against her tank. Sibyl raised a single tentacle in what seemed to be an obvious greeting. She remembered me.

"Hi, Sibyl," I whispered to her. "I missed you." I looked over my shoulder at Bradd. "Come and get a better look at her. Isn't she beautiful?"

His face was quickly turning an unpleasant shade of green. "My God, no. She's hideous." He shook his head and shuddered with repulsion. "Fucking *hideous*."

"She isn't hideous. Don't say that."

"Why? She can't hear me!"

"Yes, she can." *(Remember your miracle.)* "I told you, she can read our minds. Whatever Gus gave you was made from her."

"She looks like somebody ran a dick three-quarters of the way through a paper shredder."

"You shut your goddamn mouth."

"I'd rather eat roadkill."

I couldn't believe him. "Put your hands on the glass," I commanded, "and listen to her. Do it!"

He took another big step backward instead. "Nuh-uh. I don't want to go anywhere near her."

"You have to be kidding me."

"I'm not kidding you at all. I don't like the way she's looking at me. I feel like she wants something from me." He hugged himself. "I've seen enough. I want to get out of here. Oh, I don't like this at all."

"Bradd, what if we need to set her free? She has to be the key to all of this somehow."

"Doubtful."

"Do you think so?"

"Yes, I do. Put your fucking thinking cap on for a minute, Emma. Would Greta have left a magic octopus just sitting here if she held the secrets to everlasting life? No way. Not a chance. Just like Willy Wonka didn't let those kids go wandering around his factory unattended."

"Maybe she didn't think we would figure it out. Or maybe she *wants* us to figure it out." For the first time, it occurred to me that I could simply ask Sibyl, in a way. "You know what? Maybe Sibyl will tell me."

"How? With her *mind*?" Bradd was backed up all the way to the door; he looked ready to flee at any moment.

"Yes, with her mind. We're connected."

"Be careful, Emma. I'm telling you, I'm getting kind of a Rumpelstiltskin vibe from her."

"You're wrong."

"I don't think so. You know, I'm an excellent judge of character."

"So you've said."

I took slow steps forward until I was standing with my palms and forehead against the glass. I waited.

"I feel like I'm watching a really fucked-up prison visit," Bradd muttered.

"Would you shut up? I need to concentrate."

"Sure, Emma, give the undead sea mutant unfettered access to your subconscious. What could possibly go wrong?"

I was face-to-face with Sibyl; there was nothing separating us except the glass. Her eyes were those of an all-seeing entity adrift in an endless ocean of time, trapped for eternity in what amounted to a tomb. They were sad eyes. Her loneliness washed over me. Of course she was sad. She was a prisoner, suffering all alone so Gus could achieve his own immortality by using her to make himself a savior for mankind.

I felt a tingling sense of pressure between my eyes. I saw the wonders within Sibyl's mind. Time exploding like fireworks. The vast loneliness that was suffocating her. Gus had stumbled across a link to the sacred unknown, and he had stolen it.

"We have to set her free."

"Have fun with that."

"You're going to help me, Bradd."

"Ew. No way."

"Okay"—I shrugged—"when I kill Alison again tomorrow, I'm using a screwdriver."

He gasped. "You wouldn't do that. You promised!"

"Try me."

I could tell he was agonizing over the decision. A flicker of doubt crossed my mind. Could I be wrong about Sibyl? I wasn't wrong.

"I won't help you. And you won't kill Alison," he finally declared, "especially not with a screwdriver. You're too soft."

"Yes, I will. I'm going to kill her with a screwdriver. Then I'm going to cut off her head and put it on your pillow while you're sleeping." We both knew I was lying.

He pointed at the tank. "I'm telling you, Emma. That thing is, like, an interdimensional force of chaos. I don't think you should touch it."

"Her," I corrected him. "She's a girl."

"Jesus Christ. Whatever. Please accept my apology for misgendering the water demon."

"Nothing bad is going to happen if we touch her. I've already touched her. I already *ate* part of her. And Gus injected you with, like, a time serum that came from her body. We've already been exposed."

He stayed firm. "I won't do it. I'm scared of her. And I'm not scared of anything."

"Fuck you."

"Do you know who you remind me of right now? You remind me of that guy who went to the middle of nowhere in Alaska so he could live with a bunch of grizzly bears. Guess what happened to him?"

"Gee, hmm, I don't know. Let me guess: did he get eaten by grizzly bears?"

"He got eaten by grizzly bears."

"This is different."

"You're making a mistake," he said.

"Maybe I am, but I'm still going to try. You can't talk me out of it."

"Then you're doing it alone. I'll say 'I told you so' in the morning."

Emma

Day 33

Louis was sitting alone on the beach. It was almost sunset. He was staring at something in his hands. I crept up behind him with Maggie the mermaid's head clutched to my chest. I'd stolen it from Louis's bungalow only moments earlier, much to Connor Cackowski's disapproval. *(Evidently you think you can waltz right in here and help yourself to Louis's possessions?)*

I ducked behind a thicket of branches and lifted my arms in the air so all he could see was Maggie's disembodied head. "Louis," I crooned in a high voice, "ohhhhh, Louisssss…"

He swiveled, then started at the sight of Maggie's head. "Jesus!"

"It's only me!" I burst from my crouch to a standing position and chucked the head in his direction. He didn't raise his hands to catch it; instead, he ducked. The head landed with a heavy plop in the wet sand.

I took a seat beside him on the beach and pulled my knees

into my chest. I thought about resting my head on his shoulder—we were sitting close enough together for me to do it easily, with just a tilt—but I stopped myself. He didn't remember what I knew happened between us.

I gazed at his hands in his lap. He was grasping a small yellow comb. A few of its teeth were broken.

"What's that?" Our shoulders were almost touching.

Louis stared at the comb. "It was my brother's."

"Oh." I wasn't sure what else to say. It was so sad. But I needed Louis to open up to me—now more than ever. Even if I had to convince him of the same thing every day, over and over again, I was determined to get through to him somehow.

He was worth it.

"There's so much I need to tell you, Emma." He put the comb back into his pocket.

"You mean about your parents?"

He was startled. "How did you know about that?"

"I know." I paused. "And I know you had a dream about me last night. I was walking on the beach, and you were following me. There were octopuses all over the sand. I was helping them get back into the ocean."

Louis's eyes were huge in the moonlight. "This is impossible."

"I have a lot to tell you, too. Louis, I've been living the same day over and over again for weeks. Every day, I wake up and it's Friday all over again. I don't know how to escape, but I have an idea."

He looked at me doubtfully. "I don't believe you."

"That's all right," I said calmly, "there's plenty of time. But can you do something for me just for now?"

"Like what?"

"Can you pretend to believe me? You don't have to mean it. Just pretend. Just for today."

"But why?"

"Because I'm lonely." My voice broke a little as I realized how true it was. "And because I need your help with something. Your dream last night, the octopuses on the beach. It needs to happen for real—tonight."

"Emma, I'm not in the mood for games."

"This isn't a game. You said you'd pretend it was real, just for today. Promise me you'll pretend."

He sighed. "Just for today?"

"Just for today."

We waited until the island was fully cloaked in darkness. We took careful steps along the path, squinting to see the ground in front of us in the moonlight. Louis was unusually quiet. When we reached the door to Sibyl's room, he saw the broken padlock and hesitated. "Is there really an octopus in there?"

"Of course there's an octopus. Did you think I was making it up?"

"I don't—I don't know what I thought," he admitted.

"But you're going to help me, right? Louis, I really need your help."

"Of course, Em." He still seemed a little reluctant. "And you think this will help you by somehow resetting time?"

"I don't actually know," I admitted, "but it's an idea."

What if I didn't do it correctly? I was feeling my way around in the dark, pretty much both figuratively and literally—I knew it, but I had to try. I had to keep trying until something worked.

Louis glanced behind him, nervous. "Can we hurry? I don't want us to get caught."

I didn't want to push him too hard. I didn't want him to run away again. "Okay," I said, "there's a wheelbarrow around the corner. It's leaning against the outside of Gus and Greta's house. I need you to go get it and bring it inside. We'll scoop up Sibyl, put her in the wheelbarrow, and take her to the ocean."

"What if someone sees me?"

"They won't see you if you're careful."

"Emma, I...I'm not sure I like this." He was getting skittish, which made me nervous. A small part of me felt like I was forcing things.

"Louis, you promised." I gave him a pleading look. "Just go get it, please? It's an adventure. An adventure of Louis and Emma."

He stared at me for a minute. I couldn't tell what he was thinking. "Okay," he finally said.

He disappeared into the dark for what felt like an agonizingly long time, but in reality he was gone no more than a few minutes. I dragged the stepstool next to Sibyl's tank, found a long-handled net in a corner of the room, and got into position. I opened the heavy lid of the tank and stared inside. Sibyl was close to the surface of the water, almost like she'd been waiting for me.

"Tell me this is going to work," I whispered to her.

Louis reappeared, pushing the wheelbarrow through the wide doorway. Thankfully, it fit. Using a bucket, I scooped some water into the wheelbarrow, then grabbed Sibyl in the net and lowered her gently toward the ground. She slid herself into the wheelbarrow with a wet *plop*.

Louis stared at her. "That's the immortal octopus?"

"Telepathic, too." I couldn't tell what Louis's reaction to her was. Would he freak out the way Bradd did? He was just still staring at her, almost in a trance.

Admittedly, at the moment there didn't seem to be anything all that special about Sibyl. She just sat there like…well, not unlike an amorphous flesh blob as we wheeled her onto the beach, careful not to topple the wheelbarrow as we steered it over the rocks and sand. Once we were at the water's edge, I kneeled down next to her. I let her tentacle curl around my fingers. The feel of it made tears pool behind my eyes.

"Be free, Sibyl," I whispered.

Then I tilted the wheelbarrow forward, and Sibyl slipped into the water and disappeared beneath the surface.

We watched the water bubbling and then going calm again where she had disappeared. We couldn't see her below the dark waves.

"Now what?" Louis asked me quietly.

Now I was hoping that he'd kiss me, or confess how he felt—because I knew he felt it, too—but we just stood there, silent, and I knew it wasn't the right moment for me to speak up. There was always tomorrow, right? Unless this worked, in which case…there was still tomorrow.

If what I felt for Louis was real, it would still be there.

Emma

Day 34

It didn't work.

Be-BLAH, be-BLAH, went Carl the frog. Alison choked on my Swedish Fish. I didn't shove her. I decided to let her live. Unlike other mornings, she made little conversation as she got herself ready for the day. For once, she didn't play any music. Even as she applied her red lipstick, she was unusually somber, seeming lost in thought. When I asked what was wrong, she told me she'd had a bad dream.

Was it more than that? Was there part of her that somehow remembered what I'd done?

"Hey," she said, "can we talk real quick?"

I told her I wasn't in the mood. She seemed disappointed. "You'd better start getting ready, then," she said, "or we're going to be late."

"I'm not going to breakfast."

"Why?" she asked. "Is something wrong?"

"It's none of your business." I wasn't about to share anything personal with Alison. I wanted to cry, but I didn't want her to see me. Of course releasing Sibyl hadn't worked. Deep down, I'd known Bradd was right the whole time, but I'd stayed hopeful.

Of course I was back here again.

I don't know why I told her. I needed to tell *somebody*, though, to make it real. I heard myself blurting the words: "It's over between Auggie and me." Of course, *he* still didn't know that yet. If I remembered it happening but Auggie didn't, which version was real? What happened to the "today" that had played out days ago, to me? Where did it go? Is it buried somewhere deep within his subconscious, real but inaccessible, like every stroke of the scalpel during my tonsillectomy?

Alison's eyes lit up with interest. Her melancholy mood lifted in an instant. Something great and fun about Alison: she's a pro at gossip. Something rotten about Alison: she's a pro at gossip. (The devil's radio, as Auggie called it.) Alison was more than your average, catty, shit-talking teenager. She never repeated anything unless she was sure she had her facts straight. The juicier the information, the more thoroughly it had to be verified prior to dissemination. She was like the Anderson Cooper of our delicate social ecosystem.

"This is big, Emma. When did this happen? Tell me everything."

I didn't know where to start. As far as Alison knew, everything had been fine between Auggie and me as recently as last night. I could still remember "last night" so vividly: The adults playing cards in the common area. The way the air was ripe, heavy with a pleasant tension, like a good ache. For me it was more than a month ago. For Alison it was last night. There's no point in asking how reality can be so different for both of us. It simply *is*.

"You know what? Forget it. I shouldn't have said anything."

"Did you find out about him and Shelby?"

"Wait, you knew about that?" I felt humiliated all over again. It was awful. Now I kind of did want to kill her with a screwdriver.

"Everybody knew about that."

"Thanks for telling me."

"Oh, please. You two were never going to last." She changed the subject. "You were talking in your sleep last night."

"I was? What did I say?"

A tiny smile. "Wouldn't you like to know?"

"Alison—"

"You were saying something about an octopus." Pause. "You used to talk in your sleep all the time." She meant when we were kids. When we were friends. Good friends, the kind who spend the night at each other's houses so often that it becomes routine. We used to spend summer afternoons swimming in her pool until our fingers pruned and our shoulders burned. I had my own laundry pile and toothbrush at her house.

Then Rip Van Tinkle happened. It was the beginning of the end for us. There was no big fight, no confrontation. Just the sadness of realizing it was worth it for her to hurt me for whatever thrill or social currency she gained in return. We've never talked about it in detail.

"You say the weirdest shit sometimes. One time you said, 'I'll take the one with the waggly tail.' I should have recorded it."

"Why? To play it over the loudspeaker after morning announcements?"

"It's not a big deal, Emma. I'm just saying, you're funny sometimes. Auggie isn't funny. His personality sucks. He's always so holier-than-thou. Of course he cheated on you. He sucks."

"He's a terrible kisser, too."

"Ugh. Bad kissers are the worst." She leaned closer. Her eyes sparkled. "How was the sex?"

"We didn't have sex."

"You didn't? You've been dating him all year. What were you waiting for?"

"I guess I was waiting until it felt right."

"Then you would have been waiting forever. What did his dick look like?"

"Jesus, Alison. I'm not telling you about Auggie's dick."

"Why not? Was it ugly? I bet it was ugly. All dicks are ugly. And their *balls.* Ugh. It's like two soft-boiled eggs inside a deflated balloon. Naked men are just so…so *dangly*. And they're all so proud of their genitals, with the dick pics and all. Why do they think we want to see that?"

I didn't disagree with her completely, but I was somewhat taken aback by her over-the-top disdain for the male body.

"Look, Alison, I don't know why I even told you. I don't want to talk about this with you anymore."

"Why not?"

"Because you stole my Swedish Fish."

"I didn't eat all of them." We both looked at the remaining fish, which were scattered across the dirty floor.

"That isn't the point—it's the principle of the thing. They were mine. I asked you not to eat them. They're my favorite candy."

"I know. They're really good! Why do you think I took them? Plus, I'm addicted to sugar."

"You knew I was saving them. You knew I hid them from you. You had no right to take them, but you didn't care. You always do whatever you want, even if it ends up hurting somebody. You knew about Auggie and Shelby, and you didn't tell me. If we were ever really friends, you would have said something."

"You're right. I'm sorry." It was the first time she'd given me anything close to a genuine apology or shown any remorse. "I know I shouldn't have taken the fish. I'll buy you more when we get home."

I didn't know what to say. I didn't understand her sudden change of heart, which was so different from her usual careless glee. Somehow, she must have remembered something of her brush with death, or even her actual death. (Manslaughter. Not murder.) Perhaps it was imprinted deep within her subconscious on a molecular level, a vague feeling instead of a clear recollection. Whatever it was, something about her had changed.

"Come on, get dressed. Come to breakfast with me," she urged.

"No. I don't want to see Auggie. I haven't actually broken up with him yet."

"He's going to ask about you."

"Tell him I'm still asleep. Or tell him I'm sick—tell him I have explosive diarrhea. I don't care what you say. You can tell him I've flung myself into the sea for all I care."

"Don't be a drama queen."

"I'm upset!"

"Oh my God, you're going to be fine. People break up all the time."

"It's more complicated than that."

"Drama queen. You want me to bring something back for you? Coffee? Something to eat?"

"Whatever. Sure. Thanks." I climbed back into bed and pulled the covers all the way up to my chin, cocooning myself in sheets damp with sweat, silking the silky edge of my sheet. It was barely eight, and the air was already thick with humidity. The clouds outside were gathering momentum; the rain was coming soon.

Alison didn't come back with coffee; instead she sent Lucy Thomas. Why Lucy? Who knows? Probably to annoy me. I was surprised she'd bothered following through at all. I could barely make out the sound of Lucy's hesitant knocks; it was almost like she was hoping I wouldn't hear them.

"Come in!" I hollered.

"Can you let me in?"

Ughhhh. "Just open the door, Lucy."

"I can't. My hands are full."

I wasn't happy to leave my silky, damp cocoon. I stomped across the room to let her in. She carried coffee and two under-ripe bananas.

"Thanks," I said half-heartedly. "I hate bananas."

"Are you sick? You need to eat something. It was this or oatmeal." Pause. "Or oysters." She stepped inside the bungalow and looked around. It was a mess. Clothing scattered all over the floor, hair and makeup supplies cluttering the surface of the dresser. We were told to "pack light." Good luck telling teenage girls that.

There was a stack of magazines on a chair: *Cosmopolitan*, *Vanity Fair*, *People*, *Rolling Stone*. Alison brought photographs, which she'd taped to the wall beside her bed. Bradd and Alison at the Homecoming dance. Bradd and Alison huddled together in front of a fireplace. Alison and her horse, Noodle. Alison and her dog, Grover. Someone (not me, probably Bradd) had drawn a dick on our mirror with lipstick at the beginning of the week. I could wipe it off, but it would just come back. A half-empty bottle of rum was visible in the otherwise bare closet. There were Swedish Fish in flagrant violation of the five-second rule all over the floor.

Lucy took it all in like an anthropologist getting their first look at a newly discovered civilization. Her gaze was full of judgment. She glanced into the bathroom, saw the wet floor, dirty towels, hair dryer plugged in and resting in the sink.

"Why didn't you unpack your things?"

"What do you mean?"

"Your clothing and stuff. Why didn't you put it away when you got here?"

"What, like in the drawers?"

She nodded.

"Umm…because we don't live here."

"I always unpack, even if I'm only staying someplace overnight."

"Good for you."

Here's the thing about Lucy Thomas that eats at me: she isn't unattractive. Like, not even a little bit. And, like a millionaire who chooses to live in a shack on a remote island, she squanders it for no good reason. (Are there any good reasons?)

My mother may have some faulty wiring on the inside, but there's no denying she's a stone fox on the outside. We used to wear matching outfits when I was a kid. Back when there were moments, even sometimes whole days, when I could tell she loved me. Then, in fourth grade, I got a little bit fat. That was the end of our matching outfits and the beginning of a lifetime of constant dieting. (Part of what makes the theft of my Swedish Fish that much worse; I'm not allowed to eat sugar at home.)

Lucy Thomas played Dolly in the spring musical, *Hello, Dolly!* I was part of the background dancers. To this day, my mom talks about "that beautiful Lucy Thomas." Lucy is built like a game show hostess. She has a body that most women can never hope to achieve without cosmetic surgery. Does she show it off with stylish clothing? No. She dresses like a farmer.

In other words, Lucy is truly beautiful, and she does nothing to take advantage of it. I don't know why this infuriates me so much. And I'm aware, at least on some level, of the fact that *this* is the real reason I don't like her. It's not because of her personality; it's because of *my* personality. I've been jealous of her. I've treated her terribly for no good reason. It isn't okay. I'm not proud of myself.

"Lucy? Why don't you ever do your hair or wear makeup?" I was standing close enough to her face to smell her breath. Her teeth were, of course, straight and white. Her breath smelled of spearmint. *Did she stop at her bungalow on her way here to brush after breakfast? What about before breakfast? She probably flossed, too. She probably flosses after every single meal. She probably flosses after snacks.*

"I'm not allowed. My parents are strict."

"Well, that sounds awful. Don't they realize you're almost an adult?"

"I *am* an adult. I turned eighteen last month." She narrowed her eyes at me. "Don't you remember? I brought cupcakes to homeroom."

"I remember." They were *carob* cupcakes. Not chocolate, *carob*. Have you ever tasted carob? It tastes like chocolate that has already been cycled through somebody's digestive tract.

"Is your stomach upset? Ali said—"

"Ali?"

She blushed. "Alison."

"So, what, you two are friends now?"

Lucy bit her lip. "Something like that."

Suddenly, it all made sense: Alison's contempt for the male body; her bizarre offer to let me have sex with Bradd; her over-the-top, relentless teasing of Lucy; her love of jigsaw puzzles. Oh my God. The *song*! Alison loves "What's Up"; she loves 4 Non Blondes. She loves Lana Del Rey and Girl in Red. She loves *oat milk*, for Christsakes. How have I never realized? Alison likes girls.

"I won't say anything," I assured Lucy.

"There's nothing to say! And even if there were… It's complicated. Alison is complicated."

I snorted. "She is not complicated. She's a psychopath. She's so mean to you!"

"She isn't that mean to me."

"She isn't nice!"

"Sometimes she isn't nice," Lucy admitted, "but she's different when it's just the two of us."

"That…doesn't make it any better."

"She's confused."

"Don't make excuses for her. Lucy, listen to me: Alison is the *worst.* She's shallow; she's mean; she's superficial; she's a gossip. Have you ever heard somebody call me Rip Van Tinkle?"

"Yes."

"That's because of Alison! Alison gave me that nickname when I wet the bed at her house in elementary school!"

"There are worse nicknames."

"You sound like you have Stockholm syndrome. Stand up for yourself! Alison assumes she's the main character in every situation, but the truth is she's more like sidekick material. Deep down, she probably knows it, too."

Lucy looked like she was considering it for a second. "Alison really likes you, Emma," she eventually said. "She has nothing but kind things to say about you."

This made me pause. I almost felt bad. Almost.

"I think she has some growing up to do, that's all," Lucy continued. "It's scary to let yourself be vulnerable. It's like she thinks being mean is a way to show affection. Like boys teasing girls on the playground because they like them."

"We aren't kids on a playground."

"I know that. You know that. I don't think Alison knows it yet. She'll figure it out."

I was shocked. I was agape. "That's awfully magnanimous of you."

"Look, Emma," Lucy said, sounding very serious all of a sudden. "When you realize the person you want to be with—when you *really* know—nothing else matters. Like they say, love is blind. It makes fools of all of us." She shrugged. "Sometimes you just have to lean in with your whole self and do whatever it takes. Because you know in your heart the other person is worth fighting for."

Her words hit me right in the gut.

She glanced at the mug on my nightstand. "Your coffee is going to get cold."

"I need to brush my teeth first."

"Actually, it's best to wait until after you've eaten breakfast to brush your teeth. Otherwise the sugars will—"

"Okay, that's enough. Get the fuck out of here."

Emma

Day 34

I was sipping my lukewarm coffee, which tasted as described by Max, when there was another knock. Louis did one of those light knuckle-taps at the door as he cracked it open a few inches and peeked inside. “Emma? I came to check on you. Are you feeling okay?”

“No.”

“Can I come in?”

“Yes.”

Like Lucy a few minutes earlier, Louis looked around at the mess. Unlike Lucy, there was no flash of judgment in his eyes. “What a dump,” he said cheerfully. He sat down beside me. I was still in my pajamas. My hair and teeth were unbrushed. My heart was pounding like I’d taken some of Bradd’s cocaine.

“I’m okay.” I made a fake pouty face. “Except Alison stole my Swedish Fish last night.”

Louis looked at the floor littered with Swedish corpses. He couldn't muster the energy to pretend to care. "That monster."

"It isn't funny, Louis. I was saving those until they were the perfect level of stale." Any true Swedish Fish lover knows that said fish are best when they've been properly aged. You want them hard, almost brittle on the outside, while the innards stay chewy.

"What is it with you and Swedish Fish? They're so mediocre."

I couldn't stop thinking about our kiss. The way it had felt when his arms were wrapped around me. The way he smelled. The sound of his heartbeat against my chest. The warmth of his body. Could he remember anything at all, even in an abstract way? It had happened to Alison. Surely there was a part of Louis that had retained some awareness, however deeply buried it might be. Right?

Even if he didn't remember, it didn't change what he'd said. It happened. It was real.

It was real to me.

I rested my head on his shoulder, trying to ease us back into the comfort zone we'd found ourselves in on previous days. This time, his body stiffened with discomfort. He turned his head away. "God, Emma, you need to brush." He stood up so quickly that I almost fell over. "I should go."

"Why? You just got here."

"Yeah, but I'm supposed to be down at the beach." I noticed him trying not to look at my pajama top, which was buttoned crookedly and gaping at my chest.

"What if—what if I wanted you to stay?"

He gave me an uncertain look. "What do you mean?"

"We could spend the day together." I swallowed. "It's our last day."

"I don't think Auggie would like that."

"Who cares what Auggie wants? Maybe I don't want Auggie." I looked at the floor. "Maybe I want you."

There was a long pause. "That isn't funny, Emma."

"I know he's cheating on me. I know you know about it. Why

didn't you tell me?"

"What are you talking about? Where is all this coming from?"

"I know you had a dream about me last night."

Another pause. "How did you know about that?"

"I know a lot. Please, sit down, talk to me— Louis?" He was shaking his head and backing away like a cornered animal.

"This is too weird," he said.

"No, it isn't. If you'll just let me explain, I promise it will all make sense! Auggie and I don't make any sense, you're right—you've always been right about that. But you and me—"

"Emma, stop it. You can't use me to make Auggie jealous. It's... degrading."

"That isn't what I'm doing! Listen to me—in your dream last night, I was walking on the beach, and you were following me. Isn't that right? Please stay with me. Louis, I don't want to be alone. You're my best friend. I need your help. Please don't go."

"I ate a weed gummy before breakfast. It's starting to kick in, and this conversation is really messing with my head."

"Would you just listen to me? Please? You don't have to say anything. You just need to listen."

He sat on Alison's unmade bed. "Okay, I'm listening."

"Something really wild is happening to me, and I want to tell you, but you aren't going to believe me."

"Try me."

"I'm stuck in a time loop."

"Like *Groundhog Day*?"

"Exactly like *Groundhog Day*. But not just me. Max too. And Bradd."

"You're right. I don't believe you."

"Then how did I know about your dream? And how could I know that Max told everybody to go to the beach after breakfast to collect trash? He did, didn't he? How would I know that if I wasn't there?"

"Because you're fucking with me, and you're doing a really good job at it."

"I can tell you what everybody was wearing this morning. Max was wearing khaki shorts and a Beastie Boys T-shirt. Bradd was wearing swim trunks and a yellow polo shirt. Lucy Thomas spilled her orange juice."

"No, she didn't."

"Well, she usually does. Not everything is exactly the same every day. There are always little differences."

"Did you hit your head or something? Let me see your pupils."

"I know your parents are getting a divorce."

He stared at me.

When you realize the person you want to be with...

"Louis, I've been in love with you since the tenth grade. I thought I had no chance. Then you kissed me yesterday. Or a few Fridays before this Friday. Whatever."

"I kissed you," he echoed.

"Yes. It was nice. It was better than nice."

"Why are you telling me this, Emma?"

"Because I want you to kiss me again. I'll brush my teeth first."

"You're still with Auggie."

"No, I'm not. He hit me yesterday."

"He *what*?"

"It's so, so over between us. He just doesn't know it yet."

"Did he hit you before or after I kissed you?"

"Before."

"How did you—and Max and Bradd—get stuck in a time loop? Why is it only the three of you?"

"It's a long story. It has to do with cocaine and a sentient, immortal octopus."

Louis paused, absorbing the information, but didn't comment on it. "Will you be trapped here forever?"

"I don't know. I hope not. I really want to go home."

He studied my face, the tiniest of grins teasing at his lips. "This is a weird way to hit on someone, you know."

I covered my face with my hands. "It's the truth."

For a minute, I watched him through my fingers as he seemed to actually be considering the possibility that I was being honest. Then his expression changed, and I could tell he didn't believe a word I was saying.

"I'm sorry, Emma. This is too much right now. I'm too stoned for this."

I stood up suddenly. "Just kiss me, Louis. Please? I know you want to. I know because you told me so yourself."

"Stop it. This isn't right." He got up and started toward the door again. He paused with his hand on the doorknob, like he was about to say something else. But all he did was shake his head. Then he was gone.

Louis avoided me all afternoon, while I avoided Auggie. I couldn't concentrate during my afternoon chess game with Gianluca, which I'd been keeping up with on a daily basis, though I still beat him easily. He raised an eyebrow and winked, wagging his finger at me in playful admonishment. "Naughty girl... How can you defeat me if I am only today teaching you to play the game?"

"Pretty good, huh?"

"Excellent. Look at your big sexy brain." He watched me with great interest as I reset the pieces on the board. His smile turned downward at the corners. "Where is Emma's happy face? You are sad."

"I am a little bit sad," I admitted.

"Tell Gianluca your troubles, smart girl."

"It's nothing. Just boy trouble."

"Ahhh." He held a finger to his lips and closed his eyes in thought. I waited. Finally he said, "This is why you have the problem. Boy trouble is big problem."

"Well...yeah, I know. I just told you that."

"No, no." He shook his head. "You are misunderstand me. In my country we know the ways of love. I am expert. You have troubles because he has heart of little boy, not man." He held his fingers a few inches apart. "He is little, little boy."

"Who? Auggie?"

"Pffft." Gianluca rolled his eyes at the mention of Auggie's name. "He is clumsy lover, no? Do not answer. It is clear as nose on a face. He is show pony. You need stallion."

Emma

Day 35

B*e-BLAH, be-BLAH*, went Carl the frog. Alison's jaw went *chomp-chomp-chomp* on my Swedish Fish before choking on her mouthful. "What's Up" assaulted my ears while Alison braided her hair. I was ready to throw her speaker out the window again if she played the song for a second time, but this morning was different. After an interminable four minutes, the song tapered into blissful silence. I braced myself for a replay. Instead, Taylor Swift began to croon about whether it was over now while I brushed my teeth and washed my face, followed by "Single Ladies" while I got dressed, and finally "Rocket Man" as I did my makeup.[3]

---

3 I always get stuck on the line in "Rocket Man" where he sings about not understanding the science of his job. Surely you ought to understand the science of space travel, Rocket Man! You're an astronaut! Space is literally your job! Not to mention the part where he talks about raising his kids on Mars, but with no one there to raise them. You are there, Rocket Man! You are their father! You raise them!

I didn't so much as look in Auggie's direction when I sat down at breakfast. When he tried to touch me, I nudged him away. When he talked to me, I ignored him.

"Hey, Lucy," Bradd said, "did you know if you tilt your head back and pretend you're shaking salt onto your tongue, it tricks your brain into actually tasting it?"

"Really?" She gave him a cool look. "Show me."

"Huh?"

"Show me. I want to see you try it."

"Well, uh…no." He'll probably be running the country someday. I pictured him in a claw-footed tub in the White House, the H2Blow strapped to his ridiculous face, fellating himself while mulling over his foreign policies. Maybe not the president we need, but the president we deserve. I can already imagine his campaign slogan: *Go fuck yourself, America.*

"Emma, why are you ignoring me?" Auggie asked loud enough that there was no question of whether or not I heard him. I pretended to be fascinated by my oatmeal and said nothing.

"Hey, Emma, why don't you answer your boyfriend?" Alison's eyes sparkled with excitement at the prospect of conflict.

I am not a good public speaker and probably never will be. I didn't have a specific plan when I stood up, hoping inspiration would strike. All eyes were on me. I could still feel the sting of Auggie's hand against my cheek. I had the attention of everybody in the room.

I tried to think of the worst possible thing a person could accuse another person of being. What was so bad that it would be worthy of an immediate breakup? Slapping me was bad enough, but I couldn't say that—Auggie would deny it, which would only be fair, since he had no memory of it.

Then it dawned on me. Of course. "Um, there's something I need to share, and I want all of you to hear it. Auggie, I know I could have done this privately, but I wanted witnesses." Deep breath. "Auggie and I are broken up. I wish I could say things just didn't work out, but unfortunately that isn't the case. The truth is that Auggie is…a… Nazi."

All eyes shifted to Auggie, with his blond hair and blue eyes and western European heritage.

"I'm not a Nazi!" he insisted. "Emma, tell them I'm not a Nazi!"

"Then why do you call your penis *mein erection*? And why do you have a hamster named Adolf?"

"I don't have a hamster named Adolf! I don't even have a hamster!"

Bradd, picking up what I was putting down, chimed in to help. "It's true, guys. Auggie does have a hamster named Adolf." He glared at him. "What's even worse is that he used to have *two* hamsters. They were brothers. But one of them had a lazy eye, so Auggie killed it. You know, because of how the Nazis love eugenics." He winked at me. I gave him a subtle thumbs-up.

"I don't know what they're talking about. I am not a Nazi. Emma, you know that isn't true! Tell them I'm not a Nazi!" Auggie looked like he was on the verge of tears. "I have never been a Nazi. I am very, very, *very* anti-Nazi," he insisted loudly.

Bradd scoffed. "That sounds exactly like something a Nazi would say."

I wanted to leave then—as much as I wanted to devastate Auggie, watching him flail was too much secondhand embarrassment for me to take—but I wasn't quite finished. "Auggie, I never loved you. I never even liked you all that much, to be honest. You're arrogant and condescending." Finally, I looked him in the eyes. "And you're disloyal."

He was too stunned to respond.

The room was dead silent as I turned and walked away, hurrying toward the door, all buzzed up on adrenaline from violating the social contract so flagrantly. My ears were ringing from the rush of it all. I didn't know where I was going, but I didn't stop until I reached Gus and Greta's house, making a beeline toward the shed in their backyard. At least I could take comfort in the kittens.

• • •

Greta found me soon afterward. She gave me a sympathetic smile from the doorway as I scooted myself all the way against the wall of the shed, trying not to disturb the kittens. "Get away from me. You're a murderer."

"I'm not a murderer, Emma." Kitler was still perched on my shoulder; Frick and Frack were curled up in my lap. Greta scooped the mama cat into her arms and cradled her like a baby. "The kittens get all the attention. This girl needs some love, too." The cat purred contentedly and nuzzled Greta's cheek.

"What do you want, Greta?"

"Will you come inside with me?" she asked. "There's something I want to show you."

"Are you going to hurt me?"

She leveled her gaze at me. "No. I promise."

I don't know why I believed her. But reluctantly, I put the kittens down and followed her. We took the long way into her house, walking through the area with all the oyster tanks on our way. The room was like a huge beating aquatic heart: rows and rows of tanks, a pump for each tank, every tank layered with winding ropes of new oysters. All those delicate slivers of flesh blooming inside crusty old shells. There's something magical about their life cycles, the way each individual oyster is its own miniature ecosystem. Each one a world of pulsing cellular architecture. When you eat an oyster, you're tasting the flesh of the sea. No two oysters will ever taste exactly the same.

I followed Greta past the tanks and into her house, through the living room, down a short hallway, and into the kitchen. The fridge was covered in old photographs. A much younger Gus had red hair like his daughter's once upon a time, pre–meth Santa. He looked almost normal, but not quite. Young Gus (*young* as in his thirties and forties) wore his greasy red hair in two long pigtails. It reminded me of Louis's favorite joke: What's the worst thing you can hear after giving Willie Nelson a blowjob? I'm not Willie Nelson.

There were lots of photos of Greta as a little girl. She was an adorable, freckle-faced pixie of a child. In some of the photos, she was with a dark-haired woman who I assumed was her mother. Gus wore a wedding ring, but neither he nor Greta had ever mentioned a wife or mother. There were family photos taken in front of landmarks all around the world: the three of them standing in front of the Eiffel Tower, the three of them arm-in-arm outside the Roman Colosseum; little Greta on her father's shoulders at the Great Wall of China, Greta and her parents on an impressive sailboat in the middle of a placid blue sea. Once I had a sense of the chronological arrangement, I could start to see threads of this family's story.

There were no photos of Greta's mother after Greta was maybe ten or eleven. Whether she died or simply left was unclear. What *was* clear was that things started to go downhill once she disappeared. There were a few photos documenting Greta's decision to really lean into a goth phase. Her hair was dyed an oily jet black. Black fingernails, black lipstick, black eyeliner. No smile, not even on her mouth, let alone any trace of happiness reaching her eyes. She went from a healthy, curvy teenager to a gaunt young woman. Around the same time, according to the photos, Gus's hair began to go white. Something bad must have happened.

"That's Madeline. My mom." Greta pointed at the dark-haired woman. "I thought she was the most beautiful woman in the world. I guess most little girls feel that way about their mothers. She was way out of my dad's league, wasn't she? But oh, he loved her so much." Pause. "She was a great mom."

"Um."

"My dad's family didn't want him to marry my mom. He's a very rich man, you know, and he comes from an even richer family. Old money, you see. They were snobs. They assumed my mother must be after my dad's money. They called her an interloper, tried everything in their power to break my parents apart. In the end, all it did was ensure my father never spoke to any of them again.

"When I was a kid, it used to feel like we had the whole world in the palms of our hands. We traveled all over the globe together, as you can see. We were so happy. Then my mom got sick. I was thirteen. That's when everything started to fall apart."

"How did she—"

"She started getting headaches. Migraines, we thought. Plenty of people think they've had a migraine, but most people have no idea what they're talking about. Do you know what true, chronic migraines are like? There were days when she could do nothing but lie still in a dark room without any outside stimuli. Sometimes she vomited until she got so dehydrated that she needed IV fluids to keep her muscles from seizing and her kidneys from shutting down. It was like her own personal hell. Her vision would blur to the point where she couldn't see her hand in front of her face. Even the faintest whisper of sound was agony to her ears. I couldn't say *I love you* without hurting her. I couldn't hug her.

"My dad is a brilliant scientist, and he had access to unlimited resources and the best medical care. There was nothing he wouldn't do for her, nothing he wasn't willing to try, no matter how much of a long shot it was. He took her to so many specialists. She tried every kind of pill and therapy, every injection and diet. Nothing helped. Her body became a prison of pain. It was more common for her to be in agony than not. Sometimes she'd get three, four, even five days in a row without pain, but she could never fully enjoy those days. It was always like she was bracing herself for the next wave. Eventually there was nothing anybody could do to help her, not even temporarily. Her life became wall-to-wall pain. And then she died. She took her own life, Emma. My father never told me, and I understand why, but I knew. She died, and our hearts broke, and I thought they would stay broken forever.

"I was in so much pain, I was willing to do anything to distract myself. I started running wild, disappearing for days at a time. I made the wrong friends, got involved with the wrong boys. Drugs, alcohol, pills—I couldn't bear to be fully conscious, fully present. I became like a stranger to myself, a stranger to my father. And for all his brilliance, my dad didn't have the first clue what to do about it—my mom was always the heart of our family, while my dad was the head—all he knew was that his little girl was slipping away. He thought he was going to lose me. If I'm being completely honest, there were a few times I came close. And if he lost me, he would lose everything.

"He finally pulled me out of school and took me on a sailing trip around the world, just the two of us. It was the only way he could think of to get me away from all the people and things who were poisoning me."

"And somehow you ended up here."

She smiled. "Yes."

"Why are you telling me all this? What difference will it make? I don't care about how any of this happened. All I want to know is: how do I go home?"

"You know I can't answer that." She reached into her pocket. "I didn't bring you here just to show you pictures and tell you my sad stories. I also brought you here because I wanted to show you this." She handed me an envelope folded in half. "I think this belongs to you."

My name was scribbled across the front of the envelope in my own handwriting. Inside was a letter. It read:

Dear Emma,

Your only goal for this year is to have sex. It's the only thing that matters. You cannot go to college a virgin.

Signed,

Yourself

"You read my letter?"

"I read everybody's letters. I found them in Max's room and, well, I've always been nosy. But yours is the only one I kept."

"Why? Because you thought it was funny?"

"No. Because I thought it was sad."

My cheeks felt flushed. "How judgmental of you."

"Maybe so," she agreed. "That's why I chose you, Emma. Because of your letter."

"I don't understand."

"I wanted to give you more time. To grow up. There's so much more to life than sex."

"You—what? You had no right to make that decision for me," I said, fists clenching, vision going a little spotty with anger. "It wasn't up to you."

"That's never stopped me before."

"What you did to me was evil."

"I disagree. In fact, I'd argue it was the opposite of evil. What we've discovered is going to change the world. What we're doing here—what we've found—is so much bigger than you, or me, or even my father. The ends justify the means in this case."

"Yeah, you've mentioned that before."

"Emma, what if we could have helped my mom on one of her pain-free days? It's too late for that now, but I think about it all the time. What if we could have paused indefinitely everything bad that was happening and just been happy together forever? This could give so many people another chance."

"Putting them in a time loop?"

"We're not trying to put people in perpetual time loops. We're trying to create more time."

"Life doesn't work that way. Time doesn't work that way."

"I disagree." She shook her head. "Life is full of miracles. Haven't you realized that yet?"

"You've made me a prisoner."

"No." She smiled. "You've made yourself a prisoner by prioritizing the wrong things."

"What are you saying, Greta? Have you had the answer this whole time? Have you just been keeping it from me?"

"Here's what I will tell you: what you're going through, in a way, is a natural process. And undoing it is also natural, in a way." She paused. "It's kind of like breast milk."

"Like *breast milk*?"

"Yes. Let me finish. You know how they say breast milk is best for babies?"

"Do they? I must have missed that during one of my many pregnancies."

"Yes, they do. Breast milk is perfect. It has everything a baby needs. But some women—lots of women, in fact—can't breastfeed."

"Why? Do they have inverted nipples or something?"

"Some women just can't do it. There are lots of reasons. Low milk supply, difficulty latching... You know what, that isn't important. Just trust me. Anyway, thank God for modern science: we have baby formula for women who aren't able to nurse for whatever reason, right?"

"I'm not sure how lactation has anything to do with—"

"Would you shut up and listen to me? There's baby formula, right? And it's perfectly fine. But it isn't quite the same. Science has come *so far*, but it can't quite replicate the perfect mechanisms of the human body. Now, in your case, you want a cure for the thing that ails you—the time loop you're trapped inside. I'm telling you, Emma, you *already have the cure*."

"And it has something to do with my letter?"

For some reason, this made her giggle. "Oh, I highly doubt that. But also...yes."

"You mean you don't know?"

"Oh, I know." Another pause. "It's something you can do all by yourself."

"But I thought it had to do with my letter."

"It might. But probably not."

"None of this is helpful."

She thought about it some more—I could tell she was trying to get me to read between the lines, but I couldn't quite parse out what she was trying to say.

"Greta, *please give me a better answer.* This is only making me more confused."

"You know, sex is complicated. It's supposed to be about pleasure, but people lose sight of that. Mostly women. We're complicated, too. Men? Not so much. Sex is supposed to be about pleasure," she repeated, "but do you know what the French call an orgasm? *La petit mort.* The little death." She gave me another tiny smile. "Now I've really said too much."

"What are you talking about? Tell me more!"

She held up her hands. "I'm sorry, Emma. That's all I'm going to say. You'll figure it out eventually."

"But I want to go home now!" Then, from the corner of my eye, I spotted something on the other side of the room: a phone the size of a brick, tethered to the wall with a cord. "You have a phone."

"Of course we do. It's a satellite phone."

I thought of home—of my mother, my bedroom, my cat, my life. Tears sprang to my eyes. "I want my mom," I said. "I want to call her."

"I don't think that's a good idea."

"I want to call my mom!"

She stared at me, thinking. "Fine," she said, "go ahead."

But when I went to dial the phone, I realized I didn't know my mom's cell phone number. I don't know *anybody's* phone number. Actually—that wasn't true. I dialed the phone, my hands shaking. It rang once, twice, three times. Then, a sleepy voice: "Hello?"

"Hello?" A dawning horror washed over me as I realized what I'd done. *What I was doing.*

"Gizmo. Don't go on the trip tomorrow."

"Who is this?"

"Emma. Can you hear me? Gizmo. Don't go. Promise me!"

I'd dialed the only number I knew by heart: my own.

Auggie

Friday

Emma knows. I don't know who told her, but she knows. She wouldn't so much as look at me this morning, but I could tell right away that something wasn't right. Toward the end of breakfast—she ignored me the whole time and would only talk to Louis, which I bet he just *loved*—she stood on her chair and clapped her hands to get everybody's attention. This, I knew, was not going to be good.

"I know it isn't cool to kink-shame, but there's something I think all of you should know about Auggie." She pointed at Shelby. "Especially you, Shelby."

Not good. Not good at all.

"I caught Auggie masturbating to a picture of the Cowardly Lion. He was stroking his penis and moaning, *Put 'em up, put 'em up*! And when it was all over, he cried. I can't compete with that, so I guess it's over. He's all yours, Shelby."

Lies. All lies. Lies made worse by the fact that, through sheer coincidence, I have been the Cowardly Lion every Halloween for the past three years.

While everybody was laughing, Alison took off one of her red shoes—I guess you could say it resembled a ruby slipper—and threw it at me. It hit me on the forehead.

I guess I'm single now.

Emma

Day 41

"Auggie doesn't have genitals. No dick, no balls, nothing. He just has an asshole. It's more of a cloaca, actually, like an all-purpose hole. But I'm telling you guys, from the front, he's smooth like a doll down there."

Emma

Day 44

"Auggie likes to keep his food in his body as long as possible. He told me he can tell how it's progressing along his digestive tract based on the tilt of his hips. He likes it when he can feel it reaching his small intestine. Yeah, I know, it's super weird. But it gets weirder. He *names* his meals. He calls them his 'bits and pieces' once they've been chewed and swallowed. The last one—you guys remember the paella from dinner a few days ago—he named it the Duke of Windsor after the guy who abdicated the English throne to marry Wallis Simpson."

(I was inspired by season one of *The Crown*.)

"I feel awful saying this out loud to all of you, but I think he chose that name because the Duke of Windsor and his wife were rumored to be Nazis, you guys. He's especially attached to the duke. He's been limiting his water intake to keep it in his body for as long as he possibly can. It's not safe, Auggie!"

Emma

Day 46

Max pulled me aside as soon as he had the opportunity. "This is all quite entertaining, Emma, but as your teacher, I feel an obligation to intervene."

"I don't care what you say. You aren't in charge of me anymore. I'm going to humiliate Auggie every day for as long as it takes."

"Oh, I'm not telling you to stop humiliating him."

"You aren't?"

"No, no, no. But, Emma, it's getting a bit repetitive, don't you think? Bodily fluids, Nazis…you need to start thinking bigger."

"I'm trying," I said. "I guess I'm just not that imaginative."

"You know—and I hesitate to say this—but perhaps if you'd bothered to do some of the assigned reading this year—"

"Oh my God, would you let it go already?"

"Sorry. I couldn't help myself."

"What do you mean, *think bigger*?"

"All I mean is that you have a huge advantage over Auggie because you have unlimited time," he said. "Get creative! Have fun with it!" He paused for a beat. "And for the love of God, read a fucking book once in a while."

Emma

Day 67

I took Max's advice and expanded my skill set beyond simply humiliating Auggie each morning to ensure he wouldn't try to make nice with me for the rest of the day. I hate to admit it, but Max was right; it's amazing what a person can accomplish with endless time and a little bit of patience. It took me weeks to learn, but this morning I stood at the front of the dining hall and blew into a conch shell to play the first verse of Miley Cyrus's epic ballad "Flowers" without missing a note. It was followed by a smattering of confused applause.

"Do I have everybody's attention? Good." I looked at Bradd. "Are you ready?"

"Ready," he said.

"Then let's do this."

Bradd

Day 65

At precisely nine o'clock, Emma finished playing her song on the conch shell. Briefly, I wondered if it might be the same conch shell I'd had sex with at the beginning of the week. Probably not. What are the chances? While everybody waited to see what was going to happen next, Emma and I walked into the next room, our steps synchronized. Once we were alone, we began to wordlessly remove most of our clothes. We were both wearing black one-piece swimsuits underneath. We took off our shoes and stepped into black high heels. Mine were at least two sizes too small, but I'd managed to squeeze into them.

"I'm so nervous," Emma whispered. "I don't know if I can do this."

I was getting sick of reassuring her. I put my hands on her shoulders. "Hey. Look at me," I said flatly. I was going through the motions with my pep talks by that point. "You've got this, Emma.

Remember, left foot first. Keep your head up. Focus on the music."

We strutted arm-in-arm into the dining hall. "Oh my God," Alison said, "is that my bathing suit?" I winked at her. Even though I knew she was gay, and that she didn't love me the way I loved her, she still had my heart. She gave me a bewildered look. Emma and I ignored the stares and giggles. We stood side-by-side at the front of the room. I cleared my throat. The only person not giving us their undivided attention was Max, who was in a corner reading a book. He didn't even glance up. I looked down to double-check that none of my bits or pieces were sticking out from the sides of my swimsuit. The crowd should be so lucky.

Emma raised her voice to address the room. "Auggie," she said, "this is for you."

I pressed a button on my phone; Beyoncé's "All the Single Ladies" began to play, and Emma and I started to dance. We kicked our legs and shook our asses in perfect unison. It was the result of hundreds of hours of late-afternoon rehearsals and infinite eight-counts and missteps and frustrations. We danced like nobody was watching. We didn't miss a beat. It was transcendent. We were glorious. I might have been better than Beyoncé.

Louis

Friday

The morning was like a fever dream. I don't know where Emma learned to dance or how she and Bradd—*Bradd*, of all people—found time to practice, but they put on one hell of a show. The hip action was significant. Bradd and Emma made a surprisingly captivating pair. I could tell Bradd was giving it 100 percent effort, and he was loving every minute of the attention. He mouthed the words with bright red lips. His short hair was moussed into a high coif. He kept his expression pouty and sly throughout. He didn't miss a step.

But it was still Emma's show. I was confused as hell through the entire thing, of course, but it didn't prevent me from being blown away. Yes, she knew the steps, and she looked great—she looked better than great—but that wasn't what made it so captivating. She locked eyes with me at one point, and her smile felt like it went right through me.

It was like I could feel her body, like she was standing right next to me. I felt her breath on my face and the warmth of her skin, even though she was more than halfway across the room. I had the overwhelming feeling that I missed her, like we'd been apart for a hundred years, and now she was standing so close after an unbearably long and lonely separation. I wanted her to come closer and to stay forever.

Then the song ended. The room went silent.

Emma

Day 67

Bradd and I finished our dance. Then we waited, frozen in position with our hands on our hips, for our peers to react.

"Evidently that was impressive!" said, well, you know who said it by now.

Lily Foose clapped so hard and whooped so loud, I forgave her for making out with Louis in a different life. Almost.

Even Lucy had a slight grin on her face.

Alison was glaring at Bradd, but there was a half smile of pride lighting her eyes. "How did you get my bathing suit?"

Louis was looking at me in awe. Auggie was scowling in half disapproval, half astonishment. I walked over to him.

"We need to talk."

"About what? And what on earth are you doing with Bradd?"

"Auggie, I'm serious."

"Okay. Let's talk, then."

"Not like this." I paused. "Hey—will you play chess with me first?"

He balked. "What, you mean right now?"

"Right now."

"I thought you wanted to talk."

"I do. We can talk while we play."

He was suspicious. He must have known on some level that I didn't want to talk about anything good.

But he followed me into the great hall. We sat across from each other, a small card table between us. I set up the chessboard while Auggie watched.

"But you don't know how to play chess," he protested. "I haven't taught you yet."

I shrugged. "I've been studying on my own this week. I think I figured it out."

"It's not checkers, Emma," he scoffed. "It's a game of strategy, not a game of chance. And I've been playing since I was a kid. You couldn't possibly have 'figured out' its many intricacies in a week."

"Then you should have no trouble beating me." I looked at my watch. I had exactly twenty minutes. "But we need to hurry."

Since I was playing white, I went first. I opened by moving my king's knight. "I like to start by moving my horsey," I said, grinning at Auggie.

"You mean your knight?" He moved his queen's pawn up two spaces.

"I prefer to call it a horsey." I moved a pawn.

Auggie slid one of his bishops toward the center of the board. Gianluca had warned me about this. *"Auggie is messy, messy, messy with bishops. He has no patience."*

A small crowd gathered around us as we played. I continued stealing glances at my watch, keeping a close eye on the time. After fifteen minutes, I knew I had him beat. Gianluca, Mia, Connor, Louis, Lily, and Bradd stood near us in a semicircle, watching as Auggie grew more frustrated.

I took his queen. "Check. Oh—wait, I believe that's checkmate."

I peered at the board. “Yes, it is.”

“Ha!” Bradd, childlike, laughed and pointed at Auggie. “Ha-ha-ha! You lose! You’re the loser!”

Auggie couldn’t believe it; the shock was all over his face. His cheeks were red with embarrassment. “But you—you’re—”

“I’m what? More of a checkers girl?” I grinned smugly, but I felt a twinge of sadness at the same time. I couldn’t believe I was thinking this after everything, but it was too bad things were ending this way. “I need to talk to Auggie alone,” I told the crowd. I looked at Louis. “Can you wait for me outside? I’ll only be”—I looked at my watch again—“I’ll be there in less than five minutes.”

Then it was just Auggie and me, alone in the big, empty room. “Auggie, it’s over.”

He was frowning. “What do you mean?”

“I mean us. I want to break up.”

“But, Emma…why? What about tonight?”

“I don’t want you to be my first.” I paused. “You aren’t special enough. I deserve something real.”

“You—” He seemed genuinely devastated. It broke my heart just the tiniest bit. “You don’t think this is real?”

I stared at him. “I don’t know, Auggie. What does Shelby think?”

His face grew even redder. He lowered his gaze. “I don’t know what you’re talking about.”

“Stop lying to me.”

“I’m sorry, Emma.”

“I’m sorry, too, Auggie. But this is the right thing to do.” I looked at my watch again. I had less than thirty seconds to get outside. “Everything will be okay,” I told him.

“Emma, please don’t do this. We can work it out. I can do better.”

I thought about it for a split second. “I’m sorry, Auggie. That isn’t good enough for me.”

Louis

Friday

I waited for Emma outside the great hall. She came bursting through the double doors and strode toward me, smiling widely. She kicked her shoes off mid-pace in a way that made her seem incredibly free, then continued briskly, guiding me by the elbow as we walked. She was wearing a Mickey Mouse wristwatch that she kept glancing down at.

“Are we late for something?”

“Nope. We’re right on time.”

She stopped when we reached the grassy dune before the beach. “Chinese laundry detergent,” she said. “One broken red flip-flop. Half a Frisbee. A sharp piece of blue plastic about this big.” She held her hands apart a few inches.

“Okay, what the hell is happening right now?”

She grabbed my chin and steered my face so she could look me in the eyes. “Listen to me, Louis. Chinese laundry detergent. One broken red flip-flop. Half a Frisbee. A sharp piece of blue plastic about this big." And she continued walking toward the beach. I stared at her. She looked over her shoulder at me. "Hurry up."

We walked some more. "The devil is beating his wife," she said, shading her eyes to look at the sun.

"What does that mean?"

"Apparently, it's an expression some people use in the South when it rains on a sunny day."

"Gross," I said. "But hey, it isn't raining." As I spoke, I felt a light pelt of fine raindrops hit my face. I shivered. "You're on fire this morning. Want to tell me what's going on?"

She smiled to herself. "We're having an adventure." She slid her arm into mine, slowed her pace, and steered our footsteps closer to the water. I paused to slip my shoes off before they got wet. There was some garbage on the beach, but not nearly as much as there was on the opposite side of the island. The sand was coarse and rocky in some places, so I kept my gaze down and watched my steps while my mind kept wandering back to where the hell she'd learned to dance like that.

"I thought you didn't dance, Emma."

"I do now," she said, lightly kicking up some water, causing little circles to emanate out from where she stood.

We passed a pink plastic jug lodged diagonally in a soggy patch where the tide had only now receded all the way. I leaned over to pick it up. It was buried almost all the way up to its spout and filled with water and sand. It was a bottle of laundry detergent, Chinese characters printed alongside the faded image of a smiling child.

What. The. Actual. Fuck.

I watched Emma as she strolled along nonchalantly in her black swimsuit. Her expression was smug and amused. As she pretended not to notice my shock and confusion, I felt a sudden sense of déjà vu so powerful that I gasped. Like a reflex, tears pricked at the corners of my eyes. The world seemed to tilt on its axis. "Emma, wait," I begged her. "Will you wait a minute?"

She looked at her watch again. "We don't have time." She was calm. She wasn't smirking anymore. Her eyes were kind and searching. "Don't be scared, okay?"

"Okay," I said. But I was scared.

"You had a dream about me last night," she said.

"What the fuck? Am I in a Christopher Nolan movie? I feel like I'm in a Christopher Nolan movie."

"You might be. But I'm here, too, so it's okay. Look." She pointed at the water. I looked. A cracked red Frisbee came skimming in on the surface of the tide.

"Am I dreaming?" I asked. "I'm dreaming."

"You aren't dreaming."

"Am I dead?"

"No."

"Then make it make sense somehow."

"I'll try." She paused for a minute to think. "Do you ever think about God?" she asked me.

"I'm starting to think about him a whole lot right fucking now. Is this—are we— Okay, this is a trick somehow." She and Bradd could have been rehearsing their dance secretly for months back home, which would have been bizarre, but it was the only remotely plausible explanation I could come up with. She could have planted the items on the beach. But how could she know about my dream? Was it just a lucky guess? Is anybody that lucky?

"I never used to believe in God," she continued, "but I'm more ambivalent now. All I know for sure is that I don't know anything. I'm trying to figure it out—I've read almost every book in Gus's library, if you can believe it—but I usually only find myself more confused at the end of the day. I guess I'm trying to figure out what it all means. Like you said—I'm trying to make it make sense. I don't know if that's even possible. I can't even make sense of my own life. Like, I'm trying to grow up, and some days I think I have, but other days I just want to dance to 'Single Ladies' in a black bathing suit with Bradd. You know? I don't know if there's any point in trying to make sense of anything. The more I learn, the more I realize I don't know anything at all." She paused. "Do you believe in destiny?"

"In what sense?"

"Did you know that lots of philosophers think free will is an illusion? I think they might be right. If you imagine God as a supercomputer so powerful that it could analyze every variable from every moment since the beginning of existence at something even more precise than a molecular level, it would know everything that had ever happened and everything that was going to happen."

She was terrifying me. My heart felt like it was going to pound out of my chest. "What are you— Are you telling me you're God? Because you aren't. I could *not* fucking handle that."

"I'm not God. But watch your step." I looked down in time to sidestep a sharp piece of blue plastic the size of my brother's comb.

Suddenly, I was really ready to go home.

The waves lapped at our ankles and splashed our calves. The sun was shining as the rain fell steady and fine in a shimmery mist that only heightened the surreality of everything that was happening. "In your dream, I was walking on the beach just like this, right?" Emma said. "And you were behind me calling my name, but I wouldn't answer you. Or I couldn't."

I actually do think about God and existence and what happens when we die, a lot more than I'd like to. How could anybody not wonder? The thing is that I want badly for life to make sense. I want rules. I want answers.

But she's right, of course. Life makes no sense.

Emma guided me all the way down the beach until we reached the northernmost tip of the island. She led us away from the water and through the grass onto a pebbly path that wound through the woods behind Gus and Greta's house until we reached a small, open shed. She ducked inside. I followed her.

"Look." She pointed at a dark corner where the sunlight didn't reach. All I could make out at first was a dark, squirming mass.

I looked closer. There was a litter of kittens nursing from their outstretched mother, her lean body curved to keep their much smaller bodies nestled close to her.

"Don't touch them," she told me. "Just watch. The mama seems like she's sleeping, but she's still looking out for her babies." Emma squinted at her watch in the dim light. She didn't speak as her eyes followed the seconds ticking by. "Okay… In ten seconds, a big lizard is going to come crawling in here. The mama cat is going to look up and see him— Look, there he is!"

An iguana the size of my forearm crept into the doorway. "The mama cat is going to look up and hiss at him." She was narrating the events a second or two before they happened now. "The iguana is going to get closer and the mama's going to yowl and swipe at him and scratch him across the face and leave a big gash, and he'll turn and run away bleeding as fast as he can."

I could hardly breathe. The quick confrontation between cat and iguana lasted less than a minute and kicked up a low, dense cloud of dust and sand that drifted in a sunbeam coming through the doorway. "What happens next?" I asked.

"Next you'll notice that I have a tiny smudge of dirt on my forehead." There it was, above her right eyebrow.

"How are you doing this?" I whispered.

"I'm a prisoner of time. Today is the last day of the rest of my life, every day, forever."

"That's impossible."

"You always say that."

I wanted to kiss her. I *always* wanted to kiss her, but I was too scared. At the same time, my brain was breaking. "How—"

"Did I become a prisoner of time?" The words appeared in my thoughts as they came from her lips. "I took communion from an immortal octopus. Her name is Sibyl. Would you like to meet her?"

• • •

We stood in front of a massive aquarium. A large octopus stared outward at us, her body suspended in the center of the tank. Her tentacles dangled like vines of rippling flesh. Her head was long and narrow. Slowly, she blinked.

"She's immortal," Emma told me.

"You mentioned that." I couldn't take my eyes off her. I'd never seen an octopus up close. "She looks sad." How could an octopus look sad?

"You'd be sad, too, if you were stuck alone in a tank for the rest of time."

"Why are you showing her to me?"

"Because I want you to believe me. She's magic. She's telepathic. If you get close enough, she can read your mind. She can show you things about yourself."

I wasn't sure how I felt about the idea of letting a magic octopus read my mind. It seemed a little risky.

"It's okay," Emma encouraged me. "She won't hurt you, I promise."

I trusted Emma. Of course I did. "How do I do it?"

"Put your hands against the glass. Try to relax. Let her in."

But I was still hesitant. I put one hand against the tank, barely touching it. Sibyl raised a tentacle and slipped herself into my mind—I don't know how else to describe it. My body didn't go anywhere, but I was nevertheless fully transported. I found myself sitting in the passenger side of Emma's Toyota. We were driving down a highway at night, blasting music and singing along. The song was "Slippery People" by the Talking Heads. Emma was wearing a black sequined dress I'd never seen before and a limp wrist corsage. Her hair was in a messy updo.

I pressed my other palm to the glass and felt Sibyl's sadness lifting away. Her energy rippled through me. I felt her pulse intertwine with mine, producing a symphony of color and sound and motion. Once again, I was transported. I found myself squinting into the sun. I was in a lounge chair on the beach, Emma beside me. It wasn't a memory; we were older. A waiter in a Hawaiian shirt brought over a tray with two frozen drinks. Emma reached for hers, and I saw an octopus tattoo on the inside of her forearm. The same Talking Heads song played from a speaker. Emma lowered her sunglasses and winked at me. "Shh. This is my favorite part."

We both listened as the band sang about turning like a wheel inside a wheel. But instead of the song continuing from there, the last line repeated about turning, and turning, and turning.

My consciousness was yanked from my body on the beach, as if pulled by an invisible force. I could feel Sibyl's sadness pulsing through me again. I felt my whole self, mind and body, whooshing through a bright, winding tunnel at light speed. I realized that my sense of time had entirely disappeared. It was an incomprehensible experience, impossible to explain. Time simply did not exist. I might have been traveling through the tunnel for eternity or a split second; there was no way of knowing and no reason to care. It didn't matter. I understood that my body was far too small to contain my soul, which was as big as the whole universe. I felt an overwhelming sense of peace.

Then I was back in the room with Sibyl and Emma. My body felt clunky and heavy, like a costume I couldn't wait to take off. I kept hearing the lyrics about wheels turning, over and over again.

I wanted to see more. I pressed my whole body against the glass. I found myself in my dream from the night before. I could feel the sand between my toes and the warm breeze on my face. I was still calling out to Emma, but this time she finally heard me. She turned around. "How long have you been here?"

"I've been here the whole time."

"Then you'd better help me with this." She pointed at the octopus on the beach.

I heard a voice in my mind and knew with absolute certainty that it was Sibyl. *Don't be scared, Lulu.*

My brother used to call me Lulu.

I opened my eyes. I gasped and felt Sibyl's tentacles release from the other side of the glass. I stumbled backward as she shrank into a corner of the tank. Her color faded in a flash from red to gray as she blended into the background of sand and rocks.

"Do you see now?" Emma asked.

"I do."

"Do you believe me?"

Don't be scared, Lulu.

"I believe you. It's scary, and unbelievable, and I don't understand any of it, but I believe you."

She smiled. "I know."

"Can I ask you a question? If you've been living the same day over and over again, does that mean we always end up here?"

"You've met Sibyl before. But we've never done this—not exactly. I keep trying, though."

"How many times have you tried?"

"You don't want to know."

"So what usually happens instead? Wait—if you tell me, won't it change things? Like a butterfly effect?"

"This isn't quite the same thing. There are some things I can change, mostly little things, but there's other stuff that happens regardless of what I do. That's why I asked if you believe in destiny."

"How long has this been going on?"

"A long time. And it isn't just me. Bradd and Max are in the loop, too."

"Why just the three of you? Why not all of us?"

She told me about Gus's research then, about the Sibyl ceviche and Bradd's resurrection and Max's illness. "Greta wanted to keep Max alive. They only gave it to Bradd because otherwise he would have stayed dead."

"And you?"

"I still haven't figured that out exactly. Greta told me it was because of my letter."

"What letter?"

"The letters Max made us write to ourselves at the beginning of the year."

"What did yours say?"

"It said that my only goal was to lose my virginity before graduation. Greta found our letters in Max's room and read all of them. She told me she thought mine was sad because there's so much more to life than sex."

"She thought a teenager trying to get laid was sad? Has she ever met a teenager?" It sounded like a flimsy reason at best. I hesitated.

"Go ahead," she said, "ask me."

"How do you know what I— Oh, right."

"I didn't sleep with Auggie. I tried, but something always went wrong. I'm glad it never happened, though." She told me about the slap and the cheating.

"I can't believe he hit you. That little fucking worm. I'm going to beat the shit out of him."

"You don't need to do that. Bradd already stabbed him to death with a screwdriver. Bradd's having a grand old time living a life where his actions don't have consequences. He's really embraced the worst version of himself. He seems content to stay here forever."

"But you don't want that."

"No. I want to go home. But I don't know what I need to do to make it happen."

I looked at Sibyl. "She wants us to set her free."

Emma nodded. "I know. But we've already done that."

"Maybe we should try again."

"That isn't the answer, Louis. It doesn't work."

"Maybe this time will be different."

She tilted her head, curious. "What did Sibyl show you just now?"

"I'm not even sure how to explain it. She showed me…she showed me the universe. She showed me her sadness. She needs our help."

"You've never told me about that before."

"Maybe this is the first time she's asking me."

"Maybe." Emma seemed doubtful.

"Then let's do it. If it doesn't work, so what? What's the harm in trying one more time?"

"Okay," she agreed, "I'll try one more time. But first you have to answer a question for me."

"Shoot."

"Auggie started to tell me something about you the day he slapped me. When you were yelling at him, and he was trying to defend himself, he started to tell me something about you. He acted like it was something awful, something only he knew about. What was it?"

I didn't remember any of the events Emma was describing, but I knew exactly what Auggie would have been referencing. "I'd… rather not."

"You never want to tell me. It must be really bad, huh?"

"It isn't important. I don't even know what he could have been talking about."

"Yes, you do!" She pouted. "I won't help you with Sibyl if you don't tell me."

"Then I'll do it by myself."

"But then it won't be an adventure. And our adventures are only ours if we do them together."

Fuck. I tried to think of a good lie that she would buy as humiliating enough that I'd be this reluctant to share it. I couldn't come up with anything.

"Louis," she balked, "I'm your best friend in the world. I know everything about you. What could possibly be so bad that you can't tell me?"

"You don't know everything about me. You don't know this, and once you do, I'm afraid you'll never look at me the same way again."

"I'm sure it isn't as bad as you think."

"It's worse."

"Worse than Auggie smacking me across the face? Worse than me being trapped here with Bradd?"

"It's worse in its own way."

"Please tell me."

"Okay, fine. Do you remember when that nursing home burned down a few years ago? The one where something like fifteen people died? That was me. I did it."

"You did not."

"No, I didn't. What I did is not quite that bad. But now you're adequately prepped." I took a deep breath. "I was thirteen years old. Auggie and I weren't exactly friends back then, but we rode the same bus, and one day he came home with me for some reason, I don't remember why. We were all alone at my house, and we were starving, but there was hardly any food in the house. Eventually I found some meat in a Tupperware container in our basement freezer, which was where my mom usually kept the good stuff hidden, but that day there wasn't anything good. It was just a bunch of frozen leftovers. I assumed the meat was hamburger or something. So anyway, I started cooking it up, and it didn't smell so great, but like I said, we were starving. We were just kids. I melted some cheese and put it on a hoagie roll, and it ended up looking kind of like a cheese steak. I knew after I took one bite that it definitely wasn't hamburger meat. The texture was all wrong. It was rubbery. And the taste was gamey. My dad used to hunt small game, so I figured maybe it was rabbit meat. It wasn't like it tasted terrible; it was edible. It was just…off somehow. Anyway, I ate all of mine, but Auggie was too grossed out by the smell to try any. Then my parents came home. When my mom saw the empty Tupperware on the counter, I thought she was going to faint. She went absolutely nuts on me. Emma, it was the placenta from when she gave birth to my brother. My brother who *died*."

"That could have—that shouldn't—it's not as bad as the nursing home thing."

"When my mom told me what I'd eaten, I didn't stop vomiting for… I still haven't stopped vomiting. I'm vomiting on the inside right now."

"I was masturbating with a Ken doll once and the head came off inside me," she blurted. "It was stuck there for a week. I finally got it out with a pair of kitchen tongs. Ken's head looked like one of the Nazis at the end of *Raiders of the Lost Ark*. You know, when their faces all melt off?"

I took a minute to process the story. "How—how long ago did this happen?"

"A long time ago."

"Okay. How long ago *exactly*?"

"Years ago, Louis."

"Years ago in real time, or years ago here?"

"Why would I bring a Ken doll with me on this trip?"

"I don't know! To masturbate with?"

"It was years ago in real time."

"Right. Yeah, your secret might be worse."

"My secret is *not* worse."

"It's not worse. Let's never talk about any of this ever again."

"Oh, I think we're going to. In fact, I— "

I kissed her then, to shut her up. She kissed me back. I wrapped my arms all the way around her and lifted her off the ground. The feeling was like all the happiest moments of my life happening all at once in the same instant, each one bringing its own unique joy—and now this moment had arrived, eclipsing all of it. I wanted it to last forever.

Lucy

Friday

Alison and I had been working on a 1,000-piece puzzle together all week in the lounge. We both love puzzles. We were about 85 percent finished, and I was beginning to doubt it would happen by the end of the day. Alison could never stay focused for more than an hour or so at a time, and she was already getting antsy. "What if there are some pieces missing? There are probably lots of pieces missing."

"Don't worry about that right now. Try to stay focused."

We heard the clatter of the front doors opening and closing, followed by footsteps across the wooden floor. Louis and Emma strolled hand-in-hand into the room and came directly to our table. Emma stared down at the puzzle. "You're missing five pieces," she said. Without asking, she proceeded to shift the loose pieces around on the table. She began picking them up and putting them down in the right place on the first try almost every time. She did this until all the extra pieces were gone, leaving five empty spaces. Alison's gum fell out of her mouth.

Neither of them paid much attention to us. Emma beamed at Louis with a wide, toothy grin before she kissed him. There was a thoroughness to the way they kissed, as though they were being careful to explore every surface of one another's mouths. It looked like they were trying to eat each other's faces.

"Get some water to throw on these two," Alison told me loudly, which made them pause and pull apart.

"When did this happen?" she demanded of them. She frowned at Emma. "You know, you never even asked if you could borrow one of my swimsuits."

"I think you mean *my* swimsuit. I look better in it anyway." She nudged Louis. "Let's go drink some champagne." And they walked away, still holding hands.

Alison and I stared at each other. "I feel like I'm high," she said. "What the fuck is with this day?"

I thought about the question for a minute. "Emma figured out who she wanted, so she fought for it. Even though she was probably scared, she knows it will be worth it." I smiled shyly at Alison. "I know how she feels."

Emma

Day 67

We decided to wait until nightfall to put our plan for Sibyl into action. I already knew what to do, and I didn't expect it to work, but I didn't care. At least I would be with Louis.

We spent most of our afternoon at a secluded spot on the beach, sipping champagne and talking and kissing, our bodies intertwined. It was nothing like being with Auggie. I used to think he and I were an unlikely match, but still a good one. Now I realized that when I was with Auggie, I'd never felt like I could completely be myself. I was always trying to be whoever I thought he wanted me to be. But when I was with Louis, it was such a comfort zone. It was almost like being alone, except I wasn't lonely. I felt so sure of him. I felt so sure of myself.

"You see me," I whispered to him. "You see all of me, and you like me anyway."

"Well, what's not to like about you?"

"I'm weird. I'm a slob. I didn't enjoy *Dune*. I have a big nose."

"You are wonderfully weird. You *are* a slob, and that's fine. You're allowed to be wrong about *Dune*. And your nose is perfect."

"Ken doll," I said.

"Placenta," he responded.

I rested my head against his chest and clung to him. The day was slipping away too quickly. Soon it would be over. I was terrified. I was finally with Louis, and tomorrow I'd have to start all over again.

"I hate that you aren't going to remember any of this tomorrow."

"A part of me will remember. You said it seemed like a part of Alison remembered."

"Maybe. I can't know for sure."

He held me more tightly. "Here's what we need to do: we need to make it extra special, okay? It has to be so much different and more exciting than every other day that it creates a whole new neural pathway in my subconscious. *Emma and Louis Solve the Mystery of the Time Octopus.* And then we'll celebrate. We won't worry about what will or won't happen in the morning. We'll party like it's the end of the world. We'll celebrate like there's no tomorrow."

My Mickey Mouse watch read 12:04. (I'd actually borrowed it from Bradd; it was a gift from his grandparents, selected to humiliate him for his inability to read an analog watch.) A circle of light glowed around the full moon. Louis and I were huddled outside Sibyl's door. Louis shined a flashlight on the lock. He was holding a hammer.

"Is that a hammer? You said you were bringing a drill!"

"I couldn't find a drill."

"You can't use a hammer."

He reached into his pocket. "I brought a screwdriver, too."

It was even a Phillips head. Everything was coming up screwdrivers lately. "Can't you just use the hammer to pry the door open?"

"I can *try*. I'm not the fucking Hulk." He tried turning the doorknob. The door wasn't even locked, further proof that our effort would be meaningless.

We kept the lights off and used the flashlight to illuminate our way around the room. It was easy enough to get Sibyl out of her tank. All we had to do was climb the ladder, open the lid, and scoop her up. From my previous attempts, I knew there was a large net attached to a long pole in a broom closet that was perfect for the job. Sibyl was as agile as she was intelligent. She propelled herself smoothly into the net. She was too heavy for me to lift her out of the water all by myself, but she used her tentacles to assist me, suctioning herself to the glass as she pulled herself to the surface. Today, we couldn't find the wheelbarrow, so we lowered her onto a tarp we'd spread out on the concrete floor.

We dragged the tarp carefully out the door and through the grass, all the way to the sea. Sibyl stayed still and calm inside the net. She knew what was happening.

We eased her into the water. On our prior attempt to send her home, she'd disappeared almost immediately beneath the surface. This time was different. She swam out of the net, but she didn't swim away. She stayed in the shallow water close to the shore.

"Now what?" Louis asked me.

"Now she swims away."

"Maybe she's taking her time."

"I guess so."

We waited. We sat on the beach and looked at the stars. We kissed. The waves lapped at our toes as we held hands.

"I want to spend the night with you, Louis," I whispered into his neck.

He held me close. He was shivering. "Okay. Yes. Me too."

Sibyl was still hanging out in the shallow water. It was almost like she was waiting for something.

"Should we just leave her like that?" Louis asked. "What if she's injured?"

"She isn't injured. She's immortal."

"Right."

"She'll be okay. Let's go back to my room."

"What about Alison?"

"Alison won't be there."

I could hardly believe it was actually going to happen. Sexual intercourse! Full penetration! The beast with two backs! And with Louis!

It was the adventure of all adventures.

I noticed a flashlight beam in the distance. The light bobbed as whoever was walking down the beach got closer. "Someone else is here."

It was Bradd. Because of course it was. "I thought I might find you here. Hi, Louie." He didn't notice Sibyl in the water.

I gave him a dirty look. "What do you want?"

"I need to talk to you."

"Right now?"

"Yes. Right now."

"Can't it wait until tomorrow?"

He gave us a sly grin. "Am I cockblocking you two?"

"As a matter of fact, you are."

"I figured it out, Emma. I know how you can get home." As he spoke, I noticed Sibyl creeping slowly up behind him. She hooked a tentacle around his ankle. Bradd looked down and yelped. He tried to kick her off, but she held on. Her entire body seemed to expand as she pulled herself up his legs and wrapped herself around his torso. He screamed and struggled. Louis and I were both too stunned to move. Sibyl's body contracted and released, again and again, looking like she was squeezing the life out of him while Bradd gasped for air. She slid a tentacle into his mouth and down his throat. His back arched. He made a gurgling sound. Sibyl's body glowed in the moonlight as Bradd seemed to shrivel in her grasp.

And then, out of nowhere, she released him. He fell into the water with a smack. He was still alive. He curled into a ball and sobbed as he rocked back and forth. Sibyl vanished beneath the surface and swam toward the deep sea. She was gone.

Louis and I walked Bradd back to his bungalow. He was hysterical, inconsolable. "I told you she was evil, Emma! I told you!"

"Bradd, you're fine."

"I am not fine. She—she violated my soul."

What a thing to say. "You're okay. It's over now." We were outside his bungalow. He hugged himself, still trembling and weeping.

"I'm going to bed," he told us, sniffling.

"Not yet. You said you figured out how to go home."

He nodded.

"You have to tell me."

"I'm too traumatized. I'll tell you tomorrow. Actually, it's so obvious, I can't believe I didn't realize it a long time ago. You don't even really need my help."

"I don't want to wait until tomorrow. Tell me now."

"Emma, he's bleeding," Louis said. I shined my flashlight on Bradd. His entire body—face, arms, legs, every exposed surface of his skin—was covered in overlapping red circles that looked similar to hickies, except they were all perfectly round. Most of them were bleeding. I felt kind of bad for the guy. He'd done some really screwed-up things, but he'd also been through a lot. Deep down, Bradd was okay.

I was dreading the end of the day. Today was almost perfect. And I had Louis now. I didn't want to lose him again. But Bradd didn't seem like he'd be swayed into telling me tonight.

"Everything has to be exactly the same tomorrow, okay?"

Bradd whimpered. "I don't wanna dance again."

"But you're so good at it."

"Yeah, I know." He looked at Louis. "I'm sorry for cockblocking you tonight, Louie."

"No worries, man. The night isn't over yet." He patted Bradd on the shoulder. Bradd winced. "Go ahead," Louis told him, "get some sleep."

Bradd turned to look at us when he reached the bottom of the stairs. He raised both arms in the air. "I'll be good as new tomorrow," he declared. "I'm Braddley Hazelett, inventor of the H2Blow, and I'm unstoppable!"

Emma

Day 68

It was almost two in the morning. Louis and I were alone in my room. We were naked under the sheets. Unlike the earlier times with Auggie, the lights were on. Louis said he wanted to experience everything with me, to see me exactly as I was. To my surprise, I didn't feel the least bit self-conscious. I felt completely comfortable with him.

"Are you sure about this?" he asked me.

"I'm sure."

I thought about what Alison had said about sex: *It feels like someone is taking something from you.*

"I love you, Emma."

"I love you, Louis."

I gave myself to him willingly, and he gave himself to me. Nothing was lost. Nothing was stolen. Everything was exactly the way it was supposed to be. Our bodies bloomed together in the darkness, and

I was overcome by *la petit mort*. Little deaths, one after the next, yet I'd never felt more alive. I was right where I needed to be. I was already home.

Max

Day 15,051

I was asleep next to Greta when Gus began pounding on my door with both fists. I pulled on some shorts. Greta wrapped my blanket around her body to cover herself, seconds before her father burst into the room.

"She's gone," he said, breathless.

"What are you talking about?" Greta asked. "Who's gone?"

"Sibyl."

Greta sat up. "How?"

"I'll tell you how. That fucking kid, that's how. Bradd did this to sabotage us."

"Dad. Take some breaths. It's going to be okay. It's just a setback—we still have the kittens."

"You don't understand," he said, "it wasn't just Sibyl. It's worse than that. Bradd didn't even try to deny it: he admitted the whole thing. He was proud of himself. He broke into the lab last night, dumped the rest of the accelerant into the ocean."

"No," Greta said, going pale.

Her father nodded. "We can't continue our research without it. It's over. All that work. All that time. Wasted. It's over." He buried his face in his hands. "We're finished."

"Wait a minute." I felt clammy and nauseated. "What do you mean, you're *finished*? What are you saying? Is this the end?"

They both looked at me, stone-faced. Neither of them responded.

"So it was the cocaine the whole time?" I asked, more confused than ever.

"Not the cocaine; the *accelerant*," Gus corrected me. "And it's just a tool. But we can't continue our experiments without it."

"What kind of tool? What does it do?"

Gus shook his head. "You wouldn't understand."

"It lets us steer the wheel inside the wheel," Greta supplied, which explained absolutely nothing.

"And what about the octopus?"

"What about her?"

"This was all because of her, right? And now that she's gone, is it over?"

"Don't you get it?" Gus said, growing more frustrated. "The octopus is everything. Sibyl knew this would happen. She never belonged to us. We belong to her."

"Sibyl is never really gone. She's everywhere, at every moment," Greta said. "Whether she's in her tank or in the ocean makes no difference to your location. You're missing the big picture."

"Does that…does that mean I can go home now?" If this was it for me, that meant my life would be over in a matter of months.

Gus and Greta exchanged a long stare. "I don't know," Gus finally admitted.

I felt surprisingly at peace with his answer. Because, if it *was* the end, it had been one hell of a detour. I was ready. And if it wasn't the end, then I would always have tomorrow. Either way, I'd take things one day at a time.

Louis

Be-BLAH, be-BLAH, be-BLAH.

I didn't want to open my eyes. I was having the nicest dream.

Be-BLAH, be-BLAH, be-BLAH.

"Louis," a voice whispered in my ear, "wake up."

It was Emma.

I opened my eyes to look at her. She was standing beside the bed, wearing my T-shirt as a nightgown. Her hair was a mess. She still had pillow creases on her face.

"What is that noise?" I looked around the room. "Is that a bird?"

"That's Carl the frog. He visits me every morning." She extended her arm and offered me an open box of Swedish Fish. "Want one? It's the breakfast of champions." She climbed back into bed with me. I put my arm around her and held her close.

"I thought it was all a dream."

"It wasn't a dream."

"I guess not… But it was one hell of an adventure, wasn't it?"

She smiled at me. She was my favorite person in the world. "The adventure is just beginning."

Emma

A persistent buzzing sound woke me in the middle of the night. I bolted upright in bed and felt around on my nightstand until my hand found my phone. I squinted at the screen. The display read *UNKNOWN CALLER*.

"Hello?"

There was silence, a few seconds of static. Then a voice.

"Listen to me. Gizmo. Don't go on the trip tomorrow."

Acknowledgments

I am so incredibly fortunate to be surrounded by so many incredible, supportive people.

This book wouldn't exist without Stacy Abrams, who is somewhat of an immortal octopus herself in my eyes. You have plucked me from obscurity and brought me back to life *twice* over the course of my career. I am forever grateful. You're a joy.

Beyond Stacy, there are so many amazing people at Entangled who have worked so hard on this book. Justine Bylo, your feedback was always invaluable—and so much fun! Working with you and everyone at Entangled has been nothing but fantastic.

To my agent, Andrea Somberg—your support and encouragement and patience mean the world to me and have changed my life for the better immeasurably. Thank you.

To my children, EJ and Ezzy—I love you endlessly.

To my husband, Colin—I love you, and I love the lifetime of adventures we've shared. Thank you for believing in me and for most of the other stuff.

To my parents, who always answer their phones. I'm sorry I'm not as reliable. I will do better in the future. I love you both.

And finally, to Aunt Myrna. If you had been able to remember your wifi password while I was watching your apartment when you went to Hawaii, I may not have finished this book. Thank you for the sanctuary—I'm so grateful you've been part of my whole life.

Turn the page for the enchanting first two chapters of *Witty in Pink*.

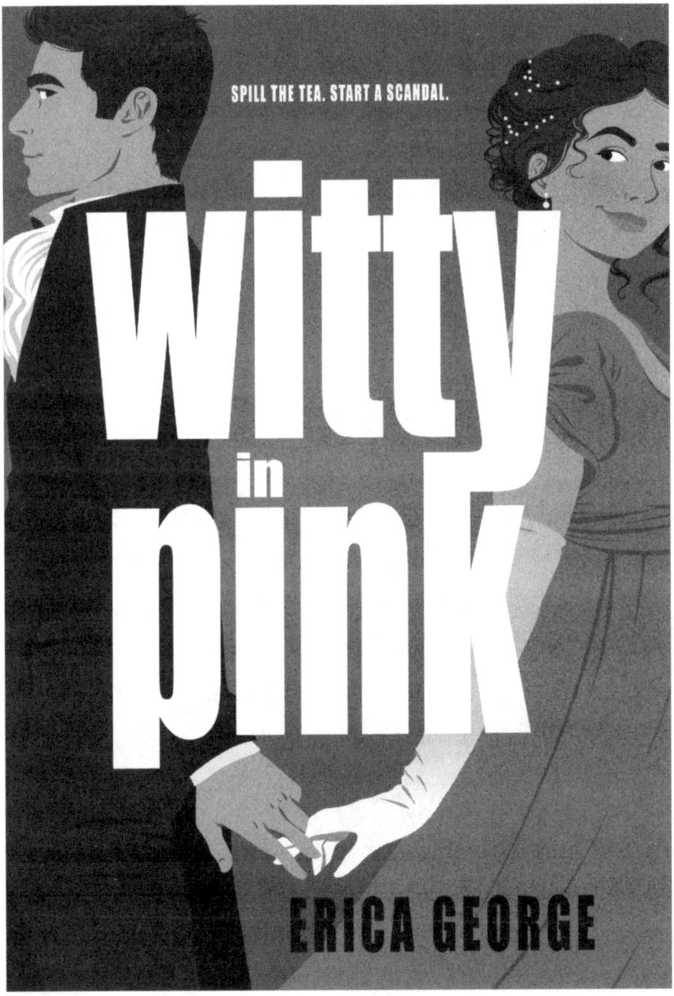

Chapter One

Blythe

Wrexford Park
Early Summer 1812

Growing up, becoming a functioning human being in an altogether relentless and trying world, is just as much a choice as it is a process. And the last time I saw Briggs Goswick, he was well on his way to becoming a certified man-child.

I can only assume that in the four years that have since passed, he has achieved that status. He must be someone unimaginably intolerable—certainly not the kind of gentleman who warrants my entire family contemplating what kind of pudding to serve at the sure-to-be-insufferable dinner party being held in his honor.

I have been sitting in Uncle Henry's lavender drawing room at Wrexford Park for thirty-three minutes—*thirty-three minutes*—listening to my uncle and cousin Charlotte debate the merits of chocolate or the downfalls of boysenberry. Briggs Goswick has been in London for several months, apparently, settling his late father's estate, and now we must celebrate his homecoming to Brumbury as the master of Mistlethrush Hall with nothing less than the perfect dinner party.

He arrives tomorrow.

Hooray.

Apparently, I am the only one dreading his return. My mother makes spirited menu suggestions to Charlotte from across the room. My sister, Amy, asks a multitude of questions about what Mr. Goswick has been up to since last we saw him. My other cousin, Julian, discusses the flower arrangements with Mrs. Sullivan, the housekeeper, and I can tell she's impressed with his ample knowledge of flora.

He offers me an exaggerated eye roll once Mrs. Sullivan turns her back, as if to suggest her taste in floral arrangements leaves much to be desired, but I know he loves coming to Wrexford Park more than Amy does, even. It's a pleasant distraction from everything that troubles us at home at Awendown House.

I wish that Papa would have joined us rather than stay behind worrying about the debts that accrue seemingly overnight.

"What about a trifle?" Charlotte suggests. The room all nods, murmuring their absolute delight at the prospect of trifle. But what flavor? What *indeed*?

I cannot indulge in this for one more second.

I rise slowly, so as not to draw attention to my eventual retreat, but the eyes of all my Barlow ancestors seem to *tsk-tsk* at me from their gilded frames.

Eat a bad prawn, Great Aunt Frances?

Charlotte turns to me. "Blythe, do you like trifle?"

"As much as I *love* trifle," I reply, slowly backing toward the door and pretending to admire the many portraits of ancestors who have passed, "the real question you should be asking is whether or not Mr. *Goswick* likes trifle. Moreover, is he sick of trifle? What if all he's had in London is trifle, and he wishes for a change of dessert as well as a change of scenery? Then what, I ask?"

"Oh, Blythe, you are so astute!" exclaims Charlotte, shaking her head. "Father, we never even considered Mr. Goswick's preferences, and it's his party. How thoughtless of us."

"How will we know what he's had in London?" Uncle Henry

asks, a tinge of panic in his voice. "How will we ascertain that information? Is it too late? I told you we should have started to plan sooner, Charlotte. I knew this would all be in vain!"

I step backward, slowly, quietly, and reach my right hand out for my book on the sideboard. In the great hall, I make a dash across the black-and-white tile floor for the kitchens, sneak one of the apples that Cook planned to bake this evening, and with a quick whiff of cinnamon and sugar, I burst from the confines of Wrexford Park and out into the glorious summer sunshine. I close my eyes, grinning up at the clear blue summer sky. Freedom, finally.

Weaving my way through the paths of the formal gardens, I break from the pruned hedges, over the green hills, and through the horse pasture, my skirts becoming tangled in the tall, tall grass.

Several of Uncle Henry's bays roam the fields, looking up briefly from their cropping of the grass and allowing me to make myself comfortable below the shade of the ancient oak. I open my book right to where I left off last night, spreading it across my lap, my back propped against the broad trunk of the tree, and read in blissful silence.

Charlotte suggested this book. Said she couldn't put it down while on her trip to the seaside, and it is just the sort of read that Charlotte would find enthralling. Handsome knights on stallions, roaming over hill and moor on dark and stormy nights, all to avenge the honor of their fair maiden. Of course, I do love it, too, though I'd never admit that to my cousin. I'd never admit that to *anyone*, actually. While romance may have bloomed in me as a lovestruck adolescent, I've been pricked by its underlying thorns before. Better to read about romance in private than allow anyone to think I'm still enthralled by its appeal in real life.

I take a bite of my crisp apple and sigh. At least I have Sir Garrett to woo me for the afternoon, and he certainly comes with significantly fewer complications than any real gentleman I've ever met. Like the kind Briggs Goswick brings with him. Lord, I cannot believe that upon my first trip to Wrexford Park in almost a year, he of all people has to show up. But I cannot let his looming return ruin my day. I'll deal with his presence when I'm forced to.

For a few minutes, I take in the serenity of my current setting, the chirping birds darting from the oak tree above me to the forest line just a few yards away, the snuffle of the companionable horses, and the rustling of the leaves as the breeze sifts through the branches. All my concerns over the return of my nemesis and my father's financial woes melt away as I find myself sucked into the story. If I didn't know any better, I would swear I could hear the thundering of Sir Garrett's noble steed.

I glance up at my equine companions, but they still munch peaceably on the grass, occasionally offering me a contented snort.

But still, the clamor of hooves grows closer. I place my book, face flat, on the ground beside me, then brush the dirt and dust off my skirts and shade my eyes with my hand to see more clearly. Becoming larger with every moment, a beautiful, dappled gray horse gallops toward the wooden slat fence that separates the pastures. Its rider is certain, leaning forward, calling out encouragingly, but once the creature reaches the divider, it skids to a sudden stop—and the rider goes flying over its head.

"Oh!" I cry, my heart pounding as I gather my skirts and race to where the gentleman lies sprawled out on my side of the fence. I kneel down beside him, skirts billowing in my haste. "Are you all right? Can you hear me?" I'm too afraid to touch him. What if he's seriously hurt?

He doesn't move. His eyes are pressed closed, his full lips parted, and his chest heaves with exertion. He has serious brows and dramatic cheekbones, a determined chin, and the slope of his eyes is gentle and smooth. A single lock of thick, mahogany hair falls down along his forehead. Clothing, impeccable. Boots, tall and shiny.

He is, quite certainly, the most handsome gentleman I have ever seen in my entire life, and conversely, he is, quite certainly, Briggs Goswick.

Chapter Two

Blythe

Damn him. His effortless good looks are irritating even when unconscious.

Suddenly, Briggs Goswick's clear, green eyes pop open, staring up at the serenely blue sky above us.

"Are you all right?" I ask quietly, my hand on his shoulder.

"Damn that horse to hell," he spits, sitting upright and then launching from the grass as though he had simply dismounted the animal rather than fly ass over head to the ground. Of course, I know better, and I can't stop the smirk that has come to my lips. "No matter how many times we practice, it's no use. He won't jump." He approaches the fence where the horse whinnies amiably and then throws his hands in the air.

"That's because he's a hunter. Not a jumper," I inform him.

Briggs stands with his hands on his hips, still breathing quickly as he stares at me. "Excuse me," he says quietly. His eyes soften, and he clears his throat. "I have been most ungentlemanly. I'm Mr. Briggs Goswick of Mistlethrush Hall." He bows. "And you are?"

I must come up with the appropriate answer to this question. He clearly doesn't recognize me, and I would prefer to avoid what will undoubtedly be our caustic reunion for as long as possible. "Well, if you would really like to apologize for your ungentlemanly behavior, you might realize that we haven't been formally introduced." I curtsy briefly and then make my way back to the tree where I left my book.

"Certainly, out here in nature, formal introductions aren't quite as necessary," he says, and when I glance over my shoulder, he's following me. Because of course he is. He gestures to the general outdoor area, then runs a hand through his annoyingly thick, shiny hair. "After all, you must be staying nearby. We will likely run into one another again before the summer comes to a close."

"And when we do," I say, bending down and retrieving my book and what's left of my apple, "I will gladly have a mutual acquaintance introduce us. Besides, this can hardly be considered *real* nature; it's a pasture."

He stands right in front of me now, hands on his hips, grinning at my lack of cooperation. Because Briggs Goswick always gets his way, and rather than being dissuaded by my impertinence, he has the gall to seem entertained.

I shake myself from staring at the perfect bow of his mouth. "I must go."

"Please don't," he says, reaching forward and touching my wrist. "I feel as though we've met before. Perhaps if you tell me with whom you're staying, I could guess." He grins again and then bites his lower lip. "I love a good game."

The way he says this makes me blush, heat pooling low in my belly. *That's quite enough of that, then.* "I really must be going," I say, heading for the fence. Gathering my skirts with my free hand, I step onto the lower rung, then hoist one leg over. Before I can clear the top, however, Briggs appears at my side, and he supports my elbow. "Th-Thank you," I say quietly, landing on the other side and pulling my chestnut hair over my shoulder and twisting it.

"Ah, now, I think I've discovered a way to learn your identity once and for all," he says. "Look there. Mr. Fitzgibbons!" he calls.

Behind me, Mr. Fitzgibbons, my uncle's gamekeeper, crosses the lower field. He waves when he sees Briggs. Lovely. It's all over now.

"Mr. Fitzgibbons," says Briggs once the man is in earshot. "Do you know this young lady?"

The gamekeeper regards me, someone he's chased out of his horses' stables since I was a little girl, his eyes darting between Briggs and me, ignoring the tiny shake of my head I try to hide and make obvious all at once. "I…cert'nly do, sir."

"Would you mind introducing us, then? Because, you see, she is a lady, and I am nothing if not a gentleman."

"Me?" Fitzgibbons asks, pointing at his own chest. "You wan' *me* to introduce you?"

"If you would be so kind."

Fitzgibbons shrugs, flummoxed but not unwilling. "Aye, sir, if'n it pleases ye. Mr. Briggs Goswick, this is Miss Blythe Rowley, niece of Mr. Barlow. She's stayin' at Wrexford Park."

"Thank you, Mr. Fitzgibbons," says Briggs quietly, his grin never faltering and his eyes steady upon me. "That will be all."

"G'day, Mr. Goswick. Miss Rowley." He touches the brim of his hat.

I raise my chin in the air in an attempt to exude whatever dignity I have left.

"Well, pluck my feathers and shove me in the oven," Briggs says, one hand on his hip and the other gripping his riding crop. "Miss Blythe Rowley, all grown up. And not altogether difficult to look at."

I cluck my tongue. "Oh, good, there you are. I was afraid you had gained manners and grace in my absence. Happy to see you're as reliable as ever."

A smug smile tugs at the corners of his mouth. "I am most surely as gentlemanly as I've ever been—the gentleman I've been bred to be. You, on the other hand, are a most delightful surprise. Hardly any dirt encrusting your person, a pretty dress, your hair tamed and fashionable. You *almost* look like a lady." He jumps the fence and circles behind me. "In fact, you sound like a lady, too. But does that a lady make?"

I arch an eyebrow, my cheeks heating at his slow perusal. *Lord, please don't let me be blushing.* "You may look like a gentleman, and if I were so fooled by your appearance, I suppose you'd sound like one, too."

He laughs.

"But you can't ride a horse, obviously, and that's a deal breaker, so I shall take my leave of you, Mr. Goswick." I curtsy low and dramatically.

"So soon, Miss Rowley? But we were only just getting reacquainted."

"I'm a busy girl," I reply, tucking my book under my arm and taking a final bite of apple. "I'm needed back at Wrexford."

"For how long will you be staying?" Briggs asks, appearing before me and trotting backward in order to keep up and be in my way all at once.

"Until the end of the week," I reply.

"Not the summer?"

"Lord, no."

"You don't sound particularly enthusiastic."

I pause. "Please don't pretend to know my innermost thoughts, Mr. Goswick. It's been quite some time since we met under less-than-ideal circumstances, and at least one of us has matured since then."

"Sharp as ever, Miss Rowley."

I skip down the slope of a hill, the clock copula adorning the arch at Wrexford coming into view. "You confuse rudeness with obligation. As I've told you, I'm needed back at Wrexford Park. There's apparently a dinner being planned."

"For me, naturally."

"So it would seem."

"So *you're* planning my dinner? How very kind of you, Miss Rowley. I am honored."

I pause at the boxwood hedges that separate the gardens from the fields, closing my eyes and allowing my shoulders to droop, even though I clench my teeth. "I am helping my cousin, who is planning your dinner."

"As always, you thrive on being enigmatic."

"Enigmatic!" I cry, that old familiar vexation bubbling in my chest again. Not five minutes in, and Briggs Goswick has already gotten on my last nerve. "I could not be any clearer, Mr. Goswick. I have told you time and again that my cousin needs me to help in preparation for your dinner. If you'll excuse me." I curtsy once again and leave him.

He's silent as I take several paces, and at last, I think, I've left him behind me.

Not altogether the worst meeting with Briggs Goswick, actually. He was cocky, no doubt, but I've experienced worse.

Until he calls out, "Will you be serving pork, perhaps?"

Slowly, I turn, regarding him in the middle of the path, riding crop in one hand and hat in the other. He is so maddeningly handsome, I see red. I hurl the core of my apple, and it meets its target, right between his eyes.

"Ah," says Briggs, offering me a slow blink. "Splendid. Right where we left off, then."

Let's be friends!

@EntangledTeen

@EntangledTeen

@EntangledTeen

bit.ly/TeenNewsletter

entangled teen

an imprint of Entangled Publishing LLC